Edward Francis Russell, Eleanor Towle

Alexander Heriot Mackonochie: a Memoir

Second Edition

Edward Francis Russell, Eleanor Towle

Alexander Heriot Mackonochie: a Memoir
Second Edition

ISBN/EAN: 9783337305161

Printed in Europe, USA, Canada, Australia, Japan

Cover: Foto ©Raphael Reischuk / pixelio.de

More available books at **www.hansebooks.com**

ALEXANDER HERIOT

MACKONOCHIE

A MEMOIR

BY

E. A. T.

EDITED BY

EDWARD FRANCIS RUSSELL, M.A.

ST ALBAN'S, HOLBORN

SECOND EDITION

NEW YORK

E. & J. B. YOUNG & CO., COOPER UNION

1890

TO

JAMES ROBERT ALEXANDER CHINNERY-HALDANE

LORD BISHOP OF ARGYLL AND THE ISLES

IN ALL GRATITUDE AND AFFECTION

PREFACE

THIS Memoir has been undertaken at the request of many persons, relatives and others, who desired to have in print some record of a man to whom they felt themselves deeply indebted. To 'praise famous men and our fathers that begat us,' is an instinct natural to our piety. Whether or no Mr. Mackonochie may justly be considered a 'famous man,' there is no doubt that a large number of persons at the present time regard him with grateful affection as a spiritual father, one from whom much has descended to them. Apart from the individual help, direction, or stimulus that any may have derived from him, the school to which he and they belong owes much of the fruit that now is being reaped to his laborious sowing. Our present peace has been to some extent won for us by the conflicts which he endured. If controversy has put on milder manners, some of the credit may not unfairly be assigned to one who habitually refused to meet railing with railing, who blessed when men cursed, to one whose whole career has been a conspicuous witness to the futility of violence, and the folly of all attempts to lay ideas with a sword.

Beyond the natural wish to perpetuate the remembrance of a benefactor, there exists the, also natural, wish to learn in such detail as may be available, how and by what methods one who had lived to such good effect managed a business confessedly so difficult. In part and in degree many of the trials which befel him, befal others, especially among the clergy. There are points on the way to the common 'goal and prize of our high calling,' at which all the paths of individual experience touch and overlap. At these points at least he will have something to teach us.[1] In spite of discouraging criticism, biographies continue to attract innumerable readers, who find in them information concerning the things which, after all, are best worth knowing, and most serviceable. They are studies in the conduct of life, and offer us in the field of spiritual economics all the help of a carefully planned and successfully executed series of experiments.

We are told that the demand for ecclesiastical biography has been more than copiously supplied. In point of numbers this may be fairly granted, and yet among the countless 'lives' it is noteworthy that not all types of character and activity find equal representation. We have the biographies of prelates, preachers, scholars, founders of works of mercy, missionaries and the like. Even the clerical humourist and the clerical sportsman have found

---

[1] These glimpses into the inner regions of a great soul do one good. Contact of this kind strengthens, restores, refreshes. Courage returns as we gaze; when we see what has been, we doubt no more that it can be again. At the sight of a *man* we too say to ourselves, Let us also be men.—*Amiel's Journal* (English Translation), p. 32.

their annalists, who have preserved these curious personali-
ties, like strange flies in amber, for the wonder of a later
time. But there are memoirs of another sort which are
by no means so abundant in current ecclesiastical literature, and which appeal perhaps to a more restricted circle
of readers. I mean, the life-story of the men who, to some
extent at least, have realised in their own person those
revived ideals of the priesthood, its supernatural character,
mission and endowments, which are filling the hearts and
firing the zeal of so many of the new generation of our
clergy. Ideals of any sort are dangerous visitants to vain
and shallow minds. In the thin soil of a poor nature they
bear ugly fruit in arrogance, or insolent pretentiousness.
It is not to be denied that instances of this 'bringing
forth of wild grapes' are not unknown amongst us. But
it is far otherwise in the case of those loftier, nobler souls,
which, thank God, are also to be found in our ranks.
Upon them the dignity of the sacerdotal character, the
glory of a divine trust for the good of human life, weighs
with the oppression of an almost unbearable responsibility. They find in it a ground, not for self-exaltation
or self-assertion, but rather for the deepest self-humiliation.
They are filled with concern how they may make good its
requirements. A sense of shortcoming haunts them. The
vision of what should be prevents all satisfaction in that
which is. Hence the feature common to the saintliest
amongst the clergy, everywhere and in all times, of a
merciless self-effacement and self-sacrifice, and, by natural
consequence, an especial devotion to the Cross of Christ.
'I am crucified with Christ.' 'They that are Christ's

have crucified the flesh with the affections and lusts.'
'God forbid that I should glory save in the cross of our
Lord Jesus Christ, whereby the world is crucified unto
me, and I unto the world.'[1]   Of Lacordaire, Henri Perreyve
wrote : ' He regarded the priesthood as an absolute and
perpetual sacrifice.   Jesus Christ nailed to the cross, dying
for the salvation of men, was for him the divine ideal of
the priest, as it was also the constant, dominant, almost
exclusive object of his piety, the daily bread of his soul,
the spiritual nourishment which he was wont to offer to
all who sought his help.'[2]

After eighteen years' service at Mackonochie's side, I
can find no better words than these with which to express his mind and method, so far as I have been able to
learn them from his lips, or observe them in his practice.
Without exaggeration, I may say that I cannot recall
any particulars in all these years which suggested self-indulgence.   Most of us have our hobbies, our side interests,
to which, alas ! more time or money is given than we can
always justify.   If he shared such frailties with us, I never
discovered them, or observed that he had any real absorbing interests outside his interest in human souls.   For
them he broke with society, refused self-gratifications of all
sorts, lived the ' separate ' life of celibacy, and gave away
all his money, allowing himself only the simplest dress and
food.   Not that he looked coldly upon the enjoyments of
other people.   Severe to himself, no one was less censorious
more indulgent to others, never sparing himself if by any

---

[1] Gal. ii. 20 ; v. 24 ; vi. 14.
[2] *Lettres à des jeunes gens*, Préface, p. 32.

means he could add to the innocent happiness and amuse-
ment of man, woman, or child.

It was from the Cross of Christ that he drew the
inspiration and the power of this life of sacrifice. An
artist friend begged one day to be allowed to do some
work in colour for him. ' Paint me for my private room,'
Mackonochie said, ' a large figure of Jesus crucified, and
paint it, as far as may be, in simple faithfulness to fact.
Let the figure be just as He was, bruised, wounded, furrowed
by the scourge.' At the foot of this austere crucifix,
marred, pallid, and blood-stained, he made his daily meditations and said his prayers and offices ; and here, too, he
matured his preparation for his very frequent preachings.
No theme was so common in his preaching as the Passion.
The subject, difficult to many, was easy to him. He moved
amongst its mysteries as one who trod dear and familiar
ground, familiar and yet inexhaustibly new, inexhaustibly
fresh, and finding in it many applications to life, much
that interpreted life.

Closely allied to this devotion to the Cross was his
devotion to the Blessed Sacrament of the Altar. The
words of the *Imitation*, which he often quoted, seemed to
have burned themselves into his heart and mind. ' When
the priest celebrates, he honours God, he rejoices the angels,
he edifies the Church, he helps the living, he obtains rest
for the dead, and makes himself partaker of all good things.'
In the last sixteen years of his life nothing but simple
necessity, such as remoteness from an altar or extreme
sickness, was ever allowed to hinder him from offering the
Holy Sacrifice every day, and he would spend much time

always in preparation and thanksgiving. At the altar his manner left no doubt about his vivid sense of the reality of the divine Presence; his movements were full of gravity, measured and precise; his air recollected and exceedingly serious. Every device and industry that he anywhere heard report of as likely to increase in others a faith in and love for this Most Holy Sacrament, he would enquire about and, if possible, employ. This is the secret of the strange fact that one to whom the world of art and music was absolutely closed—music, form, and colour were unknown languages to him—yet fought so passionately for their employment in the services of the Altar. He counted it worth much suffering if he could secure for English people liberty to use every means which might strengthen or give expression to their faith in the Real Presence of Jesus, God and Man, hidden beneath the Sacramental veils. In speaking of the absence of delight in beautiful objects, it is interesting to note that at the last, when all spiritual responsibility had been completely removed, the sense of natural beauty welled up like a flood to fill the vacant place, and he became keenly appreciative of scenery, especially of the wilder Highland scenery. This explains in part those long wanderings among the hills which ended so tragically.

The extent and limits of his powers as a preacher are sufficiently noticed in the Memoir. Something, however, should be said of his exceptional skill as a confessor. Apart from the special grace of Holy Orders, he owed this, I think, largely to his lifelong habit of careful self-observation, and to his knowledge of Holy Scripture. The usual text-books of Moral Theology reposed upon his shelves, but the dust upon them was but seldom disturbed. A few ascetical books were often in his hand, and were found after his death worn and browned by frequent use, and marked, analysed, and annotated by his hand throughout. They were the Spiritual Exercises of St. Ignatius, the works of Bellecius, and Drexelius on Conformity to the Divine Will. These books he seems fairly to have absorbed, and they supplied very frequently the plan of his Retreats, Missions, and courses of Sermons, or the framework of single Meditations. As a confessor he was exceedingly popular. All kinds of persons, learned and unlearned, rich and poor, found their way to him, literally in hundreds. Doubtless the intense reality of the man attracted them, his unclouded faith, so calm, masculine, and strong,[1] his quick sympathy, and really heroic patience. Whilst they knelt by his side they seemed to catch the contagion of his courage. Heart and hope revived, and the horizon brightened. And then they knew that for the time he was wholly and without distraction at their service. If occasion called for it, he would give hours to a single soul and betray no signs of impatience or weariness.

This individual dealing was often continued by letter for a long time after the person had left London. There are many who treasure still a long unbroken corre-

---

[1] ‘On veut savoir si l’Evangile n’est qu’une opinion plus ou moins établie, que nous devons défendre modestement contre les opinions d’autrui sans affirmer absolument les choses, sous peine d’orgueil et d’intolérance, ou si cet Evangile est la vérité même, une, incontestable, immuable, éternelle, qui doit être maintenue envers et contre tous, avec la fermeté inflexible d’une foi parfaitement sûre d’elle-même.’—*A. Monod.*

spondence, extending over years. It will be, I fear, a disappointment to some people that comparatively few specimens of his *apostolat épistolaire*, his spiritual letters, find place in this Memoir. This is due to the fact that, as a rule, the letters had to be written in great haste. They served their purpose admirably, but it was an immediate purpose, and for the individual. As a matter of fact he was almost completely insensible to the poetry[1] and charm of words. Plain and direct answers are given to plain questions, with none of those felicities of expression which redeem a correspondence from monotony.

A word should be said about his relations with his assistant curates, and the numerous workers that he gathered about him. There are not many parishes in England where the vicar has succeeded in retaining the services of so many helpers for so long a time as at St. Alban's. Of the four curates actually living in the parish, one has come since Mackonochie left, and of the other three the senior has been here seven-and-twenty years, the next, two-and-twenty, and the third, sixteen years. Of the district visitors, some are still working here who began the work with Mr. Mackonochie when he first came to the parish. The teacher of the Young Men's Bible Class has filled his post for eighteen years ; the teacher of the Young Women's Bible Class for as many. The Senior Sacristan has served *daily* at the altar for twenty years ; and one of the choir-men who sang in the cellar chapel before the church was opened, has sung in

[1] 'Je définirais la poésie : l'exquise expressi d'impressions exquises.—La poésie, c'est la vérité endimanchée.'—JOSEPH ROUX, *Pensées.*

the choir ever since—and all these workers are voluntary. One reason for this was, it seems to me, the generous trustfulness he showed towards us all, his hearty and unfeigned appreciation of what we did, and his way of dealing with us, not *de haut en bas* condescendingly, but on the level ground of spiritual comradeship. At first there was a tendency to do everything himself, but within a few years he had set this right, and divided the works according to the varied gifts of the workers. Looking back upon the years past, I feel sure that we must have tried his patience sorely at times. He had come to his maturity when we joined him, and his views of things had taken fixed shape, but some of us were anything rather than mature, and we flung ourselves with almost boyish eagerness headlong into the various enthusiasms of the hour. Startling views, religious, political, social, and scientific, were broached at the dinner-table, which must often have been distasteful enough to his conservative mind, and I still seem to see the look, part amused, part amazed, with which he listened to our suggestions for the general setting right of the universe. A smaller man would have snubbed us. He did not do so—to our gain, I think.

It may be asked how he found time to carry through the innumerable things in the parish and out of the parish which demanded his supervision and his care ? Something must be put down to his exceedingly methodical habits, and something also to the fact that he gave himself wholly and unreservedly to the work. He never seemed to forget that he was a priest, or to feel at liberty to dispose of time or strength to any other end than the service of the Gospel.

It must also be acknowledged that he stole time out of the night. Supper over, he hurried away to his room, and, closing his door, with a feeling of intense relief, set himself to make good use of the precious hours of solitude.[1]   I know not how late he worked and prayed, but when we fell asleep—and we were not early—his lamp was burning still.

I wish it had been possible to give in detail more of his inner life, the *vie intime*, the man's communings with his own heart, the growth of character and the work of grace.   Of all this, which forms so attractive and instructive a feature of foreign biographies, we knew little.

> If, in the paths of the world,
> Stones might have wounded thy feet,
> Toil or dejection have tried
> Thy spirit, of that we saw
> Nothing—to us thou wast still
> Cheerful, and helpful, and firm !

He was extremely reticent about himself, and trusted little to the insecure privacy of a journal. This is the national temperament. English reserve counts spiritual confidences almost an indelicacy, almost a failure in manliness. It is our pride to exhibit under all conditions an appearance of complete impassiveness. Mackonochie said very little about the things which were most often in

---

[1]   Dear night ! this world's defeat ;
The stop to busie fools ; care's check and curb ;
The day of Spirits ; my soul's calm retreat
    Which none disturb !
Christ's progress, and His prayer time :
The hours to which high Heaven doth chime.
                              Henry Vaughan.

his thoughts, and the finely sculptured mask of his face betrayed as little that which lay hid beneath it. He gave us results, but the processes were shut up from us as tightly as the works of a watch.

If I were asked to state in the shortest, simplest way, Mackonochie's most noteworthy achievement, that for which we are most deeply indebted to him, I should point the enquirer, not to the things he did and endured in defence of ecclesiastical right; not to the immense stimulus he has given to the revival of the solemnities of divine worship, nor yet to any of the numerous works inaugurated or developed by him, but simply to himself, to the noble manhood of the man. ' Quid docent nos apostoli sancti ? ' asks St. Bernard. ' What do the holy apostles teach us ? ' Not the fisher's art, nor yet the tent-maker's, nor anything of that sort; not, how to study Plato or pursue the subtleties of Aristotle, ever learning and never coming to the knowledge of the truth. ' Docuerunt me vivere,' 'they have taught me how to live.'[1] It is the one lesson of sovereign concern. It is the lesson for which we who knew and loved him thank him most.

It would lengthen considerably a preface already long, if I were to attempt to name and thank all the persons to whose kindly co-operation we are indebted for much of the material of this book. They will let me tender them collectively our hearty thanks.[2] One or two names, however,

---

[1] ' Putas, parva res est scire vivere? Magnum aliquid, imo maximum est.'—*S. Bernardi in festo SS. Petri et Pauli sermo.*

[2] To the kindness of our churchwarden, Mr. H. Sidney Warr, we are indebted for the use of the negative of the frontispiece. The photograph of the grave at Woking has been very kindly placed at our disposal by Mr. William Ellis, of 25 Clapton Square, E.

cannot be passed over. His Honour Judge Mackonochie and Mrs. Mackonochie have rendered invaluable help by placing unreservedly at our disposal innumerable letters and documents, and by giving every assistance in their power to enable us to complete the life record of the brother whom they so much love and venerate. The Bishop of Argyll and the Isles has laid us all at St. Alban's under such deep obligations, that his kindness in respect of this book can scarcely add to the gratitude and affection we already feel towards him. To Miss Greenstreet also, one of the oldest and faithfullest of our workers here, we owe much.

One friend, alas! whom we should have named amongst our benefactors, has passed out of earshot of our thanks— Dr. Littledale. His learning and sagacity have for years been always and willingly at our service. The legal Chapter on Martin *v.* Mackonochie, and the history of the Ecclesiastical Courts in the Appendix, are both from his pen, and stand amongst the latest labours of his laborious and suffering life. May God convert the thanks we owe him and would give him into blessing, and grant him eternal light and rest.

The preparation of this Memoir was, in the first instance, placed in my hands, and the materials were in considerable part collected. The book was also announced in my name; but in undertaking the task, I had not counted with the incessant inevitable interruptions which break up the days of the London clergy, and further, in my inexperience, I had hardly measured the magnitude of a task of this sort. After some ineffectual attempts to make way with the Memoir, I was rescued from my difficulty by the great kindness of the lady whose initials appear on the title-page. With a skill which I do sincerely envy, Mrs. Charles Towle (daughter of Sir Henry Taylor) has accomplished the work. Having followed its progress step by step, I have no hesitation in saying that it is much better done than I could have done it. For the facts narrated I accept the responsibility; they are told with truth and soberness. For the appreciations and criticisms I also vouch; they are, as far as my observation and judgment go, marked by discernment and justice. But the credit of the building of the book belongs wholly to Mrs. Towle, and all friends of Mr. Mackonochie are greatly indebted to her for her labour of love.

E. F. RUSSELL.

35 BROOKE STREET, HOLBORN.

CONTENTS

CHAPTER X.

1867–1869

CHAPTER XI.

1869–1874

CHAPTER XII.

1875–1882

CHAPTER XIII.

1875–1882 *(continued)*

CHAPTER XIV.

1882

CHAPTER XV.

1883-1887

CHAPTER XVI.

1887

ILLUSTRATIONS

ALEXANDER HERIOT MACKONOCHIE

CHAPTER I.

Birth and parentage—Early associations—Family characteristics—A student
at Edinburgh University—Religious thought in Scotland—Matriculation
at Wadham College, Oxford.

1825—1845.

ALEXANDER HERIOT was the third son of Colonel
Mackonochie, of the East India Company's service, by his
marriage with Miss Isabella Alison, of Scotch extraction,
whose family had removed to Fareham in Hampshire.

There were three children of the marriage; the eldest,
George, who died in India when a little more than a year
old; the second and sole surviving brother, James, born
August 19, 1823; and Alexander Heriot, born at Fareham
soon after his parents' return from India, on August 11,
1825.

Fareham is a small prosperous country town of about
7,000 inhabitants, situated at the head of a deep inlet of
the sea forming the western branch of Portsmouth har-
bour. Ships of 300 tons come up to the quays, and it
is busy enough with its local industries of brickmaking,

B

tanning and pottery, and yet sufficiently far removed from
the noise and bustle of the city, for life to wear a pleasant,
leisurely aspect.   There is nothing especially venerable
about the place, except the Early English chancel of the
parish church, dating from the thirteenth century ; but the
old-fashioned substantial houses, built in the days when
people had no objection to see their neighbours passing
along the pavement before their windows, have a comfortable appearance of respectable middle-age, whilst the large
gardens behind, with their smooth lawns and flower-
beds, constitute the chief beauty of the place.   To one
of these houses on the left-hand side of West Street—
a house with an old-fashioned portico and clustering
creepers—Colonel Mackonochie after his long wanderings
brought home his wife ; and the quiet, sober little town,
with its local interests, its conservative instincts, and its
air of respectability, became the home of his sons' child-
hood.   For a short time, indeed, the family removed to
the village of Wickham in the near neighbourhood, and
there, when his youngest son was two years old, Colonel
Mackonochie died ; but his widow returned to Fareham
to bring up her two little boys.

It is somewhat singular that under the circumstances
there should be no traces of injudicious fondness.   Mrs.
Mackonochie's care for her children was naturally the
chief occupation, and the engrossing interest of her life.
She put her own troubles aside to brighten their lives, and
took care for all their little pleasures ; yet they were early
taught to submit to parental discipline ; not to look for
indulgence even where affection was strongest ; and to the

little Alexander, with frequent ill-health and subdued
spirits, life was, even thus early, rather a task to be learnt
than a gift to be enjoyed. He was in these days much
with older people. Mrs. Mackonochie's mother and two
maiden sisters lived at Fareham, and to them also the two
children were objects of grave solicitude and almost parental care. And this care, with all its feminine tenderness,
was chiefly for the boy's higher interests. Bereavement
had already cast a shadow upon the home where self-
restraint had grown from a duty into a habit. There was a
deep sense of the presence of God, a constant reference to
His Will as the only guide either in the great decisions
or the practical details of life, which could not have been
without its influence upon the children. Very early there
awoke within the youngest boy the desire to devote himself to God in the Ministry of the Church, which later on
earned for him amongst his companions the nickname of
‘ the boy-bishop.’

It was a young life with few illusions, quiet, self-controlled, unemotional ; an apparently unhesitating obedience
to lawful authority, a no less ready submission to the
higher dictates of conscience ; and yet a life of natural
boyish interests and pursuits and failings ; unforced, unimaginative.

But perhaps the boy is happiest who is more or less
commonplace ; whose growth is gradual and whose con-
ceptions of right and wrong are unexaggerated ; who
fights his battles, as boys do, without counting up his
victories ; who is somewhat shamefaced as to his virtues
and not apt to dwell upon his sins.

In this small household the piety was of a somewhat severe order—a habit and a principle rather than a sentiment. We may be quite sure that no morbid tendencies would have been encouraged in the young boy, whose impulse towards a devout life came from within, not from without; assisted, doubtless, by a mother's prayers, but not fostered by any artificial means. It was a healthy plant which would thrive in any soil.

The whole tone of mind of the household was sober, disciplined, and restrained; even affection kept within the bounds of a systematic self-control. There are but few early letters, for the boys rarely went from home, but those few are singularly destitute of feeling, more noticeable perhaps on the side of friends and relations than on the part of the boy himself. There are few of those trivialities, those family jests which awaken unreasoning and yet salutary laughter, and do much to lighten the sense of growing responsibility at the outset of life. Even joy in this Scotch household seems to have been 'a solemn and a severe thing.' There is only one trace of an early enthusiasm, when his mother writes after a journey: 'We passed through Strathfieldsaye and saw at full length Arthur Wellesley, Duke of Wellington, not *in propriâ personâ*, but on a timber waggon. I thought you would have liked much even to look on that name.'

Ten or twelve years before, we read of another remote and secluded home where there were few events to disturb the even course of existence and few personal interests to interfere with those which clustered round public personages—the home of the Brontës on the Yorkshire moor—

of whom we are told that the Duke of Wellington was 'their demi-god.' But in Mrs. Mackonochie's small family circle such strong predilections seem to have been somewhat rare, and politics had apparently less interest than those religious questions which were afterwards to occupy so large a portion of the thoughts of the second son.

Within this home circle he remained for an unusual length of time ; his delicate health making it unadvisable, if not impossible, to send him to a public school. When schooling became a necessity, his mother removed first to Bath and then to Exeter, where he attended private schools ; and his education was continued later on by his studying for a short period at the Edinburgh University whilst living in Edinburgh with his mother and brother. As to his religious life before this time, we have nothing but the brief record of Confirmation and first Communion when a schoolboy at Exeter. The whole temper of the family mind was not only reserved, but averse to the manifestation of religious feeling. 'Hast thou faith, have it to thyself,' was a precept carried out with willing exactitude.

Yet, though the records are but scanty, already in these early years we see signs of that fixity of purpose, that deliberate counting of the cost, which was so far removed from unwillingness to pay, that high standard of right uplifted which was never to be lowered either for friend or foe.

At Edinburgh, under some manifest disadvantages (to which he refers when he writes to a friend, 'that he is not sufficiently advanced to profit by the lectures he attends '), he was evidently sincere in his wish not so much to excel as to make the best use of his advantages. The bent of his mind, both serious and practical, was favourable to the acquisition of knowledge, and we can well believe it was with sincere impartiality that he reports himself as having been 'very diligent.' The habit of application had already been acquired which, when every quarter of an hour had its· allotted task, was to stand him in such good stead. And it would seem as if study was at this time almost his sole occupation. We find his chief adviser in these matters counselling him for the present to 'leave Natural Philosophy, Moral Philosophy, and Rhetoric alone, and devote all his time to classical studies ; to consider history light reading, whilst divinity and church history are to occupy some hours on Sunday.' Apparently all his time and energies were to be absorbed in the painful and conscientious acquisition of knowledge ; success was to be the result of unremitting effort ; if a boyish distaste for so strict a division of time, and especially for 'divinity and church history' on his one free day, arose, it was to be sternly disregarded. The business of life already left no room for recreation.

The sacrifices made were probably, as they were throughout life, unconscious. He had no reason to be dissatisfied with the result. There are no brilliant successes to be recorded, but he acquitted himself with credit, and though his mother had wished him to go to Durham, there must have been a feeling in the family that he deserved to have some regard paid to his own strong predilections, and he had his name entered for Wadham College, Oxford.

He was there to find himself in an atmosphere so different

from that in which he had hitherto lived, that we must cast our eyes backward in order to understand something of the temper of mind (especially in regard to matters of religion) with which he entered upon his Oxford life.

Already there had been evidence that he was occupied with subjects which have usually little interest for one who was hardly more than a schoolboy. Whilst he was at Edinburgh we find a friend writing to him as follows : ' I will not engage to answer any questions your curiosity may suggest as to our present constitution in Church and State,' whilst, in evident reference to detailed questionings, he goes on to explain the constitution of the Church of England, the authority of the Ecclesiastical Courts, the questions of appeals, &c.

Yet the family traditions were altogether antagonistic to the revival within the bounds of the English Church, of which various rumours had reached them. In February 1843 we find his mother writing to him :

Sir Henry Thompson was here to-day and we mentioned your being nominated for Wadham. He said it was a very good college, the head of it (Simmons) as well as Mr. Walker ' anti-Pusey.' He thinks this wild doctrine is on the decline, which I was very glad to hear him say. Ultra views both in religion and politics lead to evil. The High Church party, as far as I have learnt their views, have not learnt humility. As far as I can see, the moderate Low Churchman who lets his moderation be known unto all men is the closest follower of Christ.

Several members of the family seem to have been much scandalised by the ' Drummondite schism.' ' All this disturbance,' as they say, with evident distaste, ' in the name of religion.' Clearly they favour order and submission to authority as well as moderation. They are very sure of their ground ; that to which they have been accustomed must be right. They have no wish to join in the battle-cry on either side ; and religious polemics are the worst of all.

One of the maiden aunts, Miss Alison, writes in 1842 of a friend who was at Margaret's Chapel and saw and heard your old master, Mr. Hutchings, who turned his back upon the congregation at the Belief, and showed by other marks independent of his sermon (which would have decided the hearers of his bias to Puseyism) that he had got the *new light*. From what I heard he never acted like a very wise man, and this confirms it. I hope it has not crept into the Edinburgh chapels. It is not countenanced in those quarters, they say, which will, it is to be hoped, give it a check.

Again his grandmother writes from Fareham in indignant distress at the innovations in church :

We have had quite a *new* service, and the Communion on Ascension Day. We none of us approved of it, and did not go to church.

There is a severe piety unconsciously arrogant in the tone of the letters. They do not expect that he will differ from them, perhaps they had no reason to do so. Novelty, especially in religious matters, is a dangerous thing, to be firmly but temperately resisted.

Professor Tulloch, in writing of this time in Scotland, has declared that there has seldom been in our national history a more fruitful epoch of religious thought. The theological mind is seen opening in all directions. Religion claims a wider sovereignty—a more powerful and extended hold of humanity ; in short, a more real catholicism than any Church had yet assigned it.

The Anglo-Catholic, or Oxford movement, had had an influence widening and spreading even into the antagonistic lines of Scottish Calvinism. For to its adherents also, dogma was (as Cardinal Newman says it was to the Evangelicals amongst whom he had been brought up) the fundamental principle of religion. 'I know no other religion,' he declares in his 'Apologia'; 'I cannot enter into the idea of any other religion'; and to the Scotch Episcopalian, who stood necessarily more or less upon the defensive, orthodoxy was not merely the groundwork but the bulwark of his faith.

It would seem, therefore, that in spite of the family sentiments and the traditions in which he had been brought up, there was need for no sudden or fundamental change in the character of Alexander Mackonochie's mind when, in a sincere and persevering search for truth, he fell back upon old beliefs. A new light was to be flashed upon the long-obscured history of the past. 'What is most remarkable to a student nowadays,' says Professor Tulloch, again in speaking of the leaders of religious thought at this time in Scotland, 'is the lack of historical knowledge in dealing with Christian dogma;' but henceforth he was to have new guides and new teachers. The principle had been there all along, it was but to be applied to the convictions which during the last year of his student life had been gathering strength within him. 'My own Bishop was my Pope,' as Cardinal Newman asserted of himself in his Anglican days, in a sentence which surely foreshadowed the allegiance he was afterwards to pay to the Bishop of Rome; and in the same way in the case of the Edinburgh student there had been the anxious search for truth's credentials, which he was to find amongst the dusty, long-forgotten records of antiquity; the feeling after some definite rule of faith as well as of life; and an ever-increasing desire to submit his strong young will to an authority whose decrees he could not question.

His unimaginative boyhood of strenuous effort and conscientious work, affectionate but unimpassioned, had left little leisure for dreams. Yet he, too, had had his visions of a Church of which the tokens should be 'simple, obvious, and intelligible. . . . God's ordained teacher in the way to Heaven.'[1] He had no revolutionary tendencies. The Church in which he believed should be no new thing; it should have its basis in antiquity. It should not be the creation of an excited imagination, nor the product of a mind supplying its own needs, but an unchangeable fact and an historical reality.

It was with these preconceived ideas, with this half-formulated creed, that, in January 1845, Mackonochie went up to Oxford.

[1] *British Critic*, Oct. 1838.

CHAPTER II.

Oxford in 1845—Religious opinions—Friends and associates—Their testimony—Political views—Charles Marriott—Extract from University sermon.

1845—1849.

IN 1845 the Tractarian movement had already passed through its first two decades. It was a time when principles were to be put into practice, and when deep religious convictions were impelling men to action. The profound discouragement which had fallen upon some of the leading spirits was but as a spur to fresh efforts. The ranks were closing up in the courageous, if somewhat futile, endeavour to hide the vacant places. In the first disenchantment of the rude awakening from a dream of an 'ideal Church,' men had begun to realise more fully that they could not defend the liberties of the Church, nor contend for the 'faith once delivered,' without engaging in the old weary quarrel with the world, the flesh, and the devil. The lines upon which they were fighting were so far defined as to show that the battle had but begun. It was still a time of struggle and conquest of difficulty and doubt ; but yet more it was a time of disappointment and failure ; of friendships broken and high hopes laid low.

Many of the first leaders of the movement were scattered. Already as early as 1823 Keble's residence at Oxford had come to an end, and his quiet pastoral life had begun. The 'Christian Year,' published in 1827, had quickened the devotional life of the Church of England, and emphasised the sacramental element in her teaching ; but its author was to be henceforth above all a parish priest, and his position with regard to the vexed questions of the day was more or less that of a spectator. In 1845 Wilberforce was about to be consecrated Bishop of Oxford ; the 'Ideal of a Christian Church' had just been published, and Mr. Ward was shortly to join the Roman Communion. Hurrell Froude, with his boyish aspirations and high imaginings, 'the knight errant,' as he has been called, of the Tractarian party, had died in 1836 ; and Newman, who since 1841, as he writes, 'had been on his death-bed as regards the Anglican Communion,' had given up clerical duty in 1843 and withdrawn to Littlemore.

All these and many others had been like a search party in a wood, intent upon the same object though wandering in different paths. Emerging once more into the light of common day, they found to their consternation and surprise how far apart they stood. Their object had been the same and the spirit which animated them one, but the search was over and they had arrived at different conclusions. They had been held together, not only by a common cause, but by the strong bond of personal affection ; it was to their honour that that bond remained unbroken, yet to the general discouragement it added the bitter sense of individual loss.

Men's minds were in an unsettled condition, either

vainly searching out old landmarks, or intent upon their destruction. Liberalism and dogmatism were contending together, whilst in an atmosphere now at fever heat a fusion seemed, for the moment, possible. 'A new school of thought was rising, as is usual in doctrinal enquiries, and was sweeping the original party of the movement aside, and was taking its place.'[1]

There remained to this new school, in the ebb-tide of the Tractarian movement, two principal guides and counsellors—Dr. Pusey and Charles Marriott. With the latter Mackonochie appears to have entered into relations of more or less intimacy, but how far he already shared his religious opinions it is difficult to determine. Undoubtedly his early training had taught him to look upon them with suspicion. One of those who had some slight acquaintance with him at this time writes : 'It seems to come back to me that we knew him in college as a man of pronounced views, I should almost have said, if I dared, of pronounced Low Church views.' But there is no evidence that this was the case. Undoubtedly the whole tone of his mind was serious and religious ; but a pronounced Low Churchman would hardly have concerned himself about Church government ; he would hardly have sought, as Mackonochie evidently sought, an historical basis for the faith that was in him. He was not so much seeking the truth itself (which no doubt he was convinced he held already), as examining with painstaking perseverance the foundations upon which it rested. His belief could never have been a vague one. One can imagine him ignoring his human

1 Newman's *Apologia*, p. 163.

sympathies and remorselessly treading down his affections, so that he might hold with stern consistency the creed of his Calvinistic forefathers ; but one cannot imagine that at any period of his spiritual life religion could have been an intangible thing, shadowy, and undefined.

He could not have lived at Oxford without being brought into almost daily contact with the controversies going on not only upon religious but upon ecclesiastical subjects. His own mind, disciplined and well regulated, demanded proportion and order in God's kingdom. The Church upon earth was a type and shadow of the Heavenly Jerusalem, 'the city that hath foundations' and 'lieth four-square'; a vision indeed, but a vision of grace and order and symmetry.

He had not been long in Oxford when we find him writing to his mother :

I heard Pusey preach on Sunday. He gave a very good sermon on the Power of the Keys, which was a continuation of the course in which he was interrupted by his suspension, to which event he slightly alluded. The sermon seems to have given general satisfaction except to a few.

And one of his friends writes :

Of course in opinion he differed widely from the warden of that day, and I well remember his extreme annoyance at having been delayed by him in college one Sunday morning when he was particularly anxious to reach the Cathedral in time to hear Dr. Pusey's first university sermon after his three years' suspension from preaching.

Another college contemporary testifies that 'he always had the same kind of opinions which he held in the latter years of his life.'

It is quite possible that his distinctively religious tone and strictness of life may have been associated in some minds with evangelical views, and thus a mistake might easily arise. To the end of his life there was a curiously strong flavour of puritanism in his religion ; his code as to the religious observance of Sunday, for instance, being of almost Jewish strictness. And he does not appear to have taken much part in the society or amusements of the college. 'He lived,' says one of those in residence with him, 'a very quiet, retired life, not belonging to any particular set, and taking no prominent part in such amusements as boating and cricketing.' To this another adds :

he was not muscularly very strong, being too long in the limb for heavy work, but he was very fond of boating, and in 1846 when all the old men had left the college boat, he was most plucky in supporting the fresh crew, and did his best in rowing whilst his strength lasted ; but a few days of racing shut him up. . . . As time went on he applied himself more and more to reading and less to athletics, but he was always keenly alive to the honour of the college. Whatever he did he did with a will and conscientiously. It was the custom when a freshman came up without friends in college for the sub-warden to ask a man who had been up for a term or two to call on him. In this way Mackonochie was the first man who called on me and invited me to his rooms, and I always felt that I owed him much for my first introduction to some of his friends, and for quiet warnings against some others who took a pleasure in leading freshmen astray.

Mackonochie was in his last year of undergraduate life when I went up to Oxford in October 1847 (writes the Rev. F. S. Lea, one of his intimate friends). Among the senior undergraduates were John Walter Lea, then, as always, a High Churchman ; his brother, whose sympathies were with the evangelical school ; John Macnaught and Walter Congreve, both Liberals ; and W. H. Stowe, afterwards Fellow of Oriel, whose brilliant career closed with his death as the *Times* correspondent in the Crimea. Differing as they did from him and from each other on many questions both religious and political, which occupied the most thoughtful minds in the Oxford of their day, all the leading undergraduates in Oxford agreed in the cordial regard and respect which they felt for Mackonochie, as those who survive will witness on behalf of those who have passed away as well as on their own. He was a man of quiet judgment who never lost his temper ; he held fast by his own opinions, but he was always fair in discussion and good-humoured as an opponent. In those days undergraduates were more given to argument than they are now ; the afternoon walk of forty years ago with its accompanying discussion is a thing of the past ; among reading men it was an established institution then. . . . He was one of a group of men who made a rule of attending chapel at both the daily services, and as far as I remember he was never absent. . . . I am writing on King Charles's Day, the now almost forgotten 29th of May, which my Oxford memories especially associate with Mackonochie. There was in the Warden of Wadham's garden an oak, reputed to have sprung from a Boscobel acorn, which provided us with sprays for morning chapel, and an undecorated undergraduate would be consoled by a ' Never mind, you can get a bough from Mackonochie's tree ; ' for the devoted Scottish Jacobite always exhibited a badge of conspicuous proportions.

Very firmly as Mackonochie held an opinion when once he had satisfied himself of its truth, he was at Oxford an adherent rather than a leader. He was very cautious, and would take up no ground of which he was not sure, and he would do nothing by halves.

After he had taken his degree and when he was preparing for Holy Orders, his scrupulous and conscientious caution suggested a difficulty in the way of his ordination by an English bishop. The second of the three articles in the 36th Canon would bind him ' to use the form prescribed in the Book of Common Prayer

and none other.'   He was a Scottish Churchman, and how could
he when in Scotland use the Scottish office? . . . I urged upon
him that the pledge was only binding within the dioceses of the
English Church.   His other friends took the same view, and the
difficulty was removed.   His reading for the schools had been steady
and methodical ; and by way of aids to memory he used mentally
to associate the events of his history or the moral and intellectual
heads of his ethics with certain points in the walls or ceiling of
his rooms—'Justice, perhaps, being over the fireplace, and Mag-
nanimity in the corner by the door.   He knew thoroughly what he
read and never crammed.

As I recall the various subjects which used in my undergraduate
time to come up for more or less eager discussion, some were merely
speculative or fanciful, having no real bearing on life or duty, and
with such, I think, Mackonochie rarely troubled himself.   His
interest was in questions influencing life and action, and among
such the relative, or, as they were often represented, the opposing
claims of reason and authority formed a very frequent subject. . . .
His way of living was careful and economical.   Few men probably
have left Oxford so absolutely free from debt.   He was ordained
in 1849, when he asked me to pay such debts and subscriptions as
were outstanding.   I have the account before me as I write, and
the amount is 12*l.* 12*s.* 6*d.*

At Oxford (writes another fellow undergraduate) he was a
poor man, and lived frugally in what was called the garret-room,
which belonged to each set of rooms.   He had not more than two
or three in-college acquaintances, and gave no parties.   But his
rowing having been observed he was made stroke of the Wadham
'Torpid.'   I was one of those who pulled behind him, and the
crew were allowed, during their training, early dinner daily with
him in his garret apartment.   Some of us who had thought him
strait-laced and unattractive, found him a genial host and pleasant
companion. . . .   Mackonochie was during all his college course
consistently religious.   I remember well his collecting in college
subscriptions for the Diocese of Fredericton, of which a Wadham

man, Medley, had been appointed bishop. It took some boldness for an undergraduate to do that.

Every letter respecting this time, whether from friends or acquaintances, is a testimony to the 'respect' in which he was held—a curious word to use in connection with so young a man. He had the courage of his opinions, and they were not so much opinions as convictions, strong and defined, not taken up lightly nor to be lightly laid aside ; yet his intimate friends appear to have been mostly men of different views. He was never one of a 'clique.' He had not the useful yet perplexing power of looking at things with other people's eyes, but at any rate he had never any desire 'to make a desert and call it peace.'

There was one thing that seemed rather difficult to understand about him (writes one of those who differed from him). His chief friend for a long time was a man who stood almost at the opposite pole of opinion from him on theological and historical questions. He was broad and liberal. The only point of similarity which seemed to outsiders to bring them together was that they both took warm interest in subjects with which many of the younger men little concerned themselves, and were both very fond of arguing.

Again, another correspondent says :

Mackonochie's warmest friends were found quite as much among the men who did not agree with him in opinion as among those who did.

It was surely an indication of strength of character, especially in this time of controversy, when party lines were so strongly marked out and party names were battle-cries or watchwords.

Nor was Mackonochie in respect to politics a party man.

He took an interest in them, not unmixed, as was natural, with a good deal of youthful ignorance and presumption, but it was chiefly because at this time political and ecclesiastical questions were as closely intertwined as they had ever been in the days of the Stuarts. Only a few years before, Newman, when he saw a French vessel at Algiers, would not even look at the tricolour, and revolutionary Paris was so hateful to him, with all its beauty, that he kept indoors the whole time he was there. . . . 'And Keble delighted to see his little nephews under his teaching snapping at all the Roundheads and kissing all the Cavaliers.'[1] All the traditions of the Mackonochie family, all the instincts of the sons were Conservative, and it is probable that his residence at Oxford deepened rather than modified his convictions. But his interest in politics was never throughout his life divorced from their bearing upon religious and social questions. He was a Tory and a Liberationist, and long after these Oxford days we find the following words in the report of a speech made at an English Church Union meeting :

He wished to refer to the impression that the English Church Union wanted to mix political questions with those that were spiritual. Now there were on the Council men of all shades of politics from Tories to the broadest Liberals, and he had never heard at any of their Council Meetings a single allusion to politics except when it was dragged in by some member for the purpose of charging them with being a political body. It was true they presented petitions to Parliament, but that was only when there was some Act of Parliament in progress which threatened the doctrines or discipline of the Church of England.

[1] *Religious Thought*, Tulloch, p. 105.

He had no sympathy with those to whom a spurious Liberalism was but a pretext for the overthrow of ancient institutions and unwelcome restrictions, involving no self-sacrifice; but his own love for the people was a wide and enduring thing; an instinct against oppression, and a pity which was almost a passion for the weak, demanding an absolute self-surrender.

> In the blossoming of lilies,
>   Christ was born across the sea.
> Since He died to make men holy,
>   Let us die to make men free.

Essentially a practical man, he was not likely at this time to have given much thought to political questions. His vocation was ever before him, and his keenest as well as his highest interests were centred upon the things which concerned it.

It is not wonderful, therefore, that he should have been attracted by Charles Marriott, whom Dean Burgon calls preeminently the man of ‘saintly life.’ He was a student and a theologian, calm, laborious, conscientious, and persuasive. Next to Dr. Pusey, he was ‘the leader at head-quarters’ of those who were searching out upon the old lines of the Tractarian movement, the historical basis of Christianity, the claims of tradition, and the catholicity of the English Church. He had had much experience in dealing with young men, owing to the position he had held as head of a theological college, and had an immense attraction for men of the most opposite minds. Frederick Maurice described his character ‘as one of the deepest and noblest to be found anywhere. His generosity and self-devotion in

the most unobtrusive way are quite marvellous. If there
are ten such, I think England is not Sodom.' And Dr.
Newman, in a letter dated 1841, wrote: 'He is a grave,
sober, and deeply religious person, a great reader of ecclesiastical antiquity, and has more influence with younger
men than any one perhaps of his standing.'

How far that influence was exerted upon Mackonochie
at this time we have no exact means of judging, but we
have the strongest possible proof of its enduring character.
For years after he left Oxford he periodically sought his
spiritual guidance. The tie was not only one of respect.
Amongst the letters which he carefully treasured we find
eight or nine notes written upon scraps and half-sheets of
paper. 'My dear Mackonochie . . . . Yours ever most
sincerely, C. Marriott ;' and that is all, with the exception
of a few lines between giving him appointments. They
were written in 1853 and 1854, and yet here they remain,
evidences of an ardent affection, to which probably a strong
reserve would allow him to give no other expression.

That reserve constitutes a great difficulty in judging of
his character at this time. His letters are so often bare
statements of facts ; even in writing to those nearest and
dearest to him there is no expansion. He touches, indeed,
upon home interests, but where his own feelings are concerned he is silent. It is not until he has entered upon the
duties of his ministry that with the formal copper-plate
handwriting there also vanish the stiff old-fashioned sentences which tell us so little of his real self.

He took naturally the recreations which came in his
way. The even tenour of his Oxford life was broken

by visits to Wales and North Devon, and by one short tour abroad. They were not unwelcome interruptions to his work, but it was then, as always, his chief object, and the engrossing interest of life. Always humble with regard to his intellectual attainments, he was fully aware that great diligence would be required to atone for early disadvantages, and he had little expectation of doing well in the final schools. When in June 1848 he writes to inform his mother that he has taken a second class in classics, he is evidently both pleased and surprised, and in simple phrase gives thanks to Almighty God.

And so this time of preparation was over. He was to enter upon the work to which he had so long dedicated himself, and as we finish the chapter it recalls his own words in a sermon preached before the University more than twenty years after.

The University life is not simply a life in itself; it is distinctly one which is preparatory to another. . . . Many of you will tell me, no doubt, that the University is not the place for self-devotion. I fearlessly assert that to say so is to libel yourselves, your university, and your God. . . . Above all things avoid an effeminate sentimentality whether about religion, or taste, or art, or some quasi-scientific pursuit . . . not to live energetically for God in your university life is to do evil . . . Live, then, within her walls ' in the Name of the Lord;' live as those who are practising in the narrower sphere of the university to work for God in the great world beyond. Take always, not the popular side, but that which is high and noble and acceptable to God. Go forth ' in the Name of the Lord,' and you will find all the blessings for which you crave and many to which you have not dared to aspire.

CHAPTER III.

Ordination—First curacy at Westbury—Early ministerial work—Removal to Wantage—Letters from Bishop Denison—Wantage in 1852—Letters from Dr. Liddon and the Dean of Lincoln—Work at the hamlet of Charlton—Reminiscences of the villagers—Thought of mission work abroad—Call to St. George's-in-the-East.

1849—1858.

IT was in Lent 1849 that Mackonochie was ordained by Bishop Denison at Salisbury, and went at once as curate to the parish of Westbury in Wiltshire.

On January 20, 1849, the Bishop's chaplain writes:

Mr. Meyrick has informed me that he has been allowed by the bishop to nominate you to a cure at Westbury. Under ordinary circumstances the bishop would require you to come to Sarum for a preliminary examination—as it is, he will not expect to see you here till the examination commences at the palace.

And on February 27, Mackonochie wrote to his mother from Salisbury:

The examination will begin to-morrow. I know I need not repeat what I said before, that I have now an especial claim to be in the thoughts of all my friends. At such times one feels most strongly one's great want of all that the intercessions of friends and fellow-Christians can obtain for us.

I am very glad (he writes again) that the examination is over, for it has been hard and exciting work and nowise conducive to such meditations as befit the work of to-morrow.

And then again, on a scrap of paper dated March 4:

I have only time to tell you that the ordination is at last over. . . . Meyrick (the Vicar of Westbury) offers me a week's holiday, but I have decided to go down on Monday.

In the preceding October, the Rev. E. W. Tufnell, afterwards Bishop of Brisbane, had recommended him to apply for the Westbury curacy.

It is (he wrote) one of the most important parishes in the county, and the curates there seem to work so happily and laboriously with the vicar that it must be a very desirable post.

The Rev. Thomas Bowles (afterwards Mackonochie's fellow-curate and intimate friend) had, however, been first in the field. He was ordained to Westbury at Christmas, and no other suitable curacy offering itself, Mackonochie's ordination was delayed until Lent. It was shortly before his ordination that Mr. Meyrick communicated with him again. He was obliged by failing health to leave his parish for some time, and wished to secure his services if he were still disengaged. This proved to be the case, and he at once closed with Mr. Meyrick's offer. As usual, he had accepted his first disappointment very quietly.

Mr. Bowles, who furnishes us with some recollections of this time, writes:

I was much more vexed at having stood in Mackonochie's way than he was with me for interrupting his plans. . . . In a very few days after his arrival he was at work amongst the poor, visiting with great diligence and at first with some difficulty of manner, though it was not long before he was much liked by his own especial parishioners as well as generally, though they thought him 'stiff,' as in those days he was. His preaching at the time I was with him at Westbury could not be called good. He wrote sermons and preached from his paper. He wrote with slowness and considerable difficulty. I have known him write most of Saturday, and, unable to make enough to fill his paper, work on into the night, till he went to bed on Sunday morning rather than Saturday night in despair, and have to fill a few more pages on Sunday morning before service. . . . It was certainly hard work for three curates, all young. We had three churches. One of them (Bratton) was more than three miles off; another (Ditton) one and three-quarter mile. Bratton had its two services, Ditton two also, and there were three at the parish church . . . From the first A. H. M. had always to preach two sermons a week.

The curates lived together, and ' I do not think,' writes one who knew them intimately, ' that they ever had a shade of disagreement. The only fault was that they did not know the limits of human strength, fasted too much and worked too hard. Mr. Mackonochie's powers of work were wonderful. At one time, when single-handed in the parish, he had four daily services in different parts of it, in addition to his other work. When he first came to the parish, various circumstances had combined to bring about a great deal of poverty in the district, and he could not restrain himself from giving what he could ill afford to those in need. On one occasion, being much pressed to go to Oxford for some interesting gathering, his friends were puzzled by his refusal, until at last the reason transpired. He had not a coat fit to go in, and as he very apologetically remarked, " I could not help it, the fever was so bad at Ditton." '

About forty years ago (writes Canon Tinling) my official duties as H.M. Inspector of Schools required me to visit Westbury. I remember distinctly the real pleasure I enjoyed in passing forty-eight hours with the curates and witnessing for the first time the community life that they were living. . . . Mackonochie was evidently a power; there was a manly vigour pervading the home.   Everything was charmingly clean, and yet no waste or luxury ; all was unselfishness, brotherly love, and earnest devotion to God and man ; all was calm, unpretending. . . . Mackonochie impressed me very deeply as a man of God— certain to draw those with whom he came in contact to a higher life of devotion.

He threw himself at once into his work with energy and zeal, and a painstaking conscientiousness as to its smallest details which was even more remarkable in so young a man.   The drudgery of parochial work, which must often precede direct spiritual ministrations, was never neglected.   He described it as ' spade husbandry,' and as absolutely necessary if the work was to bear fruit.   There was not only a singleness of aim, but a method and order in his life which shut out any thought of personal ease or self-indulgence.   One of whom he never afterwards lost sight, who was at that time Master of the Westbury Union, writes :

I knew his landlady, and she told me that he was very exact and orderly in all his movements, that he declined everything in the shape of personal indulgence, and even if she put an extra covering on his bed in cold weather he made no remark, but she invariably found it in the morning neatly folded and laid aside. He usually rose about four or five o'clock in the morning. . . . I knew several schoolboys whom he invited to his lodgings to receive special instruction from him; one of whom unexpectedly called on me the other day and feelingly spoke of him as the first person who initiated him in the study of Latin and encouraged him to persevere.   This same schoolboy has now for many years been a successful parish priest and vicar in the north of England

. . . During many years of intercourse with Mr. Mackonochie I never ceased to notice and admire his deep humility and self-abasement; his unwillingness to blame and his readiness to approve. The poor, and especially the sick and suffering, always found in him a constant, sincere, and generous friend. . . . The most desolate and least inviting parts of the parish were the places to which he dedicated the chief part of his time and the exercise of his energies. I have known him walk several miles day after day in all sorts of weather to prepare poor pauper children for Confirmation, and to minister to the sick and dying in the lowest haunts of the poor and in the Union Workhouse. One incident I will venture to notice. There was in the workhouse a resolute and abandoned woman known to my wife, for whose state she felt much concerned. She drew Mr. Mackonochie's special attention to her, but she refused with a scowl and an oath to have anything to say to the parson. After several fruitless attempts to see her, he at last only succeeded by following her and remaining with her until her passion had subsided, and by making her feel that his only object in visiting her was to lead her to her Saviour and so make her happy. Then for the first time the idea seemed to dawn upon her that she was not utterly forsaken, that she had one friend in the world who cared for her. This was the turning point in her moral history. Henceforth she honoured her pastoral friend and was always ready to receive his ministrations. From that time he often read to her and prayed with her, and the blessed Spirit carried his words with convincing and purifying power to her once cold and obdurate heart. Her early excesses had, however, impaired her constitution to a fatal extent, and she began rapidly to sink, and while dying faintly breathed out the wish that her gratitude might be conveyed to Mr. Mackonochie who had brought her to feel her sinful state and her need of her Saviour. . . . His unabated zeal and untiring devotion to his Master's service (continues this old and faithful friend) was also seen in his visits to my wife when nearing her end. He used frequently to *walk* from St. Alban's, Holborn, to Great Cambridge Street,

Hackney Road, and after performing his early morning duties as chaplain at St. Saviour's Priory, would reach my house at Bermondsey (a distance of several miles) by eight o'clock in the morning, that he might converse with his friend of the Saviour's love and administer to her the Blessed Sacrament of the Body and Blood of Christ. . . . When I look back and contemplate my intimacy with him for more than thirty years, his life appears to me to have been an unbroken series of acts of self-denial and of the faithful discharge of the duties of his ministerial commission ; and an attentive observer could not fail to perceive that he was sustained and cheered in his life of self-sacrifice by an unfaltering trust in the promise of the abiding presence of his Risen Lord.

The simple testimony bears the stamp of truth. It was for this reason that the ordinary duties of a village pastorate were neither commonplace nor wearisome, and Westbury was ever held by Mr. Mackonochie in affectionate remembrance.

To one case of great difficulty which came under his notice whilst there, he applied himself with that persistent care for the individual soul which was such a marked characteristic of his ministerial life in after years.

The child of a somewhat prominent member of the Baptist Chapel in the place had died suddenly under suspicious circumstances, and after a while (though no inquest had been held at the time) the body was exhumed, and it was proved to have been poisoned, and by its own mother, who had also, it was now discovered, got rid of her elder children by the same means. The Baptists would have nothing to do with this unhappy member of their community. It was Mr. Mackonochie who at once went to see her, and during the time she lay under sentence of

death did his utmost to bring her to repentance, never
relaxing his efforts (which were, unhappily, unavailing)
until life itself was gone. It was an early instance of that
practical love for the lost and outcast, which was, as it
were, the mainspring of his actions, and to which so much
of his influence in after life was due.

The vicar's bad health necessitating frequent absences,
led in 1850 to his resignation ; but in the short time they
had been together he had greatly endeared himself to his
junior curate, who wrote of him in 1854 :

I have had letters telling me of the departure of my dear friend
and vicar, Meyrick. His death was, as his life had been, simple,
trustful, full of faith and hope and love. Frederic Meyrick kindly
wrote to tell me of it, and said that he spoke of me among the last
things which he said about this world. We cannot wish him
back to live over again the last five years, and yet it is hard to
think of him as gone.

Mackonochie was the only one of the three curates who
stayed on with the new vicar, the Rev. Henry Duke.

The work amongst the scattered population was trying,
and in some respects unsatisfactory. His was certainly
not a restless mind, but he had now been three years at
Westbury. There was no possibility of increased organisation, nor prospect of much development in the work. He
had been compelled to buy his own experience, and had had
but little training. Moreover, he had an increasing desire
for opportunities to give practical expression to his faith.
Frequent celebrations, and even weekly communions, were
as yet seldom to be found in country villages. Long years
after, only a month or two before his death, he told of the

disappointment of the Westbury curates when they had
clubbed together to buy a pair of candlesticks, invited the
vicar to tea and presented them to him ; and how when he
had admired them enough they broke to him the fact that
they were intended for the church, and with profuse admiration he repeated over and over again : ' But you know I
cannot put them on the altar.' Still he was a kind man, and
so they got them into the vicarage, and on to the highest
shelf in the pantry ; and at last, years after, on a certain
occasion when Mackonochie returned to Westbury, he found
the lights on the altar, where they still stand.   He told the
anecdote as a consolatory one to some one whose offering
had been in like manner rejected, but it is a little indication of the state of Church feeling in his day, which must
of necessity have been a trial to him.

He was near enough to Wantage to hear a good deal
of the work going on there.   His friend Mr. Bowles
strongly urged him to apply for a vacancy upon the clerical
staff; and after an interview with the vicar, he made
arrangements to go there at Michaelmas 1852.

On October 5, 1852, Bishop Denison wrote :

I am sorry to sign your testimonials as a step to your removal
into another diocese. I cannot do so without expressing my sense
of the faithfulness with which you have discharged the functions
of your ministry at Westbury and the benefit which has resulted
from your exertions. I hope that the post of duty upon which
you are now entering may prove one satisfactory to you, and
with every wish and prayer for your happiness and usefulness
in it,

Believe me yours faithfully,

E. SARUM.

Already, in 1852, Wantage was celebrated for its elaborate parochial machinery and efficient organisation. Under the energetic rule of the Rev. W. Butler, the present Dean of Lincoln, it was especially fitted to be a training school for the younger clergy. There was no overwhelming population with which to contend, no crushing sense of multiplied duties some of which must needs be left undone; neither was there the isolation and monotony of a single-handed ministry in a country village. There was a sufficient staff of clergy with varied duties, in the town itself, in the large Church schools in the outlying hamlets, without speaking of the different works of mercy carried on by the Sisters, who co-operated with them. Men were not slow to avail themselves of the advantages offered to them of associated labour and systematic training, and it is a curious fact, which has frequently been commented upon, that so many who afterwards occupied important posts, or were in other ways especially distinguished, had been, at one time or another, curates of Wantage.

It lies at the foot of the Berkshire Down; an old country town dating from the days of King Alfred; carrying one's mind back to childish times when the stories happily connected with that Saxon monarch shed a cheerful though transitory gleam of light over the dull pages of early English history. It is an old-fashioned place, with an air of sobriety which has little in common with the noise and bustle of modern life. There is a wide market-place where business is transacted after a leisurely fashion; the foot-paths before the red-tiled cottages lead down into shaded lanes or green pastures; every now and again the

soft lines of the landscape are broken by a straight row of
rustling poplars ; patches of orchard are bounded by
clusters of houses ; a sluggish stream fringed by willows
flows under the stone wall of the churchyard and vicarage
garden ;—at every turn, with scattered blossoms and much
waving of green boughs, the country makes friendly inroads
into the town.

The fine old church with its massive central tower,
stands on the low hill-side.   At a short distance there rises
a pile of grey stone buildings, the home of the Wantage
Sisters, who have another large house, St. Michael's Home,
where they train industrial girls and pupil-teachers.   For
the old town is full of young life.   From schools of every
grade and kind there comes a cheerful sound of children's
voices, and at every turn in the green lanes on a summer's
evening you meet a group of small loiterers on their way
home from school.   The religious houses, the large body
of sisters and clergy, and the varied works of mercy
carried on in its midst, have given a curiously religious
character to the place.   People mark the lapse of time by
the Church's calendar, and life moves along sedately to the
sound of church bells.

It was with an intent purpose to use to the utmost his
opportunities for parochial work and spiritual advancement
that Mackonochie came to Wantage.   The disadvantages
under which he had unmurmuringly laboured at Westbury
were about to be removed.   For the first time he was to be
within reach of a frequent Eucharist ; the church was open
all day long for private prayer and frequent services.   He had
the constant companionship of men who were, like himself,

reaching forward to the higher life, fed and sustained by the means of grace and the Sacraments of the Church. There were not only opportunities for study, but guides in the way of knowledge, and ample opportunities for putting that knowledge into practice. From the first he had been deeply impressed with the responsibility of his position as a religious teacher. He would have earnestly corroborated the assertion that ' in every one who has a cure of souls, an accurate and habitual knowledge of the Church's formal statements of doctrine will be an essential part of his qualifications,' and all the more necessary when he is called upon to minister to the uneducated ; for ' in what manner are the unlearned and unintellectual to learn orthodoxy ?— indeed the whole subject of the religious *knowledge* of a saint-like and heavenly-minded believer who should be wholly without intellectual cultivation, is full of importance, interest, and, we may add, mystery.'

Mackonochie's work at Wantage lay principally amongst the young and ignorant. He was daily in the schools, and one of those, then a teacher, who came into constant contact with him, writes :

He took upon himself not only the teaching in the parish schools for an hour or so on certain days, but also what would be called the drudgery of the work ; in the absence or illness of the mistress, keeping school himself and giving his whole power to the most trivial detail. . . . There was in those days a school for the employment of elder girls in plain needlework, at which they partly earned their living. They were always at daily Matins, and regularly after the service Mr. Mackonochie came into the transept where they sat and catechised them on the 2nd lesson for the day. . . . His teaching, though I was then only a girl of fifteen, left a very deep impression on my mind, and though of course the subject of his sermons is forgotten, there are many passages of Holy Scripture which I scarcely ever read without recalling the fact that he preached upon them.

And in reference to this period the Dean of Lincoln writes :

The Deanery, Lincoln : July 23, 1889.

You have asked me to give you some notices of the life of our dear friend A. H. M. during the time spent by him as assistant curate of Wantage. I must premise by reminding you that more than thirty years have passed away since he left Wantage, and that therefore (keenly and clearly as in a general way his memory comes before me) it is impossible for me to recall many of those incidents which show most satisfactorily what a man really is. I remember very distinctly his first arrival in Wantage in the summer of 1852. My fellow-workers, as was our wont, were dining with me in the middle of the day, and we saw a tall spare figure standing at the door of the Vicarage, and asking to see me. He had been recommended by a curate, Rev. S. J. Bowles, who was leaving Wantage, to take his place. His manner was, as ever, simple, bright, straightforward, and we soon made an alliance and friendship, which, in spite of serious differences in some very important questions, never for a moment flagged. Soon he settled down among us, together with others, the Rev. R. Harvey, now Vicar of Sarisbury near Southampton, Rev. H. P. Liddon, now Canon of St. Paul's, and later on the Rev. W. Sawyer, Vicar of St. Luke's, Maidenhead, in a small house in the town, which they took among them, living, as I need hardly add, in the very quietest and simplest way. He came to us in the earlier days of my Wantage ministry, not long after the stir about the ' Papal Aggression ' as it was called, when every effort for improving the services or the fabric of the church was looked upon with bitterness and suspicion. The body of the church was choked up with high pews and galleries, and the chancel, though in somewhat more seemly condition, was sorely inadequate to guide the heart to realise the greatest act of Christian service. We had then to work against considerable difficulties, and it is impossible to describe how much we were aided in our struggle by the nobility of his character, his absolute self-sacrifice, and his very considerable ability. While he frequently took part in the services of the parish church, his special charge was a certain street in the town, called Grove Street, noted as having been inhabited first by sackweavers, men and women and children earning high wages, and spending as they earned, and then when this manufacture had left the town, by the same people converted into hawkers and cadgers of every kind, and a district outside the town called Charlton, where a small chapel had been built, and where the bulk of the agricultural part of the population lived. To these two he gave his whole heart, and produced very remarkable results, taming and humanising, and teaching definite doctrine, and converting souls in true Church fashion. Even at this long interval of time his name is remembered, and there are some still who love to tell of his assiduous visiting, the earnestness of his preaching, the wonderful influence which he gained over some of the most hardened and hopeless. There was in Wantage at that time a lady, widow of a former curate, wealthy and eccentric. For some reason of her own she would not enter the parish church, but she found her way to Charlton, and though by no means naturally disposed to what are called Church principles, she became a complete convert to his teaching, attended the services regularly, sent large gifts of the rarest flowers for decoration, and when she died some years after he had left Wantage, left him in her will a very considerable legacy. As a preacher in those days he was remarkably ready and often very effective, though his voice was somewhat too high-pitched to be always agreeable. I remember on one occasion when some club came to church and behaved a little disorderly, he was asked on the spur of the moment to address them, which he did so admirably, that all were impressed and made for the season reverent. At my request the Bishop of Oxford appointed him to preach the Ordination sermon in Wantage parish church in 1857. He preached, if I remember rightly, an unwritten sermon, such an outpouring from the heart, such a setting forth of the solemnity as well as of the blessedness of the ministerial office as could have been uttered by no one who had not like himself probed it to the very core. This too struck deeply into his hearers' hearts. Though not a good teacher, being from his great conscientiousness too much given to overload instruction with details, no one was ever more loving to children, or more beloved by them. With them he was always full of merriment, and knew well at our school feasts and at other times how to brighten their young lives. Thus for six years we laboured together in most loving brotherly fashion, and during that time it is no exaggeration to say the parish distinctly mounted to a higher level of spirituality than it had ever before known, from which I rejoice to think that it has never fallen. It was in 1858 that his chivalrous heart was greatly stirred by the riots at St. George's-in-the-East. He had been asked to preach at the time when the mob had been hounded on to yell through service and sermon, and it will be remembered that he was almost the only preacher who subdued them into temporary silence. He was very much affected by what he saw and heard on that occasion ; and greatly to my regret and to the regret of Wantage generally, he left us for that London work in which he lived and died.

As the foregoing letter intimates, his special charge was the hamlet of Charlton, where the simple-minded villagers in undiminished affection, even after the lapse of more than thirty years, have kept his memory green.

It was in this spring (1889) that we found our way to the group of cottages with their roofs of thick thatch or red tiles, which, on rising ground at a distance of about a mile and a half from Wantage, are closely clustered about the little church.

It is Easter-time, and within it is sweet and gay with flowers ; they line the walls above the low oak benches where in past years he gathered all the generations to be taught, until, so the old people declare, there was hardly one amongst them, except the young children, who were not communicants.

Some of his closest affections were twined about this place, to which he gave so much of his early zeal, which long years after, in his weakness and failing health, he so often revisited, almost unconsciously wandering back to his old haunts ; just as the mind, in times of depression, reverts with a happy instinct to brighter days.

On this spring evening the people have come home from their work and are at supper before the fires in their low wide hearths, or loitering in their well-kept gardens amongst the sprouting gooseberries and patches of polyanthus and wallflower. Their minds work but slowly, yet dimly they have discerned something of the meaning and motive power of his life. They are eager to tell us how he was always amongst them, a most welcome guest ; they speak of his daily visits, his love for the children, and his care for the sick and dying. ' He were a friend to *we*,' says the mother of the family as she tells of what he did for her own aged mother and for the growing up boys and girls, and then, half apologetically, with rustic simplicity she adds that she may say ' they were all friends to he.' As, one after another, one hears them talk there is no doubt about it. ' Preach !' cries the old sexton, with indignant contempt for our ignorance when we venture to ask a question about his sermons. ' He were a fine preacher. He'd rumple himself up to give it 'em straight and plain till he were red in the face. He were the

shepherd of the flock and no mistake.'   And then they tell
how, after the Sunday evening service in the little chapel
was over, half the congregation would walk down to the
town below with him to see him home.   Nothing was insignificant or unworthy of his attention, if it could in any
way raise their thoughts or brighten their lives, and in his
day the little churchyard was gay with flower-beds, because 'he was always a-tending of them.'

One of the women tells us how many hours he would
give to comfort those who were in distress of mind.   'For
there are many distresses of mind about religion,' she
asserts.   We cannot help thinking that if such were,
indeed, the case in this small hamlet, amongst these
sturdy phlegmatic villagers, it must have been in a great
measure due to the awakening power of his preaching,
when, 'rumpling himself up, he gave it them straight and
plain.'   With softened voices and the restrained and yet
outspoken expression of sorrow which is characteristically
English, they speak of his last years and death ; and one
old man is very anxious to make us understand that he
destroyed his health by overmuch study of the Scriptures,
for their respect for his learning almost equals their affection.   One and all they are proud to hear that the story of
his life is to be printed.   They little imagine that one of
its fairest records is written in their lives.

In corroboration of their simple testimony, we quote
a passage from a letter of Dr. Liddon dated February 26,
1889, when he first heard that this memoir was in progress :

I have a vivid recollection of Mackonochie's sermons at
Charlton, of our summer evening walks in the fields between

Wantage and Letcombe, and of his extraordinary care for those who were under his charge. But he was too absorbed in his work to have much time for intercourse with his fellow-curates, and too simple and humble to say much about what he was doing if this had been otherwise.

He had a way of expanding a single subject into practical details quite extraordinarily. He would, *e.g.*, begin the Prodigal Son or Psalm cxxx. on Ash Wednesday, and preach on the same subject all through Lent two or three times a week and without at all exhausting himself or the interest of his subject. The reason was that his real interests were so predominantly practical, and he had always a fund of new experiences or warnings or reflections of this kind ready at hand to illustrate the sacred words.

Nobody could enjoy the privilege of being near him when he was a young man without being braced in numberless ways by his companionship and example.

It was on Christmas Eve, 1852, that Dr. Liddon went to Wantage; in August 1854 Mackonochie wrote:

Liddon has been appointed Vice Principal of the Theological College at Cuddesdon. The work will suit him much better than this, and he is a capital man for it. There has been a likelihood of it all the time he has been here, but the matter has only just been settled.

Their work together at Wantage was not, therefore, of long continuance, but the friendship there begun was never to suffer any fluctuation or decline. To the last year of his life Mackonochie was amongst those who dined at Amen Court each Christmas Day. The invitation was sent for 1887, but was never destined to be received.

What perhaps strikes us most as thus we pass in retrospect from Oxford to Westbury and from Westbury to Wantage is the consistent and steady advance; the development of abilities until now dormant or unsuspected. There is a striking evidence of it in the fact that though his sermons at Westbury had been said to have been ordinary and laboured, already at Wantage we find that they had made a lasting impression upon Dr. Liddon, and when an ordination had taken place at Wantage Mackonochie wrote :

The bishop had made the great mistake of appointing me to preach the sermon. They insisted on my abandoning a written sermon I had prepared and preaching extempore ; so of course I made a mess of it. However, people were very good-natured, and listened better than could have been expected. I need not attempt to describe the ordination service, all who know the wonderful way in which the Bishop of Oxford executes on such occasions his office will feel what it must have been. At the end of the day we all felt as if we had lived a lifetime. I feel that it ought to be a very great thing for the spiritual state of the parish to have had such a service and such a visit from the bishop.

The reference to his own sermon is characteristic. The failure, as he considered it, accepted with composure almost amounting to indifference, with no resentment against those who had suddenly called upon him in his comparative inexperience to preach an extempore ordination sermon before Bishop Wilberforce, his own vicar, and Liddon. There is, indeed, very little about himself in any of his letters, but there is one from Bishop Wilberforce about this time, indicating that he was already intent upon practising the rigid asceticism and self-denial which was a prominent characteristic of his later life.

I do not entertain any doubt that the vicar is right (the bishop writes, in evident reference to some appeal which had been made to him). I am quite sure that with our climate and constitution such fasting would be absolutely incompatible with work, and for the sake of the parish I feel bound to forbid it. May God, even our Father, accept your sacrifices and bless your labours.

I am ever yours,

S. OXON.

We have a yet stronger proof of his increasing desire for self-sacrifice. It was towards the end of 1856, in the midst of his most congenial work at Wantage, that a desire arose within him to devote himself more entirely in isolation and hardness to God's service in mission work abroad. The Bishop of Newfoundland was seeking fellow-labourers, and he proposed to go out with him.

The Rev. E. Hobhouse, of Merton College, Oxford, afterwards Bishop of Nelson, was at this time his confessor. He had the greatest confidence in his judgment, and some years after, in 1865, we find a letter commending a young man to his care, that he might help him in any spiritual need, 'or name some one who will take the same office on his behalf, which you so kindly and forbearingly discharged for me some years ago.' He now in his difficulty turned to Mr. Hobhouse, and there are several letters from him, all referring to what was clearly a case of anxious choice amongst conflicting duties.

On November 8, 1856, he writes:

With regard to Newfoundland, if your heart bids you go, and no imperious ties forbid, I should say without doubt, go. Faults of character will not hinder there more than here. . . . It is eminently a case of *Bis dat qui dat cito.*

But there were difficulties which finally proved insuper-

His mother's strong opposition was one of them, and at her age he felt it ought to have great weight. Mr. Hobhouse wrote again, advising him to submit the case to the Bishop.

He is (he wrote) the proper authority to decide such questions. I conceive that it would be very contrary to ecclesiastical order to set up the opinion of a self-constituted spiritual guide against the authority of the superior in the diocese. The bishop will, I am sure, give you a ready and full hearing. With earnest prayers for your right guidance,

Yours very affectionately,
E. HOBHOUSE.

The Bishop had, indeed, already written on the 14th:

My dear Mr. Mackonochie,—I have given my best consideration to your question, and greatly as I shall regret losing you, I dare not offer any opposition to the desire for more difficult work for God, which He has, as I trust and believe, Himself stirred up in your soul. If, after full deliberation, you resolve on going, my prayers and benediction shall go with you.

I am most truly yours in the Faith,
S. OXON.

But when the decision was arrived at it was contrary to his wishes.

Mr. Hobhouse writes on December 12:

I thank you for the letters, though I could have wished the issue more decisive. It is satisfactory enough in one most important condition. You have got guidance and have followed it. Whatever comes you are now and will be simply walking in the appointed way and not after your own choosing. May God of His goodness always make your way as plain and enable you to walk in it.

Yours affectionately in Christ,
E. HOBHOUSE.

And on the 24th the Bishop writes to him again :

It must always be a comfort to you to know that it was in your heart to give yourself to the work, though the Spirit, I doubt not, suffered you not. . . . May God continue to bless you in your work.

I am ever most sincerely yours,

S. OXON.

The way seemed to be closed against him, and once more with undiminished energy he resumed the routine of parochial life ; but there was still within him the desire for more arduous work, and in 1858 it took a certain shape and form.

Rumours had from time to time reached Wantage of the hand-to-hand conflict with evil which was being carried on in the parish of St. George's-in-the-East. It was a forlorn hope imperatively calling for volunteers, and it was a call to which Mackonochie responded with unhesitating and yet thoughtful devotion. His enthusiasm was never allowed to carry him off his feet; his ardour gathered strength from deliberation.

On October 5, 1858, he wrote to his mother :

J—— will have told you of my intention of going for three months to the Mission in St. George's-in-the-East. . . . I shall leave Wantage with very great sorrow, especially with the feeling that if the three months' trial is satisfactory my stay there may be longer. Still, I think that I am following as well as I can the indications of God's will. I have consulted the bishop, and he quite agrees with me that I ought not to refuse to try. My only hesitation rested on the vicar's still opposing. He now withdraws all opposition on hearing the bishop's opinion, so that I am simply left to follow the advice of my bishop. I have at the same time the comfort of knowing that those who work with me here, and others who have had opportunities of knowing both myself and the work at the Mission, think that I am right.

That was now, as always, the only thing which really mattered to him. He loved Wantage, the place itself and the people. The old church and the quiet country lanes, the sick whom he had tended, the poor sinners he had sought to save, the little children he had taught ; and now, so far as anything can be at an end which has its issues in eternity, it was all past and done with. Henceforth his work was to lie amongst the streets and lanes of a city, amongst those whose claims were stronger because their need was greater than that of those to whom he had hitherto been called upon to minister.

CHAPTER IV.

St. George's-in-the-East — Characteristics of the work — Personal recollections of the Rev. T. I. Ball—Daily life in the Clergy House—Riot at St. George's-in-the-East—Correspondence with the Bishop of London—Letter from Keble—Offer of the Vicarage of St. Saviour's, Leeds—End of Mission work in the East.

1858—1862.

THE work that was being carried on by the clergy of St. George's-in-the-East differed in many important particulars from that of an ordinary rural or town parish. It could by no means be confined within the rigid lines of a stereotyped Anglicanism, and yet had little to do with the methods of the religious revivalist. It was more or less of a novelty even to those who were engaged in it.

It is an old story now. Mission after mission has since those days been planted amongst the poor and crowded populations of our great cities. One after another men have sought in their various ways to solve the great problem of the Christianising of the people. But thirty years ago, both their spiritual and temporal needs were making themselves felt with new and irresistible force. Sin abounded, grace should much more abound. It was no new disease, but in its alarming complications and rapid developments it seemed to call for a new remedy. In every section of the Church of England men were awakening to the fact that, as a writer in the 'British Critic' expressed it,

No Church ever succeeded in retaining the allegiance of the people without a larger, stronger, more searching and more elastic apparatus than is ours. The extent of the popular apostasy in our days is indeed wonderful; but not more wonderful than the degeneracy of the Church's present ways and means. Christianity did once wear that very guise which, while it was good for the rich, was also of the very sort which most appeals to the prejudices and sympathies of the poor. It was once a religion of visible self-denial and holiness that willingly took upon itself the sorrows which to the multitude are inevitable and lightened their sufferings by its own pain and privation. It was not once that umbratile thing, that feeble exotic shut up in churches, parsonages, and parlours; but walked abroad, made the multitude both the receivers, the collectors, and distributors of her bounties; compelled cities to wear her livery, and *dared to inherit the earth.*

The object of the Methodists outside, and of the Evangelicals inside the Church, had been to break down the barriers between the soul and God, and in a dual revelation to show men their sins and their Saviour. Upon this foundation-stone of faith it was the aim of the Anglo-Catholics to raise a superstructure of ordered prayer and praise, and daily self-denial; to lead men onward step by step in the life of conversion—a life of union with Christ of which the Sacraments should be no empty symbols, but the very means and pledges; the condition at once of individual sanctification and of the Church's corporate existence.

These were the principles which had been carried out in the missions connected with St. George's-in-the-East, and Mr. Mackonochie was not only prepared but anxious

to uphold them. The Christian life, with its high ideals
and paramount obligations, was to be set forth in all its
fulness, with the deep conviction that to lower the standard
of religion in order to popularise it was to sacrifice permanent stability to temporary success.

'They were,' in Father Lowder's own words, 'making
a great venture for the salvation of souls, . . . setting forth
in all its fulness the love of Jesus Christ and His grace in
the Sacraments and ordinances of the Church.' To this
end they had taught, both by word and by ritual, the
doctrine and duty of Eucharistic worship, the benefit of
confession and absolution, the office of the priesthood,
and the other practices resulting from it.

The Rev. Charles Lowder, in his narrative of 'Twenty-
one Years in St. George's Mission,' writing at this time,
says :

Wellclose Square, in which our Mission House was situated,
is a large open square forming the meeting point of the three
parishes of St. George's, St. Mary's Whitechapel, and St. John's
Wapping. . . . The poverty of the place was very great. . . . In
the midst of scenes of sin and misery the children were brought
up, the school of too many the streets, abounding in temptation,
echoing with profane and disgusting language, and forming a very
atmosphere of vice. . . . The parish had very few redeeming
features ; scarcely any residents of education and respectability to
foster a better spirit. . . . The church had little influence ; what
wonder that when the rector attempted to throw a little life into
the services and teach the doctrines of the Church faithfully, that
he should meet with opposition. . . . The mischief which afterwards burst forth in the St. George's riots had been already
smouldering. . . . It was in the presence of such a population,
and in the face of such difficulties without and trials within, that

the St. George's Mission was now making ground in its campaign against sin.

Of that campaign Father Lowder himself and his biographer have already told the story; but some more particulars of its surroundings, and a special account of those years during which Mr. Mackonochie was connected with it, has been furnished by one of his friends and fellow-labourers, the Rev. T. I. Ball.

It was during the Advent of 1859, in the chapel in Wellclose Square (he writes), that I first saw Mr. Mackonochie. The chapel was as a place for English worship, so unique in appearance, and is so associated with the memory of Mr. Mackonochie's earlier labours in London, that it deserves a word or two of description. The building, which stood in the middle of an old-fashioned square, and which was in summer-time almost hidden by trees, had nothing worth describing so far as outward appearance went, but directly you entered it you felt that you were in a church which had originally been built under other than British inspiration. It had, in fact, been erected at the end of the seventeenth century by Danish settlers in London for their own use. There was a thoroughly foreign air about it. First, it had much greater height than we should ordinarily give to a building of the same area. Then the arrangements were very non-English. At the east end was a shallow apse, open to the church above, but screened off from it below by a wooden partition, in the midst of which rose up a lofty pseudo-classical reredos, containing in the centre a large and inferior painting of the Agony in the garden, flanked by Corinthian columns, and surmounted by a pediment. In those days (1859) High Churchmen were nothing if not Gothic, and so in front of the pseudo-classical reredos the clergy of St. George's Mission had placed an altar with a mediævally designed frontal, on the gradine stood Gothic candlesticks, a Gothic cross was fastened to the reredos behind, and a Gothic cross adorned (or disfigured) the pediment above. . . . Against the lateral walls on either side of the reredos was, on the right side a royal pew or box, and on the left side an elaborately carved pulpit with extensive staircase. Between the two erections the floor was paved with black and white marble, and in this space stood mediævally designed choir stalls for men and boys. Iron gates divided this sanctuary from the body of the church, which was seated with open benches. . . . It was in this church at a week-day Advent service that I first saw Mr. Mackonochie, who at that time was barely known in London beyond a very narrow circle. I remember that the service was dreary ; there were very few people present, but the sermon spoke to the heart ; and in the following January or February I offered myself to Mr. Mackonochie as a lay-helper in his work.

I still remember, after the lapse of twenty years, as well as if it had taken place yesterday, my first interview with him in his own room in the Clergy House at Wellclose Square. The room was a back one, panelled with drab-painted wood ; well-filled bookcases stood against the walls, on which hung some pictures (mostly of sacred subjects, with one or two views of ecclesiastical buildings) ; between the window and the door of a little dressing-room stood a *prie-dieu* table with books on it, and a small crucifix in a triptych over it ; the general furniture of the room (there was no carpet) was of the plainest and severest description. . . . At that my first interview I was struck by qualities which I learned afterwards to revere and appreciate more and more as years went by. I remember so well how, on my raising or asking some question with regard to the doctrine of Holy Orders, Mr. Mackonochie expended infinite pains in discussing the matter to the very bottom, how he rushed to a cupboard and hunted out notes of college lectures in order to unearth some valuable opinion ; this kind of painstaking treatment of a question raised by an unimportant stranger impressed me very much, and I think I may say that then and there a friendship arose which only deepened and matured as years went on, and which I feel and know death has not broken, nor even interrupted, on either side.

E

In after years Mr. Mackonochie went on different occasions to take charge of Mr. Ball's mission chapel near Aberdeen ; and in reference to this he wrote :

It is a great pleasure to do something for our Lord's kingdom in the country which, though not of my birth or (*sic*) chiefly of my education, has such very deep ties for me.

And the sentence touches upon a fact which it is well to remember, and which Mr. Ball emphasizes further on :

In nature as in name, and by race, Mr. Mackonochie was eminently a Scotchman. There are many qualities in the Scotch mind which are misunderstood or undervalued because not shared in by Englishmen, and of some of these qualities Mr. Mackonochie had his full share. A Scotchman is not only undemonstrative, but he has an inbred difficulty in expressing the warmer and deeper feelings of his heart even in words. To know the extent to which profound reserve and self-continence can be carried you must study the Scotchman, and you will again and again be surprised to discover how hard it is to find out what he really feels, or *how much he suffers*. Of this tendency to reserve Mr. Mackonochie possessed his full share. Then, again, the Scotch mind inclines to give full weight to distinctions which would appear to be trivial or immaterial to the less acute and logical English mind. Mr. Mackonochie had a genuine Scottish delight in a distinction, and I am sure that this was more than once the cause of his being seriously misunderstood by the English public, through its inability to appreciate the fact that to a Scotchman's mind a distinction, great or small, is all the same a distinction, and must be taken into account and allowed for as such.

Nor was this all. From his Scottish forefathers he had inherited not only his powers of discrimination and self-control, but the moral and mental hardihood which, in the troubled times upon which he was now entering, were to stand him in such good stead. It was a temper of mind to which the fear of misconceptions or adverse consequences was almost altogether unknown; a liberty of spirit eminently characteristic of the land :

> Whose feudal faith had been her law,
>   And freedom her tradition.
> Where frowned the rocks had freedom smiled,
>   Sung, mid the shrill winds whistle—
> So England prized her garden Rose,
>   But Scotland loved her Thistle.

When in 1858 Mr. Mackonochie joined the Mission, this happy indifference to outward circumstances was more especially needed. There had been troubles both within and without. Two of the clergy had recently joined the Roman communion, and Father Lowder (though he had occasional clerical and lay helpers) was practically singlehanded at the Mission House.

We thankfully welcomed the valuable help of the Rev. A. H. Mackonochie, hitherto curate of Wantage (wrote Father Lowder). He took special care of St. Saviour's, and by his indefatigable labours, eloquent preaching, and unceasing care for souls, set us an example of what Mission work really was. He was soon joined by the Rev. H. A. Walker, and both worked together most happily at St. Saviour's, until, to our heavy loss, but to the great gain of the Church, Mr. Hubbard, with the advice of those who were best acquainted with his high qualifications, and after mature consideration, nominated him to the charge of St. Alban's, Holborn.

But these intervening years were destined to be years of conflict; not only the inevitable conflict with the poverty and misery and sins of those to whom they ministered, but a harassing frontier warfare with enemies whose only object was to weaken their position, divide their forces, and paralyse their efforts. It was a warfare in which Mr. Mackonochie had had no experience, and for which he must necessarily have been unprepared, for it was not until after his arrival at St. George's Mission that the riots in the parish church began.

For a short time, even after he took up his abode at the Mission House, the clergy were left to carry on their work in peace. Surrounded by the sinful and the fallen, they were to see 'the eternal glory shed upon the human race by the Love Christ bore to it;' and in their own persons to manifest that Love, not by the ordinary fulfilment of recognised obligations, but by the irresistible light of an absolute self-surrender. In the midst of the flagrant oppression and glaring inequalities of a degenerate world, they were to proclaim, not only by their lips but by their lives, the universality of the Christian brotherhood, and set the poor and sorrowful in those high places which (in the Kingdom of God at least) were theirs by right.

With such an object any personal ease or self-indulgence would have been manifestly inconsistent; and the daily routine at the Mission House would in any case, when faithfully adhered to, have rendered it almost impracticable.

The day in the Clergy House (Mr. Ball tells us) began somewhere about 7 A.M. with Prime said in the oratory. At 8 A.M. there was always either Matins or Celebration in the church. It may surprise some to hear that there was no daily Eucharist in the church in Wellclose Square; but in those days, while the neighbouring clergy were allowed to neglect rubrics by the score in the interests of Protestant laxity, the clergy of St. George's Mission were not allowed to transgress the strictest letter of the most antiquated rubric in a Catholic direction, except at the risk of having their licences remorselessly withdrawn. As there were but few week-day communicants in the congregation, it was not ventured to have more than a Thursday and Saint's Day celebration in order that the legal number might always receive. . . . The entire order for Matins was always read through, and Mr. Mackonochie always read it all himself; he had an invincible repugnance to lay readers of lessons. Breakfast, and Terce in the oratory followed about 9 A.M., and after this Mr. Mackonochie paid a visit to one or other of the schools where he gave Bible lessons. The discipline observed in his class was Spartan. The lesson was given from notes carefully prepared, and somehow the children did not hate these classes, as one might have expected would be the case. But though I never knew children shrink from his class or from spiritual intercourse with him, I do not think that he was a children's man. Whilst he was always gentle and kindly with children, there was in him an entire absence of that playfulness which must still linger in the mind and manner of the grown-up man if there is to be sympathetic *rapport* between him and children. But yet he could impress and win the confidence of the young. I remember the case of two big boys unbaptized, whom he took infinite pains with and whom he prepared for baptism. The City Missionary on visiting their mother was horrified to find under whose influence they had fallen. 'How can you let your boys go to Mr. Mackonochie?' he demanded. 'Do you not know he will make them go to confession?' 'And what if he does?' was the mother's reply. 'I am certain that Mr. Mackonochie would never let my boys confess *anything that was wrong.*' On the eve of their baptism he insisted that the lads should undergo a thorough ablution (at that time he considered this as a part of a proper preparation for baptism), and a missionary student who was staying at the Clergy House was sent with the boys to a public bath with orders to see that the cleansing was perfect.

After his return from the school Mr. Mackonochie's day was spent in the thousand and one occupations which came upon him as a Mission priest in a populous district, and which his growing reputation as a preacher and a spiritual guide brought upon him. Dinner and Sext came somewhere about 1 P.M. Nones at 3 P.M., but the recitation of this latter office generally fell through. Evensong was sung in church at 8 P.M., and at this service there was always a fair attendance, which was growing in numbers when Mr. Mackonochie left to go to St. Alban's. As at Matins so at Evensong, the whole office was punctiliously said and sung. . . . Evensong was almost always followed by something or other. I remember a very excellent set of Prayer Book classes which I attended ; in those days he excelled in this kind of instruction : what he said was always carefully read up and prepared before-hand ; he never aimed at originality or profundity ; but he gave you in clear, simple, well chosen words the cream of what the best Anglican authorities had said on the subject in hand. Scarcely an evening passed without confessions to be heard. Frequently it was past ten before he left the church ; some poor old voluble woman, some much-tried matron would come to pour out their lengthy griefs, or some troublesome young man or woman had been got hold of and must be reasoned into repentance. Supper and Compline ended the Clergy House day, but both were often over and done before he was back from church.

And yet, though the work was hard it was not over-whelming, and Mackonochie was not the least likely to exaggerate its difficulties.

It seems worse here (he wrote) because there is more of it and less outward pleasantness in the work itself, but I do not know that it is in itself harder ; and plenty of people for worldly gain are ready to give up as much or more.

But this time of peaceful though strenuous effort was about to be rudely broken in upon. As we have said, it was not long after Mr. Mackonochie's arrival that the riots at the parish church began, and the Mission clergy bearing their part in the conduct of the services were distracted in the midst of their spiritual work by the necessity of taking what measures they could to restrain the irrational violence of the mob. The opposition to the rector, the Rev. Bryan King, had begun almost with his institution to the parish, but it took an active and aggressive form when Mr. Allen, the incumbent of St. Jude's, Whitechapel, was (contrary to Mr. King's wishes) appointed to the office of evening lecturer at St. George's. It was then 'that, urged on by Mr. Allen's intemperate language, a few malcontents first interrupted the services of the church.' The flame once kindled rose and spread with the gusts of unreasoning passion, and burst forth with renewed fury upon the most trivial pretexts. Disorderly interruptions to the church services were organised and systematically carried out week after week, whilst the proper authorities were either indifferent, or took no efficient means to suppress them. During Mr. King's unavoidable absences a great pressure of work and responsibility devolved upon his curates. Vacillation would have been absolutely fatal, and presence of mind was of the greatest consequence, when to postpone action was to render it ineffectual.

On August 18, 1859, Mr. Mackonochie wrote :

The disturbances at the parish church have gone on increasing, till last Sunday afternoon the curate fell down in a fit in the middle of the service. This was followed by a most horrible row and at last fighting. There are to be cases on both sides tried at the police courts to-morrow, and the rector has given notice of a citation from the Ecclesiastical Court to their ringleaders. The bishop has also promised that, if the churchwardens fail to exert themselves, he will cite them. . . . However, the rector and —— have both gone away—one ill, the other for a much-needed holiday.

In this letter he states that Father Lowder was away, but did not know how bad things were, and would return at least for a time; but on August 30 it would appear that Mr. Lowder was again absent, for upon that day Mackonochie addressed a letter, from which we take the following extracts, to the Bishop of London, alleging as his excuse for doing so that he was 'the only licensed clergyman at present in the parish':

I have taken the liberty of sending to your lordship by this post (he writes) a copy of the 'East London Observer' of Saturday last. I accompany it with this letter as being unwilling to communicate anything to your lordship anonymously. The object with which I send it is connected with the disturbances, and there are two points to which I would ask leave to call attention: the position of Mr. Allen in the matter, and the conduct of the churchwardens.

In regard to the first, your lordship will, I think, agree with me in looking upon the first leading article in the accompanying paper as an impartial witness. The writer clearly does not sympathise with the rector, but merely looks upon the disturbances as a nuisance and traces out the cause. In the course of this investigation he is led, in the fourth paragraph, to describe the character of Mr. Allen's sermons. Supposing his account to be correct, it is difficult to conceive how the turbulent spirits of his hearers could be more effectually stirred up. Mr. Allen comes to St. George's Church attended, he asserts, and I have no reason to doubt the truth of his assertion, by about 1,200 people. These are almost all strangers—not people of St. George's or the neighbourhood—apparently from Whitechapel. These are his supporters, who have come, as their conduct testifies, not to be brought nearer to Christ, but first to hear an orator whose words please their ears, and then to insult Almighty God by mocking responses in the Litany, and even interrupting it, as themselves allow, by loud laughter. This being their object, Mr. Allen uses the opportunity of his sermon, not, so far as I can hear, to preach Christ and the way to Him, but to goad them on with exhortations to ' arm themselves ' and be ' ready to shed the last drop of their blood,' and in conclusion exhorts them to retire quietly. My lord, may we not ask what need of such an exhortation, if his aim in the sermon had been to teach them to know the evil of their own hearts and the exceeding love of Christ and to send them away in the spirit of the meekness of Jesus ? I hope I am not repeating an oft-told tale in saying something of the manner in which the election of Mr. Allen has been carried on. The person who claims, I know not how truly, to have suggested his nomination is a Presbyterian, who for some reason likes to go to church, while he openly avows his dislike of Church doctrines and practices. I need not say that he does not go to St. George's. He does not hesitate to say that he thinks the rector and those who agree with him the only consistent Churchmen. But he dislikes the Prayer Book, and therefore seeks the ministrations of those whom he believes most unfaithful to their ordination vows. It is not for me to endorse or reject his opinions, but your lordship will be able to judge of his consistency. His object he also openly avows to have been the desire to see the two opposing parties in the church face to face. The Church, he says, is *militant*, and he wishes to see the fight.

The letter goes on to complain of the handbills which had been put about the parish, containing much exciting language, the last being in the form of dissuasion. ' Do

not groan ; do not hiss ; do not pull the popish rags off his
back ; ' upon which Mr. Mackonochie justly remarks that
if Mr. Allen were not responsible for them he ' should have
instantly and indignantly repudiated such unworthy proceedings.'   And then he touches upon his second point—
the conduct of the churchwardens ;

I cannot conceive anything more unsatisfactory.   For three
months they have allowed these scenes to occur weekly, nor has
their sympathy with the rioters been any secret. . . . A great deal
is said about things being quieter, but on Sunday last I find that
just as the clergyman was ready to go from the vestry into church
he was told by the churchwardens that the tumult was so great as
to render it impossible to say the service at all.   As soon as the
clergyman had consented not to attempt it, the fact was communicated to the crowd in church by the churchwardens in a tone
of apparent triumph. . . . The real point which the rioters desire
to gain is not, I do not hesitate to say, the disuse of certain forms.
It is convenient to put this forward, and no doubt if permitted to
gain one point they will ask for more ; but at present they are
simply vexed that Mr. Allen is not allowed to interfere with one
of the regular services of the church, and are determined, as they
avow, that no one else shall have a service at that time.   This the
churchwardens know quite well, and when the service was given
up they felt that for one Sunday agitation had gained its point,
and triumphed accordingly.

And then, in conclusion, he adds :

I feel reluctant even now to send this, lest I should seem to
step out of my place in writing at all.   But I will ask your lordship
to excuse my forwardness, if such it is, in consideration of the grief
of spirit which it is to hear Sunday after Sunday of the violation of
God's house—my own parish church.

The Bishop's letter in reply is a lengthy one, entering

in detail into the causes and incidents of the case, blaming
in some respects the rector's action, and expressing a hope
(not well founded, as later events proved) that if the
matter were placed unreservedly in his hands he might
put a speedy end to the disturbances. He expresses himself kindly and considerately towards the young curate in
charge, whose position 'as the only licensed clergyman at
this moment resident in the parish,' is, as he remarks,
'peculiarly painful.' And a day or two after Mr. Mackonochie writes back in a tone of frank cordiality, which, the
Bishop seems to have been wise enough to see, implied no
disrespect :

I have to thank your lordship most heartily and sincerely for
your kind and ready sympathy with us in our anxiety. I need not
say how much enhanced we all find this to be by the unhappy fact
that scruples and differences of opinion have for some time past
interrupted that cordiality which we most earnestly wish to exist in
all things between the clergy and their bishop. I know well that
your lordship, while deeply grieved at any such estrangement, will
have from the first given the credit of conscientiousness to all
concerned, as also I am sure none have doubted that, while discouraging and in some cases prohibiting that which others have
thought it their duty to the Church to maintain, your lordship has
been acting only out of a single desire to discharge the duties of
your sacred office. I do not say this as of myself, but from a
certainty that all belonging to the parish, and none more than the
rector, are impressed with this view. I am sure when he is made
aware of all your lordship's kindness he will fully join in every
word which I have said. . . . You will, I am sure, feel that the
tenacity on the part of the rector has only sprung from a conviction on his part (on the rightness or wrongness of which it is not
for a junior priest to express an opinion) that he could not give
way without violating his allegiance to the Church. Short of this,

I feel convinced that your lordship's wish would have been law to him.

The two letters quoted are legible indications of a strong individuality, which, though free from self-assertion, manifests itself, when called upon to do so, without reserve. There is not the slightest shrinking from responsibility, whilst perfect loyalty to his rector is combined with an evident and almost affectionate desire to comply with his Bishop's wishes. And Bishop Tait evidently liked him all the better for a frankness to which perhaps his junior clergy had not altogether accustomed him ; for on September 15, in reply to another letter, he wrote :

My dear Mr. Mackonochie,—Let me thank you for your interesting letter. I trust by God's blessing that the efforts you have made will not fail to produce their effect, and that this disgraceful state of things will soon be ended. I am sure that the manifestation of the kindly Christian spirit of conciliation at the same time that you show your determination not to be intimidated, must have its effect. . . . I cannot but feel much for the very difficult position in which you are placed.

It is interesting to place the unsolicited testimony of the Rev. R. H. A. Bradley as a sequel to these letters :

During the riots in St. George's, East, at Mr. Mackonochie's request, I celebrated early on a Sunday morning at the parish church. On Monday the bishop sent for me, complaining of altar lights, eastward position, &c. On my telling the bishop that these were matters that concerned the rector of St. George's, and not me, he asked how I came there, and on receiving the answer that Mr. Mackonochie was a friend of mine, Bishop Tait replied, 'Well, I have not a better man in my diocese than Mr. Mackonochie.' This was when St. George's and the

Docks Mission was in the worst possible odour, and the bishop was harassed on all sides, and there was scarcely an incumbent in London who stood by Mr. Bryan King and the Mission. At the end of my interview with the bishop he urged me not to mix myself up with St. George's, and when I declined to accept his advice, he replied : 'Well, I can't say anything against your wishing to help such a man as Mr. Mackonochie.'

In the meantime, Mr. Mackonochie had not only to send reports to the Bishop and to his absent rector, but also to seek interviews and correspond with the police authorities, and with Sir George Cornewall Lewis, at that time at the head of the Home Office. In a long letter to the latter, dated September 6, there is a strain of just indignation, all the more forcible because restrained within the limits of temperate language. The indifference of the magistrates had been fruitful of too disastrous results not to be bitterly resented by those who were making unavailing endeavours to re-establish order. Mr. Mackonochie had already had a personal interview with Mr. Waddington, the Under Secretary, from whom, he writes, he 'got no further consolation than that doubtless instructions had been already given to the police, and that for the rest we must have patience.'

I cannot believe that this is really the only answer which the Crown will return to subjects seeking protection in the exercise of their religious duties ; and those subjects, too, ministers and members of the Established Church. It is, I urge, a simple question of social order. Will the law allow a crowd, merely because it is large and cannot be controlled by two men, to assemble Sunday after Sunday in a parish church and prevent the regular performance of divine service ?

He then proceeds to detail the circumstances which aggravated the causes of his complaint, but he adds :

Were the circumstances of the case the exact converse of this, I should still feel that I had the fullest right to claim for the service of the parish church all the aid which the law can give. Were it a question of a mere conventicle of Mormonites or other barely tolerated sect, the police would interfere at once and punish the offenders most severely. Why are the legal officers of the Church of England to be the only ones unprotected in the exercise of their duty ?

Mackonochie's spirited efforts—more remarkable for the cool self-possession displayed than even for their energy—were not destined to be successful. For many months the conflict raged at the parish church, although (except for a few Sundays, during which St. George's was closed) the congregations at the Mission chapels were left undisturbed. Concessions made at the Bishop's request only served to aggravate the excitement and to encourage the rioters. In November 1859 he wrote to his mother :

I thought it better not to tell you yesterday that L. and I should have to divide the services between us . . . I was interrupted several times in the sermon, so that at last I asked the people whether I should go on or not. Some said 'yes' and some 'no,' and some told me to go on and not mind the rabble. At one time I thought the 'noes' had it and was going to stop, but a cry of 'go on' changed my mind. I was less disturbed afterwards.

But from this time, fortunately, he had comparatively little to do with the miserable and protracted struggle. He was more free to give himself to his spiritual work, and tha. Lowder writes that

Mr. Mackonochie's valuable assistance at St. Saviour's was bearing good fruit. The conversion of many souls in the way of true repentance, the increase of communicants, adults and children brought to baptism and confirmation, the better organisation and instruction of the schools, and the careful administration of the charities of St. Saviour's, all bore witness to the zeal and power with which his missionary labours were carried on.

It is more than possible that his ministrations had gained in power from the trials which had beset them. Some illusions had been dispelled and some fair hopes blasted, but the great realities of life stood out all the more clearly. The fight had ended in a defeat more ennobling than an easy victory. He had been forced to think for others as well as for himself, and the sense of responsibility had matured his character and deepened his convictions without impeding his action. If the difficulties which he had to encounter had placed him in an undesired position, the uncompromising sincerity of his conduct had won the respect of those who differed from him, and the warm approval of his Bishop. Nor had there been wanting the spontaneous sympathy from without which generous spirits are always ready to accord to a well-fought battle against overwhelming odds and to an oppressed and failing cause. Men of altogether different or adverse opinions—Lord Brougham, Dean Stanley, and Tom Hughes—had spoken out strongly about mob tyranny being permitted to work its will under cover of the law. Letters of encouragement had been received from unexpected quarters. The Guild of St. Alban, then in its infancy, had forwarded an address expressing a heartfelt conviction that when 'this persecution shall cease, a great religious work will develop itself in your parish.' And then from the quiet retirement of Hursley there came help, all the more prized perhaps because given after some doubts and misgivings lest zeal for God's honour should lead men further to profane it.

I did not wish my name, being at a distance and unable to do any good, to be mixed up in the matter (Mr. Keble wrote in March 1860). It is now become a plainer case, and I shall be much obliged to you if you will kindly accept the sum I take the liberty of forwarding, and pay over 10*l.* or 20*l.*, according as the need may be, to the Defence Fund, applying the rest to any of your charities which you and Mr. Lowder may judge best. Perhaps you will kindly make my apologies to Mr. King if any good opportunity occurs ; I think I should say to him if I met with him that I hardly knew what to say or do, I was so worried and perplexed about the whole matter. Mr. Lowder knows that I could not myself 'show fight' about the mere externals if I were allowed liberty of teaching and ministration. My fancy is that if I knew of a disturbance coming on, I should dismantle the church silently on the Saturday night (as holy vessels might be buried to prevent desecration), and get some one who knew how to do it to address the people on the whole matter and try to make them ashamed.

I hope that your health is better, and I pray God to preserve you and your work and your coadjutors.

Believe me, dear Mr. Mackonochie, very truly and affectionately yours in Him Whom we would serve,

J. KEBLE.

The letter begins by thanking Mackonochie for a tract upon Good Friday, which Mr. Keble trusted would do a great deal of good. They had met two years before when Mr. Mackonochie went from Wantage to spend one or two nights at Hursley, and though the acquaintance appears to have been slight, it may be the reason why this letter was addressed to him rather than to the rector. In any case, it is a strong testimony to the righteousness of the cause to find the man of peace furnishing the weapons of war.

The reference to Mr. Mackonochie's health is almost the first indication of its having suffered. But in 1861 we find that he had a severe attack of rheumatic fever, and for some time he was subject to relapses. Laid up 'upon three chairs,' at first he writes cheerfully that he might get over in a cab to see his mother, who was also ill at the time ; but the illness increased upon him, and soon took the question of locomotion altogether out of his hands. One cannot imagine that nursing in Wellclose Square can have been very satisfactory, nor the surroundings favourable to convalescence, but he had undoubtedly great physical strength as well as remarkable recuperative power, and it was not long before he was at work again with renewed health and energy.

Had the call to St. Alban's not come, it is impossible to say how long he might have remained contented and faithful at this outpost of the Church. No prospect of self-advancement was likely to tempt him away. Already, in 1859, when things at St. George's were almost at their worst, he had been offered the Vicarage of St. Saviour's, Leeds. It was a post in many respects desirable and attractive,—an important and assured position ; a beautiful and already celebrated church, in which he would be able to carry on the Church's work, if not without fear of misconstruction, at least without the constant and harassing anxieties which beset his efforts in the East of London ; and yet he writes :

I hope to be able to refuse, but I believe all my friends except the rector and Lowder wish me to take it. . . . For me to leave the Mission, just as I am getting a little rooted, would be, humanly speaking, destruction to it. Of course, if God is pleased to bless it, it will stand whether I go or stay ; and if He rejects it, it will fall in like manner ; but I do not think I should ever forgive myself if I were, through anything which might be wilfulness, to give the last blow to it. Then it would be very barbarous to Lowder just when we are working very quietly, after all his discouragements, to leave him again alone. . . . Even if there were some one to step into my place at once, and work it far better than I can, I do not think I could go ; there are many who at the present state of proceedings depend much upon personal influence and have been drawn to myself. Of course, I hope soon to see them rooted and independent of myself ; but I should not like to leave while things are so.

And thus the offer was refused, apparently without any thought of the personal sacrifice, and in 1860, looking back upon that year of many troubles, he writes :

It is a great blessing to find health standing so well when all about us we so often hear and see people falling down. And, again, I do not think we ought any of us to forget the support and pro-tection we have had in a twelvemonth, so unlike anything which could have been expected. If the end, too, is different both from our wishes and our expectations, we must not complain, but go on working in hope.

It was the character of his missionary work until the last ; patient, persevering, and steady ; with a deter-mination to do his duty and leave the results to God, against which the waves of outward opposition and inward discouragements beat alike in vain. It was no wonder that Mr. Lowder spoke of it as a heavy blow to the Mission when Mackonochie became the first Vicar of St. Alban's, Holborn.

CHAPTER V.

St. Alban's, Holborn— Position of the parish—Character of the population—
Circumstances of Mr. Mackonochie's appointment—The Greville Street
Mission— Beginnings of parochial work—Consecration of the church—
Founder's letter to the parishioners.

1862—1863.

LORD LEIGH and the Hon. J. G. Hubbard were the two
benefactors to whom St. Alban's, Holborn, owed its existence ; the former being the donor of the site, and the
latter of the church and 5,000*l.* in Three per Cents. as
endowment.   In addition to this munificent gift he gave a
house for the use of the clergy, and for some time 100*l.* a
year for each of the two curates.

In his letter to the inhabitants at the completion of the
building, he states that he had 'been seeking a site on
which to erect a church for God's service in a destitute
part of the metropolis.'   He had not far to seek.

At no great distance from the fashionable parts of
London, in the immense parish of St. Andrew's, Holborn,
there was a district to which Mr. Hubbard's attention had
been especially directed.   It was bounded on the east by
Leather Lane, on the west by Gray's Inn Road, on the
south by Holborn, and on the north by Liquorpond

Street, now called Clerkenwell Road. Brooke Street, in which the church now stands, is not without historical associations. It takes its name from Lord Brooke, whose stately mansion, Brooke House, once occupied the site of the present church. This worthy nobleman has left further record of his name in the parish in Beauchamp Street—the Beauchamps were kin of his—and in Greville Street, his first name being Fulke Greville. The Lord Brooke of the times of Queen Elizabeth was an excellent patron of authors, and himself an author. Sir Philip Sidney was an intimate friend of his, and often found his way to Brooke House. It was in Brooke Street that in 1770 poor Chatterton died by his own hand.

Close to the great thoroughfares along which the wealth of the richest city in the world passes in a continuous flow to minister to the luxury of its inhabitants, there was within the narrow area of 500 by 200 yards, in dark courts and high tenement buildings, a population of about 8,000. The locality is described by Mr. Spiller, who was the first churchwarden and had known the place for thirty years, as full of the poorest people and a rallying point for the worst characters, and a very notorious thieves' kitchen once stood where the church now stands. The inhabitants were for the most part vendors of fish and vegetables, a few very poor shopkeepers, and many foreigners. Their earnings were very precarious, and seasons of reckless expenditure alternated with times of direst poverty. The streets were thronged every day, but on Sunday mornings they were, and still are, a perfect fair, though many of the old filthy, ruinous houses have since been pulled down, and their places taken by large factories and model lodging-houses.

The population was incessantly shifting. This has always added very considerably to the difficulties of the work, making it one continuous series of fresh beginnings with little to show. For these crowded populations close to the borders of the City have a character which is altogether distinct from those at the East End proper. It is not here, as a rule, that you find the hopeless down-trodden respectable poverty of the artisan class, who, by no fault of their own, have fallen upon evil days. The people who crowd into these low courts shut in by huge warehouses are people who would not go farther east and spend money upon trams and railway fares in order to secure more space and fresh air and bring up their children in a more decent neighbourhood. They have all their lives been used to the noise and glare of the narrow streets. They spend a great deal of time at the street corners by the ever-swinging doors of the gin-palace. They have many quarrels and many rough jests amongst themselves. They are often very wretched, but as long as they are young they are merry enough, and when they grow old they have no heart to look for anything better. They live in a crowd. The women do their marketing, jostling one another about the street stalls, where people take as much interest in their neighbours' purchases as in their own ; the girls go to work in bands, and all day long stand shoulder to shoulder in the great factories ; the rough lads herd together gambling in dark corners ; the men are more independent of one another, but after all there is no such thing as privacy in anybody's life. There are four or six families passing constantly up and down the one dirty staircase; father and mother, big sons and daughters and little children, all live and eat and sleep in the one room, where there is little or no attempt at decency or comfort. For there is a great love of display, but such homely virtues as cleanliness and thrift are almost unknown. Yet, though drunkenness and vice of all kinds abound, there are general evidences of valuable qualities not so often found in better neighbourhoods: an open-handed generosity, a disposition to take the losing side, and an affection readily offered in return for any kindness, often altogether disproportioned to the benefit received. Times of trouble or sickness draw forth unsuspected virtues; their self-sacrificing kindness to a sick or sorrowful neighbour knows no limit. Their many trials have not hardened their hearts against those even less fortunate than themselves. They have many crosses, and, as has been said, few Victoria ones. They are very poor, and must always remain so, since any money earned or received would be as quickly squandered. They have an insatiable love of finery and cheap purchases of all kinds, and, like children, will buy fruit or sweets when in need of a wholesome meal. They amaze the reasonable philanthropist by evincing more gratification at the present of a gilt Christmas card than they show on the bestowal of a coal ticket. The present is all in all to them. It is not only that they do not believe in the far-off future, but they do not even look on to the next month. They have few fears and fewer hopes, and the pressing needs of their physical existence have all but crushed out their religious instincts.

The supernatural has no terrors, and the joys of the next world but little attraction.

There was a large proportion of such people, men and women, girls and swarming child-life, in the courts lying between the coster market in Leather Lane and the wider Gray's Inn Road ; and these, with some admixture of the artisan or shopkeeper class, were the parishioners upon whom the influence of the new church was to be brought to bear.

The vast extent and the dense population of the parish of St. Andrew's had made it impossible for the clergy of that parish to look much after individuals. Some work had been done, however, and good work was being done by an excellent school conducted under the auspices and with the personal help of a Mr. Martin, of whom, later on, we are to hear more. This school was in touch with the London City Mission, who had two agents engaged in preaching in the neighbourhood. A very small Roman Catholic Chapel stood in the midst of a maze of courts and alleys, but this was given up and pulled down a few years later.

Mr. Hubbard had chosen his ground well. It only remained to find a priest fitted by past experience to grapple with the difficulties which must always attend the establishment of a new church and mission.

He had long watched with sympathetic interest the work going on against such overwhelming odds at St. George's. There is an heroic element in some failures which appeals more forcibly to a generous spirit than success, and the attitude of the St. George's clergy, quiet and determined, had gained for them, together with an unenviable notoriety, the respect of those who differed from them most widely. The work they were doing was well known, whether for good or evil; the principles by which they were actuated had been publicly discussed, misconstrued, or approved. Owing to the vicar's unavoidable and frequent absences, Mr. Mackonochie, at the time of the riots, had taken (as we have seen) a more prominent part than would naturally have fallen to one of his age and position. The lines upon which he had been working for nearly five years were perfectly well known.

Mr. Hubbard was justly anxious for a personal knowledge of the first vicar of his church, upon whose character and capabilities much would necessarily depend. He was not likely to make a rash choice, and upon January 15, 1862, he wrote as follows to the Bishop of London :

My dear Lord,—I have offered the incumbency of the new church of St. Alban's to Mr. Mackonochie, who has accepted it, and will doubtless before very long wait upon your lordship to say so.

Mr. Mackonochie has been by every one who knew him approved to me as a man of zeal, energy, and piety, and admirably qualified for missionary labour, and I have every confidence that he will fulfil my anxious desire and expectation by carrying on this work in the same spirit with which I commit it to his charge. He knows that it is my desire that the work at St. Alban's should be carried out with a hearty allegiance to the Church of England— neglecting none of the means of edification which she supplies either in doctrine or in ritual, but using the large liberty which she allows with loyalty and discretion—remembering that the *one great object* for which the church is founded is the salvation of souls.

He could not blame himself for any precipitancy in the matter, and in spite of the ample information which he had had, it is clear, from his own words, that when he made the offer of the incumbency he had no misgivings. But Mr. Mackonochie was not prepared at once to accept so serious a responsibility.

He delayed some time before giving a definite answer, consulted various friends, and finally wrote the following letter to his late vicar, Dr. Butler of Wantage :

Mission House, Wellclose Square, E.,
March 1, 1860.

My very dear Vicar,—I have just received the answer of the Bishop of Oxford. I am very sorry to say that he expresses no doubt that I ought to accept the offer if it be made to me by Mr. Hubbard.

It therefore becomes necessary for me to write to you about Mr. Hubbard's letter. I have read over again carefully all but the second page.

It certainly makes me feel a little doubtful about the matter.

In the first place I feel that a priest must accept such a position unfettered or not at all. I could not enter upon it feeling that Mr. Hubbard looked upon me as pledged to do this or not to do that. If upon enquiry he thinks that he can offer it to me with perfect confidence and leave me absolutely free to carry out the work of the church, &c., I should feel bound to accept. I think Mr. Hubbard would take the same view of the priest's position, but I doubt if he would entrust that position to me. The founder completes his work and offers it to CHRIST, exercising his right of founder in the nomination of a priest. The church then belongs to our Lord, and the priest holds it from Him, not from the founder. This might work in fairly well if it were only a question of money ; but Mr. Hubbard's name will always be associated with the church ; and if any of my views or acts came to be clamoured at (as they almost certainly would) it might seriously affect his political position. Many considerations might weigh with a political man which a priest would be sinning by entertaining for an instant. This has always seemed to me one of the great moral difficulties of a founder. The question of money may possibly also complicate the difficulty. I do not know to what extent the continued support of choir, schools, organist, &c., will depend upon Mr. Hubbard. I suppose he will hardly like to endow everything. If, however, he is to be called upon for a continued outlay of money it would make the relative position of himself and the priest additionally difficult. He might be reduced to the choice of either crippling the work by withholding funds, or supporting work which he conscientiously disliked while the priest as conscientiously held it to be necessary.

To enable the founder and the priest to begin with a reasonable hope of going on smoothly, it seems to me that they must either be entirely and essentially of one mind, or else the founder must feel content to defer absolutely to the judgment of the priest. I doubt if either hypothesis would bring Mr. Hubbard and me together. Of course the latter would not. As regards the former, I imagine his mind gravitates continually towards compromise, while mine as continually tends the other way. I have, I think, sufficiently protested against anything which I say in this or any other letter being understood as a pledge, and may therefore go on to the particular points on which you desire information. It will be seen that I should not be prepared to have such statements produced against me hereafter, if my ways in any degree seem to depart from them.

There are four points about which you ask—The sign of the cross, bowings, vestments, Purchas's book ; besides these four you make an allusion to the doctrine of the Blessed Eucharist.

1. I cannot too strongly express my conviction of the rightness and edification of the sign of the cross used at meal times. Its known origin in the very earliest ages of the Church alone would establish this. It is also (I believe) most undoubtedly a post-

Reformation practice. I have, I think, used it invariably for the last eight years. . . . I have also felt that our principle was to be very open in all such things ; as helping to impress on ourselves and others the tone which we desire to cultivate. I speak this last as my own personal feeling, not as a recognised view at the Mission.

2. It is difficult to criticise one's own manner of celebrating. If Mr. Hubbard wishes to know what my custom is in all these points his best way would be to come down some Sunday morning and stay all day. Of course in a new sphere I should not feel bound to conform my practice in all points to what it is here, but he would be able to form an idea. I believe our Ritual is very much that of All Saints' shorn of its magnificence.

3. In one sense I do most undoubtedly believe that a priest ought to introduce the Eucharistic vestments. Whether they should be exactly the shape delineated by Mr. Purchas I cannot say : and colour and material I hold to be comparatively immaterial, but in some form they ought, I think, to be the point of ritual aimed at. When they are to be introduced, and whether even by this generation, is another question. A good painter, I believe, draws his skeleton first, then clothes it with flesh, and finally puts on the garments. I imagine this to be not very unlike the process of the spiritual things of God's house. Neither the priest nor the painter would rest contented with the skeleton or the flesh.

4. I cannot say that I regard Purchas's book as inspired or an infallible guide. At the same time I think he deserves some credit for the industry with which he has hunted out old rubrics and customs, which help us to understand the mind of our own Church in her office. I believe, however, that he is often wrong even according to the old Ritual, and certainly in one case shows an ignorance of the modern rubrics. So far as I have used it at all, it has been to read what is said and decide for myself what is best to be done. I may say generally that I think the Ritual of the Altar is the thing to be striven after. In comparison with this

any amount of dignity connected with Matins and Evensong is valueless. I should like in a perfect state to arrive at both, but the former seems to be immeasurably superior. As to that ritual I believe the essentials which must be had at starting are candles lit at the Celebration, the position of the celebrant in front of the altar, the use of some veils, and the cleansing of the vessels before leaving the altar. I believe I have now done with Ritual and may go on to Doctrine.

I believe the two statements of Archdeacon Denison to be necessary inferences from the Doctrine of the Real Presence, and most important. Still I do not deny to others a right to clothe their faith in other words. My own teaching runs very much in the Archdeacon's line. Now I think I have said quite enough to frighten any member of the House of Commons from having anything to do with me, so may hope to rest here in peace again. If Mr. Hubbard should think it worth while to say definitely that such a profession of faith will not do, I should just like to know that the matter has passed over.

I ought to thank you very much for your interest about it. Even if all these points were arranged I still feel very strongly my unfitness for the work—mentally, morally, spiritually.

Though little accustomed to write about himself, there are in later years several very explicit references to his feelings at this time, and to the circumstances of his appointment. In a letter to the Bishop of London, dated July 23, 1875, he says :

I was much against my own will placed in this church, the very grandeur of which called for a corresponding dignity in the conduct of the services. I was avowedly a man of extreme views as to ritual, and of deep convictions as to the essential connection of a sound faith and the ritual expression of it. I refused to think of accepting the charge of this parish unless I could do so unconditionally, without any sort of agreement to be guided by the

wishes of the founder as to the management of the church or its
services, beyond a general desire to consider those wishes so far
as my duty to God, to His Church, and to my people would allow.
I thus deferred for ten months my being nominated to it, during
the whole of which time and ever since I have stood firm to this
resolution.

In an address to his parishioners and congregation on
St. Alban's Day, 1874, he states :

I was never a candidate for, or sought in any way, the position
which I now hold ; indeed I have always thought it wrong for a
priest to seek after any particular cure of souls. . . . So far was
I from recommending myself, that I strongly urged all the objections
which seemed likely to arise in Mr. Hubbard's mind against me ;
so that on the day on which Mr. Hubbard resolved to offer me
the incumbency a friend writes from his house to me : 'I pray you
for the love of our dear Lord to raise no further difficulties. None
need be raised. Mr. Hubbard has had put before him, honestly,
by myself, all that may be in you different from what he might
wish.' . . . Being asked by a friend of Mr. Hubbard's as to the
principles of doctrine and worship on which I should desire to
work here, I stated exactly those which have come to be called
Ritualistic, and said that I did not believe that any M.P. would
give me a 'living' on the terms I stated. This letter was sent
on to Mr. Hubbard. . . . I know (he adds towards the end of
the address) Mr. Hubbard would be the last man to wish to
impugn any of these facts ; but as others have misinterpreted his
words and otherwise dealt with them in ways for which he is not
responsible, I feel obliged to say thus much. . . . That in any
way the work done here should be a sorrow to a man who deserves
so well of this parish and of the Church of England at large as
does Mr. Hubbard, must always be a grief to me. It was the fear
of this which made me so reluctant to be appointed priest in this
place, and compelled me to make it plain from the first that I could
not accept the responsibility of such a parish, except on the basis

that my duty to God and to the souls of His people, according to the best judgment I could form of it, would have to be paramount over every other consideration. The point I kept before myself and, as forcibly as I could, pressed upon others was that when once a priest was licensed to the parish and the church consecrated, the work would be neither his nor Mr. Hubbard's, but God's. With the priest as God's steward would rest the responsibility, and therefore with him alone, after such security for sound judgment as he might be able to take, must rest the decision for which he alone would answer at the Judgment.

Such were the feelings, clearly defined and expressed, with which he entered upon his new charge ; and it is only right that, in view of the unhappy differences which afterwards arose between the incumbent and patron of St. Alban's, the facts of the case should be clearly stated. Mr. Hubbard had indeed agreed with Mr. Mackonochie's premisses ; but he was utterly unable to accept his conclusions, or to understand that his actions were the natural and logical outcome of his belief. His views of a patron's authority were wholly incompatible with freedom of action on the part of an incumbent ; and it was soon evident that they differed entirely from Mr. Mackonochie's. He objected to flowers on the altar, to the presence of non-communicants at the Eucharist, to the crucifix in the Clergy-House oratory, to the cassock worn in the house, to the sign of the cross at saying grace, and even to the hats and cloaks of the clergy ! Moreover, there were fundamental differences between him and Mr. Mackonochie which made concessions in indifferent matters of no avail. He had spent his money with lavish liberality, and the result was a grief and disappointment to him. He thought that he had made a mistake, and found that it could not be rectified.

Hence there arose disagreements which in the future cast a cloud over the friendly relations which would naturally have existed between him and Mr. Mackonochie when on each side there was so much mutual appreciation, together with the strong bond of a common interest and a common cause. As yet, however, all was full of hope, and no divergence of opinion had arisen to mar the happiness with which the little band of Christian workers set forth upon their mission of evangelisation in this dark and crowded corner of the great city.

The first service was held on May 11, 1862, in a room over a fish-shop in Baldwin's Gardens. Soon after part of a house was secured in Greville Street, and it was in the cellar of this house that the first Christmas was kept. Here, notwithstanding the difficulties of confined space, the choir were in surplices, there were altar lights ; linen vestments were used (with black stole and black maniple), and the clergy vested in a cupboard. A member of that first choir is still one of the choirmen at St. Alban's, and Mr. Stanton (who first worked in the parish as a layman and then received his title for Holy Orders from Mr. Mackonochie) here preached his first sermon, the boys outside all the time yelling through the grating.

Mr. Mackonochie had at once begun to organise operations in the parish. It was divided into districts, and one assigned to each of the clerical staff, which at first consisted of the Vicar, Mr. Walker, Mr. Doran, Mr. Ibbotson (who remained only six months), and Mr. Stanton, who came into residence as soon as his ordination had taken place. Every house was visited, every name inscribed. Mr. Mackonochie's attention to detail, and his love of system, gradually bringing order out of chaos, whilst his unwearying activity made itself felt in the most insignificant parts of the work. Two ladies (Miss Millner, who still works in the parish, and Miss Dowson) offered their services. A mothers' meeting and a girls' class were started; a little room was rented, and a school held on week-days as well as Sundays.

It is interesting to note that one of the children who belonged to this first little attempt at school, is now a valued Sunday-school teacher at St. Alban's, thus affording another instance, amongst many, of the permanent hold which the church has had upon its workers.

Mr. Mackonochie was always present both at the girls and women's classes to interest or instruct the members; and every evening the doors of the Clergy House were open to all who came, and the clergy personally investigated cases of distress and distributed relief.

None of the workers met with the slightest rudeness in their visits to the people; but it was uphill work. The small congregations gathered in were restless and curious. The clergy were objects of fluctuating interest not unmixed with good-humoured ridicule, and there was as yet little disposition to accept any religious ministrations. The staircase leading up to the mission room was dark and rickety, which was a great disadvantage in affording opportunities for 'rowdyism,' and these undisciplined children of the streets were not easily subdued or impressed. There were frequent interruptions to the peaceable conduct of the services, whilst the best disposed of the worshippers could not always be expected to resist the importunities of their friends outside.

In the character of these town populations the element of reverence is, as a rule, entirely wanting. Except when their passions are aroused they are exceptionally good-humoured and friendly; but accustomed all their lives to bargain and barter, they are not the least disposed to accept any one upon their own valuation. Open hostility to religion has for the most part died out, and in many instances the lives of the clergy have won their affectionate regard; but the natural order of things is reversed; respect may follow upon personal affection, but rarely precedes it, whilst in regard to higher things it would seem as if the love of God entered in before there was any fear to be cast out. The claims of religion are disregarded on account of their paramount nature; for life is too short to be spent upon any one thing; and the pleasure or excitement of the moment is all in all.

Gradually, very gradually, out of those who came to see and to wonder, there was gathered together a small band of people with some desire for better things. Diligent visiting amongst the courts and tenement-houses brought to light melancholy cases of sin and sickness and destitution; the personal kindness and the individual sympathy shown could be appreciated even when words of spiritual comfort or admonition fell all unheeded. A desire was awakened to make some return; and if the clergy were so singular as to prefer some regard paid to religion to anything else, well! they would make some little effort to please them. 'You see, it's this way. George likes it,' as a working man was overheard to say to one of his companions when asked why he went to church, in friendly reference to the Rev. George ——, the vicar of his parish. A poor motive no doubt, yet not altogether unworthy, since it held within it an element of gratitude and affection. So as time went on, one by one, individuals were gathered in, warned, encouraged, and instructed, and the work grew and prospered.

In the meantime the fabric of the church had reached completion. On August 20, 1862, Mr. Mackonochie wrote to his mother. 'Did I tell you the bishop inspected the church on Thursday, and proposed to have the consecration on October 30. He seemed amiable.' There were, however, various delays, and the consecration did not actually take place until February 21 in the following year, when the work had been already carried on for nine months in Greville Street. So far, in spite of many disappointments and trials, it had been singularly blessed. There had been the happiest unanimity in the little band of workers, and they had steadily increased in numbers. Zeal is contagious, and the influence of Mr. Mackonochie's restrained ardour was making itself more and more felt. But to a sincerely humble nature nothing is so humbling as success. Confident in his beliefs he was full of a sense of his own shortcomings. In answer to congratulations upon his birthday in August 1862, he writes :

Another year has gone with its blessings, its mistakes, its carelessness, and its sins. God grant that His grace may have saved me from being, where my own self would have left me, a year further from Him. . . . I have as yet received nothing from my incumbency, and much is going out, so that I have some trouble as to how both ends will meet at the end of the year. I am in very safe hands as to the future, but my head will not go through prospective calculations.

There is no expression of pleasure at finding himself at the head of a work which already promised to assume considerable proportions ; little even of natural delight in the beautiful church rising up before his eyes. Life is still, as it has ever been to him, too serious a thing to allow of any by-play; he is absolutely indifferent to worldly interests or personal triumphs. In another letter he says :

I must not do more than write a very few lines to congratulate you on your birthday. I suppose I use the word congratulate in a different sense than others. There are two senses in which I suppose it may be used ; one is congratulation that another year of preparation has been vouchsafed for the rooting out of vices and faults, and the implanting of all heavenly graces ; the other sense is that one more year of exile is over and we are so much nearer our home.

The words would be commonplace enough but for the circumstances under which they were written, in a letter of rare intimacy to a near relation. He was upon the eve of the consecration of the church ; standing in full health and vigour upon the threshold of a life to which he had looked forward from his earliest boyhood ; a life of absorbing interest, and one to which he had felt himself called by all the strongest inclinations of his energetic nature ; and yet in his own thoughts it is but a step nearer to the end.

The first foundation-stone as it were of the spiritual

structure of St. Alban's had been laid in the Greville Street Mission. The consecration of the church itself did not take place till February 21, 1863.

From the first linen vestments were used and there were lights on the altar. Bishop Tait preached in the morning, and Mr. Mackonochie in the evening ; the Bishop of Ripon upon the following Sunday. The church was densely crowded, not only by people from a distance, but by the parishioners, bonnetless women and ragged children pressing in ; some already won to some appreciation of a religious service, many others from mere curiosity.

It was on this day that the founder addressed the following letter (from which we have already given extracts) to the inhabitants of the district.

To the Inhabitants of the District of St. Alban's, Holborn.

My Friends,—When I was seeking, a few years since, a site on which I might erect a church for God's service in some destitute portion of the metropolis, it was intimated to me by Mr. Toogood, then rector of St. Andrew's, Holborn, that Lord Leigh, hearing of my enquiry, and anxious to promote the spiritual welfare of the neighbourhood in which you dwell, offered a site upon his own property, if I would build the church there. To this proposal I willingly agreed.

In fulfilling his offer Lord Leigh met with serious obstacles. He found that only on extravagant terms could he obtain possession of some of the tenements he desired to remove, but which were let on lease ; and I felt bound to restrain his liberality, and accept a diminished site, rather than subject him to an unreasonable outlay in effecting the larger gift he generously desired to make.

The site, at much trouble and cost, was at last cleared, and conveyed to me by Lord Leigh ; and upon the site so given now stands the church, consecrated to-day by the bishop of this diocese, and which, dedicated to St. Alban, commemorates the earliest English martyr recorded in the Calendar of our Church.

St. Alban's church is free. It has been built especially for the sake of the poor ; but, rich or poor, all alike may enter it without fee or payment, and may find in it a place where they may kneel to pray and stand to praise God, and where they may sit to hear the good tidings of the Gospel. Rich and poor may often meet in that church ; but as rich and poor are alike in the sight of God, so in that House of God they will meet with no distinctions. But although the church is free, and you will not be permitted to pay for entering it, you will not be debarred from the privilege of making your own free offerings to God. The clergy will be provided for without your aid ; but there will be many purposes immediately connected with God's honour, in the maintenance of the church and of its services, to which your alms can be applied. Your district is far from being wealthy—many among you live very hardly upon wages hardly earned ; but there are few among you who, if so minded, will not be able to contribute to the offertory, and none who will not find that the habit of giving for God's service tends to their own happiness, and even promotes their wealth, by providing a motive for industry in their calling and for temperance in their living.

It is now acknowledged that the English have as much ability and taste for singing as any other people ; and you will do well to apply your voices to their noblest use, by singing heartily in your parish church. An organ has been provided to assist and guide your voices, and means will be found to instruct those who desire more perfectly to enjoy together the delightful religious duty of praising God with the voice of melody.

The necessity of raising the windows of the church to a great height, and of making the east end a solid wall, has given occasion to paint the east wall with representations of the chief events connected with our Redeemer's Life and Mission, as they are recited in our Litany. It is hoped that these pictures will assist the young especially, in realising the petitions which they offer, by impressing on their minds the Humility, the Love, the Sufferings, the Power, and the Majesty of their Divine Lord.

The district of St. Alban's, as now constituted, contains more than 6,000 souls. Its existing schools, admirably directed by excellent men, are quite insufficient to receive all the children needing religious instruction, and we must look forward to the erection of other schools, which may commence the religious training to be continued at St. Alban's church, and assist the efforts of its clergy.

I desire that the church, the building of which is now, by God's help, completed, may serve as an expression of my loyal and dutiful allegiance to the Church of England, and I heartily pray that it may be the channel of many spiritual blessings to you my friends. It will not, I feel sure, fail of its object from any lack of self-denying zeal on the part of him whom the bishop has set over you. I have the strongest assurance for my confidence that Mr. Mackonochie, as a true and faithful priest of the Church of England, will affectionately teach and discreetly guide the souls committed to his charge.

To the residents in Baldwin's Gardens is especially commended the care of a fountain provided for their convenience, and erected close to their own dwellings. The church and the fountain they will protect as their own property—for they are theirs—given to them that they may, without money and without price, draw at the fountain pure water for the refreshment of their bodies, and at the church pure Gospel truth for the refreshment of their souls.

He whom God has favoured by making him, in the bestowal of these gifts, the steward of His own abundant bounty, earnestly entreats your prayers, that he may become less unworthy of the signal honour he has enjoyed in being privileged to raise an house to God's Holy Name—an honour which he would humbly and gratefully record in the words of the pious King David—'Thine, O Lord, is the greatness, and the power, and the glory, and the victory, and the majesty . . . both riches and honour come of Thee, and Thou reignest over all : in Thine hand is power and might ; and in Thine hand it is to make great, and to give strength unto all. Now, therefore, our God, I thank Thee, and praise Thy glorious Name. But what am I, that I should be able to offer so willingly after this sort ; for all things come of Thee, and of Thine own have I given Thee.'

I remain, my friends, your faithful servant,

J. G. HUBBARD.

Birchin Lane, February 21, 1863.

CHAPTER VI.

Personal characteristics—Fellow-workers—Life in the Clergy House—Family affections—Character of the services and congregations at St. Alban's—Mission held by Father Lowder in 1863—The devotion of the Three Hours first started at St. Alban's—Mr. Mackonochie's attitude towards those who differed from him—His care for individuals.

1863—1865.

IT would be easy to write the parochial history of St. Alban's during the following years. Its records have been kept with scrupulous exactitude. So far as statistics can be said to be proofs of success in mission work, that success was fully established.

But before we enter into the details of the various agencies employed, let us look once more at the central figure in the picture.

We have already seen how at Westbury and Wantage nothing was too trivial to engage his attention if it in the smallest measure concerned the interests of those under his care. Here in the midst of this teeming London population there was the same sense of responsibility towards each single soul, the same painstaking care for individuals. He did not only work for the church, his parish, his congregation, but he watched with unremitting vigilance over each man, woman, or child with whom he came in contact.

The Clergy House is a conspicuous building at the end of Brooke Street, built on to the church, divided into two portions by the entrance gate and passage to the church; the clergy occupying one portion and the servants the other. It contains a bedroom and sitting-room for each of four clergy, a spare room of very modest dimensions, an oratory, and a common dining-room. Mr. Mackonochie's sitting-room was on the first floor.

The style of living (writes one of the staff) was of a very simple kind, and the arrangements excellent for the soul, not quite this for the body. The order of the day included all the small Hours, Prime to Compline, which were said in the oratory. This arrangement it was found impossible to maintain when the work increased and it became necessary to be accessible to those who needed our help. The great trial was the difficulty of keeping the house clean. At one time it fairly deserved the character given, I think by Dr. Littledale, to another spot, ' it was like an entomological museum *without the pins.*' This was especially trying in the parish when celebrating for the sick.

Here, then, close to his church, in the midst of his people, and in daily, almost hourly, companionship with his fellow-workers, Mr. Mackonochie entered upon the twenty years of ministerial life which he was to spend at St. Alban's.

Perhaps one of its most striking features at the outset was his ready response to each separate demand upon his time and attention. When each five minutes was of value, and when with all his efforts the stress of work must last from early morning until late at night, he would bear with repeated and often unnecessary interruptions without the slightest manifestation of impatience. One of his constant fellow-workers declares that he was never so much as out-wardly hurried. It was the great secret of his influence. For the time being only three persons existed for him, God, himself, and the soul with which he had to deal. Parochial interviews, necessary visits, services, accounts, school teach-ing, sermons, confessions—all the various spiritual and official duties met one by one with the same undivided attention, though there was often hardly breathing space between, and the short time marked out in his daily rule for recreation was almost always encroached upon and frequently altogether crowded out. Perhaps it is true that if he had been given a couple of hours in which to refresh or amuse himself he would have been at a loss to know what to do with them. The fact no doubt points to a deficiency in his character. From the very first 'play' had been left out of his life, he was not likely to murmur because he had no play-time, though he thoroughly en-joyed any little distraction which came in his way. Indeed, his pleasure in any parochial entertainment or excursion was as simple as that of the youngest school-child. But he never sought recreation for his own sake, and even his reading had almost always a practical bearing upon his work. One cannot help thinking with a smile and a sigh of the poor lad who, even before he went up to Oxford, was to spend his spare time in the holidays in the study of theology. Now that his life had become that of a teacher, he was more than ever anxious to be thoroughly grounded in the science. He had a conscientious reluctance to go one step beyond what he had learned ; until he had grasped a truth for himself he would never have presented it to others, any more than from motives of expediency he would have withheld it from them. So it came to pass that the chief characteristics of his preaching were clearness and simplicity. As one of his habitual hearers observed, 'He always taught us something.' Truth had its rights as well as its obligations, it could be no part of his duty to soften or conceal it. The praise of men, the respect of those opposed to him, even the sympathy of friends, had not so much as been weighed in the balance with the aim of his life, to choose the right as he saw it, and let the truth make him free; free from fear of misconstruction, free from vain regrets, and the perplexity of side issues and the snare of a widespread popularity.

His teaching was the necessary outcome of his belief. The phrasing of one of his addresses to his parishioners is characteristic of the whole attitude of his mind. 'I believe and therefore have taught,' he begins; and in the same address a little further on, 'I believe and therefore have always taught you.' The truth had from the first been stated with uncompromising clearness, without a thought of the consequences to himself. It was the sacred heritage, the inalienable right of Christian people. As he saw it, as he knew it, so he must proclaim it to others.

It was the same when dealing with individuals. Reproof when called for was direct, telling, absolutely sincere. Though he would not give unnecessary pain he certainly never shrank from probing the wound he was intent to heal.

'Was he a severe man?' was the question put to one of those who knew him best. 'Never to those who most deserved it,' was the quick, spontaneous answer. Hard upon himself, he was also stern in his dealings with those who had adopted the same high standard. He expected a great deal from them; the demands he made were an honour, and their response required no praise; he never forgot that they were to work, not for him but for God. His trust was without reserve, and his confidence once given was not likely to be withdrawn. It was his unshaken loyalty to his workers which, amongst all the trials which beset the work, gave it substance and cohesion; and within certain well-defined limits he allowed them absolute freedom.

It has been my one great joy during my ministry in this place (he wrote) that my brother priests and I were one; there was not one single hair's-breadth of difference between us. I can always drop the *I* and say *we*. I said to them when we first came here, our strength will be in our unity. There must be a centre in a corporate body; there may be occasions in which that centre must moderate with his own opinion the opinion of others; and when his opinion differs from the opinions of the others, he may have to overrule the opinions of those who work with him. But we are all priests; one may be leader, but we have the same orders, and therefore our strength should be in unity. Whatever then is done at St. Alban's is not done by one or the other, but emanates from all; one may act in the body, we all act in the spirit.

There is a strong practical testimony to the truth of this assertion in the fact that there are still two men at St. Alban's who worked with Mr. Mackonochie almost from the first—the Rev. A. H. Stanton, and the Rev. E. F. Russell who joined him five years later; whilst Mr. Walker, who went there at the time of his appointment, only left in 1872. There were, of course, from time to time changes in the clerical staff, yet we think it would be true to say that no one severed their connection with it without regret. It seems necessary to touch upon this point, because it forcibly illustrates the subordination of natural characteristics to the singleness of his purpose. Confident and determined, very sure of himself and of his conclusions, with a taste for method and organisation, and a great sense of the importance of details, one might have expected that his parochial rule would have been a beneficent despotism, and that it would have been hard to co-operate with him upon terms of equality. But such was not the case. The purity of his motives freed him from any touch of jealousy, and when once assured of a bond of union deep and enduring as a common creed and a personal devotion, he was ready to allow free play to individual instincts and capabilities. The liberty of action and speech which he claimed for himself he freely allowed to those who were working with him, recognising that in so wide a field there must of necessity be a varied and experimental husbandry. At Oxford, to the surprise of bystanders who thought him narrow or bigoted, he had chosen his friends chiefly from amongst those who dissented from his religious opinions ; and now his closest companions were men whose views upon political and social questions differed in some respects widely from his own. It was enough that through all the varied texture and crossed threads of life there ran the one strong cord of a practical and unhesitating allegiance to the absolute claims of fundamental truth.

It was the more remarkable since his very single-mindedness made it difficult for him to see both sides of a question, and his scrupulous conscientiousness had, at least in his earlier years, engendered a certain stiffness in the attitude of his mind. 'Save me from my virtues, I can save myself from my vices,' might well have been his petition, lest hatred of evil should degenerate into harshness and resolution into obstinacy.

He stood in the position of one of the leaders of a new movement, but he had been forced into it by circumstances ; the post he held had been unsought for, undesired. There was enthusiasm indeed, but of so severe a kind as to be most generally unperceived. The force of the torrent was, as it were, veiled by a thin coating of ice. Its strong current flowed steadily and in silence.

When you spoke to him of your interests and your troubles (writes one of his friends) you felt that for the time being you really were his one object of thought and attention, and that his whole mind was bent on understanding your story. Many professional men are successful in assuming this attitude towards those who consult them, but one feels instinctively that the interest is after all only professional and conventional. But with him you felt that all was real and genuine, and you felt it all the more because of the amount of reserve which never left him. . . . His small clear hazel eye looked straight at you, not with the searching, enquiring gaze that one meets with in some who have power over souls, but rather with the fearless, candid look of a child, who has nothing to conceal and takes it for granted you have nothing to conceal either.

Such testimony does not stand alone ; from every side and from the most opposite quarters there come examples of his power over individuals; but it would seem as if he needed a distinct personality upon which to exercise his influence. There was no sense of inspiration from a crowded congregation; no eloquence kindling into passion in quick response to the sympathy of the multitude; his curious absence of self-consciousness made him too indifferent to be greatly moved by a public verdict; too self-confident to need the support of public approval. He can hardly be said to have looked at himself from the outside at all, not even with other people's eyes. He had that element of fanaticism which resolves itself into an unconscious aloofness from other men's minds; and we see one result of this in the fact that he had more intimate relations with those to whom he looked up, or with the persons of all classes whom he guided and helped, than with those with whom he consorted upon terms of equality. It was with them that he was most reserved; perhaps with an instinctive feeling that confidence in their case must needs be reciprocal, and with a natural repugnance to accept that for which he was unable to offer an equivalent.

He had few near relations, but perhaps for that very reason the tie of kinship had a peculiarly strong hold upon him. Some part of his short holidays were invariably spent in his brother's home, and the children were always objects of his care and interest. Until the spring of 1865, when she died, his mother was living in London; and whenever he could gain a little breathing time from the troubles of St. George's-in-the-East, or the responsibilities of St. Alban's, it was spent with her. Upon his birthday in the August of the year of her death he wrote to his brother:

It is quite true that the great earthly loss which it has pleased God that we should experience this year comes back with an especial force on this day. In one way especially to me you are now the one only close earthly tie that I have or ever shall have . . . Of course I make friends—friends whom I value and even love, but this is very different from what we have known as the love of our little home.

These affections which had struck their roots so deeply into the past were undoubtedly in some measure fostered by that almost necessary separation from the engrossing and yet transitory interests of other men which comes upon one to whom earthly gains and losses are of little or no account, and for whom the precepts of the Sermon on the Mount have a literal signification. He lived as a poor man all his life, not only upon principle, but because he had in truth but little value for the personal gratifications which money can purchase. His income, never large, and during some part of his life what most men would have considered barely sufficient for his own needs, was freely shared with others; not only with the members of his own family, and with those in his own parish, but with many others whose straitened means and secret privations had become known to him; the simplicity of his character often enabling him to give friendly and timely help where mere charity would have been at once rejected.

Such were to ordinary observers the most prominent characteristics of the man who, after thirteen years of diligent ministerial work, had been chosen as the first Vicar of St. Alban's, Holborn. When the church was opened in 1863 he had already been for nine months at work amongst his people. They had learnt to know him. As yet he had been brought into no undue prominence, no one could have foretold how, under the pressure of circumstances, his influence would hereafter be extended far beyond the bounds of his own parish. Here for the present he had ample scope for all his energies as day by day he laboured to bring the Gospel message to bear upon hard hearts and wasted lives. The church had been purposely erected in a rough neighbourhood.

Wild girls and lads after work hours (writes the Rev. E. F. Russell) engaged in the roughest horse-play. Fights were very common, especially amongst women, and Saturday nights on into Sunday mornings were most often times of hideous uproar and sometimes criminal violence. Where Brooke Street widens at the church end of it there stood formerly a large iron pump with a capacious iron trough. Much happened at this point. It was a favourite fighting ground, conveniently furnishing water to wash away the stains of battle. Cases of sprain or bleeding in the neighbourhood came here to be pumped on, and here on certain days costermongers were wont to wash the carrots and turnips that they sold. One day we found the iron trough full of human skulls and bones. The enterprising youth had discovered them in the excavations of the Farringdon Street Station and had brought them up to sell at the rag and bone shop. Later on, when the inhabitants began to take an interest (in their way) in what was being done at the church, the pump was made to serve as a pulpit, mock sermons were preached by the wild girls (the girls were always the worst), mock confessions were made, and, alas ! mock baptisms of cats. The number of dead cats surprised us. They were a very favourite local weapon and very unpleasant.

But the months in the Greville Street Mission had not been spent in vain. When the church was opened there were many of the poor of the parish who had already come to look upon it as their own. Speaking of the day of the consecration, one of the daily papers says :

The church was kept open all day that the inhabitants of the district might see for the first time the interior of the building designed for their use, and very many availed themselves of the opportunity . . . At the Evensong of the same day it was literally thronged with a congregation such as one, judging from past experience, would hardly have expected or hoped to see in so stately a pile. Not merely those fairly well-to-do were there and the less struggling class of poor, but those whom want of means and insufficient apparel too often keeps away. The bonnetless and shoeless were in numbers amongst them, and as there are no pew rents and no appropriations they were enabled to feel that they had as good a right to their church as any one else. The demeanour of the congregation was reverent and attentive . . . The work is likely for a long time to be of a distinctly missionary character.

It was true ; but the preceding sentences prove that the foundations of that work had been already laid. There are no statistics before 1863 ; but in that year we find that 295 persons, many of them adults, were baptized, whilst in 1864 the Easter communicants already numbered 291 ; in the following year they had increased to 453. Of course these numbers included many persons outside the parish. The work as soon as the church was opened became not only parochial but congregational. Union within brought as a natural consequence hearty co-operation from without, whilst the very dissimilar characteristics of the clergy attracted different classes of people. The poorer worshippers were supplemented by a large body of middle-class young men (for whom the church has always had a great attraction), of tradesmen and their families, and of young women in business, whilst it was also frequented by many from other parts of London who were drawn to it by the preaching or the services. Yet those amongst whom Mr. Mackonochie had been working in Baldwin's Gardens and the adjacent courts and alleys were by no means wanting. As he justly remarks in a letter to the ' Times ' dated August 1866 :

A poor man or woman does not come to church for many Sundays in bad clothing. He gives up buying gin and gets good clothes. I ought to thank you for your testimony as to the manner and heartiness of the congregation—made up, let me observe, after allowing for a few rich and a good many poor, of shopmen, warehousemen, tradesmen, professional men, students of medicine, &c. ; the very men whom the Church generally finds it so hard to hold together.

As we shall see further on, nothing was done for the sake of popularity. From the first the services (so far as means allowed) had emphasised and, as it were, illustrated the doctrine taught. Some special offerings had been made to the church, two altar cloths, red and violet ; and the linen vestments which were the gift of the founder. They had been used from the beginning, together with the lights and ceremonies, which, now in so many places matters of course, were as yet comparatively unaccustomed. The St. George's Mission hymn-book was used, and many of the hymns were very popular in character, but the office hymn and the chief part of the music was Gregorian.

The work of Dr. Pusey, and of the great men who with him were instrumental under God in the latest of the many reformations of the Church of England, was mainly the restatement of forgotten or half-forgotten truths ; . . . but it was the work of a younger generation of clergy and laity to apply these truths to the hearts and consciences of the people, . . . to teach men to use the penitential system of the Church as Christ's means of restoring and assisting the sinful ; and to awaken men not only to the duty of Communion, but also to the duty of Eucharistic worship. For these ends, with simple common sense, devotion, and reality, Father Mackonochie lived and worked.

Such was Canon Knox Little's testimony in a sermon preached soon after Mr. Mackonochie's death, and at the very outset of his incumbency the words were as true as they were at its conclusion.   He valued ritual as the exponent of his belief; it was no empty symbol, but the outward and rightful expression of the faith which he held and taught. There was in him a complete absence of the artistic sense of beauty.   As one of Nature's children in field and hedge-row and plot of garden-ground he had not failed to learn her secrets, but of form, colour, architecture, and music he had but little appreciation.   It was the fitness and not the beauty of ceremonial which commended itself to him.

People have taken to call us ritualists (he wrote in 1867, in an address to his parishioners).   Knowing how small a share in my own thoughts (and I believe in yours) the mere question of ritual occupies, I confess to thinking the name a somewhat unsuitable one . . . You very well know that the value we attach to these things (he continues, speaking of the ceremonies of the Eucharistic service) is not for their own sakes, it is because of the special service in which they are used . . . It ought to mean something. It does mean something.

Matters which were mere matters of taste or opinion

he was ready to relinquish, but throughout the long and wearisome battle he held to his flag (his rebel flag, as his enemies called it) with undismayed tenacity. In all simplicity he might have given the same answer as the drummer-boy when ordered to sound the retreat, ' I have never learned it.'

Without any love of novelty he was yet anxious to use all means to reach those to whom he had been sent, and had no sort of respect for old prejudices and conventional barriers. Already, in 1863, Father Lowder had preached a successful mission at St. Alban's, and it was also the first church in London where the devotion of the Three Hours was started, on the Good Friday of 1865, two years after the consecration. It called forth many and various comments from the public and the secular press, being regarded as a startling and somewhat dangerous innovation upon the ordinary services of the day, which could only have been attempted in a church already noted for its ritual and frequented by an extreme section of the Anglican Communion. It is a curious instance of the change which time has wrought to note the numberless churches in which this service is now a matter of course ; and when contrasted with the timid or condemnatory judgments from some high quarters to which it gave rise in 1865, the fact that in this present year (1890) the Bishop of London has preached the Three Hours at St. Paul's Cathedral is not without its significance.

The verdict of an irresponsible public had never much weight with Mr. Mackonochie ; but secure in his own position, he could afford to be just to those who differed from him. Over and over again we find words of exhortation to charity.

You will need patience (he writes in 1869, when judgment had just been given against him) ; patience with your opponents lest you lose love ; patience with your friends lest you break up your forces ; patience above all with yourselves lest you lose heart. You must be patient at home and patient in society, patient in discussion and patient under abuse.

And with an extraordinary power of self-control, he carried out his own precept. Whilst the stormiest discussions were going on around him at the most tumultuous meeting, he would remain apparently unmoved ; if he spoke his words were few, sometimes abrupt, but never discourteous ; the fire of his speech never lighted upon a personal enemy, nor was kindled at the smouldering remembrance of a personal wrong.

When misrepresentations were most rife and ignorant prejudices were apparently gaining ground ; when every attempt was being made to counteract the influence of his self-denying life ; when the walls in his parish were placarded with outrageous accusations and warnings, ' Beware the wily demoralising priest, the cunning emissary of Rome. He is a traitor to his Church, a disgrace to England which gave him birth,' &c. When Dr. Cumming in Covent Garden and the Rev. F. Laing at the Italian Church close by were from their different standpoints lecturing against him, he himself rarely spoke upon controversial subjects except in self-defence. As has been well said, ' Prosecutions, persecutions, admonitions, abuse, ridicule, calumny—all ran off this robust constitution like water off a duck's back.' He was keenly sensitive to the adverse verdict of a friend, but he gave no heed to the scornful or condemnatory judgment of ill-informed critics; it was not his business to justify himself to them.

Yet with the difficulties or prejudices of those who had a claim upon him he had an infinite patience; and in this manner many an overt enemy or indifferent bystander was won over to espouse his cause with a zeal which only needed to be directed or kept in check. There is an instance of this going forth to meet an enemy only to find a friend, in the case of one of the churchwardens brought in as the spokesman of the Protestant party in order to counteract his influence and head the opposition at a time when the strife was fiercest and party feeling at its height. He came to the church prepared to do his best or his worst, the doctrine taught was abhorrent and the ritual distasteful, but he was met with friendly courtesy, invited into the Clergy House, and time after time reasoned with and directed, until in no long while Mr. Mackonochie had the satisfaction of preparing him for confirmation, and he became one of his staunchest adherents and a faithful communicant at the church.

It was only one instance among many. Grave and self-contained, with a touch of austerity both in his looks and manners, there was the real personal love for souls which breaks down all conventional barriers. He never for an instant supposed that 'the sphere of Christian duty was to be narrowed to suit the lukewarmness of Christian feeling;' and so, not only in the abject and in the fallen, but in the crudeness and self-confidence of youth and in the self-sufficiency of respectable middle age, through all the poor disguises which the world puts on, he saw the marred reflection of the Divine Image, and time and strength and effort were ungrudgingly spent in the work of its restoration.

CHAPTER VII.

Growth of spiritual work at St. Alban's—Influence of the church and clergy—
Doctrinal teaching—First prosecution—Direction—Sermons.

1862—1867.

THE five years from 1862 to 1867 were years of uninterrupted progress. The congregations were large and increasing. It was soon no longer a question of a knot of people gathered about the pulpit on Sunday evenings, whilst in the background ragged children ran in and out and played among the benches. Classes had been formed for instruction, schools were in working order, and every effort was made to raise the tone of the neighbourhood. There was, even in these early days, one means to this end which especially occupied Mr. Mackonochie's attention. Confronted with the difficult problem how best to awaken those so long sunk in apathy and degradation to a sense of universal sonship, conferring undoubted rights to the good things of a spiritual kingdom, one of his first desires was to deprive the outward circumstances of death and burial of those ghastly and expensive adjuncts which were still so much matters of course, and at the same time to dignify and Christianise the careless and slovenly funerals of the poor. Remembering the place of his own burial, it is interesting to find an entry in his handwriting in the parish book kept at Wantage when he was a curate there.

We have had in the parish since Saturday one of the Baverstocks. His father was formerly an inhabitant of the town. We had much talk with him on different subjects, especially on the efforts now making by the Guild of St. Alban (of which he is a member) in the district of St. Barnabas, Pimlico, to Christianise the burials of the poor, and one would hope through them those of their betters. Among other things he told me that the Woking Cemetery Company had offered to set apart for their use a part of the Cemetery and let them erect in it a churchyard cross. At present some difficulty has prevented their accepting the offer.

This subject was even then constantly in his thoughts, and he often erected, at his own expense, a simple oak cross to the memory of some of those to whom he ministered. When he went to London, the Burial Guild which he started at St. Alban's, the mortuary chapel attached to the church, and the ground secured at Woking for the last resting-place of members of the congregation, all bore witness to his strong feeling upon the subject. It was one which especially appealed to working people. The care and reverence shown to their dead were often the means of awakening the deeper and tenderer feelings which had long lain dormant; and in times of sorrow the bonds which united clergy and people were more closely drawn.

In some respects it was almost more difficult to deal with those who were outside the parish than with parishioners, and the attendance of strangers at the church was large, though fluctuating. Already, in 1863, Mr.

Mackonochie issued an address to the 'strangers attending the services.'

Those services were in all essentials what they afterwards became, though there were differences of detail. But from the very first two fundamental doctrines were not only taught but practically brought into prominence :

(1) The position of the Holy Eucharist as the only divinely appointed act of worship ; and (2) the right of every soul which felt its need to seek in the Sacrament of Penance the absolution and remission of sins.

From the first there was, in addition to the early services on every Sunday and holy day, a celebration of the Holy Communion, with accessories of music and ceremonial. In 1863 Mr. Mackonochie writes : 'I most earnestly entreat you all to remain from beginning to end of the service for Holy Communion.' Whilst the communicants were as earnestly requested to make their communions fasting at one of the early celebrations.

When it became necessary to arrange the services for this church so as to suit the wants of parishioners (wrote Mr. Mackonochie) I saw two things which had to be thought of. One was to have many services, none of them of too great length ; the other was to respect the integrity of the Church's Offices. . . . As the morning service is one and has no break, so the service for Holy Communion is also one and has no break . . . There is not one word in our Prayer Books about those withdrawing who do not intend to communicate. This becomes the more remarkable, because in the First Prayer Book of Edward VI. those who did not intend to communicate were desired to leave the choir (not the church, let us observe), but this order was withdrawn at the first revision of the book. The Church has therefore deliberately taken away the word of discouragement from those who, though they do not communicate at that service, yet desire to be present and worship their Lord.

It was particularly difficult to train a congregation where a great many of those composing it came from outside the parish and could therefore only be reached by sermons, unless brought into personal contact with the clergy, and for some years they were slow to put into practice the teaching which they received ; even in 1866 we find that nearly half the communicants communicated on great festivals at late celebrations, but by degrees the character of the congregation underwent a change. Those who came merely from curiosity or love of novelty dropped off, and those who remained accepted the doctrine and discipline of the church. To those who came from a distance, Mr. Mackonochie added a few words at the conclusion of his address for that year.

London is full of churches with early celebrations of Holy Communion. Surely at some of these the Holy Communion might be received early according to the unvaried rule of the Church ; then if you like to worship here later in the day well and good.

The words incidentally show how little he valued numbers ; how averse he was to attract to his church those who could elsewhere more consistently carry out his teaching.

From the first he sought to make his people regard penance as an ordinary means of grace, to which they had an undoubted right. He was most anxious to take from those who frequented it all sense of singularity, and his straightforward teaching as to its blessings and obligations at once pressed home a duty and satisfied a need. The practice of confession thus made plain was adopted by an ever-increasing number of those who came under his influence; whilst many who had never heard or seen him came from long distances—from remote country parishes, and other parts of London—to make their confessions at St. Alban's.

It was the practical result of the teaching of the old Tractarians, in those days more or less of a novelty, even to those who shared their convictions. Mr. Mackonochie's temper of mind would naturally have inclined him to press upon his people the life of penitence and self-denial as the only possible preparation for the fulness of Christian joy, and his own force of character and definite beliefs were strength and consolation to the weak-hearted or doubtful. His views upon this subject, which never wavered, are fully expressed in a private letter, dated 1870.

The only way is to put the matter simply as Holy Scripture does. We are ambassadors for God, and as such have a message of forgiveness for sinners. Come and receive it. No one doubts that to come to confession without true contrition is sacrilege, but so too it is sacrilege to make a bad communion. In both cases God ultimately throws the responsibility on each conscience, but in both cases He expects His priests to tell their people clearly of the privilege and of the responsibility. This done simply makes the act of confession a straightforward, brave, and manly act. . . . For the last twelve years I have had experience over an area extending more and more widely every year, and now, supported as it is by that of my brother priests, here and in other parishes, a very wide one. What is the result? Souls by the scores, not to say hundreds, thanking God for the plain outspoken teaching of God's mercy to sinful souls—souls in ordinary states of sin, having no health in them, as we say daily—and grieving that the partial and hesitating utterances of those who have told them only of absolution for exceptional cases should have kept them back so long from a means of grace which has made God's command 'be ye holy' a word of possibility to them, clearing away the entangling past, smoothing the path of the future, and giving strength for the present contest.

This plain and explicit teaching, illustrated as it was by the character of the services, was not long in arousing opposition. It was known that the founder of the church was dissatisfied, and would not be likely to take up its defence ; indeed, the differences between him and Mr. Mackonochie had assumed so grave a character that Mr. Mackonochie had already offered to resign. The proposal, however, fell to the ground ; and after some preliminary threats and warnings, the first prosecution was instituted in the spring of 1867.

I am very thankful to say (wrote Mr. Mackonochie, in his parochial address of this year) that it proceeds neither from the Bishop nor from the parishioners. The nominal prosecutor is, as you know, a gentleman [Mr. Martin] who has an official connection with school premises in Baldwin's Gardens, and thereby is legally a parishioner, but who lives out of the parish and has allowed his name to be substituted for that of another who had taken steps to begin the suit on the general ground of his belonging to a party in the Church adverse to the views of her teaching which I believe to be the truth. The real prosecutor is said to be an irresponsible Society, formed with the object of forcing upon the Church of England one particular form of opinion, not easily reconciled with her own Prayer Book.

Upon this there follows some explanation of his own

position and line of defence, but we do not propose to enter in this place into the account of the prosecutions, which will be dealt with in a separate chapter, and it is the less necessary as they interfered very little either with the daily routine or the aim and scope of his ministerial work, which was every week becoming more and more of an individual character.

It is difficult to select from the many recollections furnished by those who made practical experience of his ministrations. There is a singular unanimity in their testimony. Never in a hurry, always willing to listen ; and then prompt, decided, gently immovable ; so that you felt when once his judgment had been formed and his advice was given, that any expostulations or remonstrances would be absolutely useless. In his opinion, if you voluntarily sought his guidance you must be prepared to follow it. He was ready to teach and to explain, but not to argue; indeed, controversy in any form or shape was distasteful ; he never lightly fenced with weapons in order to prove them, or for the sake of practice in the art. One who was for many years a Nonconformist writes :

About the time I made his acquaintance I was terribly harassed by doubts as to the Faith. I wanted to believe, I tried to believe, but believe I could not. I was, I suppose, what is nowadays called an honest doubter. In this state of mind I consulted him. . . . He never expressed surprise at my doubts, he never treated them as sins, but he never reasoned about them, he never argued. All he said was, 'Use the light you have and do your duty. Leave your doubts to God, He will solve them.' I must confess that at first I was considerably taken aback. My doubts were important factors in my life ; they had caused and were causing me real grief and pain, and now they were to be passed over in this fashion. The remedy 'use the light you have' was a great deal too simple to be palatable. I was ready for any amount of mental analysis and study and discussion. How could I use light at all so long as any part of the horizon remained dark ; and so, like Naaman, I was about to go away in a rage, when it flashed upon me that I had heard somewhere the same advice before ; and following up the thought link by link I lighted upon this, 'If any man will do His Will, he shall know of the doctrine.' So I thought Mr. Mackonochie is not so far wrong after all,—first the doing of the Will, then the doctrine. I resolved then and there to take Christ at His Word ; and I will only say that the Master honoured the servant by confirming the message—yea, abundantly.

I soon found, moreover, that Father Mackonochie's apparent lack of sympathy did not spring from any want of feeling for me in my trouble. It arose from the fact that to himself doubts were simply non-existent, mere negations, phantoms with which personally he could not fight. Before his strong positive faith they vanished as do the shadows in a firelit room before a clearer light . . . His way of dealing with these questions used to suggest to me in those days a rather curious parallel. Before I knew him one of the great motive powers in my life had been Thomas Carlyle. Probably no two men were ever more dissimilar than Father Mackonochie and Carlyle. . . . Nevertheless, their teaching, wide apart as were their opinions, was in one respect similar. To the soul that is 'groping painfully in darkness and inexpressibly languishing to work,' Carlyle says : 'Do the duty which lies nearest to thee which thou knowest to be a duty ; ' and to the soul beset with doubts and liable to exhaust itself in combating them, Father Mackonochie says : 'Use the light which thou hast which thou knowest to be light, and—do thy duty.' Thus the remedy of both was action, work, duty. The difference of the teaching of the two, to my mind, lies in the fact that Carlyle's counsel was single, 'do the duty ; ' Father Mackonochie's was two-fold, 'Use the light and do the duty.'

I

The fact was that Mr. Mackonochie's own life, though, in one sense of the word, an uneventful one, was pre-eminently a life of action. Speculative thought, or the imaginative day-dreams of a prophet or a poet, held no place in it. His strong grasp of eternal truths was never relaxed, because to him they were absolute realities; the only immutable substances in a changing, dying world. As a natural consequence, his obedience to what he believed to be God's Will was as simple as a child's. His ' happy conscience,' as one of his friends calls it, was untroubled by misgivings as to motives or consequences. *Fais ce que tu dois, advienne que pourra* was the keynote of his teaching, and his confidence that to see the right was of necessity to do it, was very happily contagious. His irrepressible hopefulness, all the more remarkable because unsupported by natural buoyancy of spirit, awakened new hopes in the faint-hearted, and morbid scruples, doubts, and fears vanished in a healthy and invigorating moral atmosphere.

Yet his rule was by no means a lax one. Both in the outward and the inner life there should be method and order. From the first, as we have seen, he was scrupulously exact and punctual in all the duties of his office ; and in church more especially anxious that everything possible should be done to render the service both reverent and edifying. In a letter of advice to a young curate in 1867 he writes :

I have been wanting to write to you about the Bishop's letter. Now I have lost sight of it and I can only remember this, that it exactly puts in better words what I wanted to say to you when we last parted. I did not say it because I did not quite know how to

express it. The Bishop calls it 'hardness.' I think this fairly
expresses the idea ; perhaps I should have said sharpness, the ring
of steel instead of silver. I noticed it in your reading of lessons,
saying of offices, celebrations, perhaps in preaching. The manner,
I mean, is one exactly to make things disliked which would be
liked if done by some one else. I do not like to write this because
it seems merely to lead to self-contemplation, but I do not know
how to say it otherwise. The Bishop thinks it co-exists with a
mind unable to tolerate the difficulties of unbelievers. I could
fancy that it would be incompatible with a keen perception that a
Presbyterian was bought with the same Precious Blood as ourselves. I fear I must leave this in its own bald state, simply
because I do not know how to put it better. I know you well
enough to know that you do wish to cultivate both inwardly and
outwardly the Love of Jesus for souls, and therefore I am sure
that if the Bishop and I are right, and you can at all make out
what the evil is, you will be glad to know in order to correct it.

Your most affectionate Brother in Our Blessed Lord,

ALEX. H. MACKONOCHIE.

The letter is very like himself, eminently practical, and
yet searching at once into the root of the matter. It was
not a question of mere edification, though that too was of
importance ; there was another consideration of yet greater
moment ; did not the ' ring of steel instead of silver ' indicate
that the natural self-assertion and aggressiveness of youth
had not been thrust out of sight by the humbling responsibilities of the Christian ministry ; so that the Gospel message
in his mouth sounded like a declaration of war, unbefitting
the sworn ambassador of the Prince of Peace ? And thus he
makes his protest with affectionate directness, and without
any sort of suspicion that it is likely to give offence.

His feeling of awe for his office is well expressed in a

letter about this same date (1866) to a candidate for Holy Orders.

I promised to write you a few lines about your approaching entrance into the priesthood. I feel that it is utterly superfluous, as you will doubtless in your preparation have every thought which I can suggest pressed home to you with a power which I am wholly unable to give to it. Still (since you ask it) I will say a few words committing them to God.

1. I suppose that the first thought with which one would try to approach the subject would be the great goodness of God in accepting one to be His Priest. And this in regard both of the greatness of the office—whether as teaching with authority, or dealing individually with souls, or above all in ascending to Heaven upon the Son of Man, in offering the Divine Sacrifice, and descending with Him in our hands to give to His people ; and also in regard of our own unworthiness generally as man, particularly as such a man. The whole past comes up before our eyes, as we can conceive its coming before the eyes of the redeemed at the hearing of the great acceptance in the last day. The heart exclaims : 'that I, being what I am, should obtain such an inheritance !'

2. The difficulty and danger of the priest's life ; such that if the disciples might exclaim, 'Who then can be saved?' we may still more exclaim what priest can be saved, and more still, 'how can I be saved in so dangerous an office?' The many bad among those who have been called especially near to God, from Lucifer to those sad scandals which so often turn up among ourselves, fallen priests ; scandals to the faithful, warning beacons to us. Then will come your own special temptations, whatever your confessions have revealed to you ; perhaps levity and keenness of perception of other people's faults ; leading to a resolution of indifference to circumstances of work, &c.

3. I think this will lead to a more and more earnest prayer for perseverance, that the fear and the resolution with which you

accept the office may never fail you. That on your death-bed
you may be able to return to God the office of the earthly priest
with the remembrance of purposes fulfilled, reverence deepened,
and love more burning for each year of your ministry.

You see I have fallen rather into the line of heads for meditation. I think, perhaps, you will be able to gather from this, better
than from anything else, such material as you want.

God bless you. In Him, your affectionate
ALEX. HERIOT MACKONOCHIE.

The very same idea is brought out in a letter written to
Bishop Smythies upon his consecration in 1883. Nearly
twenty years had elapsed, but the habits of a lifetime had
but served to deepen the almost melancholy sense of high
responsibilities which no human sympathy can lighten.

The office of bishop (he writes) is not one to be desired in
this world, and therefore I cannot in the common sense congratulate you ; but as you will, by the Grace of God, administer it, it
will no doubt, by its burdensome anxieties, be the choicest treasure
you can possess on this side of the grave.

If in St. Chrysostom's time it was so fearful a responsibility, as
he saw it to be, what must it be now, when the fierce strife is so
exaggerated in proportion, by the progress of knowledge most
unevenly balanced with faith, and so embittered in all its most
evil characteristics, as it is now? Your own case will be the harder
by its removing you from all your immediate associations, and by
your having to throw yourself into a new sphere, with all its new
angles.

In regard to all this you are much to be envied. Of course
the joy of Christian life is to suffer, as the very title tells. Instead
of flying like St. Chrysostom from the burden, it will in your case
be only the burden which makes it bearable to you. All the
Saint's apprehensions fled when fairly in his work, and God has
given to men of successive ages gifts of strength and perseverance

from the blessed Spring out of the Pierced Side, the only source of victorious strength through suffering.

You will have many before you watching you—dear F. O'Neill, the great Bishop Milman, the Mackenzies, and hosts more, not only of the Episcopate, but also of our own order and the laity. However scattered, it will be our own faults if, by grace, the Kingdom of Christ be not deepened in the hearts of men ; and men like yourself will make ample use of the gifts which will be yours in a few hours. The Hands from Heaven will have touched you, as did the live coal the prophet's lips, and in the full panoply of Christ's armour you will be one of His Generals. 'Be thou faithful unto death and I will give thee the Crown of Life.'

Asking earnestly your blessing, believe me yours affectionately,

ALEX. HERIOT MACKONOCHIE.

The two letters to the young deacon and the Bishop curiously illustrate the unity of his character. In both there is the same strain of strongly expressed awe and reverent hope ; it marked his dealings with individuals, his public ministrations, his spiritual letters, and his sermons, with the deep impress of his own nature.

'Was he a great preacher?' The question is one not easy to answer. He was undoubtedly not a great orator. He had no rhetorical power, nor striking felicities of expression. His sentences in the pulpit were short, and his language unstudied and perfectly simple ; it was the vehicle of his thoughts and nothing more. His delivery at once arrested attention ; his voice was not especially powerful, though clear and penetrating ; and his gestures were, though emphatic, abrupt and almost ungainly ; but as he stood with his searching eyes upon the congregation he had a curious power of making each separate individual feel

that he was speaking to *him*.   He not only taught
the great truths of religion in explicit language, but he
pressed them home to the individual conscience with a force
by which they became the very foundation-stones of the
Christian life.   And so it is that from the rustics in his first
curacy to his educated hearers at St. Alban's ; from the
poor and from the men of the world, there comes the same
witness.   ' I remember the sermon he preached years ago.
I have never forgotten it.'

After a lapse of many years, with a vivid recollection of
his impressions, one of his hearers writes :

I went on eight successive Good Fridays to St. Alban's.   I
was a layman then.   The last time I went was in 1878.   I
remember what most impressed me in all those wonderful
addresses, which he always took himself, was his tenderness and
keen sympathy when speaking on the word of pardon to the dying
robber.   He used to linger on it, and I used to watch his features
with the bright eyes, and the strong yet trembling hand as it
seemed to be pushing through the veils of earth ; and how his
eyes kindled with a look of inspiration and eagerness and steadi-
ness of gaze as he spoke of Paradise, until I was (and I think we
all were) lifted out of ourselves and St. Alban's and were at the
foot of the cross outside Jerusalem.

One feature of his preaching was clearness both of thought
and expression.   He had a definite plan, and he had given
time and trouble to the work of preparation.   Not, of course,
as years went by, the laborious preparation which was
only too apparent in his early sermons at Westbury, but a
patient and thoughtful consideration of his subject resulting
from old habits of conscientious application and the strong
sense of ministerial responsibility.   If eloquence is, as

French writer has expressed it, '*l'art de bien dire quelque chose à quelqu'un*,' he was eloquent, but it was not the eloquence of fluent language, nor, except upon rare occasions, that of the inspiration of the moment. His delivery was rather rapid than slow, yet his words came out in order as befitted the representatives of a truthful nature.

With so many really holy and saintly men that one knows or has known (writes one of his friends), one cannot but feel that, especially at certain times and seasons, they are acting a part—a beautiful and edifying part, a part that costs them a great deal, but still a part ; their goodness is not yet quite the same as themselves ; but you never felt this with Mackonochie. He was always himself ; his tenacity, his stiffness, his reserve, his tenderness, his sympathy, his modesty, his deference to others, his manliness, his temperance, were all real manifestations of the man himself. You could not help trusting so *true* a man as this.

And then he goes on to speak of his 'perfect naturalness.'

This last quality was perhaps even more noticeable in the pulpit than elsewhere. Words and manner, expressions and gestures were alike free from the slightest touch of self-consciousness. It was not that his hearers were forgotten ; on the contrary, he was intensely conscious of their presence, and spoke directly to them with a vivid realisation of their personality and their needs, but he thought of them only in relation to the message he had to deliver, not in relation to himself ; their judgment was of but little account ; he asked neither for their criticism nor their praise ; he only knew that he had something to say to which they were bound to listen ; and so it was that, though he never drew a bow at a venture, many a shaft sank in deeply where it might least have been expected.

There are not many of his sermons in print. Latterly—indeed almost always after entering upon his London ministry—he preached extempore ; and his sermons were always of a kind to lose much of their life and force when written down. One of the few published verbatim was a sermon preached before the University of Oxford in December 1867, from which we have already given an extract. He appears to have had some hesitation as to accepting the offer to preach upon this occasion, and Dr. Liddon wrote to him :

Accept the turn by all means. I am sure you might do an immense deal of good which nobody else could do, and certainly not the select preachers. . . . I should think you would best serve the Church's cause by taking a subject on which you would speak with the authority of an experience that none could gainsay. I mean the blessedness of hearty work for souls. This would very naturally commend itself with the Advent, as being on the one hand an extension of the Divine Incarnation, and on the other a preparation for the last judgment.

And then again he writes after reading over the manuscript :

I have made the few corrections which seem possible, without altering the character of the sermon. I am so afraid of making patchwork of it. I hope that the few little words I have altered will meet with your approval. The sermon was a great blessing to a great many souls, and a rude hand might easily damage its beautiful self-consistency. May God strengthen and support you ever. In all love, your most affectionate

H. P. Liddon.

And then again, upon receipt of the printed copy, he writes :

I am rejoiced to possess a copy from its author. It will do a great deal of good of the best kind, and I never was more sure of being right than in begging you first to preach and then to publish it.

These words, as well as those already quoted with reference to Mackonochie's earlier sermons at Wantage, are of especial value coming from so high an authority. The verdict was not merely that of a friend, but of a critic touching upon a subject peculiarly his own. It was an opinion, moreover, delivered in cold blood apart from the accidents of delivery.

' It was valued; for the three little notes had been carefully docketed and put away; and it was no doubt all the more appreciated because Mackonochie's estimate of his own preaching was not a high one. In his earlier letters we find occasional references to his sermons as not worth sending home; he considered the ordination sermon, by which Dr. Butler was impressed, a failure; and though he was by no means given to undue self-depreciation, and as time went by could not but be aware of increasing powers both of thought and diction, he never studied preaching as an art. By sheer force of directness and simplicity he said things very well; and an old truth came with fresh force and freshness from the lips of a man to whom it was the very anchor of the soul.

During these first five years at St. Alban's he preached chiefly in his own church. He often touched upon dogma, but seldom upon controversial subjects; and his practical sermons on the everyday duties of his hearers, when, as a newspaper remarked, 'he talked very pleasantly,' were

both encouraging and instructive ; his counsels were those
of a man who had found life eminently worth living, to
whom, though the conflict might be long, the victory was
sure. Though less subject to moods than most people, like
every other extempore preacher he varied a good deal both
as to matter and to delivery ; and no doubt his sermons
suffered at times from almost inevitably hurried preparation, or from preceding over-exertion. Already in 1868
(a year when, it is true, he had been harassed by prosecutions) we find the Bishop of Brechin (Forbes) writing
to him :

My dearest Friend,—The love and respect I entertain for you
forces me to use my Episcopal authority in the way of urging you
to economise your strength more. You are working yourself fast
out. Both the sermons I heard, especially the evening one,
exhibited the effects of a worn body telling on the brain. You
will not go on three years at the present rate, *experto crede* ; on the
other hand, by delegation of duty where possible, and by other
management your valuable life will be long spared to do your
Master's work.

Bishop Forbes's apprehensions were not justified by the
result ; but they point to a temporary failure of strength
which was only to be expected when the pressure and the
responsibility of the work is taken into account. Into the
details of that parochial work we intend to enter later on ;
but that it did not ordinarily affect his sermons is proved
by the fact that he would carry on as many as six courses
of sermons at the same time ; all clear and well-reasoned
expositions of his subject preached with fresh energy and
vigour day after day ; and the strain of a misson wen the

him as full of spirit and strength at its close as at its beginning. Perhaps it was because his whole life was the preparation for what he had to say, and no single sermon was, as it were, an isolated effort. As some one said who knew him well :

He carried everywhere with him a good savour of Christ, and I should feel quite sure that if I called him away from the middle of a dinner-table to hear my confession, I should find him in as spiritual a frame of mind as if I had come upon him at his prayers.

It was the result of a close correspondence between the inner and the outward life ; between thoughts and words, ideas and actions, as they were together brought into conformity with the high ideal of the Christian life ;—it was the consequence of that unity of motive and singleness of aim which constitutes the impregnable strength of the Christian character.

CHAPTER VIII.

Work outside the parish of St. Alban's—Confraternity of the Blessed Sacrament—Society of the Holy Cross—Letters from abroad—Chaplaincy of St.
Saviour's Priory, Haggerston—Letter from Bishop Tait—Position of affairs
at the time of the first prosecution.

1866—1867.

BUT though Mackonochie's name must always be insepar-
ably connected with the church and parish of St. Alban's,
Holborn, his work with individuals, as we have seen, extended far beyond its limits, and his sympathies (always
readily enlisted in any effort for the cause which he had
so much at heart) led him to take an active part in organisations and societies whose objects were coextensive with
those of the Church herself.

In the annual address of the Superior, Canon Carter, at
the meeting of the Confraternity of the Blessed Sacrament
in 1888, he referred to the loss they had sustained in the
death of Alexander Heriot Mackonochie, and 'we can
mention,' he adds, ' no one more distinguished, more single-
hearted, or more devoted as a witness to the truths we are
leagued together to promote.'

The Anglo-Catholic movement had been essentially a
revival, and the central doctrine, so long obscured or practically ignored, which it was destined to revive, was 'the

honour due to the Person of Our Lord Jesus Christ in the
Blessed Sacrament of His Body and Blood.' They are
the words in which the first object of the Confraternity is
set forth, and that object was one which Mackonochie
had especially at heart. His public teaching, his personal
practice, the ritual for which he afterwards suffered were
all most intimately connected with it. He was one of the
first Priest Associates of the Confraternity, and, fostered
and directed by him, the ward in connection with
St. Alban's grew and increased year by year until at the
present date it is one of the largest upon the roll of an
association which numbers 12,500 lay associates and 1,400
clergy.

This was only one result of his consistent upholding of
a high standard with regard to the duty of Eucharistic
worship and frequent Communion. In 1867 he wrote to a
younger priest who had consulted him :

I think myself that we ought to put before all who are in
earnest about their souls the standard of Sunday and Festival
Communion. I see no lower standard unless the carelessness of
the receiver obliges us to restrain him and insist on a very special
preparation before each Communion. Of course it is much more
satisfactory that such should come to confession ; but where their
not doing so seems to spring from the invincible ignorance of
inborn and engrained prejudice, I do not think—always supposing
they possess a proper amount of spirituality in other ways—that
they ought to be limited. Indeed, we may hope that the grace of
frequent Communion will make them wish for that which they
have not yet learned from other sources to desire.

And with regard to this subject, in every annual
address, whilst warning his parishioners against judgments

formed as to spiritual advance being based upon statistics, he records with deep thankfulness the increase of communicants, and the evidences of greater devotion and self-denial in the larger number of those who received fasting.

So far, thank God (he writes), the gradual increase of celebrations has been marked by a steady advance in the desire of His people to show their love for Him by their use of this increase—I hope I may add by a corresponding growth of the interior life.

And in 1867, referring to his first prosecution, he says in his address to his congregation :

The battle must be fought in your prayers and before God's Altar. If our daily Eucharist be attended by double the present numbers ; if there be a great and growing increase in communicants and in the frequency and devotion of their Communions, we shall prevail. If we lose, it will not be because we have broken the law, but because we have not deserved God's help.

Always anxious to lead people on to the highest Christian privileges, he was keenly alive to the demands they made upon them for corresponding spirituality and strictness of life. He was not only one of the first Priest Associates of the Confraternity of the Blessed Sacrament, but he was the Master of the Society of the Holy Cross, 'founded for the primary purpose of deepening by means of a definite rule the spiritual life in its brethren.' This Society was, in accordance with the terms of its constitution:

restricted to bishops, priests, and deacons, and *bonâ fide* candidates for Holy Orders. The originators of the Society were convinced that work for Christ in His Church could only be effectively done by those over whom the Spirit of His Own Life on earth had gained some hold ; and on the other hand, that this spirit can only retain its hold upon the character of a priest when it finds its expression in vigorous action within the sphere of his calling.

Hence the features of the Society are two-fold ; its interior rule, acting upon the character and its outward work, leading the brethren to take their position towards the world as possessors of a supernatural life and commission which must either die out or extend its influence to others.

There was an obligatory rule binding all associates to certain definite religious duties and strictness of life, and two voluntary rules, one of which was restricted to celibates, recommended to those who ' feel called to seek in them a means of closer union with God.' From the first it was the stricter rule which Mr. Mackonochie adopted ; and willingly conformed to its obligations.

The ordinary routine of life at the Clergy House was only broken in upon by the necessary interruptions and exigencies of parochial work, and one is glad to find in 1866 mention of a real holiday and short tour abroad. In October, 1865, he had gone for a short time to Aix-la-Chapelle, when a sharp return of rheumatism had obliged him to seek the remedy of the baths ; but he was without a congenial companion, and more or less of an invalid, and it would appear from his letters that his enforced idleness was rather a duty than a pleasure. In the following year, however, we find a long letter from abroad full of pleasant accounts of the places he has seen and the people he has met. The city father with his invalid son, a nice young fellow with a cough that, Mackonochie fears, he will only lose in Paradise ; George Williams, of King's College, Cambridge, with whom he dined in Paris ; and various other travellers with whom he appears at once to have entered into friendly relations. At Paris he did not like the Madeleine, 'it has so very much the character of a show place'; but he was much struck with the various services he attended, and remarks, 'I think I have seen people communicating at most of the masses to which I have been, and sometimes in great numbers.'

From Paris he went on to Dijon to see Citeaux, the cradle of the Cistercian Order of Benedictines, and to visit Les Fontaines, the birthplace of St. Bernard.

I saw (he writes) the room in which St. Bernard was born. I bought two of the books, one for Mrs. N——, who greatly loves St. Bernard. The priest met me as I came away. He knows Perceval Ward. As we parted he said, 'Je vous souhaite un pas de plus vers l'unité.' My next resting place was Villefranche, on All Saints' Eve. Having slept and been to the services, all very crowded and many communicants, I then started for Ars, where the great Curé lived and worked and died. If you see Stanton tell him that I visited Ars on All Saints' Day. I saw his bedroom, dining-room, confessional. I did not see his altar, for, leaving the building of the little old church untouched in other ways, they have taken down the east wall and built on a very fine addition of transepts and chancel, a handsome new altar standing under the lantern tower . . . I shall tell you much, if you care to hear it, when I come back. I was shown about by the dearest and most simple Brother, who had been with the dear Curé for years.

From Dijon he went on to Grenoble, and as they passed through the hills and valleys he writes that

involuntarily one could only exclaim, 'Oh my God, is Paradise like this?' Till again the thought came, 'If Thou hast given such loveliness to us sinners on earth, what hast Thou not reserved for Thine elect hereafter?'

K

It is one of the very few references which we have in his letters to his love for natural beauty. It was not the educated appreciation of the artist or the poet, but something at once simpler and deeper; an instinctive, childlike delight, mingled with wondering reverence for this outward revelation of the mind of God.

Perhaps the feeling gathered strength from the fact that he was rarely able to indulge it. Nearly all his life after he left Wantage was spent in London. His holidays were rare and brief. Already, in this year 1866, he was at home and at work again within the month. There was one more winter before him of undisturbed parochial progress; though, indeed, there were indications of rising opposition and of the storm which was to break in the spring of 1867; but they were the natural, perhaps almost the inevitable, accompaniments of a success which was at once a surprise to his friends and a practical answer to those who condemned the course of action he had adopted.

As we have seen, it was in March 1867 the first prosecution had begun; and it does not seem out of place to relate one or two facts which curiously illustrate the condition of his own mind at this critical time, and the friendly relations he still maintained with those who might naturally have been supposed to be antagonistic to him.

As we have already seen, the work of his own church and parish by no means absorbed all his energies; but it is a very remarkable instance of absence of pre-occupation with his own concerns that in this very year when he was first exposed to the open attacks which were unhappily such familiar incidents in his after life, we find him voluntarily taking up a fresh work, and one certain to land him in new difficulties and subject him to further misconstruction.

Sisterhoods in the Church of England were still in their infancy. Most of those who theoretically approved of their constitution and objects looked upon them as experiments ; whilst to many more they were objects of ridicule or suspicion. The old ' No Popery ' cry had been raised against them with some show of reason, since the secession of some of their earliest members to the Roman Communion had awakened a not unnatural fear as to the ultimate influence upon young and enthusiastic minds of a life to which the engrained prejudices of the average Englishman were so absolutely opposed. It was easy enough to awaken popular antagonism ; it has taken many years of patient perseverance and of still more convincing practical experience to allay it. And in 1867 there were as yet few parishes in which the work of organised communities of women had been tested, though the names of Dr. Neale, Canon Carter of Clewer, Dr. Butler of Wantage, and many others, were sufficient proofs of the stability of its foundations and the purity of its aims.

In 1865, the Sisters of St. Margaret's, East Grinstead, had started a new mission in Haggerston. It now embraces the three parishes of St. Augustine's, St. Mary's, and St. Chad's ; but in those days it was comparatively unknown ground, with an overwhelming population, scanty church accommodation, and, numerically, an altogether inadequate clerical staff.

The Priory was opened with its full contingent of Sisters and workers on May 3, but besides the difficulties and disappointments which were naturally to be anticipated, it was almost at once beset with unexpected trials. Dr. Neale, whose last work had been the planting of this offshoot of his Sisterhood, upon whom the Sisters had depended as their counsellor and stay, died in the August of the same year, and the sympathies of the people amongst whom they laboured had hardly been enlisted, and early prejudices overcome, before the struggling mission received a yet greater shock in the secession of its Chaplain to Rome.

Mr. Mackonochie was not only a strong man, but he was a strong Anglican, and it is not surprising that the minds of the small and disheartened community should have turned to him as one most likely to assist and guide them in their need.

Little as many would have given him credit for it (writes one of his intimate friends), Mackonochie was a staunch, I had almost written a bigoted, Anglican. Even when I first knew him he had passed the insular limits of mere Anglicanism ; but from first to last he was Anglo-Catholic. The only occasion on which I remember coming into anything like collision with him was once when (early in our acquaintance) I ventured to exclaim in somewhat a disparaging tone, in answer to something he had said, ' Yes, but—the Church of England !' His eyes flashed with indignation, and with one angry look he swept out of the room without deigning to give me one word of reply. . . . The Bishops of the Church of England never made a greater mistake than when they treated this man as a Romanising traitor ; he was, at the first at all events, the most rigidly loyal of Anglicans, and if he at all receded from this position it was because he was forced, to some extent, out of it by the oppression and suspicion with which he was treated by Anglican authorities.

But at this time, at any rate, the one amongst those authorities who had come into personal contact with him, and most closely observed his line of action, both at St. George's-in-the-East and at St. Alban's, spontaneously confirmed his friend's verdict by giving him the strongest proof of confidence in his power.

It must be remembered that St. Alban's had been the subject of more or less embittered controversy in the public press. Various circumstances had combined to set a mark upon it. Mr. Martin had instituted his suit in March, the Ritual Commission was sitting during the summer, and Lord Shaftesbury, in a letter to the 'Times,' had made strong objections to Mr. Hubbard's position upon it as being the founder of the Church of St. Alban's, 'which is the head of all the offence in this matter.'[1] Even friends were doubtful and uneasy, opponents loud and clamorous in denunciation, and the press almost without exception ranged on the adverse side; but Bishop Tait's last dealings with Mackonochie (then comparatively unknown, except to his Bishop, as curate of St. George's-in-the-East) had not been forgotten; and widely as their views might differ, he would not withhold the tribute due to his personal integrity and consistent conduct. On hearing that the distressed community at Haggerston desired to secure his services as Chaplain, the Bishop wrote to him as follows:

I am told they are in much perplexity from the secession to

---

[1] In July 1866 Lord Shaftesbury had made the following remarkable note in his diary: 'On Sunday to St. Alban's Church in Holborn with Stephens and Haldane. In outward form and ritual it is the worship of Jupiter or Juno. It may be Heaven itself in the inward sense which none but God can penetrate. . . . Do we thus lead souls to Christ or to Baal?'

the Church of Rome of Mr. Tuke, who has been their clerical adviser for some time, and are most anxious to avail themselves of your assistance and advice. I have carefully inquired into the circumstances, and am most anxious that everything possible and right should be done to prevent these ladies from being unsettled in their allegiance to the Church of England by what has happened, and that they should have whatever assistance and advice you are able to give them. I understand that they have confidence in you, and are more likely to listen to you than to any one else. Although I have reason to believe they depart from the model I approve, I hear from undoubted testimony how great is their self-denial in nursing the sick, by exposing themselves to so many dangers for Christ's sake, and I cannot, therefore, withhold the expression of my sympathy with their ceaseless labours for the poor and afflicted. If by kindly advice and guidance, and such help as you can afford, you can be of use to them at this crisis, I shall be well pleased. I have full confidence in your conscientious desire, according to your own views, to uphold the Church of England, as against the slavery of the Church of Rome, and I think it right you should give what assistance you can to these ladies, and especially to endeavour to save them from following the example of Mr. Tuke, and taking a step which, I fear, could never be retraced, and would be found most injurious to their soul's health.

And in the midst of his own difficulties at St. Alban's, when most men would have considered themselves already overwhelmed with work, Mackonochie accepted the chaplaincy. The post was not only an unpopular one, but it was beset with perplexities. Suspicions had been aroused which seemed to be justified when a few months later a number of the Sisters and their Superior followed their late chaplain to Rome. The reduced members were left almost without friends or funds; and the relinquishment of the work in Haggerston seemed to be a foregone conclusion. Still one person was determined that, triumphing over all temporary discouragements, it should in the end succeed. Mr. Mackonochie at least would uphold it with all the power of his strong will and undisturbed confidence in its ultimate success. Year after year in the midst of his own anxieties, with ever-increasing responsibilities at St. Alban's, with a sphere of work which, as his powers became more known, was opening out in all directions, he yet found time to guide and guard the little community, putting aside his own weightier interests to enter into every detail of the Sisters' work ; until in the end it grew and prospered even beyond the most sanguine expectations. For a while the Sisters occupied small and inconvenient premises in the Kingsland Road, but in 1870 they moved back into the parish of Haggerston. There they still remain, and in the year 1889 have seen the opening of their new Priory house, from which all the various machinery of mission work is successfully brought to bear upon the adjacent parishes. The value of the devoted labours of the large staff of Sisters who inhabit that house cannot be estimated, and in all human probability Haggerston would never have benefited by them if the struggling community had not been upheld in its earlier days by Mr. Mackonochie's resolute will and wise judgment.

There was an obvious reason for the reliance placed in that judgment, not only at this juncture nor by one class of people only, but by so many who at some turning point in their lives felt the need of counsel or assistance. It was a judgment singularly free from personal bias or subsequent vacillations. There is a self-confidence which justly awakens distrust in other people, as being the natural result of egotism or prejudice. But this was rather the confidence of a mind at once candid and clear-sighted following an argument without hesitation to its practical conclusion. In a letter dated 1865, he wrote :

I always think of ——— as a 'moderate' man. This I abhor because it seems to me that it commonly means a man who lacks courage, either moral or spiritual, to carry out his principles to their legitimate issue.

Before we begin the story of the hostile legislation upon which we are now about to enter, we would once more emphasise the fact that the spirit in which Mackonochie met it, though far enough removed from conciliation or compromise, was absolutely free from personal bitterness. Neither at any time was he so absorbed in the pending suit and the verdict which so intimately affected him, as to forget for one moment the interests of the Church at large, and the furtherance of those interests in his own parish. The various religious organisations with which he was connected, and which he had done so much to form and guide, were as much to him as ever. Individual souls with their various needs claimed and received an attention undisturbed by the anxieties which were pressing upon him.

New efforts were made for the evangelisation of the poor people in the courts and alleys about St. Alban's. The unremitting care of the clergy for the children in the day and Sunday schools was bearing good fruit ; the young men and women found not only guides and teachers, but friends at the most critical period of their lives ;

ignorance was in some measure at least dissipated and prejudices overcome; moreover, the sympathies of the working men were enlisted in the Church's cause; and when the conflict came they were not only ready to range themselves upon the losing side, but they had attained to an intelligent appreciation of the principle for which they were contending, and were well aware that it was not merely a question of a posture or a vestment, but of the doctrines, rights, and liberties of the Church.

CHAPTER IX.

MARTIN *versus* MACKONOCHIE.[1]

THE situation in 1863, the year when St. Alban's Church was consecrated, was a critical one for the Church of England. The High Church revival had been largely directed, from the delivery of the judgment in Liddell *v.* Westerton, to the adornment of public worship, so as to bring it into more harmony with the newly restored or newly erected churches whose beauty and magnificence contrasted so strongly with the squalor and meanness which had been prevalent earlier in the century. If the judgment itself had been intended to check the beginnings of ritualism, just faintly discernible at its date, the unfamiliarity of the Judges with the subject-matter prevented them from noting how much more the positive factors in their finding—those admitting the legality of all the Edwardine ornaments, and the permissibility of subsidiary articles not

---

[1] [The following chapter and the history of the Ecclesiastical Courts, given in the Appendix, were written by Dr. Littledale.—ED.]

prescribed by any rubric—made in favour of ritualism, than the negative factors and specific prohibitions made against it. Consequently, the spread of ceremonial observances which had been long in abeyance was both wide and rapid from this time forward, and caused as much resentment amongst the members of one school in the Church as satisfaction to those of the competing school. And it happened that just then various circumstances combined to put the Evangelical party into a very favourable position for organising a campaign against the innovations which were so unwelcome to it. The most prominent member of their party was a nobleman universally respected for his ardent philanthropy, which made the Earl of Shaftesbury a tower of strength to any cause he was willing to champion, and he was heart and soul opposed, not only to the external observances of ritualism, but to the whole theology from which they sprang. His influence with Lord Palmerston, his near connection, enabled him virtually to nominate the bishops appointed during Lord Palmerston's ministry, and thus in 1865 the proportion of Evangelicals in possession of Sees was larger than it had been since the time of Queen Elizabeth, while several prelates who could not be classed along with them were, from other points of view, quite as hostile to the ceremonial movement. Not more than six bishops could be accurately described as High Churchmen, though a few were found including the Primate, Archbishop Longley, who were so styled because they could not be reckoned as either Broad or Low Churchmen, but not because they had any firm grasp of High Church theology, or any sympathy with the new development. Thus a powerful majority of the Episcopate could be safely depended on to do what they could for the suppression of ritualism ; and at the same time a like hostility was felt by some of the principal lawyers of the day, who were all but certain to find a place on any Committee of Privy Council before which suits to repress ceremonial might be brought. These facts did not escape the observation of the Evangelical leaders, who had noted all along from the date of the Gorham Judgment the temper of the Judicial Committee, and felt that it could be relied upon as their firm ally. Accordingly, a new organisation was set on foot in 1865, in opposition to the English Church Union, which was to be specifically occupied with counteracting ritualism, and that not only by the ordinary methods of controversy, but by stirring up litigation, instituting prosecutions, and supplying the funds to meet the legal expenses, and it took the name of the ' Church Association.' Nor was this all. Two years later, the weapons which the new society had so far lacked were forged and placed in its hands by its unacknowledged allies. Its own most prominent member, Lord Shaftesbury, was preparing a Bill for putting down ritualism by the direct action of Parliament, and without any reference to the Church, for which scheme he had secured the support of the greater number of the Bishops, who did not at first see the grave peril of such a course, almost certain as it was to have provoked a schism.

They had come to this conclusion upon the receipt of an elaborate report on the subject of the ritualism recognised in the Prayer Book, drawn up by a committee of the

Lower House of the Convocation of Canterbury, to which they had replied in the following terms :

Our judgment is that no alteration from long-sanctioned and usual ritual ought to be made in our churches until the sanction of the bishop of the diocese has been obtained thereto.

When it was made clear to them that they could not safely unite themselves with Lord Shaftesbury in his legislative plans, their next idea was that the Archbishop of Canterbury should himself introduce a Bill into Parliament on very similar lines, and with a like neglect of the constitutional initiative of the ecclesiastical assemblies. The history of the crisis can be read in the 'Life of Bishop Samuel Wilberforce' (vol. iii. pp. 204–210) ; and the salient facts are that Lord Shaftesbury's Bill was to make the fifty-eighth canon (which enjoins the surplice for use in all ministrations) the sole rule for the ornaments and vestments of the Church of England, and that the whole of the Northern Bishops and all the Southern ones save three were in favour of it. The Bishop of Oxford drew Mr. Gladstone's attention to the serious peril thus threatening the Church, and he succeeded in dissociating the Primate from the coalition, and inducing him to obtain from Lord Derby a Royal Commission of inquiry into the whole ritual question, instead of the summary process of an Act of Parliament.

Lord Shaftesbury, however, did not await the result of this step, but introduced his Bill into the House of Lords, where a majority of the Bishops (eleven as against eight) voted in its favour ; but it was thrown out by a majority of fifteen votes, mainly in consequence of a speech by the

Bishop of Oxford, who pointed out that the principle on which the Church of England was constituted was not that of compromise, whereby one neutral type of opinion was made the only standard for all its members ; but that of comprehension, so as to include men of widely differing schools, and that it would be most unwise to destroy this comprehensiveness by legislating in the interest of one party exclusively.   Accordingly, upon the rejection of the Bill, the alternative method was proceeded with, and a Commission was appointed, consisting of fourteen ecclesiastics and fifteen laymen, but so composed that eighteen out of the twenty-nine were certain to report against Ritualism, whatever the evidence might be, and only six who were likely to give it a fair hearing.   Five of the Commissioners were ultra-Puritans, six were Bishops who had all pronounced against ritualism, two were Broad Church deans who had done the like, three were high and dry Churchmen who had also declared against the ritualists, and two were lawyers who had been active upon the same side.   It should be said here that in 1866 a carefully garbled case was drawn up on behalf of the Archbishops and several of the Bishops, in a sense adverse to the revived ceremonial, and an opinion had upon it, signed by the then Attorney-General, Sir Roundell Palmer (since Earl of Selborne), Sir H. M. Cairns (afterwards Earl Cairns), Mr. Mellish and Mr. Barron.   They took the view that the Statute of Elizabeth had been altered by the document known as the Advertisements of 1564–6, that having been the 'taking of other order,' as provided for in the Statute, and that this other order had prevailed down to

1662, while no change was introduced then, the new ornaments rubric pointing merely to the retention of such ornaments as had continued in use, and not to the revival of such as had become obsolete. . . . This opinion was delivered on May 29, 1866, and is the instrument whereby the findings in Hibbert *v.* Purchas and Ridsdale *v.* Clifton were effected. Its legal untenability will be discussed presently, it suffices to set down the fact alone now.

An opposing case was drawn up on behalf of the English Church Union, and submitted to nine counsel of at least equal distinction, none of whom, besides, were so definitely committed by obstinate prejudice to one side in the controversy as the two most prominent of those named above. They were Sir R. J. Phillimore, the chief ecclesiastical lawyer of his day, Sir Fitzroy Kelly (later Lord Chief Baron), Sir William Bovill (later Lord Chief Justice of Common Pleas), Mr. W. M. James, Dr. Deane, Mr. J. D. Coleridge (now Lord Chief Justice Coleridge), Mr. C. G. Prideaux, Mr. J. Hannen, and Mr. J. Cutler. These nine advised with entire unanimity in favour of the legality of the vestments, six of them in favour of altar lights (one, Sir Fitzroy Kelly, was unable to give his opinion, having been raised to the Bench meantime), and they were variously divided upon the remaining points in dispute, except that they were generally agreed against the legality of the ceremonial use of incense. This opinion was delivered by instalments between July 13 and November 17, 1866 ; and these two competing documents formed part of the apparatus of the new Ritual Commission. The Commission began to sit on June 17 1867 and examined seventeen

witnesses, of whom eight represented various shades of
Anti-Ritualism, and nine as many of its opposite. A careful analysis of the evidence yields the following results:
Only eight of the witnesses touched upon the question of
vestments—obviously the most contentious element in the
inquiry—and of these eight four spoke definitely in support
of the vestments, stating that they were very popular where
used, and had helped to fill once empty churches ; while,
curiously enough, the only direct testimony of a contrary
kind came from one gentleman who had seceded from the
Church of England in a parish where ritualism prevailed,
and had opened a meeting-house, ministered in by a Nonconformist pastor. But it came out in the course of his
evidence that his quarrel with the clergy dated from 1844,
of course many years before any ritualism had appeared,
that he had opened the meeting-house in 1860, some years
before the adoption of vestments in the parish church, and,
finally, that only two of the parishioners attended his
services, while it was not alleged that even these two had
ever been Churchfolk, and not Dissenters. Consequently,
as a matter of the evidence adduced before the Commission,
the case against the vestments broke down utterly. Nevertheless, in their first Report sent in upon August 19, 1867,
the Commissioners spoke as follows :

We find that while these vestments are regarded by some
witnesses as symbolical of doctrine, and by others as a distinctive
vesture whereby they desire to do honour to the Holy Communion
as the highest act of Christian worship, they are by none regarded
as essential, and they give grave offence to many. We are of
opinion that it is expedient to restrain in the public services
of the United Church of England and Ireland all variations in

respect of vesture from that which has long been the established usage of the said United Church, and we think that this may best be secured by providing aggrieved parishioners with an easy and effectual process for complaint and redress.

They were not content with thus misrepresenting the general tenor of the evidence as to this part of the inquiry, but were almost more culpably silent concerning faults of omission. For they were not commissioned to examine one part of the question solely : their duty was to inquire into the whole subject of public worship in the Church of England, for the terms of the Commission run, that as

differences of practice have arisen from varying interpretations put upon the rubrics, orders, and directions for regulating the course and conduct of public worship, the administration of the Sacraments, and the other services contained in the Book of Common Prayer, according to the use of the United Church of England and Ireland, and more especially with reference to the ornaments used in the churches and chapels of the said United Church, and the vestments worn by the ministers thereof at the time of their ministration, . . . it is expedient that a full and impartial inquiry should be made into the matters aforesaid, with the view of explaining or amending the said rubrics, orders, and directions, so as to secure general uniformity of practice in such matters as may be deemed essential.

Thus, as just said, the entire subject was intrusted to the Commissioners, and they were bound to report upon all of it. But although a large body of evidence was laid before them of systematic violation of plain directions of the Prayer Book by members of the Puritan school, and also that these violations caused much distress and pain to many persons, even driving them from their parish churches (just the kind of testimony which was *not* forthcoming upon the other side), not one syllable in the Report so much as hints at this aspect of the matter. Nor did the Commissioners say anything as to the legal merits, although this issue came up directly before them, seeing that the High Church witnesses alleged themselves to be complying with the clear intention of the law in adopting the vestments and attendant ceremonial ; while, contrariwise, the Puritan witnesses did not allege the law as justifying them, save in respect of omitting daily service, and wearing the black gown in the pulpit.

But, unfair as the Report was, it did not content the party in whose interest it was framed, because it not only expressed no condemnation of the doctrines connected with the revived ceremonial, but by using the word 'restrain' instead of 'prohibit,' in reference to the vestments, it left a loophole open for their use wherever the authorities happened to be favourable, or where no formal complaint by three aggrieved parishioners was lodged.

The force of this difficulty in the path of those who were resolved on extirpating ritualism was felt to be considerable, and all the more because the legality of the vestments had never been seriously contested at any time since the Restoration till quite recently, for all the older liturgical writers and others who have occasion to discuss the question are absolutely unanimous in pronouncing them legal. So the Presbyterian ministers at the Savoy Conference ;[1] so Baxter, 'Considerations on the Book of

---

[1] Cardwell, *History of Conferences*, p. 314.

Common Prayer;'[1] so Delaune in 1704;[2] so Dr. Nicholls
in 1710;[3] so Wheatley at the same date.[4] Indeed, the first
attempt to contest this position seriously was made in 1830
by Bishop Mant of Down and Connor, in his treatise 'The
Clergyman's Obligations Considered,' wherein he argued
that the actual usage and the assent of the governors of
the Church thereto abrogated the former law, and made
the vestments illegal, though of course at that date the
question was a purely abstract one, and not so much as
dreamed of as being within the range of practical politics.
But he was directly confuted by Dr. Stephens in his 'Book
of Common Prayer, with Notes Legal and Historical,'
wherein he observes :

The irresistible answer to Bishop Mant's argument is that
neither the 'governors of the Church' nor 'usage' can supersede
the positive enactments of the Statute Law. . . . All the directions contained in the First Book of Edward VI. as to the ornaments of the Church and of the ministers thereof at all times of
their ministration are, by Stat. 14 Car. II. c. 4, the Statute Law of
the Anglican Church.

It is important to keep these facts in mind, as they
establish that the legality of the vestments was no novel
idea suddenly evolved by a few black-letter ritualists, and
sprung unexpectedly upon a public reared in a contrary
belief, but the opinion which had been held consistently by
all serious students of the question for the two centuries
which had elapsed since the last revision of the Book of

———

[1] Sylvester's *Life of Baxter*, ii. 371.
[2] *Plea for the Nonconformists.*
[3] *Commentary on the Book of Common Prayer.*
[4] *Illustration of the Book of Common Prayer.*

Common Prayer. And consequently those clergymen who revived their use had ample reason for holding that they were not merely availing themselves of an indirect permission, but obeying a definite injunction of the law.

Such, then, was the general position when the recrudescence of litigation began. From the consecration of St. Alban's, Holborn, in 1863, the ritual of the Holy Eucharist adopted there included the eastward position, unleavened bread, the mixed chalice, altar-lights, and linen vestments, the last-named having been provided by the patron. In 1864 coloured silk vestments, presented by the congregation in the previous year, and incense, were added. No objection was raised against any of these details by those practically concerned, the regular attendants at the services ; but they gave great offence to the Church Association, which was quick to see much more danger to the system it upheld in the spread of ornate services to the classes represented in the congregation of St. Alban's than had threatened it so long as they were confined to the section of society attending such churches as St. Paul's, Knightsbridge, and St. Barnabas', Pimlico.

Accordingly, a prosecution was resolved upon, and a technically qualified prosecutor was found in a Mr. Martin, a solicitor residing in the parish of St. George, Bloomsbury, and having his offices in New Square, Lincoln's Inn, but whose name stood on the rate-book of the district of St. Alban's in consequence of his holding the office of secretary to some schools situate therein. He was not the first person selected as promoter in the suit, but was chosen to occupy the vacancy left by the death of the gentleman first selected. He was not himself specially anxious to move in the matter, but pressure was put upon him by the Church Association.

The Bishop sent Letters of Request to the Arches Court on March 28, 1867, and the citation to Mr. Mackonochie issued thence on April 5, but the case did not actually come on for hearing until June 15. The Dean of Arches was then Dr. Lushington, and had he heard the case to the end, there is no doubt that he would have condemned Mr. Mackonochie upon all the issues involved, which were the mixed chalice, altar-lights, kneeling during the Prayer of Consecration, elevation of the chalice and paten, and censing persons and things. But Dr. Lushington retired from office soon after the opening of the case, and was succeeded by Sir Robert Phillimore (who had previously been retained as counsel for Mr. Mackonochie in this suit), before whom the case was heard, and who decided it, together with the cognate action of Flamank *v*. Simpson, in a single judgment, pronounced on March 28, 1868, the anniversary of the day upon which the Letters of Request had been issued.

This judgment, a very learned and careful one, was to the effect that (1) it is not lawful to elevate the cup and paten during the celebration of the Holy Communion in a greater degree than is necessary to comply with the rubric ; (2) it is not lawful to use incense for censing persons and things, or to bring in incense at the beginning of or during the celebration, and to remove it at the end of the celebration, and to remove it at the end of the celebration ; (3) it is not lawful to mix water with the wine during the celebration ; (4) it is not unlawful for the celebrant to kneel during the Prayer of Consecration, at least unless the Bishop has in his discretion made an order forbidding it ; (5) it is lawful to place two lights upon the Holy Table during the celebration. A further point was also ruled, but it concerned the other suit only, and need not be cited here.

On these several points it should be said that in respect of the first-mentioned, that of elevation, Mr. Mackonochie had discontinued the kind and degree of elevation which he had previously practised, having had a conference with his diocesan, and having agreed to modify his usage ; while the censing of persons and things had been discontinued from the date of the opinion of the nine counsel consulted by the English Church Union ; and the disallowance of the ceremonial mixing of the chalice was based upon the ground of the omission of any such ceremony from the manual acts prescribed in the existing rubric, though a non-ceremonial mixing in the sacristy before service was pronounced admissible. No order was made as to costs, partly because some of the points were given in favour of the defendant, while he had spontaneously altered his procedure as to others before the institution of the suit ; but still more because the promoter was neither a churchwarden nor a resident parishioner, whose business it might be to interfere, but had merely the technical right conferred by the diocesan's acceptance of him as promoter in the suit.

Further, two principles of interpretation laid down by Sir Robert Phillimore in this judgment directly negatived two of the main arguments relied on and urged by the prosecution : in that he set out with much force and clearness the historical and legal continuity of the pre-Reformation and post-Reformation Church of England, as against the contention that a wholly new body was constituted by the changes in the sixteenth century ; and that he dwelt upon the legal distinction between ' non-user,' the mere abeyance of any once lawful practice, and ' dis-user,' its formal repeal, which the prosecution had treated as convertible and even identical terms, although the leading advocate upon that side was the very Dr. Stephens who had confuted Bishop Mant upon this precise issue.

And consequently, though most of the secular journals agreed in treating the judgment as a very heavy blow and discouragement to the ritualistic school, and it was known that Mr. Mackonochie had expressed his readiness to submit to it, yet the Puritan school was far from content with it, and notice of appeal to the Privy Council was lodged immediately. The case was argued before the Judicial Committee from November 17 to November 20, and the Court which sat to hear it consisted of Lord Cairns, then Chancellor, Lords Chelmsford and Westbury, Sir William Erle, Sir J. W. Colvile, and the Archbishop of York. The appeal was limited to the permission of kneeling in the course of the prayer of Consecration, the use of altar-lights, and the disallowance of costs, and on all three the decision was given in favour of the prosecution, which was also allowed the costs of the appeal.

This partisan finding was not only discredited alike by the dissent of the two ablest lawyers composing the Court, Lord Westbury and Sir William Erle, by the neutral position taken up by Sir J. Colvile, and by the adhesion of the

Archbishop of York (by whose casting vote it was thus carried), but it proved exceedingly distasteful to the very party which had invited it. For in order to compass the condemnation of Mr. Mackonochie upon the count of kneeling during the prayer of consecration, the Court ruled thus :

Their Lordships entertain no doubt on the construction of this rubric, that the priest is intended to continue in one posture during the prayer, and not to change from standing to kneeling, or *vice versâ* ; and it appears to them equally certain that the priest is intended to stand, and not to kneel. They think that the words ' standing before the Table ' apply to the whole sentence ; and they think this is made more apparent by the consideration that acts are to be done by the priest before the people as the prayer proceeds (such as taking the paten and chalice into his hands, breaking the bread, and laying his hands on the various vessels) which could only be done in the attitude of standing.

But this ruling at once struck at and made unlawful the ordinary Puritan usage of removing the bread and wine from the centre of the altar to the north end, and proceeding to consecrate there. And this view of the ruling was at once acted upon by many persons who had till then been in the habit of consecrating at the north end, including Bishop Wilberforce, and was accepted subsequently in the Court of Arches as decisive upon this issue.

The judgment, however, by its condemnation of the altar-lights, contrived to evacuate a good deal of the finding in Liddell *v.* Westerton, in accordance with which, as already stated, all articles or utensils 'used under' the First Book of Edward VI. continue to be lawful. The Court

upon this latter occasion, while ostensibly agreeing with
the ruling of the earlier judgment, that the words 'authority
of Parliament' in the ornaments rubric apply solely to the
Act legalising the First Book, or do not cover any injunctions or the like having statutory authority at that time,
yet practically reversed its conclusion upon a vital issue:
that the ornaments rubric legalises all articles actually
used *anno* 2 Edward VI. in the course of divine worship,
but does not touch mere inert decorations, such as an altar
cross or a banner. The limitation now introduced was
that instead of all that was 'used under' the First Prayer
Book being legal, nothing remained so except what was
'prescribed by' that Book. As the candles upon the altars
of SS. Paul and Barnabas were not lighted at the time of the
suit of Liddell *v.* Westerton, and as the lawfulness of the
candlesticks and unlighted candles had been ruled by Dr.
Lushington, this particular count had not come up before
the Judges on that occasion, since there was no appeal raised
upon it ; but it is reasonable to conclude that the Court
would have ruled the legality of altar-lights, as unquestionably 'used under' the First Book.

Another dictum of the Mackonochie judgment was of
an even more sweeping range, namely, that 'by necessary
implication a rubric abolished what it does not retain': a
thesis readily confuted by such disproofs as the failure, at
the very outset of Morning Prayer, to prescribe the dress,
the place, and the posture of the officiating minister ; the
existence of formally prohibitory rubrics, which would be
superfluous if the dictum were true ; and such a fact as the
absence, ever since the substitution of the Second Book of

Edward VI. for the First Book, of any direction to pour wine into the chalice. There is a positive direction of the kind in the First Book :

'And putting the wine into the chalice, or else in some fair and convenient cup, prepared for that use (if the chalice will not serve) ;' but nothing equivalent is in the present Prayer Book, nor has there been in any Prayer Book legal since 1552, so that, on the showing of the Court in this case, it has been illegal to put wine into the chalice for the last three centuries. No more crushing demonstration of the mingled bad faith and ignorance of the judgment could be adduced. And the animus displayed in the matter of costs is in notable contrast with the action of the Judicial Committee in the case of Liddell *v.* Beal in 1860, when Mr. Beal complained that the monition directed to Mr. Liddell had been disobeyed on three points. The Court found against Mr. Beal on all three counts, and mentioned further that Mr. Beal had no *locus standi*, and was heard merely because Mr. Liddell had consented to waive the objection of his being no longer a parishioner ; yet it allowed him his costs. But in the Mackonochie case, although four out of the six points charged had been given for him in the lower Court, and the promoter had never been a parishioner, the whole of the costs were given against him.

The monition to refrain from sundry specified ceremonial acts issued upon January 19, 1869, and was complied with at St. Alban's. Nevertheless, the Church Association, acting through Mr. Martin, lodged a complaint on December 2 against Mr. Mackonochie before the Privy

Council for disobedience to the monition in continuing to elevate the chalice and paten, in using lighted candles when not required for necessary light, and in kneeling and prostration during the prayer of Consecration. Mr. Mackonochie conducted his own case on this occasion, and the Judges were Lord Chancellor Hatherley, Lord Chelmsford, Sir J. W. Colvile, Sir Joseph Napier, and the Archbishop of York. On the first count he pleaded that he had obeyed the monition, which had forbidden one kind of elevation only, that above the head of the celebrant, and had practised only the lesser elevation conceded by the Arches judgment; on the second, that the lights were no longer used at the time prohibited; and on the third, that he had entirely ceased from kneeling, had not at any time practised prostration, but that he had bent his knee in the course of the consecration prayer, and might possibly have once or twice touched the ground when doing so, but not intentionally. That genuflexion is not kneeling, and therefore he was entitled to construe a penal injunction in the narrowest way, a literal compliance being all that the law exacts in such cases, and thus he was free to use the less demonstrative gesture.

The decision of the Court was that he had established his compliance with the monition on the two counts of lights and elevation, but that he had disobeyed it in genuflecting, which was constructively forbidden by the prohibition to kneel, as being *in pari materia*, and he was condemned in the costs of the appeal, for having adhered to the letter of a criminal judgment, though it is a recognised maxim of English jurisprudence that every such judgment shall be construed in the narrowest and most rigid manner.

Ten days after the delivery of this finding, the Church Association again sent spies to St. Alban's, and on receiving their report, again charged Mr. Mackonochie with disobeying the monition by sanctioning on the part of others the acts he was forbidden to do himself, to wit, elevation and kneeling, or prostration ; and affidavits were filed describing the acts done by the officiating clergy upon seven Sundays in the months of December 1869, January and February 1870. The hearing was appointed for March 26 ; but Mr. Mackonochie, acting under legal advice, did not appear by counsel to defend himself, but filed counter-affidavits from the accused officiants and from the churchwardens, denying the truth of the charges alleged.

Hereupon he received notice that the case would not be proceeded with ; but, nevertheless, three fresh affidavits, said to be in reply to those he had put in, were filed in July ; but, in point of fact, they also related to an alleged offence committed by himself upon June 17, and the hearing came on before the Judicial Committee (consisting of Lords Hatherley and Chelmsford and the Archbishop of York) upon November 16 and 18. Three counsel, Dr. Stephens, Mr. Archibald, and Mr. Benjamin Shaw, with their proctors, appeared for Mr. Martin, the promotor ; Mr. Mackonochie was unrepresented, and the matter turned entirely upon the credit to be attached to the rival affidavits. Those filed by Mr. Mackonochie and the other clergymen charged not only specifically denied the truth of the charges, but brought counter-charges of grave misconduct in church against the informers, to which they in their turn replied in a supplemental affidavit, denying the charges. The first day's proceedings were mainly formal, and the principal matter which occurred was the permission granted by the Court for the very unusual course of oral examination of the witnesses whose affidavits had been put in. Mr Mackonochie himself was the first to be examined, and his testimony was to the following effect: (1) that when the monition issued, he had told his curates that he intended to obey it, but did not remember giving them any directions to do the like; (2) that he had never practised the forbidden elevation since 1866, and that he had told the curates that there was henceforth to be no genuflexion in the course of the consecration prayer, and that he himself intended to bow instead of kneeling; (3) that his object had been to obey the law of the Church without disobeying the law of the State.

Judgment was pronounced upon November 25, and was to the effect that Mr. Mackonochie had not complied with the monition in respect of elevation; that the low bow he had substituted for genuflexion was 'a humble prostration of the body in reverence,' and was also a disobedience to the monition, and therefore that he should not only, as on the former occasion, pay all the costs of the application, but be suspended from office and benefice for three months; and it was specifically observed that his main offence was that he had 'carefully scanned the monition and the Order in Council, to see how nearly he could preserve the prohibited ceremonies . . . without disobeying the law of the

State ; ' but that he had been again foiled in his 'attempt to satisfy his conscience, and shelter himself behind a strictly literal obedience.'

This monstrous outrage upon justice falsified the first count, by declaring that acts had been done which were denied on oath, not only by those charged, but by the churchwardens and other members of the congregation, who must have seen them if they had taken place ; and violated the laws of English and of common sense by putting an untenable gloss on the word 'bow,' to make it include the forbidden prostration ; and which made it a chief ground for censuring the defendant that he had followed the invariable rule of law in construing a penal sentence in the most literal manner. One remark upon the condemnation of any kind or degree of elevation, beyond what is necessarily involved in the act of the priest taking the paten and chalice into his hands, as enjoined by the rubrics, will not be out of place. In the 'Essays and Reviews' suit, the charge against Mr. Wilson that he had offended against the formularies by denying the eternity of future punishment was dismissed by the Court on the ground that the omission from the Thirty-nine Articles of the clause in Edward VI.'s Forty-two Articles, condemnatory of such as denied that tenet, is fatal to a prosecution of any such persons ; even though it be not disputed that no corresponding change in the doctrine of the Church, so as to bring it into agreement with such denial, has taken place.

Now, the case of elevation is legally identical with this ; for it was prohibited explicitly in the First Book of

Edward VI., but the prohibition was struck out in the Second Book, and has never been replaced. Nor can the last clause of Article XXVIII. be imported into the question, as helping to decide it. For that document is not a law or rubric affecting the conduct of public worship; it confines itself to making a statement of an historical kind, and contains no words declaring any of the four usages it mentions in connection with the Holy Eucharist (reservation, carrying about, lifting up, and worshipping) either illegal or even morally wrong; and there is besides one convincing piece of contemporary evidence by way of practical exposition of its degree of bearing upon the point at issue: that in the Latin Prayer Book, issued in Elizabeth's reign for use in the Universities, there is a rubric prefixed to the office for the Communion of the Sick, as follows:

If the sick person cannot come to church, and asks that the Sacrament may be given him at home, he is to signify the day before or early in the morning to the parish priest how many are willing to communicate with him.

And if it happen that the Lord's Supper is celebrated in the church that same day, then the priest shall reserve so much of the Sacrament in the Supper as suffices for the sick person, and presently, when the Supper is ended, he shall go to the sick person, together with some of those who are present, and shall first communicate those who are tending the sick person, and were present at the Supper, and lastly with the sick person.

Here, then, are two of the usages named in Article XXVIII., to wit, reservation and carrying about of the Sacrament, expressly enjoined, and the book so enjoining them continued in legal use till a date long subsequent to the promulgation of the Thirty-nine Articles; whence it follows that as Article XXVIII. cannot be construed as forbidding reservation and carrying about, it cannot be construed as forbidding elevation or worship either, seeing that all four acts are on precisely the same footing in that Article.

An attempt was made by the faction in whose interest this judgment was delivered to palliate its iniquity, by alleging that it merely aimed at foiling Mr. Mackonochie's disingenuous evasions of the previous monition ; but to this he made a conclusive reply in the letter which appeared in the 'Church Times' of December 9, 1870.

The services were carried on without any change during the term of Mr. Mackonochie's suspension, and resumed by himself at its close precisely as before, but no fresh action was taken thereupon by the prosecution at that time.   However, at the annual meeting of the Church Association on March 27, 1874, the chairman informed the audience that a fresh suit was to be instituted against Mr. Mackonochie, not only renewing all the former complaints, but introducing a new count, that of having erected a confessional in the church, and given notice of the times at which confessions would be heard.   Hereupon, the congregation of St. Alban's began to take measures to protect themselves against such external interference with their concerns ; and the first step taken, under the advice of the Bishop, was the removal of a large crucifix, which had been employed during the then recent mission of 1874, and also that of the curtains hung up to secure privacy for persons coming to confession at the church.   But as these concessions in no degree checked the advance of the fresh litigation, the congregation held a large meeting, and addressed a memorial to the Bishop, to which the following Memorial and Protest against the interference with religious liberty were appended, both documents being signed by nearly two thousand communicants :

MEMORIAL.

To the Right Reverend Father in God, the Lord Bishop of London.

The humble Petition of the undersigned Parishioners and Members of the Congregation of the Parish Church of St. Alban the Martyr, Holborn,
Sheweth :

I. That your Petitioners learn with great sorrow that the clergy and congregation of the above church are threatened with a renewal of the annoyances and prosecutions to which they have been before subjected with regard to certain observances which are highly esteemed by them as exponents of the Catholic Faith professed by the Church of England.

II. That your Petitioners, knowing from past experience the grievous injury done to the work of the parish by that which they deem to be an unwarrantable interference with their privileges as loyal members of the Church, and fully believing in your Lordship's sympathy with every work which tends to the glory of Almighty God and the salvation of souls, beg very respectfully to lay the following statement before your Lordship :

(*a*) This petition emanates solely from the laity who worship at the Church of St. Alban the Martyr, and they have taken this step in order to show to your Lordship that they consider themselves deeply aggrieved.

(*b*) The ritual that has been gradually developed has been re-

M

quested at each successive stage by the laity, so that there is no pretence for saying that it has been forced upon an unwilling congregation.

(*c*) We feel that the interest taken by us in the work of the parish sufficiently warrants us in petitioning your Lordship ; and although unwilling to speak of our personal deeds, we cannot on this occasion forbear to state that a great amount of actual work is done by the laity, and that a very large sum of money, not less than 50,000*l.*, has been expended during the past eleven years upon the services of the church, the schools, and various works of mercy.

(*d*) We firmly believe in all the doctrines of which ritual is but the outward sign. We value lights, incense, and kneeling, because they teach the Real Presence of our Blessed Lord in the Holy Eucharist. We lament the removal of the Crucifix, because it so eloquently preached Christ crucified. And we regret the removal of the Confessionals, which has been caused by an interference which is inconsistent with religious liberty.

(*e*) We feel that if the opposition be honest, it is aimed rather at doctrine than at ritual ; so that while we have the plain words of the Prayer Book to teach us the former, we claim the right of having the latter to set it forth more clearly.

(*f*) We further believe that the ritual used is entirely in accordance with the law of the Church of England, and with the spirit of the Prayer Book, which cannot be interpreted by the neglect of past years, and upon which the conflicting judgments in recent suits throw no light whatever.

III. That your Petitioners in laying this statement before your Lordship, simply ask for toleration. And that they pray your Lordship to protect the priests of this church, whose self-denying labours have, under the blessing of Almighty God, resulted in such a marked way in the spread of our Holy Religion and in the due observance of its ordinances.

And your Petitioners will ever pray, &c.

PROTEST.

To the Right Reverend Father in God, the Lord Bishop of London.

My Lord,—Before the preceding Memorial could be presented, we learnt that a prosecution had commenced, and therefore venture to protest to your Lordship, as strongly as we can, against the course adopted by our opponents, and to submit that we feel most deeply in the first place, the great evil which must result to this parish from the interference with the work of our priests ; and secondly, our annoyance at the attack on religious liberty to which as Englishmen we feel that we are justly entitled.

My Lord, this question touches the laity very deeply. We ourselves feel that the time has arrived when we must speak and act publicly in this matter, and declare that we fully believe in all those doctrines which are really being attacked under the pretence of an attack on the outward symbolism of ritual. In this belief, my Lord, we do not stand alone ; there are thousands of members of the Church of England who think as we do ; and we venture to assert that the events of past years point unmistakably to the fact that the laity will not be content unless their faith is set forth by a corresponding ritual.

In conclusion, we declare our unfeigned devotion to our branch of the Church Catholic. We beg your Lordship to remember that the Church of England has under its present constitution always embraced men of various schools of thought. And we venture to leave in your Lordship's hands this our strongest possible protest, desiring only that liberty and toleration which is extended to all other schools in the Church.

We must consider this letter, together with the draft Memorial and your Lordship's reply, as intended for publication.

We are, my Lord, your Lordship's humble and faithful servants.

M 2

But neither these documents themselves nor the oral remonstrances of the deputation which presented them prevailed with Bishop Jackson to withdraw his sanction from the new proceedings, and they came on in due course in the Court of Arches, where Mr. Mackonochie appeared under protest.

The charges were: use of lighted candles during morning prayer; undue elevation of the paten and chalice; processions with banners, crucifix, and candles; singing the *Agnus Dei* after the Consecration; making the sign of the cross; kissing the Prayer Book; wafer-bread; vestments; and the eastward position.

An acquittal was pronounced upon the charge of undue elevation, but Mr. Mackonochie was condemned to six weeks' suspension upon all the remaining counts.

Mr. Mackonochie at first entered an appeal against the judgment, but subsequently withdrew it, and addressed a letter to the Bishop, giving his reasons for so acting.

Upon the sentence of suspension taking effect, the congregation of St. Alban's addressed the following protest to the Archbishop of Canterbury :

May it please your Grace :—We, the undersigned, churchwardens, parishioners, and members of the congregation of the church of St. Alban the Martyr, Holborn, desire to make a respectful remonstrance and protest to your Grace against the sentence of suspension pronounced in the Court of Arches against the Rev. Alexander Heriot Mackonochie, vicar of this parish, as being morally indefensible upon several distinct grounds :

I. In the first place, the sentence has been obtained on the promotion of the office of the judge by one person only, namely, Mr. John Martin, who is not legally a parishioner, such as even the Public Worship Regulation Act requires as a complainant, and who has no moral claim to interfere, as he has never been a worshipper at the church of St. Alban, nor has contributed a penny towards its expenses.

II. On the other hand, a large and devout congregation, averaging 700 persons, and amounting in the aggregate to 2,000 persons, accepts entirely Mr. Mackonochie's view of the matters in dispute, and has testified its sincerity by contributing upwards of 50,000*l.* to the church expenses.

III. Whereas Mr. Mackonochie, whose blameless character is undisputed even by his chief opponents, and whose pastoral diligence has won high commendation from those best fitted to judge, has been singled out for repeated prosecution for what, at the worst, is over-zeal for the beauty and order of divine worship; on the contrary, no attempt whatever is made to bring legal coercion to bear upon clergymen notorious either for immorality, for gross neglect of duty, or for defiant violation of what they confess to be the law ; several of whom receive, not merely impunity, but countenance and encouragement from those in authority.

IV. That Mr. Mackonochie cannot be justly charged with resistance to the law, nor with obstinate refusal to modify his practice, since he made at once and without difficulty, though sorely against his own wishes and convictions, many concessions in the mode of performing divine service on the injunction of the Court of Arches, which other clergymen who have never been presented have never made at all ; so that under these circumstances he was fairly entitled to consideration which he has not received.

V. That several of the matters upon which the sentence of suspension rests are in truth unsettled, are under discussion by the lawful assemblies of the Church in both provinces, and are likely to be made the subject of speedy future legislation, so that it is contrary to public policy to make them the ground for criminal prosecution now.

VI. That the Court of Arches, in pronouncing sentence,

followed, as a matter of precedent, the finding of the Judicial Committee of the Privy Council in the case of Hibbert *v.* Purchas; a finding in an undefended suit, marked throughout with the strongest partisan bias, disfigured by serious misquotations, interpolations, and misconstructions of the evidence to which it professes to refer, widely discredited amongst the legal profession, and openly disavowed in more or less of its statements and conclusions by such eminent lawyers as Sir John Taylor Coleridge, Lord Coleridge, Lord Cairns, and Lord Selborne.

On all these grounds therefore we appeal to your Grace against Mr. Mackonochie's suspension, as having no moral ground whatever, and a legal ground which is not only much disputed, but which few competent authorities believe to be as much as tenable.

The correspondence which ensued is here appended :

Lambeth Palace, S.E., June 26, 1875.

Sir,—I beg leave to acknowledge the receipt of your letter, dated the 23rd instant.

You inform me that 'at the request of the churchwardens of the parish church of St. Alban the Martyr, Holborn, in the diocese of London, you forward to me a copy of a protest against the suspension by the Court of Arches of the Rev. Alexander Heriot Mackonochie, vicar of the said parish, which was adopted at a meeting of the congregation held on Monday, the 21st instant ;' and you further request me ' to appoint a day, after the 5th of July, when it will be convenient to me to receive a deputation to present the protest in due form, with signatures thereto.'

I have read the printed copy of the protest which you have forwarded to me, and must point out that it would be quite inconsistent with my duty formally to receive the document in question. You appear to desire to appeal to me personally against the decision of the Judge of my Provincial Court, and to cast the gravest censure upon the judgment pronounced by him as Official Principal of the Metropolitan.

The constitution under which we live in Church and State has provided proper means whereby any proved violation of duty on the part of a judge may be dealt with. On this point the best way to inform yourselves how to proceed, supposing you are convinced that there has been any miscarriage of justice, will be, if you think it necessary to do so, to consult your legal adviser ; but the reception of such a protest by me individually would be a most irregular proceeding, and could lead to no good result.

I shall however be always ready to give my best advice to any members of the Church of England who may desire it, provided I am approached in a way consistent with the constitution of our Church ; and if there is any point on which you at present desire my counsel, I shall be glad to advise you to the best of my ability.

Believe me to be yours faithfully,
A. C. CANTUAR.

G. R. Jellicoe, Esq.

My Lord Archbishop,—I am directed by the churchwardens of the parish church of St. Alban the Martyr, Holborn, acting on behalf and with the authority of the congregation, to acknowledge the receipt of your Grace's letter of the 26th June, declining to receive a deputation with protest against the suspension of Rev. A. H. Mackonochie.

I am further instructed to beg of your Grace to reconsider your purpose, and to lay before you some comments upon your letter which may perhaps induce you to do so.

1. Your Grace observes that it would be inconsistent with your duty to receive an appeal against the decision of the Judge of your own Provincial Court, which involves the gravest censure upon him. I am instructed to remind your Grace that you made no difficulty, on May 5th, 1870, in receiving and welcoming a deputation whose practical object was to protest against the acquittal of Mr. Bennett, in the case Shepherd *v.* Bennett, both by your Official Principal and by the Final Court of Appeal, and to complain of the toleration thus allowed to a great historical school

within the Church of England ; and further, to point out that if we were indeed bringing a charge against your Grace's Official Principal, it would in that case be your Grace's imperative duty to receive it, inasmuch as that officer is directly responsible to your Grace for the fitting discharge of his duty, and you would therefore be the proper person to call him to account for any malversation of his office.

But we allege no graver charge against Sir Robert Phillimore than that of his having given a piece of mere professional etiquette the preference over the superior duty of rightly interpreting the ecclesiastical law of England.

What we ask of your Grace is to uphold the decision of your Official Principal in the case of Hibbert *v.* Purchas, which has been set at nought and overridden by the Judicial Committee of the Privy Council, whereby your Grace's authority in your own Court has been materially infringed and lowered in the eyes of the public.

We desire to remind your Grace that the finding of the Judicial Committee in the case of Hibbert *v.* Purchas, upon which the suspension of the Rev. A. H. Mackonochie rests, is a patent and notorious miscarriage of justice, which, to use your Grace's own words, ‘misinterprets the law for unrighteous party purposes.’

It is no part of the ‘constitution under which we live in Church and State,’ to which your Grace refers us, that four men should be empowered to set aside the statute law of the realm, when, and because, it happens to conflict with their private bias in matters of religion.

Not merely does the judgment in Hibbert *v.* Purchas directly conflict with that in Liddell *v.* Westerton (delivered by a Committee much more respectable for numbers, attainments, and character), which laid down explicitly that the same dresses and utensils which were used under the First Book of Edward VI. may still be used ; and with that in Martin *v.* Mackonochie, which ruled that the words ‘standing before the Table’ apply to the whole rubric of the Prayer of Consecration ; but the notion of bad faith is inevitably suggested by its incessant misquotation of the documents to which it professes to refer as evidence.

Errors on points of religious opinion, such as those which disfigure the *obiter dicta* of the Privy Council judgment in Shepherd *v.* Bennett, may be reasonably ascribed to unfamiliarity with theology and to unconscious prepossession ; but a much more charitable hypothesis is needed to palliate continual misrepresentation of plain matters of historical and legal fact, which misre presentation, moreover, in order to be even colourably plausible has to rest on inaccurate citation of the evidence in several particulars. We may draw your Grace's attention especially to the manner in which the word 'only' has been twice interpolated after the word 'surplice' in two separate documents (*i.e.* the Advertisements of 1564, and the Canons of 1603), so that it appears that the exclusive use of that vestment was intended ; and to the substitution of the date 1687 for 1627, when it was sought to show that Cosin's visitation articles supplied a comment on the Rubric of 1662 unfavourable to the action of Mr. Purchas. We are not unaware that an attempt has been made to deny the existence of this last-mentioned error in the original text of the judgment, and to ascribe it to a mere misprint in unofficial copies; but such denial is confuted, not only by the authoritative documents themselves, but also by the internal proof that the true date, 1627, would have been quite useless for the matter in hand, which was to show how the Rubric of 1662 was subsequently construed by the person supposed to have framed it.

2. Your Grace is good enough to point out to us that the Constitution provides 'proper means whereby any proved violation of duty on the part of a judge may be dealt with.' We are not unaware of this fact, but as the persons inculpated in this case are members of the House of Lords and of the Final Court of Appeal, the means are practically limited to impeachment, and we beg to point out that your Grace, as the chief official of the body whose laws and discipline have been thus trenched upon, is

the proper person to make that impeachment from your place in the Upper House of Parliament.

But your Grace's duty in the matter has yet a deeper basis than that of your rank as Primate of the Established Church. Your Grace is also the chief minister of the Christian religion in this country, and should therefore be principal guardian of morality and piety. No sin save the shedding of innocent blood is so sternly denounced in Holy Scripture, and has such awful penalties threatened against it, as the wresting of judgment and the condemnation of the guiltless.

That this sin has been committed, in its very gravest form, by the Judicial Committee of the Privy Council is widely believed by a powerful section of the English people, and any attempt to stifle inquiry will be very perilous to the characters of those who resolve on such a line of policy, and to confidence in the integrity of our highest courts of law.

Your Grace, by receiving our deputation and furthering its prayer, will deliver yourself from this responsibility, and will materially aid in vindicating that justice which has now been denied to faithful members of the Church of England.

On these and other grounds, I am requested to repeat the prayer contained in my first letter, that your Grace will be pleased to appoint an early date on which it will be convenient to receive a deputation.

I am, my Lord Archbishop,

Your Grace's humble and obedient servant,

GEO. R. JELLICOE,

Hon. Sec. to the Committee in the above matter.

Lambeth Palace, S.E., July 9th, 1875.

Dear Sir,—I beg leave to acknowledge the receipt of your letter of July 4th, in which you repeat the request contained in your previous letter of June 23rd, that I will appoint an early day to receive a deputation from the churchwardens and parishioners of St. Alban the Martyr, Holborn, to present a protest against the suspension by the Judge of the Court of Arches of the Rev. A. H. Mackonochie ; and in which you urge various reasons why I should comply with your request. On carefully considering your second letter, I am constrained to abide by my previous decision, and I can give no other answer to your request than that which is contained in my letter to you of the 26th June.

I would, however, repeat what I have already stated, viz., that I shall be ready to give you my best advice in the difficulties which you at present feel, provided that I am approached in a way consistent with the constitution of our Church.

Believe me to be, dear Sir,
Yours faithfully,

G. R. Jellicoe, Esq.   A. C. CANTUAR.

14, Clement's Inn, W.C., London, 13th July, 1875.

To his Grace the Lord Archbishop of Canterbury.

My Lord Archbishop,—On behalf of the Committee of the congregation of St. Alban the Martyr, I have to acknowledge the receipt of your Grace's letter of the 9th instant, and I am now instructed to say that we regret that your Grace still adheres to your decision not to receive our deputation. We had hoped that your Grace would have been willing to listen to an alleged grievance of even the humblest members of the Church in which you hold the highest office, more especially as that grievance arises from the fact that the Judge of your own Court has adopted the decision of the Judicial Committee of Privy Council in the case of Hibbert *v.* Purchas, the injustice of which is notorious, and which is more widely discredited every day ; and we are at a loss to conceive how we could act in any way more in accordance with the constitution of our Church. The only course now left open to us, therefore, is to publish the correspondence with your Grace.

I am, my Lord Archbishop,
Your Grace's humble and faithful servant,
GEO. R. JELLICOE,
Hon. Sec. to the Committee in the above matter.

The Bishop of London took practically the same line as his superior, and directed Mr. Stanton, the senior curate of St. Alban's, to carry on the services upon the lines of the Purchas judgment during the term of Mr. Mackonochie's suspension ; a proceeding which drew forth a strongly-worded remonstrance from the Committee of laymen acting for the congregation, who reminded the Bishop that he could not possibly believe the Purchas judgment to be an honest exposition of the law, and that he had thus no moral right to enforce it ; while Mr. Mackonochie also addressed an individual remonstrance to a similar effect, further pointing out that whereas the Purchas judgment told against every school, nay, every clergyman in the Church of England, it was nevertheless put in operation against those of one school exclusively, while entire impunity was granted to all others. After the close of the term of suspension, there was a virtual truce for a time, so far as St. Alban's, Holborn, was concerned, but a circumstance connected with another of the Puritan prosecutions, that of Mr. Tooth, calls for mention, as having a direct bearing on the closing incidents of the long-protracted litigation of which Mr. Mackonochie had been made the subject.

It was incidentally remarked that the Public Worship Regulation Act, as passed against the express protest and repudiation of Convocation, has never been a valid statute of the realm, being in conflict with Magna Charta and the Statute of Appeals, and certainly not cured of this defect by the votes given for it by Bishops in the House of Lords, since they sit there not as officers of the Church, but as temporal barons, in which capacity they have no spiritual powers. But it was not then added that the two Archbishops who engineered the Bill were bent on disguising the real character of the tribunal to be set up under it, in order to prevent the clergy from noting that a very grave encroachment upon the liberties of the Church was thus being made by the civil power. If it could be made to appear that nothing more was effected by the Bill than to modify the procedure of the ancient ecclesiastical Courts in particulars where the assent of the lay Parliament was clearly necessary to give coercive legality to such changes, they introduced clauses into the draft that upon the avoidance of the judgeships of the Provincial Courts of Canterbury and York, the judge of the new Public Worship Regulation Act Court should succeed to both vacancies, and exercise all jurisdiction thereto attached ; and that, as regards the Province of Canterbury, proceedings taken in this Court should 'be deemed to be taken in the Court of Arches.' From the date of the passing of the Act, then, Archbishop Tait invariably professed to speak of the new Court as though it were the old tribunal, and Lord Penzance, the person whom he and the. Archbishop of York selected as a suitable instrument for their purpose, has systematically posed as Dean of Arches, and given himself out as such, from the time when the contingency provided for in the Act became fact by the resignation of Sir Robert Phillimore.

But when Mr. Tooth's case for wrongful imprisonment came before the Queen's Bench Division, represented by three exceptionally strong Judges, Chief Justice Sir

Alexander Cockburn, and Justices Mellor and Lush, on November 19, 1877, this very contention, that Lord Penzance had tried the case as Dean of Arches, was adduced by the counsel on his part. But the Chief Justice said :

This Act—the Public Worship Regulation Act—is the foundation of a new jurisdiction. Mr. Benjamin has argued that the jurisdiction of the Dean of Arches is not touched by this Act ; but it is not as Dean of Arches that Lord Penzance has this jurisdiction. . . . The jurisdiction is the creation of the statute ; . . . it is undoubtedly, to my mind, an entirely new office, and one with which no former Dean of Arches had anything to do.

Justice Mellor was not less emphatic in refuting the pretended claim. He said :

I cannot doubt that it had occurred to Parliament that the existing law and tribunals were not sufficient to meet the exigencies of the case, and that what was to be done was not merely to improve and extend the jurisdiction of the Dean of the Arches, but to erect an entirely new tribunal, which has no relation at all to the office of Dean of Arches.

And when to these weighty words the fact is added that in the only patent ever conferred upon Lord Penzance for his new office he was not named Dean of Arches, it is plain that he never has enjoyed that dignity, and that the claims he still lays to it are untenable ; so that he is merely the secular judge of a secular (and therefore illegal and unconstitutional) Court for the trial of spiritual causes which it is not competent to evoke before it.

The importance of these considerations is due to the fact that when the prosecution of Mr. Mackonochie was resumed after a brief interval, it was under the Public

Worship Regulation Act that proceedings were taken, and in Lord Penzance's Court that the issues were tried.

In March 1878 an application was made to Lord Penzance to enforce upon Mr. Mackonochie the monition issued by Sir Robert Phillimore in 1875, already cited. But Lord Penzance said that as no attempt had been made on the part of the prosecution to get the monition enforced within a reasonable time after its issue, being content to let it lie dormant for some years, he would pronounce no fresh sentence then, but would give Mr. Mackonochie the opportunity of conforming himself to the decisions affecting him, on the understanding that a severe sentence would be passed in the event of his refusing to do so ; and, while thus refusing the application, sentenced Mr. Mackonochie to pay the costs of it. The application was renewed upon June 1, 1878, and upon evidence being adduced that Mr. Mackonochie had not in the meantime conformed to the monition, Lord Penzance sentenced him to suspension *ab officio et beneficio* for three years. The technical ground upon which this sentence was based was that the monition appended to the earlier finding was of the nature of a perpetual injunction, so that any breach of it constituted a continuance of the former offence, and could be dealt with under the judgment already delivered, not requiring a fresh suit to be instituted. But the Queen's Bench Division held that this reasoning was unsound, and granted a writ of prohibition to Mr. Mackonochie against the sentence of Lord Penzance, on the ground that an entirely fresh trial should have preceded the issue of any such sentence. And the Chief Justice specifically added, in reference to the precedent set by the Judicial Committee by its suspension of Mr. Mackonochie for three months for contumacy, that the Court then 'usurped an authority it did not possess,' and delivered a judgment 'contrary to fundamental principles.' The former of these two charges against the Privy Council was explained thus by Sir Alexander Cockburn :

The authority and power of a Court of Appeal, however high its position, can be no greater than those of the Court appealed from. It can annul the judgment, or it can confirm it, or in some cases it can reform it ; but it can pronounce only the judgment which the Court below should and could have given.

And no precedent for any similar sentence pronounced by the old ecclesiastical Courts could be produced, as was acknowledged even by the very wording of the judgment which was thus illegally delivered. This finding of the Queen's Bench Division was appealed against, and was reversed in the Court of Appeal by a majority of one in a court of five Judges on June 28, 1879; whereupon, as Mr. Mackonochie declined to appeal at this stage to the House of Lords, the sentence of suspension for three years was pronounced anew in the Public Worship Regulation Court by Lord Penzance on November 15, 1879, to take effect upon November 23 next following. Upon that day, a Sunday, the Rev. W. M. Sinclair, a chaplain of the Bishop of London, accompanied by Mr. Lee, the Bishop's secretary, presented himself at St. Alban's Church, and tendered a licence which the Bishop had issued to him, appointing him curate-in-charge, to conduct the services during the continuance of the suspension. Mr. Mackonochie declined to acknowledge the validity of either the suspension or his own supersession as minister of the church, and Mr. Sinclair withdrew, no further steps being taken at the time.

In June 1880 a fresh application was made to Lord Penzance to decree deprivation against Mr. Mackonochie for having disregarded the various decisions against him, but it was dismissed on the ground that no steps had been taken to enforce the former decree of suspension, and that the Court could not well issue a second sentence of a different kind while its previous finding remained inactive. Mr. Mackonochie appealed from the decision of the Court of Appeal to the House of Lords, which dismissed the appeal with costs on April 7, 1881, and affirmed the three years' suspension pronounced in 1878.

On the other hand, Lord Penzance's judgment, refusing to pronounce deprivation as a punishment for continued disobedience to the monition issued to Mr. Mackonochie, was appealed from by Mr. Martin, and the Privy Council, on February 3, 1882, reversed that finding, remitting the case anew to Lord Penzance to decree punishment. Before this matter proceeded any further, Mr. Mackonochie, acting on the counsel of the Archbishop of Canterbury, resigned the incumbency of St. Alban's, and was appointed, with the consent of the Bishop of London, to that of St. Peter's, London Docks, thus legally ending all proceedings against himself in his quality of incumbent of St. Alban's. Nevertheless, when the suit came once more into the Public Worship Regulation Act Court, Lord Penzance declared that no substantial change was made in the situation by this avoidance of the benefice, that if Mr. Mackonochie had been

N

unbeneficed, the appropriate sentence would have been perpetual inhibition from officiating, but that as he held some benefice, it was immaterial where it was situate, and that sentence of deprivation should accordingly be pronounced, as was done then and there, July 21, 1883. The Bishop of London soon afterwards issued a writ of sequestration to the churchwardens of St. Peter's, London Docks, appointing them sequestrators during the vacancy thus occasioned ; but no overt act followed to remove Mr. Mackonochie, and he continued in possession of the incumbency till he resigned it on December 31, 1883, thereby, as the event proved, terminating his official connection with the temporal side of the Established Church, and so wherewith, but so only, bringing to a close the rancorous persecution with which he had been harassed for more than sixteen years, with no support from those whose duty it was to have upheld him in his compliance with the ecclesiastical laws of this Church and realm.

It is plain, from the details thus accumulated, that a persistent miscarriage of justice marked the proceedings from the first, and that a travesty of law was all that the Courts concerned vouchsafed to administer. And the conclusion hence is that the whole application of the Royal Supremacy in the ecclesiastical sphere has become disorganised, and is in need of wholesale reform and reconstruction.

The facts are simply that, while the personal supremacy of the Sovereign is still the legal theory in both Church and State, yet for the temporal side of government this has long been fundamentally modified, and the Sovereign now exercises supreme authority, not directly, but through the instrumentality of Ministers virtually elected by Parliament, to which they are responsible, as well as to the Crown. But as the Church is a body politic in itself, diverse in origin, and in the nature of its sanctions, from the civil society of the nation, the Sovereign must act in the same manner towards it. Unless it is merely a department of the Civil Service, it cannot be constitutionally brought under the supremacy of Parliament, to which it owes, upon its spiritual side, no allegiance whatsoever, though Parliament can unquestionably enact laws affecting its temporal accidents. No statute can be adduced merging the Church in the State, or transferring the rights and liberties of the Church to the State, nor the powers of the Crown over the Church to Parliament. And therefore it may at the very least be said that the largest and most ancient religious body in the country is entitled to as much freedom in the management of its own internal concerns as any of the sects tolerated and protected here, and which are to the full as much 'established' by that legal fact. That Parliament has failed when endeavouring to legislate for the Church is openly manifest and indisputable : the laws affecting ecclesiastical matters have been clumsily and ignorantly drafted, and have proved futile too often, when they have not been actively mischievous ; the tribunals set up by the State for the trial of ecclesiastical causes have become a by-word for gross incompetence and grosser partisanship ; the whole system is branded with disgrace and failure.

What is needed is simply the recognition of the change

which has passed over society since the laws which originally erected the Royal Supremacy were enacted, and the reconstitution of the relations between the Crown and the Church on those yet older bases which are practically identical with those now admittedly the only valid ones in the civil sphere, namely, that the Crown may not act despotically, nor through any alien instrumentality, but must govern through ministers belonging themselves to the body politic which they administer, and responsible to that body for any malversation in office. But a mixed Parliament, containing a large element which is outside the Church of England, an element which may quite conceivably at any given time constitute a majority in the Legislature, and which must always contain a considerable body of non-English members having no direct concern with the Church of England, is for the purpose in hand an alien agency, and not constitutionally fit to intermeddle with the internal concerns of the Church. Free election of Bishops, granting the Crown a vote; free Convocations, as unfettered in their sphere as the lay Parliament, which they far exceed in age, and of which they served as the model; and freely constituted ecclesiastical Courts, in which it shall be impossible for judges to sit who are totally ignorant of the system they are called on to administer; such are the necessary factors in any wholesome reform, which shall readjust the relations now disorganised and thrown out of gear by the incapacity or the bad faith of Crown nominees in high places, of Church and State alike.

CHAPTER X.

Alexander H. Mackonochie under prosecution—Testimony of friends and of the public—Indifference to public opinion—Sympathy from without—Unity within—Letters from Dr. Pusey and Liddon—Views on secession and disestablishment.

1867—1869.

FROM the March of 1867, when Mr. Martin first instituted legal proceedings against him, until 1882, the date of his resignation of St. Alban's, Mackonochie's ministerial life was thus, as we have seen, harassed and broken in upon by frequent prosecutions. There were, it is true, long intervals of peace, but there must always have been a sense of insecurity, since immunity from these troubles could only have been purchased by an almost unconditional surrender of the principles in whose defence he had first entered upon the contest.

In the eyes of the world he was somewhat in the position of a rebel leader at the head of a small and yet dangerous party. The purity of his motives was questioned; his conduct loudly condemned as at once rash and disloyal; some of his earlier adherents withdrew from him in disapproval or alarm; on every side and from every standpoint, it was easy for the dispassionate spectator to note some flaw in his argument, some weak point in his defences.   Not even his own supporters could foretell the final issue, nor feel more than a general confidence in the ultimate success of what they believed to be a righteous cause ; whilst from year to year the end of the struggle was indefinitely postponed.

Perhaps one of the most trying parts of the position was the consciousness that to the large majority of indifferent on-lookers the stakes appeared to be so small as to be hardly worth playing for ; added to which there was a well-grounded fear that a religious controversy, even at its best, could hardly fail to have a bad effect upon those who held themselves altogether aloof from Christianity.

Mr. Mackonochie was by no means backward in vindicating his position, but it was difficult to make those who were only anxious to seize him at a disadvantage give any time or thought to the serious consideration of the doctrines or principles involved.   It was easier for the ' Times ' to stigmatise his teaching as ' outrageous ' and his doctrines as ' the most obnoxious doctrines of Roman Catholicism,' than to define them more accurately ; or enter into a theological discussion, which would not, indeed, have befitted the columns of a newspaper.   But, unfortunately, it is from newspapers that many people take their opinions, especially upon subjects with which they are not altogether conversant, and it is not surprising that misrepresentations, arising either from ignorance or prejudice, should have been readily received and widely circulated.

When one correspondent wrote that the chorister boys all wore ' chasubles ' over long gowns and that two of them ' carried thurifers,' the blunder, though somewhat funny, was of no moment ; but the matter became more serious when persons unacquainted with the rudiments of theology delivered opinions upon articles of faith ; and even Lord Westbury, one of the Privy Council Judges, spoke of one of the 'Inferior Persons of the Trinity.'

The personal attacks and unjustifiable accusations brought against the clergy were rarely noticed either by them or their adherents, although the most trifling matters were often distorted or magnified into causes of offence. There is hardly a letter from Mr. Mackonochie in reply, until he somewhat significantly broke the silence by the indignant repudiation of an assertion that one of his clergy had refused Communion to a dying man, because the sick man or his friends objected to lights at the Celebration.

It was only one amongst the many unfounded accusations which served to increase the accumulation of unsifted evidence. Embittered feeling was aggravated, and opposition justified, and yet, as we are told,

nothing could disturb his equanimity nor tempt him to say an unkind or ungenerous word of those opposed to him. Nay, further, 'that his tone and manner of handling the whole subject were such as at once to allay expressions of anger or impatience in others.'

In an address to his parishioners, dated 1867, he says :

I think that one of the greatest dangers in a case like the present is that people may lose charity by thinking evil of those who take a different side from themselves. It is quite natural, though not the less quite wrong that it should be so. We know that our object has been the honour of God, and our motive the love of God. Now when we find people reviling that which we do from such a motive and for such an object, it is often hard for us to believe that they are animated by the same motive as ourselves, and striving for the same object. Yet such is undoubtedly the case. With regard to many of our most strenuous opponents we know it to be so by all the tokens which we could desire ; in few do we know anything to the contrary ; and therefore with regard to the majority we are bound to believe in their entire sincerity. . . . We shall thus be kept from that most unchristian tendency to look out eagerly for faults in others and to rejoice in such faults when they appear ; and moreover we shall know that on both sides the strife is for the same thing, the one object of our lives—the honour and glory of God. Hence, without abating in the very least our own efforts to advance that object, in the way which we conceive to be according to His Will, we shall the more rest assured that as both sides are seeking to forward the same objects, it must eventually by God's Help be attained. It will keep us certain of the ultimate result, and therefore comparatively indifferent to the intermediate steps.

Speaking at a meeting after his death, Sir Walter Phillimore said :

Others would speak of Mr. Mackonochie as the devoted parish priest ; and many in that room did not need reminding of that striking element in his career. To him Mr. Mackonochie was the man who had suffered, and suffered severely, for the maintenance of the Faith. It had been his province to have frequent interviews with Mr. Mackonochie in those troublous days at St. Alban's. He had on these occasions to point out to him the full bearing of these questions both upon the Church and upon Mr. Mackonochie himself personally. The way in which he behaved struck him most forcibly. It was then that the saintliness of his life and character shone forth. . . . He never showed one atom of fear, and then again there was an entire absence of anger ; he was purely and absolutely free from any sign of it. He had frequently heard him express his conviction of Mr. Martin's sincerity and conscientiousness in what he was doing. What did he not go through in those twenty years, quietly doing what he thought right without the slightest regard to consequences?

Although it is forestalling events, it is interesting to note, in corroboration of Sir Walter Phillimore's words, the anxiety which Mr. Mackonochie displayed to obliterate any embittered recollections, and do away with any possibility of sore feeling between himself and Mr. Martin, in whose name the prosecutions under which he had suffered had been so long conducted.

In 1880, hearing of Mr. Martin's serious illness, he had, through some mutual friends, expressed his sorrow and sympathy, together with a wish to be allowed to pay him a visit, and, though this was impossible, Mr. Martin wrote to him in the following terms :

I fully accept your assurance that you never entertained any ill feeling towards me ; and I have no hesitation in saying, as indeed I have done on a former occasion, that I never entertained any unkindly feeling personally towards yourself. I thank you sincerely for your kind sympathy and for your prayers, but in reference to your proposal to pay me a visit, although much appreciating the feeling which prompted it, it strikes me that such an interview would under all the circumstances be undesirable. The fact would in all probability get into the newspapers, and be productive of all sorts of absurd rumours and misconstructions, which might prove embarrassing and unpleasant to me and possibly to yourself also.

I am, dear Sir, faithfully yours,
JOHN MARTIN.

And to this Mr. Mackonochie replied :

Your reception of the expression of feeling which I had made to some mutual friends is a great satisfaction, and although it would have been gratifying to have said in person what I have written, had it seemed desirable, I fully realise the objections which you suggest and quite agree with them. I hope that nothing which has followed from my reply to kindly meant communications from your friends, has caused any addition to the anxieties of a sick bed. With the assurance of my continued prayers and sympathy with your illness,

Believe me yours faithfully,

A. H. M.

Sir Walter Phillimore's testimony, thus corroborated, is that of a man whose relations with Mr. Mackonochie were of a peculiarly intimate character; not the verdict merely of an enthusiastic partisan, but the calm, dispassionate judgment of a layman and a lawyer who had watched the case throughout with the closest attention. Self-interest may well urge a man to self-control in the immediate presence of his enemies, a higher motive is needed to keep him silent in the company of his friends; and yet again one of them writes:

Through all that most trying time, though his feelings were (as they must have been) intense, he never allowed himself to be swayed by them one way or the other, but only sought still the one thing, viz., what was the *right* step to take. I often wondered how much this decision in the choice of the right step from time to time must have cost him. But he never let me into that secret. How naturally he hated notoriety, and felt the lash of public misconception and abuse, and how by the grace of God he learnt to take it all with unruffled heart as in the day's work of his life, he did once let out to me. We were walking short cuts (as his manner was) through narrow slummy passages from one street to another, on the way to whatever next he had to do, when he told me he had been to some public meeting or other, and in reply I expressed a doubt as to whether much good was done by such platform efforts. He at once replied with the simplicity of a child: 'Oh! I go to all the meetings I can just now, and speak if I can, just in order to show people after all I have really not a cloven hoof and a tail.' Once it fell to my lot to warn him against some damage that was deliberately sought to be done against his spiritual influence in one department of his work by an individual who had boasted of what he was doing in my hearing. A. H. M. manifested, and I am sure felt, not the slightest shadow of resentment, but only seemed to be amused by the fact, that knowing the secret hostility of the man, he had imagined the attack was being carried on in some quite different manner. The idea of taking any notice of it evidently never entered his head.

It was not that he did not feel the attacks, which, often insignificant in themselves, yet, like little pin-pricks of pain, were perpetual reminders of the existence of the evil ; but he accepted them simply as part of an anticipated trial He would have said with Frederic Robertson :

It seems to me a pitiful thing for any man to aspire to be true and to speak the truth, and then complain in astonishment 'truth has not crowns to give but thorns.'

He had never with youthful assurance looked upon happiness as a right, nor offered up to it in vain propitiatory sacrifice the claims of duty or of conscience. Referring to temporal anxiety, he writes :

The only way to escape from that anxiety and be calm, is to be as the captain at the helm in a tempest. We all know that our course in life is beset with stormy winds and waves and sunken rocks which may in one form or another make shipwreck of our dearest interests in a moment (I do not mean spiritual interests, which can never be wrecked except by our own consent), but we can steer on, making as sure as we can by God's help of the rightness of our course, using to the utmost the skill and energy which He gives, and then, 'having done all to stand.'

The metaphor is somewhat characteristic. He was emphatically the captain of his own ship, never anxious to shift a responsibility which was rightfully his own on to other people's shoulders.

Through all the worries and anxieties by which his life was beset (writes one of his friends), at times too when all the world around him was feeling and saying how much depended on what Mackonochie should do, he never for a moment lost his head, or did anything but what he saw clearly to be the right thing for him to do, and because it *was* the right thing, without any regard to consequences whatever. I was a good deal with him at the critical time when he finally resigned his benefice, and it became my duty to summon a number of priests from all parts of the country to confer with him upon the subject, and I remember how when we got him upon his legs, all he had to say was—very courteously but very firmly—that while he should be thankful to hear whatever his brethren had to say, that it was he himself that had to decide what was right for him to do, and he should do it.

It was the determination of a man who had, as a matter of course, brought each difficulty and perplexity to be solved at the bar of conscience, and saw no possibility of reversing its decisions. The 'Saturday Review,' though it might not form an altogether just estimate of his character, no less truly than graphically described one side of it, when it said of Mr. Mackonochie that he had a strong power of will and a still stronger power of *won't*. He was like a hard rower who grasps his oars more firmly and pulls the harder as he feels the force of the current. And yet few men put a higher value upon the sympathy of those whom he cared for or respected. It was very dear to him. Every evidence of it was treasured up, from the warm commendation and generous encouragement of distinguished theologians like Dr. Pusey or Canon Carter, to the indignant wonder of his poor parishioners that any one should want to do any harm to 'dear Father Mackonochie.'

Injustice, as ever, defeated its own ends, and in a natural revolt against it, people who in many instances dissented from his teaching ranged themselves upon his side. Gradually it began to be understood that, rightly or wrongly, he was contending for a principle which the integrity of his purpose forbade him to relinquish, and that his so-called contumacy was due to pure conscientiousness; whilst those who were brought into personal contact with him found their preconceived prejudices and half-formulated ideas disturbed or altogether removed under the influence of his unmistakable sincerity. Mr. Dorling, of the 'Christian World,' who made his acquaintance on a railway journey, writes :

Since then I have taken much pains to speak the best words of him of which I am capable. Opinions, creeds, formularies, seem almost vanity when a pure Christian soul is in clear view before us.

'It is lamentable,' writes Lord Shaftesbury, referring to Mr. Mackonochie, 'to see a high self-denying and self-sacrificing spirit in such a quandary of conflicting duties.' Even in the days when the clamour was loudest and party spirit at its height, a noted Nonconformist lecturer could be found to declare that he who supposed that the leaders in the ritualistic movement were men to whom outward forms

were matters of interest except as indicating a doctrine or setting forth some great truth, must have ill read the lives and the doings of these men, in whose ranks he found some of the choicest scholars, the most hard working men, and men of the purest lives and tenderest consciences.

And again, in 1877, we find Lord Shaftesbury writing: 'All zeal for Christ seems to have passed away. The Ritualists have more of it than the Evangelicals.' Such evidences of Christian charity did much to soften the sense of injustice, but they were but as dust in the balance to the deeper sense of thankfulness for the unshaken loyalty of his friends.

I have cause specially to thank God that He still continues to me the help of those other priests with whom in His Goodness He has so long joined me (wrote Mr. Mackonochie in his annual address in 1869). Under God, nothing seems more to help the work of the Church than the continuous united help of the clergy, one in heart and mind and intention to co-operate fully for the glory of their Lord in His work. It is just such a little band, as you know, that He has given to be with me here.

It was thus that at the time of the prosecutions the garrison had the surest element of success in unity within ; and nevertheless it would have been difficult to find men who, in temperament, in personal characteristics and pre-dilections, differed more widely than the four men who were then living and working together at St. Alban's. They had many interests besides those to which they were primarily pledged, in the political, intellectual, and scientific world ; but they were fighting for a cause which united them in a bond even closer than that of personal friendship—the old cause of liberty, though under a new flag ; the cause which under so many different leaders had many times before been lost or won. As Lord Halifax said, in a speech at an English Church Union meeting soon after Mr. Mackonochie's death :

It was a battle to vindicate for the Church of England in regard to her ritual, her doctrine, and her jurisdiction, not only the historical and constitutional rights recognised and secured to her by prescription and statutes, but also her inherent and indefeasible rights as a portion of the one Holy Catholic Church.

It was no wonder to any of those engaged in that vindication that the struggle should be severe and protracted. They were well aware that freedom's banner

torn though flying,
Streams like a thunderstorm against the wind,

and had never reckoned upon an easy victory. It was enough that a common danger but served to deepen their sense of the importance and justice of their cause, gave cohesion to their plan of action, and gained them fresh supporters, who strengthened and extended the lines of their defence.

Mr. Mackonochie had had some correspondence with Dr. Pusey upon doctrinal questions, and it was in 1866 that he wrote :

My dear Mackonochie,— . . . . In the theological statement which you have sent me my only theological misgiving relates to the comparison of the Presence of our Lord in the Holy Eucharist *in regard to space*, with that of His Godhead in his Manhood. And that in regard to ubiquitism. For you are comparing the *local* Presence of His Godhead, with the local Presence of His Godhead and Manhood. This I should think would be confusing. I do not understand a Presence which is *not* local. Still De Lugo (who is a high authority. I have quoted him somewhere) denies that the Presence of our Lord in the Holy Eucharist is local. And this satisfies people that the Presence which we believe is not a carnal corporal, *i.e.* an unspiritual Presence of His Natural Body and Blood which is denied in the 'black rubric.' I should think it then charitable to deny this. I do not see how the passage is to be altered without destroying the whole antithesis. However, I have written something (such as I should write it) embodying a sentence of yours, for the words, 'so I believe in Ascension in the Flesh ;' saying always, that what I say about 'locally' I say simply on the authority of De Lugo, who is regarded as a very accurate and primary authority.

I do not myself think that anything depends on the word 'faithful' in the Catechism. For since it is speaking of the H. Eucharist as a means of Grace, even if the word 'faithful' were taken in the more popular sense, it would not deny its reception by the unfaithful not as a means of grace. For the assertion of the saving gift to the one (of which this whole section of the Catechism is treating) does not involve either doubt or denial of the condemning reception to the other. I mean if you take faithful as *fideles*, this asserts the reception by all ; if 'faithful' is taken in the narrower meaning, the reception by the wicked to their hurt is not indeed asserted, but it is involved in the other.

I do not quite understand the antithesis in the last clause, viz. how the faith is to be taken away. In the first clause, ' Take from me my faith in God's Word, &c.'—you mean that you could not believe in one, if you did not believe in the other, because the truth of ' God's Word Incarnate Present in the Sacrament ' is so embodied in ' God's Word written,' that if you did not believe It, neither could you believe anything else to be written in It. Do you mean in the same way, that the same truth is so clearly expressed in the Prayer Book and Articles of the Church of England, that if you ceased to believe in the one as part of the teaching of the Church of England, you must cease to believe all the rest. If so I think you must bring it out more clearly. For people talk of throwing away the P. B., &c., in a very different sense. I have suggested B. to bring out this.

All joys of the season. Yours affectionately in Christ.

E. B. PUSEY.

F. of S. Stephen.

A. The Presence of Christ in the Holy Eucharist is not of His Godhead only, but of the Manhood also which He vouchsafed to take without confusion of substance into His Godhead, but not making it ubiquitous like his Godhead. Christ is present in the Eucharist supernaturally, but (it has been said by most thoughtful theologians) not locally. I believe Him to be locally present only in Heaven, which He has localised by His Ascension in the Flesh. This in no wise interferes with the Divine, ineffable, sacramental, supernatural Presence of His Body and Blood in the Holy Eucharist, which He has promised by virtue of His Words, 'This is My Body,' which is spoken of also in the Book of Homilies in the terms 'The receiving of the Body and Blood of Christ under the Form of Bread and Wine.'

B. Both rest on the same authority. If I did not believe my Redeemer's word, 'This is My Body,' on what ground could I so detach It from His other teaching, that, while refusing to believe one word of His, I should believe the rest? If I held that the Church of England taught me untruly that the Inward Part, the *res*, the reality of the Sacrament is the Body and Blood of Christ, on what ground could I trust any of her other teaching?

It was in this year also that Mr. Mackonochie received many letters of approval and sympathy from those whose opinion he most valued.

It is quite true (wrote Dr. Pusey again) that I should not

O

have taken the line of the ritualists ; but it is utterly untrue that I do not most heartily sympathise with them for our common faith and for their work.

God be with you and uphold you.

Yours affectionately in Jesus Christ.

E. B. PUSEY.

I will not take up time with vain regrets and needless expressions of sympathy (said Archdeacon Denison at the end of one of the many notes which Mackonochie had carefully preserved). All this is fully understood between us. God help and guide us all in this great strait.

Your ever affectionate

G. A. DENISON.

Bishop Forbes of Brechin, too, writes to wish him 'all success and the aid of God in his great cause.' Dr. Liddon, in reference to the Defence Fund, writes :

If you think that it will help your subscription list, pray print my name. I wish I could have given more when so much more is needed. You will, I hope, not be run down by your many anxieties.

In December 1866 Canon Carter wrote :

My very dear friend and brother,— . . . I feel the anxiety and trial it must be to you to decide, and I pray you may be guided for the glory of God and good of our distracted Church. Whatever you decide, you will be the same you have ever been to me, our thoughts of affection and admiration cannot alter.

And Mr. Skinner of Newland, the Rev. T. C. Chambers, his old friend Father Lowder, and numberless others, were all in various ways strengthening his hands and working for him. This sympathy, felt and expressed, was no doubt one result of the interest which he himself took in what others were doing. He might be holding an important position against the enemy, but it was not from one side alone that attacks were to be apprehended. He was not only very sure of his own ground, but anxious to encourage and establish those who, beset by difficulties and doubts, were inclined to seek a refuge in another communion.

At the end of an address in 1867, in which he had put his position with regard to doctrine and ritual before his parishioners, he said :

People will tell you all this must end in your becoming members of the Roman Communion. In answer to this I honestly tell you that if a man has no stronger ground against Rome than some contest about what he calls 'Catholic and Protestant,' or some isolated doctrines however important, I can easily imagine his going to Rome in these days of convulsion in the spiritual world. Indeed, if he be an earnest man it is difficult to see where else he can find a rest. But I thank God that He has given to the Church of England a very different position. She takes her stand not on Acts of Parliament or a Royal Injunction, or even a purer faith or greater manifestations of the spiritual life—all this might one day fail her. She is the one Christian body having mission from Christ in this land, and on this she founds her claim to your allegiance. She is the only Church in the world which can claim the joint British and Saxon succession. . . . It is on this footing we may rest secure. So long as by the grace of God she shall be enabled to hold fast the deposit of truth which she has received and kept, she alone can claim to have stewardship from God towards us. . . . In her we shall rejoice to be joined to Christ ; separation from her will be separation from the Church Catholic which is His Body, in her and for her we shall strive to live ; with her if God so will we shall be content to suffer ; and with God's blessing bestowed upon us by her, we shall hope to close our eyes in death.

In this year it would seem he had heard some rumours of Dr. Pusey being unsettled in the Church of England, and in answer to a letter from him Dr. Pusey wrote :

Christchurch, Oxford, August 5, 1867.

My dear Mackonochie,—I am altogether puzzled how Mr. E—— could have got the notion. My friend Dr. Newman knows very well that I have no misgivings about the Church of England as it is. He knows equally that if (which God avert) she were formally to reject the Faith, I could not remain in an heretical body. He knows too that I wish and pray for the reunion of Christendom (as indeed everybody knows). But while I should be thankful for a healthy reunion, I have seen these 23 years the great evil of individual secessions. But for them we should not have had this rampant rationalism. The Church of England held it at bay or converted the rationalists until the secessions. Even lately those Balliol secessions checked the tide of conversions. But for the secessions England would have been Catholic by this time.

I have no idea what the 'one point' can be. I suppose it must be my faith as to the Church of England. If I believed the Church of Rome to be alone the Catholic Church, I could only go as a little child ; but while I do not, I have no temptation to leave the Church of England, in which I have seen these many years God is working so marvellously. I have often said, 'Where God the Holy Ghost is, it is safe to be,' the more as He is working sacramentally.

You may show this letter to any one. God be with you.

Yours affectionately,
E. B. PUSEY.

Again, it was in the spring of this year that his active mind, ever seeking for fresh means to enlarge the sphere

of the Church's work, had given special consideration to
the claims of educated men, who, though making some outward profession of religion, were yet at heart doubtful or
unbelieving, and he appears (in a letter which has not been
preserved) to have made some suggestions, in reply to
which Dr. Liddon wrote :

Men of the class for whom apologetic conferences would be
designed would never put their foot within a church on a week-
day, and the preacher would address a few good people who had
no doubts about the Faith.   I think that any such lectures could
only be given on Sunday if they are to succeed. . . . People who
do not believe, or who believe only in bits of Christianity, will go
to church on Sunday from sheer ennui, and then they might by
God's grace be got hold of.   But a week-day has Parliament, the
Clubs, Rotten Row, and plenty of business—serious and the
reverse.

Yet the suggestion, though at the time rejected, was a
strong proof of Mr. Mackonochie's clearsightedness.   It
is a curious commentary upon Dr. Liddon's words, and
surely a most encouraging sign of progress, to note the
hundreds of men who on week-days assemble at this present time under the dome of St. Paul's, to hear not only
the great preacher who twenty years ago doubted the possibility of attracting them, but many other special preachers
less well-known to fame.

It was inevitable that the prosecutions should raise
complex questions and open out wide issues on every
side.   In the revolt of a violent partisanship against 'the
merciful compromises of the Church' there was the desire
to drive out from her pale those who claimed an equal

right with their opponents to interpret her formularies and give expression to her spirit.

We could wish indeed (writes Matthew Arnold) that the Church had shown the same largeness in consenting to relax ceremonies, which she showed in refusing to lighten dogma or to spoil diction. Worse still, the angry wish to drive by violence when the other party will not move by reason finally no doubt appears, and the Church has much to blame herself for in the Act of Uniformity.

It was an Act which the party to which Mr. Mackonochie belonged never desired to enforce. The liberty which they claimed for themselves they freely allowed to others. In a letter to the 'Church Times,' dated January 1869, Mr. Mackonochie wrote :

I did not suggest that we should move for the repeal of the Act of Uniformity, but the omission was of less consequence as it is no original idea, and others have put it forward. Surely we ought to get a large measure of support for such a petition. I suppose it was never obeyed from the second year of Edward VI. downwards. Certainly the Puritans never kept it. They knew quite well that its provisions were aimed at them, and they eluded it in every way. Catholics I imagine were beset by these same Puritans whenever they tried to obey it, so that it fell practically into disuse. From time to time some unhappy being (like myself) has been spitted upon it ; but for securing uniformity of worship it has done nothing. Is not King Log dangerous to all his subjects when he is found to be a box of fireworks ready to spit out a rocket or a squib at any unlooked-for moment and on any side?

Upon the question of disestablishment his views were no less pronounced. In a letter to the 'Daily News,' January 1869, upon the Privy Council judgment, he wrote :

If I may judge from the reception which was given to a few words of mine at the meeting of Tuesday in Freemasons' Tavern, the conviction is gaining ground that the time has come for the Church to claim deliverance from the yoke of State control. I do not believe it to be a question belonging to any political school, for I constantly find myself at one on this point with men of views differing as widely as possible from one another and myself on political questions. Even if we look at the matter from a State point of view, the principle for which I contend lies deeper than any differences of modern politics; for thus regarded, an equitable union of Church and State is only possible where the two terms are co-extensive. In any other case one of two difficulties will arise—either the influence of the Church in the affairs of State will be a burden to those subjects of the State who do not belong to her pale, or else (which is the more probable alternative) the yoke of the State will press heavily upon the conscience of the Church. The English establishment dates from a time when the two were co-extensive, and a continuance of this condition was assumed at the Reformation, but has not been realised, nor will any one dare to predict that it is likely to be realised; so that even from this point of view the union of Church and State is an anachronism and ought to be swept away. But it is in the interest of religion solely, not in that of politics, that the question has to be viewed by us. . . Once free from State control, we shall begin, I trust, to feel as a body, and not merely as individuals, that we belong to the Kingdom which is not of this world.

These utterances belong to the period between March 1867, when proceedings were first instituted against him, and the January of 1869. But later he wrote an article upon Disestablishment, which attracted a good deal of attention, in the 'Nineteenth Century,' and it was apparently in answer to some letter from him upon the reform of Convocation that in 1874 Dr. Pusey wrote:

I am very much afraid of any question of the reform of Convocation, because the question of the laity would be sure to come up (as the Archbishop of Canterbury threw out the other day), and I would rather have an imperfect instrument than a wrong one. I think that the less we ask for now the better. The rest will come by-and-by : the less we have to settle, the less pleas there will be for a great measure and change to effect it. If we are able to make our ground good as to those things which bear upon the Holy Eucharist when people are accustomed to these, they will not [stumble ?] at the rest. I remember when stained glass began to revive, and of this there were only small medallions, unintelligible except by explanation. If in those days the Exeter reredos had been attempted, instead of commanding general sympathy people would have been afraid of it as against the second Canon. . . . Your strength is, and will be, in the hearts of your people. These you have won wonderfully. Courts cannot really move you while you have them. They will be just as much your strength, being lifted out of their sphere, or more so. If the younger clergy will but win their people first as you have. Mr. Hilliard in his speech the other night, when speaking of his ultimate success, owned that he had driven away a certain number at first, for he said that they came back afterwards, some sooner, some later. This may have been no great evil in a town so full of churches as Norwich, but it was a bad precedent. It was a grand Roman boast : *volentes per populos dat jura.*

The tone of the St. James's meeting was delightful. If we could but remain as one as we were that evening.

The action of the laity in the United States can do the less harm because they are a separate house. They are much like our Parliament, only Churchmen. Still, it is a bad principle. For a body, as you say, must find something to do, else there is no good in its existence. And a general necessity of finding something to do would very probably end in doing mischief, like children who break things for something to do.

I am very sorry for Lord Selborne's line. The ex-Chancellor

has been too strong for the Churchman. But people have been more provoking in their random speeches than their acts. As for the 'Guardian' I gave it up long ago. It always deserted us at a pinch. God guide us safe. Your very affectionate

E. B. P.

June 28, 1874.

Briefly recapitulating the chief incidents of the various prosecutions (from which there was no real freedom until 1871), we shall proceed to give some account of Mr. Mackonochie's ministerial work during the five years from 1869 to 1874, both in his own parish and elsewhere.

CHAPTER XI.

Sequence of legal proceedings—Inhibition by the Bishop of Ripon—Speech at the Liverpool Church Congress—Visit to the Cove, Aberdeen—Mission preaching—First mission at St. Alban's, 1869—Establishment of Clewer Sisters in the parish—Letter from the Mother Superior—Ideal of co-operation—Various parochial agencies—Chaplain to Lord Eliot.

1869—1874.

IF we take a brief review of the prosecutions with regard to the ritual at St. Alban's, we shall see that during the years 1867, 1868, 1869, and 1870, they followed one another very rapidly.

In March 1867 the Church Association, in the person of Mr. Martin, first instituted legal proceedings against Mr. Mackonochie. In the spring of the following year Sir Robert Phillimore delivered the judgment in the Court of Arches to which Mr. Mackonochie conformed. Against this judgment Mr. Martin at once appealed to the Judicial Committee of the Privy Council, and in the December of the same year judgment was given and Mr. Mackonochie was condemned with costs. Charged with non-compliance, the case was taken again before the Privy Council in December 1869, and finally, at the close of 1870, Lord Chelmsford declared judgment, and on Advent Sunday a sentence of suspension for three months was delivered to Mr. Mackonochie.

The details of these prosecutions have already been given ; we only refer to them now because, though in themselves much to be regretted, they had no doubt an immediate influence in consolidating and extending his work during these successive years. The notoriety which unavoidably attended these various suits and appeals had its advantages as well as its drawbacks. Rites and doctrines which had perhaps at first been adopted by many people more as matters of taste than of principle, were found to be links in a chain binding the English Church by an indissoluble bond not only to the early days of Christianity, but to the rest of Catholic Christendom ; and in the midst of discord, amongst the strife of tongues, there was a strong and ever-increasing desire not so much for outward peace as for inward unity.

In the spring of 1869 Mr. Mackonochie had gone up to attend an English Church Union meeting at Bradford, and was announced to preach at several churches in the town and neighbourhood, when he received a most unexpected communication from the Bishop of Ripon inhibiting him from preaching at all in his diocese. This unprecedented proceeding called forth a good deal of feeling, and awakened a not unnatural suspicion that Mr. Mackonochie and the party to which he belonged were not having fair play. It might easily have led to bitter recriminations and aggravated discontent ; but a slight reference to it in Mackonochie's speech at the meeting manifests, with what one of the daily papers called 'his high tone and admirable temper,' nothing but a desire to allay irritation. He did not regard the Bishop as responsible for what had been done, and believed he had only acted in the matter under pressure. He made that statement with the greater pleasure because, being quite removed from the local associations which surrounded his hearers, he was saved from the blame of transferring the responsibility to any particular person. There was one thing which confirmed him in the impression he had about the subject, and that was that only once in his life had he come into direct intercourse with the Bishop of Ripon, and on that occasion nothing could exceed the kindness and consideration with which the Bishop thought of his feelings and consulted him in every way ;

and then passing from the subject in a few short sentences, he goes on to speak upon questions of general interest to the Church. In a note to his brother referring to this incident he writes :

You will be gratified to know that I have drawn out Leviathan with a hook. In plain English the Bishop has inhibited me from officiating in the diocese without his written permission. Happily the Saturday night and Sunday have made a considerable impression, which I trust has been deepened by an address to the Guild of St Alban and a few select friends on Monday evening, so that the inhibition will just tread in the seed.

He had meant to spend some time in Yorkshire preaching and lecturing upon secular platforms, but this was now at an end, and he used to say that he had to thank the Bishop for a pleasant fortnight's holiday. But though he accepted the inevitable with undisturbed composure, he was by no means anxious to shut himself up. He had been brought before the public as a culprit, and he was not inclined to maintain a silence which was likely to be misunderstood. Not only was his preaching attracting increased attention, but his wide experience and practical suggestions made him a valued speaker at public meetings and upon occasions which called for the co-operation of men of all shades of opinion. It was in this year that he was announced as one of the speakers at the Liverpool Church Congress ; and though Dean McNeile declined to appear upon the platform if Mr. Mackonochie's name were retained on the programme, it is pleasant to find that the good sense of the committee refused to give way to the Dean's scruples, and at a full meeting the proposal that Mr. Mackonochie should be asked to withdraw was negatived by a large majority.

The subject upon which he proposed to speak, ‘ Improvement of the Church's Services,’ was one upon which he was well qualified to give an opinion ; but he probably took a good many of his hearers by surprise when he rose in the midst of a good deal of excitement and said that he intended to speak from a practical point of view, and deprecating a rigid uniformity, pleaded for simple and elastic services to supplement the ordinary ones of the Church.

If one section of the Church—those who agree mostly with me—think that such additional services as I have spoken of help their belief most, let them have them. But why should we grudge to others the use of a prayer meeting or extempore prayer in one form or other by which they can best lay hold of the souls of their own people?

He then described how in Scotland he had held a service at the house of a poor fisherman upon the Presbyterian model as one best suited to those to whom he was called to minister.

The experience was a recent one and fresh in his mind. He had sought change of air and scene in taking charge of a Mission Chapel at the Cove near Aberdeen for his friend Mr. Ball. He was delighted to find himself amongst the simple fisher people, and with characteristic energy at once set himself to see how he might best bring home to them the Gospel message.

I have charge of the little mission here (he wrote on August 17, 1869), which is very delightful. Ball lets me have a daily celebration, to which from ten to fifteen come. Then on Sunday I have in addition Matins, Litany, and sermon at 11.30 ; and Evensong at six, also with sermon. At 3 P.M. I go down to a fisherman's cottage in a Row called *Balmoral* and give a cottage lecture. Her Majesty was not there in person last Sunday, but all the corners were stuffed with fishwives, fishermen, and great lads. We sang a Psalm sitting, then extempore prayer standing, then chapter of the Bible and another Psalm as before, then exposition paraphrases, extempore prayer and blessing. I should like to be here for a long time.

And with reference to his first Sunday services he wrote :

I have got through yesterday. T—— came and sang, so we had lots of noise. In the Psalm he had a strong predilection for the two endings of the 7th tone which are given in Helmore, while the children would hear of nothing but the 4th ending. The Te Deum also was contested by Tone 2 and Tone 8.1, the last eventually gained the day. But all went well as far as the service was concerned . . . . The Revivalists are here in great force. A man whom you will know as ' Charlie' preached and prayed and sang from soon after 3 P.M. till about 8, when I was resting after my labours. I think he would be going on now, only a short but sharp shower of rain fell at that period . . . . I hope I edified the fishwives more than I did myself. I never felt more like a fish out of water in my life. I find I made them sing one more Psalm than usual to make up for not being able to sing myself. I read them St. Matt. xvi. and made my text ' What shall it profit ?' Certainly the old women looked impressed, but I do not know what about. Afterwards we had a talk about *Abinadab* and his sons, also Melchizedec, the sons of Eli, Judas, and generally the peccability of priests—including St. Peter, with whom by-the-by it began . . . Now ' Charlie ' has given me an idea, and I want to know what you think. I heard some bits of his sermon. There was the new heart—then grace and salvation only through our Lord—then Faith. So far all was very good ; but next came an attack upon works. He gave an account of some conversation which he had had, he described the religion of the other as all do, do, work, work ; but *he* is straightforward, &c. Now if I could do it and carry the people with me I should like next Sunday to talk to the fishermen about the whole Gospel, not saying anything about Charlie, but speaking of salvation by grace through our Lord's merits, then justification by faith, then sanctification. Do you think one could get them to take it in ? Then the last Sunday might be ' the Christian's life.'

Here at any rate is ample testimony that he was ready upon occasion to carry out his own advice with respect to elasticity in public ministrations. It was not a question of Church ceremonial or the Book of Common Prayer ; he prized these things, as many people would have asserted, far beyond their worth, and yet, when the occasion demanded it, he could lay them as easily aside, and was ready to take a lesson from ' Charlie ' if by any means he might save some.

He found much refreshment of spirit in this quiet time at the Cove. He had indeed, even upon his holiday, a large correspondence with which to deal, and many anxieties which could not altogether be put aside, but he had a happy faculty of living in the present, as far as the things of this world were concerned; and no dark forebodings overshadowed his future. He made new friends amongst the small population at the Cove, and returned with renewed pleasure at different periods of his life to the quiet little bay.

He always seemed to enjoy Scotland [wrote one who knew him there]. We have many recollections of long walks with him, and he was so kind and genial with the children, reading aloud on one of his visits the 'King of the Golden River' with great vigour. . . . Some of the most beautiful sermons I ever heard from his lips were those preached in the little Cove chapel, and they are still remembered.

He had, no doubt, for so reserved a man, an unusual capacity for adapting himself to his congregation, and this constituted one of his most important qualifications for mission preaching. In 1865, after a mission held at Plymouth, he wrote:

We got on very well (thank God) at Plymouth. I think that no doubt the mission has been made the means of establishing and deepening the spiritual life of those who had been already seeking God, and I hope also of removing some shyness. Prynne said that he was almost overcome by the number of officers whom he saw at the Holy Communion of the Sunday, and whom he had not seen for a long time—some for years.

In reference to this first mission, the Rev. G. R. Prynne, the Vicar of St. Peter's, writes:

I think he was one of the most effective mission preachers I ever heard. Not simply because of his eloquence, though that was often great, but because of that tone of thorough and honest conviction which characterised every word he spoke, and which, therefore, as if by an electric current, carried conviction to the hearts of his hearers. The reality of the impression which he made was evidenced by the numbers of people he had never seen before who came to him to make their first confession. . . . He was most unsparing of himself, and gave himself with the most absolute self-surrender to the work which he had undertaken.

In addition to the missions which he preached, he held many retreats for clergy, for religious communities, and for others. They were marked by the same directness of aim which characterised his ordinary preaching. Some of these retreat notes lie before us now, and are chiefly remarkable for wideness of scope combined with definiteness of arrangement, the gathering up of the different threads of thought having always a practical bearing upon the circumstances of every-day life.

From November 14 to November 25, 1869, a mission, conducted by Father O'Neill,[1] of the Society of St. John the Evangelist, and the Rev. G. Boddington of Willenhall, was held at St. Alban's. It was the first London mission, and indirectly affected large numbers who took no practical part in it. It had, unlike many isolated individual efforts, received the formal approbation of the Bishops in whose dioceses it was to take place, and was a united and vigorous effort on the part of clergy differing as widely as possible from one another as to the ordinary means to be employed in furthering their common end. Its very

---

[1] Father O'Neill remained ever after one of the best beloved and most valued among our friends. The last years of his life were spent in India, far away from European society. He lived among the natives as a native, and died in their midst of cholera. In the parish of St. Alban's, Holborn, he is still lovingly remembered by some, who speak of him always in terms of deepest respect as ' that apostolic man.'—ED.

P

novelty insured a certain amount of transitory success, but nevertheless its ultimate effect remained uncertain, and in default of experience it could hardly be regarded by even the most sanguine as more than a hopeful experiment.

A mission is a call from God (wrote Father Mackonochie in his opening address). In a mission God calls us all. He calls us as sinners to repent. He calls us as beginners to go on well. He calls us as lovers of Him to perfection.

The services, various meetings and instructions, were arranged to suit the convenience and needs of all classes of people, and differ in no respect from the ordinary means employed during a mission week, now so well known as to excite no attention outside the limits of a parish or congregation. It is curious to refer to the lengthy accounts in the daily papers, entering into every detail of the proceedings, at that time the subjects of widespread interest and public criticism. The congregations at St. Alban's were so crowded that it was necessary to have supplementary meetings in the schoolroom, and the mission ended with a public renewal of baptismal vows. It was in reference to this that Mr. Mackonochie wrote :

I never saw anything so touching. Old white-headed men, young children, rich and poor, many old men with tears on their cheeks. Surely the Spirit of God was with them. . . . It has been a great, quiet, calm success. *Deo Gratias.*

And by the time that his annual address was issued on the St. Alban's Day of the following year, that success was established and assured, and he could write :

The chief event of our year has been the twelve days' mission in November. I trust that the effect of this will long endure.

. . . It was shortly followed by a special confirmation, most kindly accorded to my request, held in St. Alban's by the Bishop of London two days before Christmas. About 115 of our own people then received the Holy Ghost from the hands of Christ's chief Pastor in this diocese.

This is only one instance of the large, and in some respects rapid, advance which the Church had made ; an advance which had, to some extent, insured the success of the mission. The preparatory work had been real and thorough, and no artificial means had been used to force the growth of either personal spiritual experiences or outward religious observances.

There was a large band of district visitors, and an Association of laymen, in connection with the order of St. John Baptist, Clewer, had its headquarters in the mission-house in Greville Street, and was doing good work. The Mother of Clewer (Harriet Monsell), with her keen insight into human nature and practical knowledge of parochial work, had from the first felt a special interest in St. Alban's. She had been the means of bringing the work of the Association to bear upon the parish, and as soon as it became possible she willingly acceded to Mr. Mackonochie's anxious desire to have the co-operation of resident Sisters.

In 1868 he wrote :

It would be impossible to over-rate the help which would be derived from the residence among us of a small band of Sisters;

and in 1869, already two choir and two lay sisters were in the mission house in Greville Street.

It is not yet easy to say what we are doing (wrote the Mother soon after their arrival), because we are just getting into work; but that which is specially committed to our care is the work which lies too deep for the district visitors to do. The care of the sick, the getting at the people in their own homes, the bringing what Mr. Mackonochie calls the sacramental power of the Sisters' life to bear upon all the sin and sorrow and misery of the parish. . . . It is a great blessing to enter upon work in a parish where you have such clergy to help you —and I, having some little experience in work, say with my whole heart that it is impossible to find more excellent, devoted, and self-sacrificing men than those working at St. Alban's; this little time of trouble will pass away, and their work will remain. I could not but marvel the other day, when at the midday celebration, at the good sense of England spending thousands to put out those two innocent candles, placed there for the one aim of pointing out Christ as the Light. Oh how the angels who look into these mysteries must marvel to see what man can and will do to mar God's work !

On New Year's Eve we had a tea for the parents of the school-children. Nearly 300 were fed most comfortably, then they had a few songs, and then Mr. Stanton told them we were going into the church to sing a Te Deum in thanksgiving to God at the close of the year, and that whoever liked might come; and every one of them turned into the church, and so in the midst of evil times we sang our thanksgiving, surrounded by the people who throughout eternity will, we trust, thank God for the church which God put it into Mr. Hubbard's heart to build for His Glory.

The small community thus established increased and prospered. In 1870, speaking of the Sisters, Mr. Mackonochie wrote:

Their presence, bringing the power of the religious life to bear on all the parochial works of mercy and charity, is an unspeakable blessing.

And again in the following year:

We are getting, I think, to the right idea—different works each with its own head, and with more or less independence, according to the character of the work and the power of the worker ; but all making the Sisterhood the centre round which they work.

Here, too, Mr. Mackonochie was specially fortunate in retaining for many years the services of those who had zealously co-operated with him from these early days. In writing about the Sister-in-charge of this branch of the community, who was only removed in 1882, he says :

One prominent figure in all that was good and active in the parish disappears from the midst of us this year—I mean Sister Georgiana Mary. . . . She is a loss, a great loss to the parish, not to say to the neighbourhood . . .

and he goes on to speak of 'the womanly tact and perseverance she carried into work which few men would care to attempt.'

As the parochial organisation was extended, the work naturally became of a more varied character. Already, during the period of which we are writing, some of the most valuable parochial agencies were in active operation. The Choir School ; the Orphanage, started on a small unpretending scale after the visitation of cholera in 1866 ; the Infant Nursery ; the Youths' Institute ; the Sunday breakfast for really destitute boys, 'every care being taken to avoid its ever seeming to be a trap to get them into church ;' the Soup Kitchen, assisting about 150 families weekly during the winter months ; and all the other means employed for raising the physical and spiritual condition of the people, were in good working order ; and in the midst of many inevitable disappointments there was cause for deep thankfulness that so far the efforts made had been sustained and blessed.

The years 1871, 1872, and 1873 were years of peace. It was during this time that the new schools were built and opened, the Working Men's Club established, and various other additions made to the parochial machinery. But there was no change in the main scope and object of the work ; it had not ceased to be of a missionary character, though year by year the church undoubtedly influenced a larger number of outsiders. In earlier days, one of the Sisters had spoken of ' Father Mackonochie doing all the work of everybody.' The saying was no longer true. It was now rather his desire to secure for those in co-operation with him an appropriate sphere of action. He himself took as keen an interest as ever in the affairs of the parish, but in many respects he was content to leave the conduct of them to others. He was day by day in St. Alban's, constantly preaching, instructing, hearing confessions ; and undoubtedly as time went on his life became less one of ordinary parochial duty, being almost altogether engrossed by direct spiritual ministrations. He could well afford to turn a deaf ear to the angry clamour of opponents, whilst hearts were touched and consciences awakened, repentance deepened, and the old wounds of sin healed by his ministry ; when, moreover, the glaring injustice of repeated prosecutions served but to kindle fresh enthusiasm and generosity, of which the following letter is by no means an isolated example. It was on the occasion of his first suspension by Lord Chelmsford in November 1870 that Lord Eliot wrote :

Dear Mr. Mackonochie,—I am going to make a request that you will, I hope, at least not think an impertinent one.

As a peer I have a right to name a domestic chaplain ; it of course entails no duties, and I fear conveys no privileges, and if I venture to offer you such a title it is only with a sincere desire to give a proof of my gratitude for the comfort and, I hope, profit which I have derived from the service which the Privy Council is attempting to put down.   That the attempt will be successful I do not fear ; but, feeling that it is the duty of every one to do what he can to protest against this monstrous iniquity, I venture to make this offer, well knowing that all the honour will be on my side if you kindly consent.

I have the honour to be yours very faithfully,

ELIOT.

The offer was accepted, and the connection thus begun was only severed by death.

CHAPTER XII.

1875—1882.

IN reading the history of the repeated prosecutions—of
condemnations, inhibitions, suspensions on the one side,
and of refusals to recognise jurisdiction and to submit to
authority on the other—it is very necessary to remember
that a life of contention is by no means inconsistent with a
desire for peace. There were not only to be no reprisals,
but there was to be no desire to retaliate. All 'this fighting,' writes Mr. Mackonochie, with a confident simplicity
hardly justified either by the experience of individuals or
the history of nations—'all this fighting must be in the
spirit of love.'

Over and over again, both in private letters and public
addresses, we find expressions of thankfulness when freedom
from litigation has brought peace to his parish and congregation. He was able by the force of his strong will
to bear anxiety and suspense without manifesting any un-
easiness, but he dreaded its effect upon others.

My feeling about ritual (he wrote as early as 1865) is to get the actual law of the Church generally observed in order to give people's minds rest. At present the great anxiety on all sides is to know ' how far you have got.' Thus ritual takes a wrong place from which it cannot be dethroned till the chasuble at the altar is at least as common as the surplice in the pulpit. Then people will know that in a church of a certain type they will certainly find the legal ornaments ; thus they will cease to be disquieted on this head. Of course there are some people who will always be found to run after something : and if they have a chasuble everywhere they will then think about details in music, &c. But there are many to whom this growth of ritual is very trying, and to them I do earnestly wish to be able to say—' there you see the whole.'

His keenest anxieties were, however, never personal. In 1874 he wrote :

The year must be a most anxious one, and probably one of great importance to a much wider range of persons than merely myself and my people. . . . However, God sitteth above the water-floods, and if we do our best He will win the battle for Himself even with our mistakes if better may not be had.

And again :

No doubt our walk through this little world is through much fog and darkness and many alarms ; but it is wonderful when one looks back to see how little the evils of life have been allowed to leave real marks upon our course, or upon our present state. It seems as if we have only to go on with our eyes fixed upon God and somehow the mist disperses at the critical time.

It is, no doubt, in the last sentence that we have the real groundwork of his composure ; but he had at the same time powers of mental and physical endurance which were rather the results of nature than of grace.

Delicacy of health had passed away with early youth,

and occasional attacks· of illness had left his vigorous
constitution unimpaired. This was in one sense a snare;
for no physical weakness nor overwhelming sense of
exhaustion gave timely warning that it was being subjected to too severe a strain. It sometimes appeared
as if the ordinary accidents of life—pain and weariness,
heat and cold—were alike indifferent to him. If he suffered,
he gave no sign either of physical distress or mental dis-
quietude.

A little incident curiously illustrating his habitual
stoicism took place in 1874. He had been calling at a
house in Portland Place, when his foot slipped on the
door-step and he fell, dislocating his shoulder. He had an
appointment at Haggerston that afternoon, and conceiving
this trivial misadventure to be unworthy of attention, he pursued his road. By the time he reached St. Saviour's Priory
he was not unnaturally a good deal worse, and after a while
consented to go home in a cab. On his arrival at the
Clergy House one of the Sisters came to attend upon him,
and perceiving the nature of the injury, without waiting for
his permission, sent off for a doctor. In the meantime
nothing could be done. Knowing the pain he must necessarily be suffering, the Sister, in a good deal of anxiety,
went back into his room to find him still apparently unmoved. His arm hung helpless, but voice, manner, looks
were unaltered, as he quietly observed, 'Perhaps, Sister, it
might be as well to send for a doctor.'

By this time the journey to Haggerston, the jolting of
the cab over rough pavement, and well-meant but ignorant
efforts at relief, had aggravated the mischief. It was not

without difficulty that the surgeon did his work, and the
Sister was thankful when the last wrench was over and she
could follow him out of the room, but she was taken by
surprise at his first words : ' That is a *good* man.' His
professional knowledge had rightly estimated the agony so
unflinchingly endured, and in the one short emphatic sentence he summed up his verdict.

It was the same with regard to fatigue and fasting. On
Good Fridays, for instance, he would be at St. Alban's taking
services and hearing confessions from an early hour until
12 o'clock. He would preach the Three Hours, and afterwards remain at his post seeing people until five ; then for
the first time he would break his fast, walk down to Haggerston to his duties at the Sisterhood, and return to preach
at the evening service at St. Alban's, the day of incessant
mental and physical strain not being ended until midnight.
In one of his letters he speaks of having preached twenty-
three sermons in seven days, and he would carry on as many
as six courses of sermons at a time, keeping his subjects
perfectly well defined, and handling each of them separately
with clearness and power. It would have been only possible
to a man who was at once singularly clear-headed and
physically robust, and these sustained efforts having apparently no ill effects at the time, established dangerous pre-
cedents for future exertions. One secret of his strength
was no doubt to be found in the power he possessed of
laying aside the burden of the day in those times of
spiritual rest and refreshment which are amongst the
necessities of the Christian life. Every year he went into
retreat, and no need of relaxation nor press of business

could induce him to forego that period of closest self-communing, of silence, and of prayer. Exact in all things, he was more especially careful lest the 'fightings without' should destroy the peace within. Yet he was so lavish in placing his time at other people's service that when at last he broke down, those who watched him most closely could only wonder that the natural result of his persistent disregard of ordinary precautions should have been delayed so long.

The second London Mission took place in the spring of 1874, and, as in 1869, was fruitful in blessings to the parishioners and congregation at St. Alban's. Mr. Mackonochie was absent from his church, being engaged to preach at St. Paul's, Knightsbridge; he returned full of thankfulness for the mercies vouchsafed there and elsewhere, to carry on and consolidate the work to which the Mission week had given a fresh impulse; but he was not long destined to do so undisturbed.

Already in May the fresh suit 'Martin *v.* Mackonochie' began in the Court of Arches, and was followed by the events which have been detailed in Chapter IX.: Sir Robert Phillimore's judgment on December 7, against which Mr. Mackonochie appealed; the withdrawal of the appeal on May 21, 1875; and finally, on June 12 of the same year, Mr. Mackonochie's suspension for six weeks.

The storm which broke with the renewed prosecution in 1874 had been threatening for some time; and those most deeply interested in the affairs of the Church observing the ominous signs of its approach were not slow to perceive that in all probability it would first burst over St.

Alban's, and that weighty interests (by no means affecting that church and parish alone) would be involved in the line of defence which should be adopted ; and already in March 1874 Mr. Mackonochie had received the following joint letter from Dr. Pusey and Dr. Liddon :

Christ Church, March 14, 1874.

My dear Mackonochie,—You will have seen from the newspapers that we are threatened with legislation having for its object the summary enforcement of recent disputed decisions of the Judicial Committee of the Privy Council. If, as is apparently the case, we can trust the articles which have appeared in the 'Times,' the Episcopal authority is to be shared—in the work of diocesan administration —with laymen elected by the nominees of the ratepayers, and therefore not necessarily Churchmen or Christians ; while it is also proposed that those directions of the Prayer Book which are notoriously disregarded by the Low Church and Broad Church clergy, shall no longer have the power of law.

We will not characterise this project as it deserves. But we wish to submit to you, that even if, as we trust will be the case, it should be defeated, it points to a permanent source of danger to the progress of Church work and life among us.

There are, of course, opponents whom nothing that we can do or say will ever conciliate, since, unhappily for themselves, they reject the revealed doctrines of Sacramental grace, and, not infrequently, the more central truths of Christianity from which these doctrines directly radiate. But if such persons are assisted by others who seriously believe what God has revealed, or wish to do so, we have reason to ask ourselves whether we ever act or speak in a way calculated to cause needless ' offence,' and so to retard that very work of God which we have at heart.

Must it not be acknowledged in view of the exaggerated ceremonial and ill-considered language which are sometimes to be found among (so-called) ' Ritualists,' that there are grave reasons for anxiety on this head? We at least cannot help thinking so,

and we are therefore writing to ask you to use your great influence
with many of our brethren, in favour of a course which appears to
us to be recommended alike by charity for souls, and by loyalty
to the common Truth.

Would it not be possible to take some early opportunity of
considering how much of recent additions to customary ritual
could be abandoned without doing harm? We will not attempt
to go into details. But surely matters of taste or feeling, not
necessarily or of long habit associated with the enforcement or
maintenance of doctrine, yet calculated to alarm the prejudiced
and uninstructed, ought, on St. Paul's principle, to be at least
reconsidered. If we could show that we have unity and humility
at heart as truly as we have at heart the loyal maintenance of the
Church's faith and worship, much of the existing opposition would
be disarmed, and we might hope by God's mercy to escape from
dangers which are more imminent and serious than appearances
would suggest.

You will, we are sure, understand this appeal in the sense in
which it is addressed to you, viz., that of a sincere wish to secure
whatever has really been gained of late years in the way of faith
and reverence, to the glory of Our Lord and the good of souls.

Your faithful brethren in Him,

E. B. Pusey.

H. P. Liddon.

To this letter Mr. Mackonochie replied as follows:

My dear Liddon,—I suppose I am right in addressing what I
can say to Dr. Pusey and yourself, to you, as the writer and sender
of the letter, rather than to him as the one chiefly to be regarded
as its author.

In the first place, I am most sorry for the long delay, and hope
that Dr. Pusey will believe that it has arisen from no disrespect,
but on the other hand, from unwillingness to send anything which
must have been hasty and ill-considered, in the midst of the constant pressure of work, seldom leaving me many minutes quiet for

thought at any one time. Somehow or other one gets to be so much the slave of everybody as to have little control over time, except, perhaps, late at night when men of small mental power, like myself, are too worn out to think, or at any rate to rely upon the wisdom of such thought.

The letter, moreover, is one of great difficulty. It appeals to me as a man of influence with many, whereas I suppose that there is hardly a man connected with the 'movement' who is more utterly destitute of influence. Then there comes next the difficulty of the subject-matter.

The principal point, I suppose, to which to address myself is the practical one : how far any agreement might be come to for some kind of compromise about Ritual.

(1) I would venture very respectfully to suggest that such a step on our part would be attended with the greatest danger. It we could proceed in the matter under authority the case might, and no doubt would, be different ; as it is we should simply be in the condition of an army attempting to change its face in the presence of an assailing force. In 1865, under strong pressure from Sir R. Phillimore, dear old Mr. Richards and Perry, I tried the experiment, and was dragged into Court and condemned by Sir R. P. for the very things which I had given up. It is to be remarked that my being singled out for attack has not been owing to my being foremost in ceremonial. Except the early days of the church when I was wearing the white linen vestments, and before other churches had adopted vestments at all, I have never been in the front ranks of ceremonial. Doubtless the apparent weakness of compromise encouraged an attack on me rather than on those who showed no signs of surrender.

(2) Then at that time we had a meeting of priests who were committed to extreme ritual as it was called. With what result? No two agreed in any one point, except that each meant to go on as he was doing ; I gave way, and I suffered as being the only one attacked.

Nor can I find fault with this spirit. You think us impracticable. But just consider. We have taught the people that ceremonial is the legitimate expression before God of the Faith. We have taught them the special significance of the great Eucharistic ceremonies, and the secondary but not insignificant symbolism of ceremonies at Matins and Evensong . . . and of minor ceremonial at other times. Then we have repressed and regulated the desire for these things, and finally granted them, some in a less, some in a greater degree. . . . What are we to expect if after such careful advance, after teaching the people to value each act and each object as a sermon preaching Christ to them, we are to sweep all away for fear of deprivation or the more remote possibility of imprisonment. Can we expect our people to honour us or our teaching?

Those who are not mixed with the class of people who come in contact with us cannot imagine how deeply they have been outraged by the loss of . . . things which to outsiders seem so small. . . . They know that they are giving not money only, but themselves in countless ways to it and its work for God's sake, and they are to be robbed for the gratification of cold-hearted partisans. You see whose interests they are we have at stake, and can we be other than careful of them? They have more than built the church twice over with money scraped out of hard personal self-denial, and all this is to go to the winds because puritans, who have shown over and over again in each generation since the Reformation that they are insatiable, demand it.

No doubt ceremonial has a double aspect. That of the Altar is beyond question that on which we set the greatest store; . . . we believe that in handling the Divine and unspeakable mystery of the Eucharist we are bound as Catholics to the utmost of our power, and entitled according to the fair reading of the Church of England Prayer Book, to surround it with all the reverent adjuncts which the Catholic Church has from ancient times attached to its celebration. This is certainly our great point, but the other aspect is also of great value. This which I have spoken of we may call the Sacrificial aspect, the other I call the Missionary. If you want to touch people's hearts and rouse them, give them a procession.

It may be dull and stupid and unmeaning to you and me, but it comes home somehow to the poor people with a loud call. . . . It is certainly manifest among our people. Then other things do the same in perhaps a less degree. . . . Still this last, important as it is for the sake of poor souls, is little compared with that in which we do honour to God. If each priest were fully at liberty, to celebrate Mass in the way he thinks most pleasing to God and most in accordance with the mind of the Prayer Book, we might forego the processions, &c. . . . If we could retain the full Eucharistic ceremonial—lights, vestments, wafer-bread, mixed chalice, &c., to be used in old Catholic ways, and the general ordering of the ceremonial acts to be also after the like old Catholic ways ; if we could do this and regain peace and forbearance—I was going to say mutual forbearance, but we have forborne beyond all bearing—if we could do this the sacrifice would be worth making. . . . It has been the mutilation of our altar ritual which has driven people into less definitely ordered ceremonial of other kinds. If we may not have what we ought, we must take what we can ; and this warfare, guerilla though it be, we shall have to pursue. . . . If you ask if I have anything to propose, I confess that I see no other course than that which the Bishop of Lincoln [Wordsworth] indicates up to a certain point. I can imagine a satisfactory issue if the Bishop would have the courage to face these facts :

(1) That a time when men's minds have been lashed into a ferment of excitement by reckless persecution on one side and perhaps recklessness in changes on the other, is no time for legislation either civil or spiritual.

(2) That most of the Bishops brought up in an opposite school of thought are utterly incapable of forming the slightest conception of what ceremonial is to us ; that they cannot imagine the ceremonies of the Mass being anything but child's play, when to us they are the barest alphabet of reverence for so Divine a Mystery.

(3) That the defects of others are at least as great a scandal to

us as our excesses (real or supposed) are to them. . . . By using
the influence which their office gives them, they might insist on
toleration on both sides, so long as no grievous outrage was committed on the great mass of the communicants worshipping in
any particular church ; and thus give time for a more general
understanding of our respective positions by means of which it
should be possible after a time to establish some basis which
should be sufficiently wide to embrace all who can honestly accept
the Prayer Book, and not so indefinite as to leave the Church
open to the charge of having no law at all on so grave a subject.
Nothing, it seems to me, can be more ruinous than the course
taken by some, who are, as a matter of fact, quite at one in
principle with us extreme men, *e.g.* our dear friend —— and
others in Convocation, of having a kick at us every few words.   If
they throw us off and we are smashed, they will, I fear, share our
fall. . . . I hope you will kindly express to Dr. Pusey my great
regret for the long delay and seeming disrespect, but I have been
simply unable till now to get the time, and even now hardly know
what I have written, as it has been a scramble between other calls.
        Yours most affectionately in Our Blessed Lord,

                                               A. H. M.

This letter is all the more valuable because he rarely
wrote at any length about matters which might have been
supposed to touch him most nearly ; and it is not surprising
that his self-restraint should have occasionally been mistaken for want of feeling.   It is very rare to find anything
more than a short commonplace reference to any fresh
aspect of pending trials or to his own conduct upon critical
occasions.

The Bishop of Gloucester and Bristol has *asked me not* to
preach at All Saints' [he wrote in 1875].   This I expected from
the moment that Randall asked me.   I never like an ill wind to

blow nobody good, so I mean to avail myself of your pressing invites and come to you on Tuesday.

Then again, on November 21, 1879, he writes :

We do not anticipate any row next Sunday, although, of course, there may be one. The Bishop and I have through his secretary made an amicable arrangement. His chaplain will come down attended by the secretary. He will exhibit the Bishop's licence. I shall read and deliver to him my grounds for not accepting him, and they will go.

This was on the occasion of the sentence of deprivation passed by Lord Penzance, when, in obedience to the Bishop's orders, his chaplain, Mr. Sinclair (now Archdeacon of London), came down licensed by the Bishop to take the services. The sentence of suspension had been tendered to Mr. Mackonochie and nailed on the door before the bell began to ring ; but when Mr. Sinclair arrived he found Mr. Mackonochie already vested and in the vestry with the churchwardens preparing to go into church. Mr. Lee, the Bishop's secretary, at once proceeded to state the object of their visit, and read the Bishop's licence appointing Mr. Sinclair curate-in-charge of St. Alban's until other arrangements could be made. Mr. Mackonochie replied by reading his protest ; Mr. Sinclair said he understood he was not to take the service, though perfectly prepared to do so. Mr. Mackonochie replied, ' Distinctly so ; ' and the interview, conducted with courtesy on each side, came to an end. As Mr. Mackonochie had foretold in his letter, Mr. Sinclair went, and the service proceeded as usual without any public reference being made to this preliminary episode.

It was a typical instance of his way of dealing with

difficulties of this kind ; and he had, moreover, the unusual faculty of rather under-estimating than exaggerating the evils which affected either himself or his cause.

In legal matters and in the public courts he sometimes made the mistake of arming himself with the untried weapons of lawful casuistry, but in personal intercourse silence was his only resource when in a difficulty. He had no aptitude for evading a question or parrying a thrust ; in short, no mental agility. A half-truth, if not exactly ' the blackest of lies,' was at any rate to be reprobated and condemned. He was rigidly and literally truthful, and indeed in this world of compromises the remorseless manner in which he would drag unwelcome truths to light was found by many people to be extremely inconvenient.

To return to the events of these years, from 1875, the date of his second suspension, to 1882, his last year at St. Alban's, we shall see that, though broken in upon by the sentence of suspension for three years under the Public Worship Regulation Act in 1878, there was a period of comparative peace. In January 1880 Mr. Mackonochie thankfully records the fact that since the preceding Advent Sunday ' St. Alban's has been a parish without a history.' It was in the September of this year that Father Lowder died, and he writes :

You will have seen the accounts of dear Lowder's funeral. It was most striking, when compared with twenty-five years since, to see the patient crowd on each side lining the way, many in tears, some audibly praying for the rest of his soul, while a long, slow procession of surpliced clergy and weeping parishioners first met the body at Old Gravel Bridge, conducted it to the church, after service again escorted it to the bridge, and returned at the same slow processional pace to the church. Traffic, of course, was stopped, but all was most reverent and respectful. The scene at Chislehurst was almost equally striking, as we walked across the great common amid throngs of people and stood in the crowded churchyard. Clergy of all schools of thought came to show their respect for the man whom they were obliged to look up to, though they differed from him.

It was in the August of this year that he had paid his first and last visit to America. Landing at New York, he subsequently, in the course of a few weeks, visited Philadelphia, Baltimore, Washington, the mountain region of Wyoming Valley, and Niagara. He preached three times on one day in Toronto, and spent a Sunday at Montreal. He was much struck with the country, but still more interested in the people, and both at New York and at Boston spent a great part of his time in the poorest quarters, asking eager questions of those best able to give him information about social and political matters, the various charitable institutions, and the condition of the people ; whilst upon his side he was perfectly ready to speak with absolute openness about his own views and work, the state of things in the Church of England, and the position of religious parties. His practical insight was, perhaps, what struck those who 'interviewed' him most forcibly. As a correspondent of the ' Boston Herald ' remarked, ' He is a champion apostle of the practical element in modern Christianity.'

This practical element in his character was no doubt as strong as ever ; but during his last years at St. Alban's he had less and less to do individually with the details of parochial work. Not only was he to a great extent relieved from the mechanical duties which are a necessary part of all pioneer labour, but he had no longer to contend with harassing and distracting questions arising from perpetual lawsuits. He was already permitted to see some result not only of his work, but of the battle which he had been fighting. For the time it seemed as if an honourable truce might lead to a lasting peace. Others, it is true, were as yet fighting the same battle at an apparent disadvantage, and their losses had been heavy ; but, though an outpost might be lost here and there, there had been a steady and general advance along the line. Those who might possibly have blamed him for extreme opinions or precipitate action were unconsciously reaping the result of the bold enunciation of long-forgotten truths and the uncompromising attitude which he had adopted. All over the country—in the midst of the dense populations of manufacturing towns, in London itself, and in remote country villages—open churches, frequent Eucharists, reverent ritual and increasing congregations, were all testifying to the revival which had taken place since first the old Tractarian leaders pleaded as for high privileges hardly to be allowed, for daily services and weekly Communions. And it was with sincere and sympathetic pleasure that the Vicar of St. Alban's marked every sign of progress.

There was not only hope for the future, but there was much to be thankful for in the present and satisfaction in retrospect. Naturally sanguine, his hopes for the Church of England were based upon a foundation of faith too sure to be shaken by temporary discouragements or individual reverses. The history of the past thirty or forty years was, moreover, the surest guarantee of ultimate success. It was in July 1876 that he wrote :

God works out His own work in truth and power, but through the weak and wavering agency of fallible humanity. The mind that is bent upon an unerring regularity and an infallible certainty will not find it either in God's ruling of the universe or in His dealings with His Church. . . . Young people find it so hard to be patient. We who have lived through the marvellous revival, of which we can remember more than forty years, have in it a testimony to the abiding and active energy of the Holy Ghost in this Church of England which they cannot have. Every wave is to them—as to children—a terror, whereas to us it is a token that the Spirit of God breathes upon the water and causes those waves which are carrying forward the Church to her final haven.

It was upon this confidence that he rested in times of trial or moments of despondency. Yet it never led him to be either mentally or spiritually inactive. The work was to be done because it was God's alone, the battle which He had already won was to be fought out. There was no new creed to be accepted, no new ritual to be enforced ; no desire to establish an unelastic uniformity and shut out from the pale all who declined to conform to it ; the contention was simply for the Church's rights and Christian liberty.

> For whom the truth makes free
> Sacred as law itself is lawful liberty.

CHAPTER XIII.

Religious aspect of Mr. Mackonochie's work—Spiritual letters—Dealings
with the young—Thoughts upon death.

1875—1882 (*continued*).

WE have said that Mr. Mackonochie's life during these
last years at St. Alban's was neither pre-eminently parochial nor controversial. Not only in its motive power,
but in its ordinary everyday occupations it had become of
an almost exclusively religious character. No doubt 'the
ideals of conduct require,' as it has been said, ' to be constantly reasserted and applied with renewed earnestness
to the individual, social, political, and religious life of mankind ;' but it was with the individual and religious life that
he was chiefly concerned.

He had not the breadth of vision which with a sort of
prophetic instinct sees the influence of extraneous elements
upon the one object in view, and instinctively recognises
the almost invisible links which make the interests of the
individual inseparable from those of the community. He
may almost be said to have had no theories ; no schemes
of widespreading social or legislative reform. When he
had dealt with these questions at all it had been in a practical manner ; and from the beginning he had been chiefly
concerned about the highest interests of his people. From

the day of its consecration the Church had been the centre of the work at St. Alban's, and the mission of the Church is evangelistic. It was no question of civil rights, of temporary alleviations, or mere philanthropy. The Apostles of the Redemption must of necessity be lovers of men, not merely of mankind in the abstract, but of each separate soul, and their work is consequently of an essentially personal character.

No doubt this is more especially the case with those who by reason of their office, and with a full appreciation of its obligations, are constantly becoming acquainted with the sins, temptations, and deeper spiritual necessities of their people ; and, as time went on, it was inevitable that Mr. Mackonochie should be more and more engrossed in ministering to persons who came under his own immediate influence or voluntarily sought his help. From the first he had had the power of inspiring confidence in those who were absolute strangers to him : and now, after more than twenty years at St. Alban's, and after holding numberless missions and retreats, the large and varied experience which he had gained in dealing with all classes of people and with all sorts of mental or spiritual difficulties had naturally led many who had no connection with his church or parish to seek his ministrations. Every week he was occupied in hearing confessions in his own church for many hours, irrespective of his work at St. Saviour's Priory, whilst he may be said to have been almost always at the command of those who sought his help ; sacrificing his time and convenience without hesitation to claims which were often unreasonable or inconsiderate.

His correspondence was large, but mostly not of a character for publication. His letters were, as a rule, short, very much to the point, and frequently only of interest to the person addressed. Their very brevity and decisiveness is, however, characteristic, and amongst those entrusted to us we have selected the following as specially illustrating the intimate connection which existed in his own mind between spiritual insight and moral sensitiveness ; the 'absolute harmony of inward desire with outward obligation,' in fact, the influence of unseen things upon the ordinary circumstances of every-day life.

'*On a first Confession.*' October 24, 1878. A first confession, especially if made when any one has reached your age, is a great point in the spiritual life. It looks both backwards and forwards. Looking backwards it gathers up the works of the 'Old Adam' in us and forces them to appear in judgment before the great Judge of all the world ; not merely with the object of forgiveness, and the varying of these old works ; but even more for their expulsion, and for a fresh gift of strength from God to lead a life free from them. Looking forward it faces the long battle of life, pledges the soul to perseverance through the Blood of the Lamb of God and the Anointing of the Holy Ghost, and then presents to the soul the last confession, which we hope to make calmly, quietly, resolutely, once more of our whole life, when the shell of this world's existence is going to break and the true life to shine from within us.

Remember specially these things :

(1) You cannot get the benefit of this great Sacrament, except in the Power and Anointing of the Holy Ghost. Our Saviour was Incarnate, was baptized, was tempted and conquered, was agonized in His Passion, was crucified, died, rose, ascended— is enthroned in Heaven, all by the anointing of the Holy Ghost. He is emphatically *the Christ*, i.e. the Anointed. And we too are

what we are, *Christ's* anointed ones in Him. Therefore prepare in the power of the Anointing of the Holy Ghost ; make your confession in that Power, receive Absolution, and do your penance in the same Power.   Remember

(2) That in Absolution the Holy Ghost not only washes your soul in the Blood of the Lamb, but in the same Blood promises to you special gifts of strength for future battles, first against fresh temptations to the old sins, and then against any other temptations by which the devil may assail you.

(3) Remember, not as an oppressing thought, but as one full of joy and satisfaction, that those about us have a right to expect visible results (I do not mean instantaneous) from habitual confession.   They have a right to see habitual faults giving way, especially any by which we observe that we give offence to others as well as to God.

(4) Remember that your Communions are the seal of the confession.   Therefore be specially careful to keep the grace of the Absolution intact as far as possible, till after your Communion. . . .

(5) Remember that we each have an inner life in which we are already by baptism, in a literal sense, dead, buried, risen, ascended, seated at the Right Hand of God. . . . Read Ephesians iii. 21, and see what is the work which God is seeking to carry out in us, and how He is not satisfied till He has completed it by our being filled with all the Fulness of God—literally filled *even up to* all the Fulness of God.   It is this inner life which will eventually shine forth gloriously from *within us*, as the Christ-life in the manifestation of the sons of God.

How habitual and intense his own realisation of that inner life was is apparent in all his letters upon religious subjects.   Often commonplace, always unargumentative, there is a direct truthfulness of feeling and expression which could only proceed from a pure and simple nature, living in intimate communion with God.   Take, for instance, the following, written in a time of great anxiety in answer to some remonstrances as to the line of conduct which he thought it right to pursue :

April 10, 1885.

I am not going to write much. I see the force of all you say, if there was not something else to be said.

We are not put into this world to find our life but to lose it. This is the very foundation of Our Lord's Kingdom and also His plain teaching . . . our gift is the cross. God lived and died in misery—not to make us comfortable but that we should live His Life in ourselves, as far as we can in this world, and then be seated on His Throne for ever in Heaven. I do not think there is one promise in the Gospel that we shall be *happy* in this world— it is impossible, this world is under the curse, and our Baptismal life, the life which we are called upon to live, is a life in a hostile country. . . . From the Beatitudes to the end of Revelation you find no other promise for *time*. But what for eternity ! What will not have been secured by Christ for us if we will enter into His Sorrows, and abide in them with joy in this world ; when He shall come with His 'Come, thou good and faithful servant, enter thou into the joy of Thy Lord.' . . . If soldiers of earth can give up their lives—perhaps without a hope for the next world—in obedience and enthusiasm for a human leader ; what ought we not to be ready to do and to suffer when led by the King of Kings?

Again on Easter Day, 1882, he writes :

This of all the great seasons is the one in which all can join because it is the festival of the Eternal joy. Others in some way think of earth ; but the day on which the Saviour conquered death and made life the trading time for heaven—in which the more we lose of the interests of the dying earth, the more we may gain of the land which is very far off—speaks only of things certain, founded upon the Kingdom of the risen Lord,

And yet this spirit of almost instinctive detachment, this constant looking beyond the horizon of this present world, never made him lose interest in the ordinary joys and sorrows, cares and pleasures which in any way affected other people's lives. In times of sickness or bereavement he would enter into every circumstance of the case with the most sympathetic appreciation of its special trials, being always particularly anxious that physical weakness or depression should not be confounded with spiritual failings.

I am very sorry indeed that you have that terrible cloud hanging over you (he writes to one of his spiritual children). Still I can but tell you the truth : that it is more closely allied to the *back* than anything else. I would gladly say otherwise, because it would be easier to prescribe spiritual remedies than to give hope out of bodily ailments, when they take this very common, though most trying form. . . . Try to commit thy way unto the Lord. . . . The darkness is His first, yours only in a shadow.

Here again is a practical answer to some questions which had been addressed to him on the subject of vocation :

The objections and the answers rest on the same mistake. Sisters are not angels. . . . They take into the cloister the flesh and blood and the same imperfect interior that they had in the world. In the cloister they find a rule, a habit of devotion and other things which help them; and a far harder assault of the devil than they ever had in the world. If they have chosen their vocation rightly, they will on the whole serve God better in religion than out of it, but still with many things which hastily judged may cause scandal to outsiders. If they have not chosen their vocation rightly, the issue may be a terrible downfall, and will certainly be a fierce struggle. An outward call does not mean a person being without a happy home, and driven to a convent for sympathy. A vocation might possibly arise under such circumstances, but would need to be very carefully sifted. If God calls you into religion you ought to go, but if He does not, it is certain (not probable only) that you can serve Him much better out than in. It is also most certain that you ought not to seek such a life from cowardice. There are some to whom God has not given strength for the struggles of the world ; these might seek a convent, not from cowardice, but as one catches at a post to avoid falling. Excuse this hasty reply. I do not like to delay longer, and think this really covers the whole ground.

Here is another letter to one troubled about the apparent and visible triumph of evil :

The hypothesis is not true. It is not true that x bad men can do more harm than x good men can do good. They seem to be able to do so, because the evil which already lies dormant in a man's nature is a much more active and volatile principle than the good, so that converts to evil are commonly made much more rapidly than converts to good, but then the evil to which they are converted has no real foundation to stand upon, and is therefore only upheld by the powers of evil. If they are withdrawn for a moment the edifice falls, and the spot is again clear for God to work upon. The point where you went astray was in not seeing from the first that the evil man is just as much under the power of God as the evil spirit, but God all the time keeps the ordering and governing of their devices in His own Hand. Hence neither one nor the other can tempt a man more than that man is able to bear, or afflict a man more than is good for him, or do anything which shall not in the end turn to the great increase of sanctity and the glory of God. Many things tend to give a false appearance to the power of evil, but this is the truth. One thing is the great difference in the way in which God and Satan work. God never enslaves a man's will. The will is God's own Image and too noble for Him to wish to enslave it. The moment it is enslaved it is destroyed. God's work is to set it free ; to open its eyes to show it the beauty of the things of God, and to strengthen it to act according to the right reason with which He has endued it. In proportion as God's work succeeds, the will sees the nothingness of its own manhood, and on the other hand the infinite goodness and attractiveness of God. It therefore abhors itself and willingly enslaves itself to the Will of God. This is the slavery of which St. Paul speaks, which is perfect freedom.

What strikes one perhaps most forcibly in so many of these letters is the tone of absolute and unhesitating confidence ; a confidence more active and buoyant than resignation, which not only touches the present, but reaches onward to the future, and interprets the past. It had always been his safeguard in moments of success, and his support in failure.

Those who work honestly for God, to the best of their power (he wrote to an elementary teacher) may not produce the best result, but the work will be true and thorough, full of life and hope, and will receive God's blessing—will accomplish the work whereto He sends. This work which God does through our work is not always such as can be written down in statistical returns or class lists.

Here again is a letter of practical advice to some one in a difficulty about obtaining ordinary means of grace :

We must be satisfied with what God gives us—it is to us our 'daily bread,' or, as the Greek word most likely means, our *sufficient* bread. . . . What you say about the difficulties, about manner in church, &c., is quite true ; but I think the need of self-restraint in such things in certain places is good for us. It helps us to see that such things are matters of reverence dependent upon circumstances, not necessaries for the protection of interior reverence.

You will, I think, value them the more for the having to give them up for a time, especially if you can be careful to make them (as it were) inwardly in thought and intention.

In September 1879 we find a letter of advice of another kind, its tone of decision upon the one point in question, irrespective of minor considerations, illustrating at once his own temper of mind, and also what he understood by ' counsel " in the theological sense of the word.

My dear child,—My advice is not to read *non*-Christian books. Such are not simply non-Christian, but un-Christian. Christianity is the revelation of God and admits no rival. The theory of non-Christianity is that against which Christianity has from the first had to contend. The world was perfectly ready to accept Christ, provided He would have allowed non-Christianity to live alongside of Him.

Do not let yourself be deluded by the sophistry that ' one's religion cannot be worth much if one cannot read a book by a non-Christian.' You might as well say that one's constitution cannot be worth much if one cannot take poison. Of course, the Faith would not be worth much if it could not be tested, but it is not every one that is called of God to test it. The principles of physic, surgery, law, mechanics, &c., would be worthless if they would not bear testing, but it does not follow that every one is called to test them. Avoid non-Christianity in all its forms. Strengthen your spiritual intellect by the positive study of Christianity, and you will find no difficulty in throwing off its opposite. You may not be always able to give a scientific answer to every objection—though the Christian instinct will seldom fail even in that—but you will feel that it is, what it calls itself, non-Christian, and therefore false. Keep as much as possible aloof from people who are non-Christian, and remember that when with them you are sent to them from Christ, that your life and patent loyalty to your Master may be His witness to them. He does not want you to be a skilful fencer in the school of polemics, but a manifestly devoted Christian in the school of Christ.

The letters which follow are addressed to young people or to children, and, as we have seen, though fond of children, his very reverence for their innocence and simplicity generated a sort of constraint, whilst in teaching he undoubtedly expected too much from their restless bodies and volatile spirits. But it was altogether different in his dealings with the individual child. His brother's children looked forward to his visits as the happiest times in their lives; to them he was the most sympathetic of companions, entering with all possible zest into their schemes and pleasures, and it was the same with his friends' children, or indeed any with whom he was brought into direct personal contact. They shared the confidence which their elders reposed in him, and showed it with all the simplicity of their age. A Sister tells how she one day observed two little girls waiting for a long time patiently in the part of the church where he was hearing confessions, and at last, perplexed at the businesslike aspect of these very small penitents, she asked them what they wanted. 'They were waiting,' they answered, 'for Father Mackonochie;' and then in reply to further inquiries they confidentially disclosed their further object—'They wanted to see Father Mackonochie to show him their new dollies!' It is a trifling incident enough, yet not without its significance; and here is a note to a small godchild, written in large hand, which bears upon the same point:

Mind you must be a good little governess to yourself. Whenever self wants to play at wrong times or do things which are not allowed, you must put her in the corner of your own little heart, which is self's own room, until she is good again, and then you will save other people the trouble of keeping you in order.

God bless you.   In Him, your affectionate godfather,

A. H. M.

Love is no doubt in its right place in the heart of any one (he wrote again), but if it has an earthly throne it is the child's heart.

And with tender vigilance he guarded it, lest by careless handling it should be rashly profaned.

Thirteen years old ! (he wrote in February 1876 to one of his little nieces). What a sage person both in the French and English sense you ought to be ! Thirteen years of Christian life and more than one of communicant life are a great treasure to have to thank God for ; and like so many talents have to multiply in the use of them. So far they have been laying the foundation of the life yet to be lived—one foundation more in the Heavenly City—now they have to be built upon. Think how life with all its powers, and joys, and knowledge, and hopes, and purposes, and bright careless happiness for a child in the protecting hand of God, has grown and developed itself in these thirteen years. And then there is the future for development, and fresh joys and wider knowledge and more happiness, some perhaps as careless as the past and some other whose very essence will be its fulness of care. . . . Before you get this you will have made your birthday Communion, and I shall have remembered you in the best way I can at the altar. So many blessings upon the day, and upon all the years, be they many or few, which lie between it and the brighter eternity. God bless you in Him. Your most affectionate uncle,

ALEX. HERIOT MACKONOCHIE.

Again, on the occasion of a confirmation, he writes :

None put on the armour of the Holy Spirit without having to prove its temper . . . The enemies who seek to mar your warfare are not far off, it will be for you, in the power of the armour which you will wear, and of Him Whose it is and Who will clothe you in it, to make each conflict an occasion for learning better to handle your weapons and to keep unsullied the brightness of your robes and arms. Jesus Christ the same yesterday, to-day, and for ever will be your watchword and your strength; study and learn Him in your Bible, and work Him out in your life, and each day and year will fill you more and more with the bright joy of conquest. To copy Him we must rub out self. Our souls are like those old manuscripts on which once God's word was written, and men have rubbed It out to write instead some common poem. The poem of self is written upon our souls in some language or other, but it is the Word of God which lies underneath, and the words of which we are so often seeing glimpses in our prayers and holy desires. We must rub out the poem and restore the Word.

Space does not allow of many more quotations, and with some extracts from letters to an older person upon the subject of death we must close the chapter.

The ministering to the bodies of the departed is most painful and most blessed. There is such a stern reality about it. The fight is over and God has recalled the spirit to His Own Presence, whence it came forth to earth, and the earth is claiming its own. We see ourselves as we shall soon be. . . . Then the last struggles, however faint, tell one of the mortal part of our being in terrible conflict with the invisible enemy. We see the instinct which God has implanted—that which is simply mortal refusing as it were to die . . . There is no haste, each struggle seems to end in the triumph of the victim, but each ends in the firmer closing in of the arms of the enemy—then the last drop of life is sucked out and death has conquered. But all this makes one ask, is this all? and the glorious words ring in one's ears, From death to life; from sorrow to joy; from a vale of misery to a Paradise of mercy. The house has fallen to pieces, but the inhabitant is first sheltered in the courts of his Father's Palace. Then the mystery of the unseen world. What is the vision of the soul now? Has it seen Jesus? How has it borne that awful moment —the first of true and unclouded knowledge of Jesus and of herself. Has he seen those of his own friends who have gone before him? What has been the face of his guardian angel? Has he seen the sweet face of Blessed Mary? Till at last our own soul finds rest only in the profession of its own faith.

> Simply to His Grace and only
>   Light and life and power belong ;
> And I love supremely solely
>   Him the Holy, Him the Strong.

And again ; you will naturally be turning your thoughts mostly to him who is keeping his first Sunday on the other side of Jordan. It is so hard to realise the strangeness of new revelations in that world which is so near and seems so far off from this in which we live. And it always seems that when God has taught any one so little as He seems to have your brother, that the beatific vision must be something so infinitely more startling than to those who have realised it ever so little in this life. It seems so no doubt, and yet perhaps it is not. I often think in those lives which seem to be left so much to themselves and the light of nature there may be manifold operations of the Holy Spirit working out the implanted life of Christ in ways none the less real though unseen by us and perhaps realised by him. Then the passage through the veil would be a marvellous opening out of instincts, suggestions, hopes, of movements of the soul hitherto unintelligible ; it would be a reading into sense of voices heard in the soul but as yet not comprehended, an interpreting, in fact, of the enigmas of life.

There is something remarkable about the absolute truthfulness of tone upon a subject around which so many tender fictions have naturally twined themselves. There is no suggestion of any false comfort to the mourner. The separation is a stern reality, and death is terrible ; and faith, though it shines upon the mysteries beyond, fails to solve them. Here by the grave-side, if anywhere, he must be true. His earthly life is drawing to a close, but no familiarity has deadened his sense of reverence, and the great secrets with which he is so soon to become acquainted are as full of awe for him as ever.

CHAPTER XIV.

St. Alban's parish in 1882—Renewed prosecution—Correspondence with
Archbishop Tait—Mr. Mackonochie's motives—His resignation—Letters
from Dean Church and the Bishop of London—Meeting of parishioners—
Farewell sermon at St. Alban's.

1882.

TWENTY years had elapsed since the first Mission service
had been held in the newly-formed district of St. Alban's,
Holborn, awakening, as it would have seemed, but a transitory and half-indifferent interest in the minds of its inhabitants; but since those early days, in spite of many
drawbacks and disappointments, much had been accomplished.   The contrast between St. Alban's in 1862 and in
1882 was marked, and such as to strike even the most
superficial observer.   Even in material matters there had
been a great advance.   Many old courts and dilapidated
tenement houses had been pulled down, giving place to
widened streets and model lodging-houses.   There were
large parochial schools held in commodious buildings with
an annual expenditure of 1,383*l.*   The church offerings,
inclusive of special subscriptions for church purposes, were
over 1,000*l.* a year.   There were numberless organisations
for teaching every section of the population.   A Recreation
society, cricket and swimming clubs, night schools, guilds

for men and women, girls and boys. The Perseverance
Association, for keeping together the boy and girl communicants upon their leaving the Sunday schools, having as
its aim 'to pilot them through a difficult period of life,
and keep them together in a simple bond of good living.'
The Church of England Working Men's Society and the
English Church Union had each branches in connection
with St. Alban's ; nor were efforts wanting to reach those
not immediately connected with the parish. Already, in
1877, Mr. Stanton had started St. Martin's League for
men employed in the Post Office. About fifty sorters and
letter-carriers joined it at the inaugural service, and since
then it has year by year increased and prospered until there
are now over 700 men upon its roll. It was in this year
also that a series of lectures to men on science and literature
were started in one of the schoolrooms after the Sunday
evening service, and proved a decided success, attracting
an average audience of about a hundred. In 1882 Mr.
Mackonochie, in giving his usual report, was able to speak
of the satisfactory state of the various organisations, and
observe upon the bright outlook for the future.

It was in this year that Mr. Hubbard ceased to be
patron of the living, handing over all the property which
he had in the church and its surroundings to the Dean and
Chapter of St. Paul's.

It might have seemed that now at last peace might be
expected. The various prosecutions had been singularly
fruitless of results. Even those most opposed to the
church and parish were forced to acknowledge that whilst
the latter was not neglected, the former had attracted a

large and united congregation, whose only desire was to
be let alone.   But it was not to be.

In the spring of 1882 the irrepressible Church Association prepared a fresh lawsuit, with a view to enforcing Mr.
Mackonochie's deprivation.   This was a result which Mr.
Martin, the original promoter, had especially deprecated ;
but it had become apparent that nothing less would satisfy
those who now for the last fifteen years had been relent-
lessly prosecuting him.

It was on March 3 of this year that, being brought
before the Royal Commission, he wrote to his brother :

As to yesterday it was very interesting.   The questioners
were the Archbishop of Canterbury in chief, the Bishops of
Winchester and Oxford, and one or two side questions from people
I did not know.   One was Sir Richard Cross, but I only knew
that from some one saying, 'You answered Sir R. Cross so
and so . . . York was not there, nor did I see any one who
looked like Coleridge.   The Archbishop tried hard to get me to
accept the spiritual validity of Lord Penzance.   He pressed that,
as the two Archbishops had agreed to appoint him, his jurisdiction was valid, although the Act might be a bad one.   We went
into Disestablishment and to remedies short of it.   Also they tried
to push me into allowing that if all jurisdiction of courts had been
got rid of, the personal jurisdiction of the Bishop revived.   I had
a hard fight with Winchester over that.   As remedy short of disestablishment I gave free election of Bishops by the whole
Episcopate, subject to a vote of either the clergy or the lay
communicants of the diocese.   This, I believe, is the ancient state
of things.   They asked me how long I thought this lapse dated
from, and I said Constantine.   They thought this a long time,
but I said I could not help that—it was not my doing !

Matters were at a deadlock.   It was perfectly clear

that Mr. Mackonochie had no intention of receding an inch from the position which he had deliberately adopted. Every possible argument, threat, and means of persuasion had been tried, and tried in vain. During these past years of enforced warfare, with all their consequent suffering and weariness of spirit, his courage had never deserted him, and practically, in spite of adverse judgments and condemnations, his position was stronger than it had been at the beginning.

With a general desire for peace upon both sides there seemed little prospect of it so long as one section of the army was obstinately bent upon the prolongation of the contest. No doubt the vast majority of what has been called the Evangelical party in the Church of England had ceased to desire a temporary triumph, if it were only to be achieved at the cost of ultimate disruption ; but the Church Association was pledged to fight to the last. Its promoters were slow to perceive that victory might be too dearly purchased. The Public Worship Act once put in motion was like a destructive engine over which its originators had lost control, and which could not easily be arrested. Its very approach was to have struck terror and cleared the course ; it had not been anticipated that so many would have thrown themselves directly in its way.

There was one person upon whom the state of affairs weighed very heavily, and that person was the Archbishop. He was not only conscious of the importance of the crisis, but he felt very strongly the pressure of personal responsibility. He was well aware that his time for dealing with these and all the other vexed questions of the day was drawing to a close.   As the 'Spectator' justly remarked :

Smaller and weaker men than the Archbishop would have tried to forget these prosecutions. . . . He would have pleased himself with the recollection that Ritualist controversies might fairly be handed on to his successor, and that in his state of health he was no longer bound to set right with his own hand mistakes which had been honestly made.   The Archbishop did not so read his duty.   Sickness only quickened his desire to undo his own error, and in the feebleness of approaching death that desire possessed him more and more.

Hence there arose the following correspondence between him and Mr. Mackonochie, of which the first letter was from the Primate :

Addington Park, Croydon,
November 10, 1882.

My dear Mr. Mackonochie,—My thoughts, so far as I am able at present to give steady thought to public matters, have naturally dwelt much upon the troubles and difficulties which have made themselves apparent in connection with recent ritual prosecutions. I am exceedingly anxious that the result of the Royal Commission on Ecclesiastical Courts should, by the blessing of Almighty God, be such as to allay disquiet, and by meeting any reasonable objections to existing procedure, to set men's minds free for the pressing duties which devolve upon the Church in the face of prevailing sin and unbelief. Anything which at this moment increases bitterness of feeling may do permanent mischief to the cause which we all have at heart. Anything which tends to preserve peace now will make a satisfactory solution of our difficulties far easier. I venture, therefore, privately to write to you, though I cannot yet do so with my own hand, to invite you seriously to consider whether you can in any way minimise the present feeling of bitterness which undoubtedly exists in some quarters.

I need not assure you that I do not wish in any way to dictate to you a course of action, but if you feel it possible, consistently with duty, to withdraw voluntarily by resignation of your benefice from further conflicts with the courts, I am quite sure you would be acting in the manner best calculated to promote the real power and usefulness of the Church to which we belong. I make this appeal to you under a strong sense of responsibility. You will, I think, feel with me that the circumstances under which I write are altogether exceptional, and you will, I know, give prayerful thought to the subject. I commend you to the guidance of Almighty God, and ask that He may give to us in these difficult times a right judgment in all things.

I remain yours very truly,
A. C. CANTUAR.

To this letter Mr. Mackonochie at once returned the following reply :

St. Alban's Clergy House, Brooke Street, Holborn,
November 11, 1882.

My dear Lord Archbishop,—Your kind letter of yesterday reached me last night. Your Grace will understand that in a matter of so deep importance I shall not answer definitely without that time for earnest seeking after the guidance of Almighty God to which you refer me, although, indeed, your Grace will not doubt that I have endeavoured to gain it and to act upon it throughout the troubled circumstances of the last sixteen years. It is a great regret to me that any of my concerns should be adding to the pressure of your Grace's anxieties under the severe illness which our Lord has sent to you. Therefore my final answer shall reach your Grace with as little delay as possible.

With earnest prayer for your Grace's restoration to health,
Believe me, my dear Lord Archbishop,
Yours truly and very respectfully,
ALEX. HERIOT MACKONOCHIE.

It was true that on all accounts he was most anxious that the time of suspense should not be prolonged. His own mind was one to arrive at a conclusion rapidly. There was not the haste of impatience, but rather a sort of instinctive desire to bring an argument to its legitimate conclusion and to convert thought into action. Moreover, the appeal addressed to him came from a dying man. The Archbishop had said that he could not yet write with his own hand ; Mr. Mackonochie well knew that he would in all human probability never write again, and in the Archbishop's weakness his anxiety for an answer gathered strength, until his son-in-law, Mr. Davidson, felt constrained to write :

I think it only right to tell you that among the very few matters concerning the outside world which at present find a recurring place in his [the Archbishop's] thoughts, and in his conversations with me, is the private correspondence on which he has entered with you. I tell you this merely in case you should suppose from the doctor's bulletin that the Archbishop is at present too ill to receive any letters. It is not quite so, and he asks me every day if there is any letter for him from you. I am sure you will not misinterpret this letter. It is merely intended with the utmost respect to relieve you of any doubt you may be feeling as to whether you would be justified in writing at present to the Archbishop should you find it possible to do so.

It was in answer to this that Mr. Mackonochie at once promised to send a speedy and definite reply. No great time had elapsed ; it will be remembered that the Archbishop's first letter was dated November 10, and this was only the 21st ; but, as Mr. Mackonochie said, it had been ' much on his mind ' not to have answered sooner, fearing delay might have been causing the Archbishop anxiety; anxiety in his own case also being probably even harder to bear than the full force of the blow which he already believed to be almost inevitable.

But yet he had not acted unadvisedly. As usual, he had referred the matter to his own court of appeal—that supreme tribunal of conscience whose decrees he had never as yet put aside, from motives of expediency or in deference to the adverse verdict of the world. He had from the first found his own mind tending in one direction, and felt that the responsibility of a final decision must rest with him; but he did not oppose the general wish that a meeting of the clergy should be convened to take counsel with him upon a question in which so many interests were involved. It was immediately after this meeting that in a letter dated November 23, 1882, he wrote:

The meeting which I was asked to wait for did not help much . . . it was opposed for the most part to my own convictions; and yet with me it is immensely difficult to decide. The illness of the Archbishop and the tone of his letter as if from his grave has certainly weighed mostly with me; which perhaps is hardly right, as even the most pressing personal considerations have to give way before the public interests of the Church. However, I suppose I have determined to comply with the Archbishop's request. It seems to be God's will. I do believe I am quite indifferent personally. Indeed personally the line I am taking is a certain loss—not in money perhaps, but in leaving this place . . . Whatever happens, my leaving this will be, at first at any rate, set down as a victory for our enemies, both by friends and foes. I feel myself a little like Rehoboam, between his father's counsellors and his own, with the exception that I am following the elder counsellors and he the younger . . . I have promised to send off my letter to the Archbishop not later than to-morrow, so that the suspense will not be much longer.

As we read the short note we experience a momentary surprise. For the first time there is an expression of fear lest his heart should play the traitor to his conscience. But what are these pressing personal considerations which might, in his opinion, unduly affect his judgment? They have nothing to do with the question of individual loss or gain, they do not even touch upon the personal aspect of the sacrifice, the severance of old ties, the bitterness of parting, the apparent acknowledgment of failure. He notes these indeed, and they must have been vividly present to his mind; but, just to himself as to others, he sees no danger lest they should outweigh weightier considerations. With absolute unselfishness he is preoccupied with the sick Archbishop, and is conscious of a strong and almost exclusive desire to afford him consolation, which for the time casts a shadow of doubt upon the grounds upon which he had arrived at a conclusion. But such a doubt could be only transitory. And now he had taken counsel with his brethren, and his first determination remained un-altered, and on the evening of the same day upon which he had written the preceding note he wrote as follows to the Archbishop :

St. Alban's Clergy House, Brooke Street,
November 23, 1882.

My dear Lord Archbishop,—I am sorry to have been obliged to add to your Grace's anxiety by a less speedy reply to your letter than I could have desired.

The subject of your letter has, I think, rarely been out of my mind since I received it, except when at times driven out by the press of active work.

The conclusion at which I have arrived is to acquiesce in you Grace's wish that I should resign my benefice. You will understand that it is to myself and will be to my people a great sorrow, but one which I hope we shall be willing to bear, if the true peace and liberty of the Church can be obtained by my compliance.

My life hitherto, since my ordination, has had for its object the seeking of those gifts for the Church, and I am contented, if so it be, to give up my peace for this.

Your Grace will, I am sure, understand that I cannot in this matter act otherwise than with that obedience to my conscience to which you refer me, so that you will not think that I have changed my conviction as to the State Courts. I accept the line of action which your Grace has indicated simply in deference to you as supreme representative of Our Lord Jesus Christ in all things spiritual in this land ; and not as withdrawing anything I have said or done in regard to those Courts. This I cannot agree to in any way whatever.

No one can deny that the bitterness which your Grace would abate is altogether an exceptional circumstance, giving rise to exceptional remedies to avert, if it may be, by the Goodness of God, ruin from His Church ; and leaving her free for the future discharge of her great mission, at home and in foreign lands. For myself I hope I may depend upon your Grace's good offices with the Bishop of London, so that I may be licensed or instituted at once to whatever work in the diocese may offer itself to me. Thanking your Grace for your commendation of me to the guidance of Almighty God, and with my own unworthy prayers for your Grace in all your sickness, believe me, my dear Lord Archbishop, yours truly and very respectfully,

ALEX. HERIOT MACKONOCHIE.

Mr. Davidson replies on November 25 :

I am directed by the Archbishop of Canterbury to express to you with how strong a feeling of thankfulness to God he has received your letter of the 23rd inst. . . . . It will, I feel sure, be a satisfaction to know what pleasure your letter has brought to the Archbishop in these, his last days, as it would seem, upon earth.

That satisfaction was not, and could not in the nature of things, be unalloyed. The sacrifice was ungrudgingly made, but it was impossible not to feel a deep regret for the disastrous and irremediable line of action which had rendered it necessary. Even Mr. Mackonochie's most inveterate enemies must have felt it was but a poor triumph to deprive a united parish and congregation of a Vicar who now for the last twenty years had, in the teeth of a vigorous and relentless opposition, been striving with an absolute disregard of personal considerations to vindicate what he believed to be the truth. And in fact, when looked at, not only from the vantage ground of Ritualism, but from the points of view of the dispassionate lay spectator, it was clear that the great engine of his adversaries, the Public Worship Act, from which they had expected so much, had, as the 'Saturday Review' remarked, received , its fatal shock from the Archbishop's deathbed,' and the proceedings connected with Mr. Mackonochie's resignation were 'a moral condemnation from which it could never recover.'

Not only had the Archbishop himself signed, as it were, that moral condemnation, as the first article of the conditions of peace, but the Bishop of London had at once shown an anxious desire to lend his aid to insure their permanence.

On November 25 he had received the following letter from the Archbishop :

My dear Bishop of London,—I enclose to you a copy of a correspondence that has passed between Mr. Mackonochie and myself. I have of course in no way committed you by the action I have thought it well to take in the interests of peace. It appears to me a great blessing that a gate of reconciliation should have been opened by Mr. Mackonochie's willingness to resign. He has of course, in coming to this decision, had great difficulties to contend with from the advice of his friends ; and it seems to me that he has in this case shown his consideration for the highest interests of the Church by sacrificing his own individual feelings in deference to my appeal.

I remain, &c.,

A. C. CANTUAR.

And Bishop Jackson's letter to Mr. Mackonochie upon the receipt of his formal resignation is conceived in the same appreciative and generous spirit :

Fulham Palace, S.W.,
December 5, 1882.

Dear Mr. Mackonochie,—I did not write to you on Saturday when I accepted your resignation, because I understood from Mr. Lee that I was about to hear from you ; but having read, as you are aware, the affecting correspondence between the dying Archbishop and yourself—so honourable to both—I wish to be allowed to express my satisfaction with the conclusion at which you arrived, and my appreciation of the motives which led you to it. I can well understand the difficulties of your position, which must have been great and perplexing, and only to be met by courage of the true stamp and under a firm sense of duty. God grant that it may tend to the Church's peace ! I have never ceased, I can say in all sincerity, to value your own worth or that of your work ; and I venture to hope that under altered circum-

S

stances those strained relations may be relaxed which arise so readily between those whose duty it is to administer the law and those who consider themselves unable in conscience to observe it.

Believe me to be very faithfully yours,

J. LONDON.

In a brief reply, Mr. Mackonochie touches once more upon the motives by which he had been actuated.

I felt it impossible (he writes) to refuse acquiescence to such a letter as the most Christian and touching one of the Archbishop, carrying with it the gravity of his Grace's spiritual position, the emphasis of his approaching departure to his rest, the very exceptional circumstances of the present condition of the Church, and the generous consideration with which he urged upon me the line which seemed to him to be my duty.

And already, on December 1, he had written to the Archbishop :

Your Grace will, I think, like to know that I have to-day formally resigned this benefice. . . . I shall probably be nominated to the benefice of St. Peter's, London Docks, from which Mr. Suckling will be transferred to St. Alban's. Allow me to express at this time my deep gratitude for your Grace's kindness and generous consideration towards me ever since the time that I entered the diocese of London in 1858 ; and that often in critical circumstances.

And thus the correspondence closes. The act was accomplished, the resignation was accepted, and he was no longer Vicar of St. Alban's.

This, then, was to be the end of the protracted struggle. Each side might claim the victory. Yet it would be well to remember that the voluntary withdrawal of a leader by no means involves capitulation. He left St. Alban's in order that the truth which he had so perseveringly taught might still be proclaimed there, and that the congregation which he had built up might not be scattered, but might still worship there in peace.

There were no difficulties to be met with from the patrons of the living. Already, on November 19, the Dean of St. Paul's had written :

I hope that you will believe that at any rate I sympathize much with you in your trouble.

And again on the 24th :

You will let me give you my thanks at least for the sacrifice you have made. I will do my best to bring about the arrangement which seems to you the best.

But what that arrangement might be remained doubtful. The idea of St. Peter's, London Docks, had been pressed upon Mr. Mackonochie by others. He wished to remain in his old diocese, but in some subordinate position, relieved from pressing responsibilities and at no great distance from his old parish, so that he might still be amongst his own people. He had been too long in the *mêlée* of London life to wish for retirement in the country ; but the strain had been severe, and it had told even upon his healthy frame and vigorous spirit. Worn, and mentally wearied, he would have remained at his post to the last, if he had been permitted to do so ; but he had no desire to accept a fresh command. Too careless of his health to be very observant of symptoms, he was perfectly aware that he was not what he had been. The time when he could give an equally undivided attention to parochial organisation and spiritual direction was past.   He could no longer subject himself to unusual mental or physical exertion without being made conscious of its subsequent ill effects.   Long years of overwork were telling upon him, and nature was taking her revenge.   But even now he had no thought of rest, still less of inaction ; and various circumstances had combined to make an exchange between him and Mr. Suckling appear to many whose opinion he most valued to be the easiest solution of the difficulty. He himself appears to have had no strong wishes upon the subject.   Having made the one great sacrifice, it would seem as if for himself he had nothing to wish for.   On November 24 he wrote :

Friends have been looking out about me.   The idea of an exchange between Suckling and myself has been revived.   I have seen J. B. Lee, who says that the Bishop is quite prepared to accept it *without conditions.*   Suckling is favourable, but asks for a week's consideration.   The St. Paul's people (or at least the Dean, to whom I wrote) will forward any arrangement which I suggest. If this scheme goes through it will be remarkable.

There is not a word as to personal predilections—in all probability he did not even pause to ask himself if he had any—and on December 1 he wrote :

In a few days I shall (D.V.) be Vicar of St. Peter's, London Docks.   There are certain formalities which will take up a little time, but which will be run through as soon as possible.   The case of Martin *v.* Mackonochie is at an end.

What will be the next phase of the conflict between Christ and the world remains to be seen.   There is no doubt of the truth which Monsignor Talbot is said to have propounded as the fruit of his morning's meditation, that the Spirit of Christ and the spirit of the world are diametrically opposed to each other, and therefore if this resignation brings peace for the time, war must arise from some other quarter. For the present we must be content. Of course it is a wrench to sign oneself out of St. Alban's, but it will be a counterbalancing satisfaction to take up Lowder's work.

And a few days later, December 4, he wrote that he should probably be instituted on Friday,

if it were not for the Archbishop's funeral. . . . Affairs are being kept very quiet, but I dread a *dénouement* daily. It will be a great relief when that is over.

It was no wonder that even his courageous spirit shrank from the moment when the news would have to be made known to his congregation. There had been not only the ordinary bond of union between priest and people, but it had been of unusually long standing, strengthened and cemented by every fresh assault from without, by every fresh opportunity for mutual forbearance and endurance within. Moreover, it was obvious that the step which he was taking was likely to be misunderstood by those whom it would touch most nearly.

He was very anxious to be the first to speak to them of the contemplated change ; but the secret had not been well kept. When Mr. Mackonochie found that the intelligence would be in the papers, all that he could do was to announce a meeting of the parishioners and regular congregation for the Saturday night which followed the publication of the news. 'This,' he wrote, 'will a little take off the bitter edge. I am, however, very sorry not to get the first word.'

It was a natural and legitimate regret, for if anything could have allayed bitterness and lightened the blow, it would have been to feel that it was dealt by one who would most gladly have spared them if he might, whose loss was even greater than their own.

The church, in which the meeting was held on Saturday night, was, as might have been expected, filled to over-flowing, and amongst the large congregation, with the exception of a few indifferent spectators, there was no one whose aspect and tones were so entirely free from agitation as Mr. Mackonochie's whilst he addressed them for almost the last time as Vicar of St. Alban's. Deeply moved and yet absolutely self-controlled, he stood facing his congregation whilst in forcible and temperate language he put the whole case before them.

He began by reading the correspondence which has been already given in this chapter, with perfect openness giving every detail of the proceedings, and freely explaining the motives by which he had been actuated ; and then he went on to speak of what lay so near to his heart—the past years he had spent in their midst, and all which they had meant to them and to him.

As time went on (he said) they had grown to understand one another better and to work together better, and their love had got cemented more and more . . . The great glory of Christianity was in some way or other to suffer for Christ and with Christ. Now, if by such action as he had taken there could be a little ease granted to the Church, a breathing time of peace in which Church parties might look one another in the face, and learn perhaps that their features were not so unlike one another, ought they to shrink from taking it ? He thought that they could see that many rough corners had been rubbed off, in spite of hindrances which seemed insupportable to one another, as the result of increased intercourse. Those who claimed for themselves the glorious name of 'Evangelical,' if they marvelled at the Catholic's ways which they did not understand, began a little to see that they who had received Catholic truth held Evangelical truth just as much as they did Apostolical order ; for what was Apostolical order unless it was built on Evangelical truth? . . . Of course those who had been gathered in in the infancy of that church did not like to think of a successor; but there was one Lord, one Saviour, one High Priest. Let them get out of the way of thinking about an individual priest. . . . All earthly priests, as he had told them over and over again, were nothing more nor less than the outward signs and visible instruments of their great High Priest Jesus Christ. Then let them not think for a single moment that they had lost anything because they had lost the priest who had been with them these twenty years.

Then Mr. Stanton, who had worked with him from the time of the church's consecration, spoke a few words, too, of consolation and encouragement—consolation in that though the separation must be in many respects a very real one, yet their old Vicar was not going very far off, and encouragement because the man who had been appointed in his place would carry on his work in the same spirit and on the same lines.

On the following Sunday Mr. Mackonochie preached his farewell sermon upon the text (Isaiah liii. 10): 'When thou shalt make an offering for sin, he shall see his seed, he shall prolong his days, and the pleasure of the Lord shall prosper in his hands.' The prominent thought in this, his last sermon, was the necessity and joy of sacrifice. He referred with deep thankfulness to the many blessings which, as a congregation, they had received ; to the peace vouchsafed among themselves ; to the continued presence amongst them of clergy whom they knew so well—Mr. Stanton and Mr. Russell having worked with him almost from the first, and the youngest member of the clerical staff having been with him for the last eight years, and then he commended his successor to them and said :

If Almighty God had blessed his ministry and been pleased by His Holy Spirit to shed abroad upon them grace in this church, let them return Him thanks for that grace and show their thankfulness by still worshipping at its altar. . . . It had pleased Almighty God to give them a grief—in a certain very feeble sense He had been pleased to make their souls an offering to Himself— they must bear it, they must do more—they must thank God for it.

The words had all the force of reality. He had already put them into practice, fully recognising the truth that a voluntary and ungrudging sacrifice is alone worthy of acceptance.

He had nerved himself for the inevitable trials of these last days ; the pain of natural misconstructions, the disappointment of friends, the sense of personal loss, the dreariness of a fresh beginning amongst comparative strangers, deprived of the support and companionship of his old coadjutors, and now in one sense the first bitterness was past.

On St. Stephen's Day he wrote :

Christmas Day passed off I hope well. Probably we have had a certain sense of farewell which did not at first sight brighten the angels' song ; although at the next thought it was clear that only ' Glory to God, on earth peace,' could soften the sorrow. Happily we are all behaving very well, and talking at least, if not thinking, little about it.

But those amongst whom he had lived and laboured so long would not part with him without some tangible evidence of their unalterable regard. On the following St. Alban's Day they presented him with the sum of 1,800*l.*, together with the following address :—

Rev. and dear Father in Christ,—We, the clergy, sisters, parishioners, members of the congregation, and friends of St. Alban's, in presenting you with the accompanying testimonial, desire to express our unfeigned sorrow at your departure from the parish where you have so faithfully ministered for the past twenty years. We are not unmindful of the great personal sacrifice which that ministry has entailed upon you, nor of the noble and unflinching stand you have made during that period for the doctrine and principles of the Church of Christ in this land, and for which, not only your own flock, but all English Catholics owe you an eternal debt of gratitude. It is our fervent hope that God will bless your labours in your new parish as abundantly as He has blessed them in the past, and that when the Chief Shepherd shall appear you may receive a crown of glory that fadeth not away.

Signed on behalf of the Committee and subscribers.

E. CHURCHILL.
B. G. LAKE.
G. R. HOGG.

It is a curious commentary upon his character to observe that those who knew him best would by no means consent to place the sum mentioned at his own disposal. It was spent in purchasing an annuity, no one of course supposing that his life upon earth was so soon to be cut short.

When this address was presented he had already, since the middle of January 1883, been established in the scene of his old labours at St. Peter's, London Docks.

CHAPTER XV.

St. Peter's, London Docks—Fresh prosecution—Advice of friends—Resignation of St. Peter's—Failure in health—Visits to Ballachulish—Life at Wantage—Final sacrifices.

1883—1887.

IT was from a sense of duty that Mr. Mackonochie had accepted the charge of St. Peter's, London Docks; and it was in the same spirit that he set himself to carry on the work there, but the highest motives are not always the most effectual.

The transition from St. Alban's had been abrupt; and his first experiences of an unfamiliar, though well-trodden, field of labour could hardly fail to be dispiriting.

St. George's-in-the-East had indeed undergone surprising changes during the last twenty years. Unbridled mob violence was at an end, and open hostility to the Church had died a natural death. On every side there were signs of improvement and of progress. Churches, missions, and schools abounded, and every agency of religion and philanthropy had been brought to bear upon the neighbourhood and population. And yet there was but little relief from the uniform picture of poverty, too often worsted in the struggle to rise above the grinding necessities of a bare existence, or destitute of hope to make the attempt, and indifferent to the possibility of a higher life, here or hereafter.

It is easy for an onlooker to examine statistics, and to contemplate with satisfaction the general improvement in the condition of things to which they bear witness, to point triumphantly to the reform of old abuses and to the diminution of crime. It is not so easy to live month after month in the depressing moral and physical atmosphere, and, as in a long and almost unbroken procession each individual case of misery passes before your eyes, to call to mind the counterbalancing good, and thankfully recognise the unmistakable signs of real and lasting progress. Of those to whom these evils are matters of daily experience, it has been well said that 'in the arithmetic of woe they can only add and multiply; they cannot subtract or divide.' Within the bounds of St. Alban's parish there were great evils to contend with, but they had been to a large extent overcome. Destitution and overcrowding, with their almost inevitable attendants of intemperance and vice, were still to be found there; but there was not the dull dead level of unredeemed poverty with which the district round St. George's-in-the-East 'stagnates with a squalor peculiar to itself.'

Moreover, though Mr. Mackonochie had now for two years been entirely dependent upon voluntary offerings, the stream of liberality had never ebbed, and it had always been found sufficient to relieve the necessities of the deserving poor. In 1881, for instance, the Sisters alone made themselves responsible for over 1,200*l.* to carry on mission work in the parish, the offertories were large and evidenced the sympathy of a comparatively rich congregation ; and the sole burthen of pecuniary anxieties had never rested upon the Vicar.

With failing health and spirits, he was now to separate himself from the close companions of twenty years ; from his tried fellow-workers, and all those who had, as it were, grown up about him. Amongst comparative strangers, he was again to enter upon a hand-to-hand struggle from which no great or cheering results could be confidently anticipated by a man whose expectations would necessarily be based upon past experience.

There was a great deal of more or less mechanical work to be done ; accounts, parochial relief, &c., to be attended to ; work to which, for a long time, he had been personally unaccustomed. There was, indeed, in the midst of the surrounding dreariness, the well-appointed church of St. Peter's, with its faithful worshippers and daily Eucharists ; but it could not, in the nature of things, altogether take the place of the church of which he had built up the spiritual fabric, and of which the very stones were dear to him. He was physically and mentally in a condition to have successfully carried on his work upon the old lines and in the familiar places, but the spring of youth was gone, his belief in himself had withdrawn like a retreating wave upon the shore, it would never touch the same high level of confidence again. The year which he spent at St. Peter's was probably the saddest year of his life.

Nor was he long to be left in peace there. Already, in July 1883, another prosecution had culminated in a

sentence of deprivation which clearly would not be allowed
to be a dead letter. If his object had been to take sanctuary at St. Peter's, that object was manifestly defeated.
But, in truth, accustomed as he was to personal sacrifices,
the threatened deprivation was a matter rather affecting
the parish than himself. The endowment of 300*l.* a year
could be hardly spared. The conflict with the civil authority, even if successful, would have disastrous effects upon
a poor congregation, gathered and held together by a long-
accustomed form of worship, and by the unrelaxed efforts
of those who ministered to them ; whilst there was the yet
more alarming prospect of the patronage eventually lapsing
into unfriendly hands.

All these various difficulties were evident enough ; the
aspect of the immediate future could hardly fail to be
gloomy. It had become a matter for serious consideration whether Mr. Mackonochie might not best further the
interests of the church and parish by sending in his resignation to the Bishop.

Once again in the face of conflicting duties it had
become necessary to take a decision vitally affecting the
interests, not only of the people under his own charge, but
of the Church at large.

In this instance he was not perplexed by divergent
counsels. His friends were almost unanimous. Their verdict was based not only upon the legal and parochial aspect
of the case, but upon various considerations which were
peculiar to himself. The general opinion was to a certain
extent embodied in a letter from the Honourable Charles
Wood, now Lord Halifax.

It is now (he wrote on December 10, 1883) some six months ago when Mr. Walker mentioned to me that he was sure St. Peter's was too much for you for the moment, that he felt you were killing yourself, however little you might think so, or be ready to admit the fact yourself . . . it was evident to all who love you that you wanted a complete change and rest in order to avoid a breakdown. . . . On the top of all this comes the action of Lord Penzance, which, putting it roughly, deprives you and St. Peter's of some 300*l.* a year. . . . If there was the strain before, how much greater the strain in the future ! . . . I am sure you can fill up the outline of some of the possible troubles I see ahead without my amplifying upon them. . . . On the other hand, if you gave up St. Peter's *now*—which I feel sure on other grounds you ought to do—you can save the church from being thus compromised, patrons and parish from another conflict which must certainly be disastrous to them, release the 300*l.* a year for the purposes of the parish of which it is now deprived, and, except for the fact that they will have succeeded in persecuting you personally, emphasise the real defeat of the enemy.

Mr. Mackonochie was quite ready to take advice in a matter which was rather one of expediency than of principle. He had undoubtedly felt the strain of which Lord Halifax spoke, and if he had had any strong personal predilections he would have been, as usual, ready to put them aside ; but in point of fact the time was past when any change of place or sphere of labour could materially affect him. The one great blow had left him more or less insensible to pain ; and when he quitted St. Alban's all that was over. Others felt far more strongly for him than he felt for himself. From every side there came notes of indignation, re-echoed even from the opposite camp, when it became apparent that even now he was not to be left in peace.

Upon the first intimation of the renewed prosecution Mr. Davidson had written

that he (Archbishop Benson) deeply regrets to hear that an endeavour is being made to impugn the action taken with such good intention respecting your resignation of St. Alban's a few months ago. He prays that you may be given a right judgment in all things, and may be guided and blessed by God in your work.

And the Bishop of Bedford [Walsham How] wrote, on September 28, 1883 :

Dear Mr. Mackonochie,—I am grieved to see an announcement in to-day's paper as to the sequestration of your benefice. I have never had any knowledge of matters connected with you except what is public in the papers. Will you kindly tell me how this step affects your position? Am I right in thinking it touches only the endowment and is no endorsement of the sentence of Lord Penzance's court by the Bishop? I trust it is not this, as I believed he would never take such a step.

And Dr. Liddon wrote :

January 1, 1884.

My dear Mackonochie,—It is impossible for any of your friends to read the announcement of your resignation in this morning's papers without a heart-ache. I have no doubt that you will have acted rightly, and I pray God that you may yet have many years of usefulness before you in some way which does not yet appear. Your immediate duty ought to be to recruit your health. . . . As to all that you have gone through there is so much to be said, that it would be difficult to begin or to end anywhere ; only my earnest hope and prayer is that, as hitherto so to the end, all may promote increasingly your sanctification and peace.

Ever affectionately yours,
H. P. LIDDON.

Such sympathy was doubly valued for the sake of those who proffered it, and was very general, and nevertheless it was certain that at this crisis many of those whose battles he had so long been fighting were more concerned for the success of their arms than for the person of their leader. It would have been easy enough to indulge in somewhat bitter reflections and unavailing regrets. If the exchange to St. Peter's had been, as it now appeared, an error, it had been a noble one, and it was hard that Mr. Mackonochie alone should be called upon to expiate it. Yet there was some foundation for the fear that he was endangering the position which he held by remaining at his post. He had himself come to the same conclusion, and on December 23, close upon the anniversary of his resignation of St. Alban's, he wrote to the Bishop :

. . . Your Lordship will remember that about this time last year you consented, in consequence of the dying request of the late Archbishop of Canterbury, and after his death, to institute me to this cure of souls. You have, I know, regretted the perseverance with which some other persons have striven to disturb the state of things which was then accepted. It seems that there is little hope of this opposition—now become simply personal against myself— being abandoned by them. Therefore I must ask your Lordship to allow me to withdraw from this cure. This withdrawal I make unreservedly. At the same time it will be a great satisfaction (if your Lordship thinks fit) to be allowed to hold a general licence in the diocese till something else presents itself.

In writing to his brother in reference to this, Mr. Mackonochie characteristically remarks : ' I must say as little as possible ; ' but he encloses a copy of the Bishop's answer, which was as follows :

My dear Mr. Mackonochie,—I shall willingly give you a general permission to officiate in the London diocese ; but I offer it for your consideration whether it might not be well, in the interests of peace and for your comfort and mine, not to take duty at present at St. Peter's or St. Alban's, say for a couple of months.

To this suggestion Mr. Mackonochie at once acceded, and sent the following letter to the daily papers :

Sir,—I shall be obliged by your insertion of the following statement in your next issue. I have been forced by the logic of facts to see that I ought not any longer to impoverish a parish too impoverished already by its own circumstances, by keeping from it the income which is due to it from the Ecclesiastical Commissioners. I have therefore asked the Bishop of London to allow me to withdraw from this benefice, and his Lordship has very kindly consented to my request.

The act was accomplished, very simply and unostentatiously ; in his own words ' he said as little as possible.' But though the sense of injustice might not be allowed to rankle, no man could be indifferent to what he justly stigmatised as personal animosity. He rarely referred to the circumstances of this second resignation ; it was the final stroke which separated him from the fair promises and hopes of his earlier years.

He had no thought of again taking a parochial charge. St. Alban's claimed him as a free lance. He had his own rooms in the Clergy House ; and in the old familiar places, in the church thronged with memories, surrounded by the affection of those whose love was of such long date, he was once more ' at home.' No jealousies of the old *régime* or of the new came to disturb the harmony of so unusual an arrangement. It was often observed that when any fresh parochial plans were to be carried out. Mr. Mackonochie was the first to wish them success.

For some time he undertook a good deal of clerical work, both here and at other places. In 1885 he wrote to ask the new Bishop of London (Temple) for a renewal of his licence, asking at the same time for a confirmation at St. Alban's (there had been but two before in all the twenty years since the consecration of the church), and he notes with great satisfaction that both his requests were at once granted. We find him constant in his visits to St. Saviour's Priory ; and in 1884 he preached the Three Hours on Good Friday when staying with the Bishop of Argyll. In the autumn of the same year he gave a retreat at Cumbrae, but it was clearly an effort. He writes of 'having got through it with satisfaction to the retreatants, but thought it advisable to beg off another for December, as the pressure was sufficient to make me feel that I must not do more in the way of clerical retreats for some time.' In reference to these two occasions the Bishop of Argyll remarks that there was a certain amount of hesitation and perhaps a little confusion at times, but what he said was always helpful and edifying.

From this time, however, it was apparent to those who watched him with the close observation of keen-sighted affection, that he was unequal to any sustained mental effort. His interest in all that went on around him was as great as ever ; his mind in one sense as clear, but he could not always put his ideas into words ; nor weave into a single strand the disconnected threads of thought. There was no jar or discord in the instrument, but something had mysteriously affected its delicate mechanism and silenced a note here and there.

It is curious to note the attitude of his mind at this period. For the first time his keen observation was directed to himself. As slowly and yet surely his illness increased upon him, he was the first to notice each warning sign of its insidious approach. With all his old resolution he set himself to ward off its attacks ; patiently adopting every precaution and remedy which medical skill could devise ; at first believing the failure to be merely temporary and not perceiving that the battle was one in which, in spite of his high courage, he must be ultimately worsted.

I have fought against my stupidity (he wrote in February 1884), but stupidity has beaten me for the time. After all, I must own that since 1858 I have had little except strife—so that I may be thankful to have survived it all. Perhaps after a time I may be allowed to do more work.

And again, in the following year, he wrote :

Dr. Carfrae advises my going off to Ballachulish to feed upon Scott's novels and Seaside Studies, but will not let me do anything harder than that till I get quite sound. I am quite well *bodily*. Almost every priest of any standing seems to have had to get through the same difficulties.

And again, in July 1886 :

I am still not able to do much writing or anything else. This is very much due to my folly in trying (from about November 1884 to about this time last year) to do *some work*. Since this I have been unable to do any intellectual work. It is to be hoped, if it is God's Will, that I may be allowed to be once more in the vineyard, and I think there are symptoms of recovery. In the body I am quite well, but cannot think to any purpose or speak what I want to say, even in a common conversation. I sometimes see what I want to say, and the moment I begin to speak the sentence has flown from me. However, God has let me do something, and if it is right He will let me do more.

In later letters he speaks of hoping to get ' out of the fog,' and again, as late as 1887 :

I am still out in the bush intellectually . . . You are right in supposing that I am out of town and unfit yet for work. Doctors say that I am advancing, and indeed I feel it myself, but it is still slow work, and work that must not be forced.

His habitual reticence and the self-control which was the habit of a lifetime stood him in good stead. It is only now and then that he speaks of himself. The quick response to a word of sympathy or affection was as ready as ever, the strong clasp of his hand as warm, his friends could still speak of him to one another as ' happy and content.' The secret struggle, the anguish of a foreknowledge more crushing than bereavement and bitterer than death, was known only to himself and his God.

And in truth there was much to lighten the tragedy of these last years. Mists might shroud the immediate future, but the line of light was brightening upon the wide horizon, and his eyes were fixed upon it. His spirit rose strong and serene from the grave of earthly hopes and joys, and the thought of the other world was as near and almost as familiar as that of the one in which he lingered.

He was often at Ballachulish, Oban, the loved and honoured guest of his friend the Bishop of Argyll. He had been with him in 1883, on the occasion of his conse-cration, and the Bishop, who had then leant upon his counsel and sought his spiritual help, was (now that the position was, as it were, reversed) only glad and anxious to minister to him, and to welcome what he spoke of as the 'sanctify-ing influence of his presence' in the house.

The free life, with its background of quiet domestic happiness, was eminently congenial, whilst the fresh mountain air brought healing to the malady which no earthly physician could cure.

It was from Ballachulish that in 1885 he wrote to the members of the Haggerston Guild over whom he had watched so long :

I am writing just before going to bed, with the mighty bellows pouring out their hurricanes from the recesses of Glencoe and Glen-Etive. They have been in more or less activity for some days. This very house, built of solid granite, shakes at their voice. Imagine from the secret places of the numberless crevices in these mountains, some 4,000 feet high, and some more, God calling the winds, so destructive, if it seem good to Him ; or, on the other hand, so laden with health and power, to great and small, to do His Will, . . . held, guided, laden with freshness, free as air, we say, giving out all that is necessary for our lives ; and yet, perhaps, while ministering life to the living, also what we call death to others. . . . Perhaps such a place as this wakens up such thoughts more than anything else . . .

and then he adds :

I suppose the soul will have through some fierce energy to go forth into the storm ; beyond which is the Bosom of the Holy Ghost for those who will trust themselves to Him.

Here in these mountain solitudes Nature was, as it were,

making herself more intimately known to him, opening out her treasures and revealing her secrets, until fears were stilled and pain itself forgotten in the pure pleasure of her close companionship.

But though he was often at Ballachulish or at St. Alban's, and occasionally absent from England, paying short visits, which he never failed to enjoy, to the continent, his chief home and resting-place was in his brother's house at Wantage. He had always loved the place, where in early days he had spent so much of youthful hope and energy. It was associated with holiday times, when he had left the dust and din of London life behind him, and come down to spend the long summer days in the garden with his brother's children. Here once more there was a promise of spring in the young lives so closely connected with him; here, amidst the darkened days of declining years, hopes sprang up and blossomed.

His tall figure was once more a familiar sight as he passed along the streets of the little town, or bent his head at a cottage doorway with his friendly, courteous greeting; and knelt morning after morning in his accustomed place in the old church. He spent a great deal of his time out of doors, wandering over the downs, sometimes missing his way, but always returning with the instinct of affection to his old haunts, the little hamlet of Charlton, the cluster of almshouses, the well-known cottages where he would enter and sit with his old friends by their firesides; a gentle familiar spirit, the shadow of himself.

He who had ever been in the fore-front of the battle, and for so long in a position of command, was now content to take the humblest place in the ranks ; what did it matter, if only his remaining strength might be spent in the same service ?

I am a kind of lay curate here (he wrote to the Bishop of Argyll). I offered to take two sets of almshouses, about twenty houses in the town and sixteen on the down. I am afraid I have not been very industrious, but can carry about magazines, &c.

The words, in their absolute simplicity, speak for themselves. With severe self-abnegation, upon the first intimation of failing powers he had relinquished the duties to which he might possibly be unequal, and after a time, those highest privileges of his office which had been the very life of his life. He rarely preached after 1885, and, though he occasionally heard a confession, he would not trust himself to celebrate except upon very special occasions. It was the supreme sacrifice of his life, and into that inner sanctuary of pain it does not befit us to enter.

> Dear Christ, when Thy new vintage fills the cup
> His hand shall shake no more nor Thy Wine spill.

CHAPTER XVI.

Last official acts—Visit to St. Paul's Cathedral—Taking leave of Wantage—
Visit to Ballachulish—His death, December 15, 1887.

1887.

In the May of 1887, Mr. Mackonochie went, as he had often done before, to the Home of Rest of the St. Saviour's Sisterhood at Herne Bay, but in June he was again in London, and present at the services on St. Alban's Day. To many his presence as a guest had a mournful significance, as they remembered other St. Alban's Days, and all that he had done and suffered. They sought out his tall figure, so easily distinguished amongst the crowd at the public luncheon, and noted the storm-beaten expression upon his worn features.

Looking on as a spectator at the scene in which he had so often played the principal part, he was probably the only person present who did not feel that for that very reason there was something missing. He had been especially anxious to see the Bishop of Lincoln, who was to be there that day, and with characteristic humility noted with pleasure in his diary the greeting which the Bishop gave him.

There might be sadness indeed, the inevitable sadness

which accompanies the loosening of old ties, the filling up
of vacant places, the relinquishment of everything which
bound him most closely to the past, but there was no single
drop of bitterness in the cup.

His birthday fell on August 11. He was sixty-two,
and in one sense his life, which had so long been one of
incessant mental activity, was over. Yet no word of complaint escaped him. To God alone he breathed the prayer
wrung from him by the momentary pressure of an incurable
evil that he *might not cumber the earth*. They are the
very words in which he emphasised the desire by noting
it in his diary.

I wish I could put my hand on Mackonochie's last letter to
me (writes Dr. Liddon). We had met at Wantage in July 1887
when he was staying with his brother. He then asked me to take
some young women in whom he was interested over St. Paul's in
August, and to my surprise he came himself as one of the party,
going all round the building as though he had everything to learn
about it, and showing the greatest interest in everything. On his
way back to Wantage he appears to have got out of the train by
mistake at Didcot Station, and to have wandered about in roads
and villages between Didcot and Wantage during a part or the
whole of the night. He described this to me in the letter which he
afterwards wrote from Wantage, thanking me for the afternoon
in St. Paul's.

And in warm and affectionate response to this letter
from Mr. Mackonochie, we find Dr. Liddon's note, dated
'August 26, 1887,' which had been carefully preserved :

It was a great pleasure to me to see you the other day, as it is
to get a letter from you this morning . . . You know that I am

one of the many who will always love and honour you, and pray constantly for your restoration in God's good time to stronger health.

Ever your affectionate
H. P. LIDDON.

The missing of his way, to which these letters refer, had always been a symptom of his malady. One of his friends might well write that 'his mental state was a puzzle.' His spirit at one moment so unclouded, his intellectual grasp so strong, the consciousness of his own failure so keen, and yet all this combined with a vain groping in the labyrinths of his mind for a forgotten word, or, as upon this occasion, wanderings out of the right road, even in well-known and often frequented places.

As to the condition of his mind during his abode with us (writes the Bishop of Argyll), there were no fancies or delusions such as come to some people. He was only forgetful of names and words, and incapable sometimes of expressing himself clearly. He was, I may say, holy and happy in his tone of mind to the last. He took a great interest in all the small events of our daily life, and was enthusiastically delighted with the beauties of this place.

It was the same at Wantage. None but those who were his constant companions knew how naturally and simply he accepted each incident of his difficult position ; how gratefully he welcomed any casual event which gave him pleasure, from the visit of an old friend, to the blossoming of a favourite shrub in the garden ; nor how readily he entered into all those trivial anxieties and joys which belong to the life of a large family.

The death of his brother's eldest son in the September

of this year was a great shock to him, and though after a
time he regained his quiet cheerfulness, there was a change
as if his life had imperceptibly fallen into a lower key. He
was again for a short time in London in October, and once
more in his old place at St. Saviour's Priory, taking part in
a Guild service ; but here too his work was over, and for the
last time he went back for a few days to Wantage.

The autumn days were darkening into winter, and a
shadow had fallen upon his spirits. If he had suffered, at
least he had suffered in silence, and he had battled with
a foreboding which was nevertheless gathering strength
because he had thought it cowardly to relinquish hope.

He left Wantage on October 19, and as he took leave
of the place where he had known so many joys and so much
sorrow, and said good-bye to those who had made their
house his home, for once, under the pressure of that parting
hour, truth leaped to light.

'When you come back—when you are better,'—so
they said with that desperate clinging to the future which
tells that the present has failed us, with that blind reliance
on a hope which we guard as a starving man guards his
last crust, when those whom we love are sick. 'When you
are better,' and for once the answer came, ' I shall never be
better.' He walked away and stood looking out at the
bare wind-swept garden and patches of leafless orchards
below ; struggling in silence with the pain which, having
once found a voice, was now striving for the mastery, until
in a few moments he could turn, gentle and composed as
ever, with his kindly farewell words to each member of the
household. He never saw Wantage again.

On his way to Scotland he passed through London, and spent a few days with connections in Yorkshire, and some time with his old friend Mr. Ball in Edinburgh. Dr. Teape, of St. Andrew's Church, at whose house he attended a clerical meeting, writes as follows :

Mr. Ball wrote asking if he might bring Mr. Mackonochie as a visitor. I was very happy he did so. He sat next to me, and looked so happy and guileless and pleased. He listened at the clerical meeting, but made no remarks.

It was the last place where he met any number of the clergy, or appeared at any general gathering.

He parted from Mr. Ball in good spirits, and on December 10 reached Ballachulish. On his way he met the Bishop of Argyll in the train, and they travelled together as far as Dalmally, where they parted, little thinking it was for the last time. For years past, as we have seen, it had been one of his favourite resorts. Its wild and picturesque surroundings of loch and mountain ; its winds, free yet soft like the soft-tongued Celtic peasantry ; the vivid contrasts of its snow-covered hills and blue waters, had an attraction which outweighed in his mind the charm of Southern skies. North Ballachulish lies in a curve of the Lochaber shore, about ten miles from the head of Loch Leven. Beyond it, stretching inland, is the desolate and almost trackless forest of Mamore, separated by the Kinloch hills from the pass of Glencoe, or the 'glen of weeping,' which Macaulay describes ' as the most dreary and melancholy of all the Scottish passes, the very valley of the shadow of death,' and now for ever since the times of which he wrote overshadowed by the memory of an awful crime.

Mists and storms brood over it through the greater part of the finest summer. All down the side of the crags heaps of ruin mark the headlong path of the torrents. Mile after mile the only sound that indicates life is the faint cry of a bird of prey from some storm-beaten pinnacle of rock. The progress of civilisation, which has turned so many wastes into fields yellow with harvests or gay with apple blossom, has only made Glencoe more desolate.

When Mr. Mackonochie arrived the weather was intensely cold, but he had not suffered from it, and his friends found no lack of cheerfulness either in his looks or conversation.

The day after his arrival was a Sunday, and he went to church with Mrs. Chinnery Haldane. In the afternoon he took a walk with the dogs, but did not go far, as the snow was beginning to fall in large flakes. In the evening all were weather-bound, and he talked a great deal, especially upon the subject of burials, and of the portion of Woking cemetery set apart for the St. Alban's people, the Christianising of funeral and burial arrangements having been (as it will be remembered) always very near to his heart.

On the Monday morning (writes Mrs. Chinnery Haldane) he spoke a great deal about the 'little old moon' which he had seen early in the morning over Donald's Peak, and wanted me to look at it, and see a star near it which I could not make out.

During the next days he both read and talked with interest upon various subjects. An article in 'The Church Quarterly Review,' which he had read aloud, called 'A French Diocesan,' led him on to speak of a journey which he had taken with his friend Mr. Russell, and what they had seen of Sunday-school organisation and teaching abroad. And a copy of the St. Alban's magazine which was lying about recalled old times, of which he spoke freely, but with an emotion which made his friends glad to change the subject. Then again, in the ordinary course of conversation during the long dark evenings which followed, he talked of French politics, and the attempt upon Jules Ferry's life; of Mrs. Scurfield's efforts on behalf of the London flower-girls; of the death of Chatterton in reference to a club connected with St. Alban's which had been called by his name; and of many other things naturally and easily as they recurred to his mind, or were mentioned by other people.

On Wednesday the frost had given way, and about mid-day drenching rain came on. He had gone out, and came back wet through two hours late for luncheon, apparently unconscious of the lapse of time, observing that he had not been far from the head of the loch, and was not at all tired. When the evening came and the household assembled for prayers in the private chapel, he said the office of Compline for the last time, and thus unconsciously with the ' Nunc Dimittis,' and the commendation of the souls of the faithful departed to the mercy of God, brought his long ministry to a close.

Thursday, the 15th, his last day upon earth, was clear and fine, and he was eager to accomplish the walk he had planned the day before. He was urged to take some food with him, and a stick, and he acquiesced in both suggestions, observing in reference to the latter that ' a stick was always company.' 'You will be back before dark?' his hostess said ; and with one of his bright looks he answered, 'I hope so, I hope so,' twice over. They were the last words which any of his friends heard him utter. A few minutes later he started at his usual rapid pace, walking with firmness and vigour, the two dogs running at his side.

There was no thought of danger, no foreboding of what was to happen. He had always been perfectly independent in his habits, and that morning especially it seemed as if amongst the hills which he loved, he was stepping out from the shadow which lay across his path of life into the sunshine. He reached Kinloch before two o'clock, and was observed by a gamekeeper eating his luncheon on the hillside above the bridge. After this it would appear that instead of turning homewards he went up the glen, following the course of the river Leven, and making his way ever eastward toward the desolate country of moorland and marsh and lakes which extends towards the mountainous outskirts of the vast Mamore deer forest. From this point all is necessarily conjecture.

It is supposed that as the evening fell he may have mistaken the glimmer of the dim pools for the head of the loch which he was leaving behind him, and still he pursued his way, the two dogs following, perplexed but faithful. On and on into wilder and deeper solitudes, ever further from the friendly lights and anxious watchers at Ballachulish, until to his weary limbs and bewildered brain, it was only the way to Heaven which still lay open.[1]

---

[1] When a snow-storm drove St. Cuthbert's boat upon the coast of Fife, his companions cried in despair, 'The snow closes the road along the shore, and the storm bars our way across the sea,' and he replied, 'The way to Heaven still lies open.'

At first no great apprehension had been felt. The Kinloch road was well known to him, and when towards evening the darkness came on it was supposed likely that he had taken refuge in some cottage, or in any case, if anything had happened to him, that the dogs would have come back. But when time passed and no tidings came, the Bishop, who had returned that afternoon, grew uneasy, and then there began that long and weary search which lasted with but little intermission, and with ever-deepening fears, from that Thursday night until two o'clock on Saturday afternoon :

Of all our searchings (writes the Bishop) I have the most terrible recollection of our Friday night's work among the hills between the head of Loch Leven and Glencoe. It was pitch-dark, except for the light of our storm lanterns, which were every now and then blown out by the force of the wind. We stumbled on over rocks and ice and sometimes through deep snow, whilst the howling tempest and driving hail were at times almost over-powering.

By Saturday the news had spread all over the district, and roused the keenest sympathy.

The Bishop was accompanied by a crowd of men and dogs, who had come in from all quarters, when, after a short rest at a shooting lodge near Kinloch, he started out again. For hours the search was protracted and in vain. It was not until the afternoon that some of the foremost men raised a cry that the Bishop's two dogs had been sighted in the distance. A few minutes more and the search was over.

He lay outstretched upon the snow, which half shrouded

THE MAMORE FOREST, WHERE THE BODY WAS FOUND.

his limbs, and wreathed his uncovered head, in an attitude of undisturbed repose. Righ, the deer-hound, sat bolt upright beside him, whilst the little Skye terrier lay at his feet, alert and vigilant, growling at the approach of strangers. It was about twenty miles from the house which he had left more than forty-eight hours before.

The day had been overcast, but as the Bishop knelt and kissed him, the clouds divided in the west, over the Glencoe and Glen-Etive mountains, and the light which overspread the wild and rugged landscape rested upon his calm features still in the peaceful majesty of death.

He had never been easily vanquished, and he had fought hard for his life. There had evidently been a long struggle in the darkness amongst the rocks ; the snow all around the spot where he lay was trampled and trodden down, and beyond the wire fence, which he had apparently followed, his footsteps had only been arrested by an impassable snow-drift ; but strong as he was, death was stronger. Silently, resistlessly, but in no unfriendly guise, it had drawn near. The physical conflict and the mental perplexity were for ever ended, as under that touch, chill yet gentle as the falling snow, he sank down to his last sleep.

And who could doubt that after his long restlessness and weary wanderings that night at least he slept well? For him already 'the crooked was made straight, and the rough places plain.' The darkness deepened and the snow fell ever faster, blurring the outlines of the rocks and hills and blotting out the homeward track ; but it did not matter to him any longer ; as his memorial tablet in the Bishop's

U

chapel fitly expresses it, he had 'departed into his own country another way.'[1]

They lifted his body after some prayers had been said, and laid it upon a bier formed of cross sticks and a plank, which the shepherds found a little lower down,[2] and so whilst the Bishop walked behind supporting his head, they began their journey to Kinloch. It was a rough and rocky way through swollen torrents and drifted snow, and their

[1] Fall, snow ! in stillness fall like dew,
    On temple's roof and cedar's fan,
And mould thyself on pine and yew,
    And on the awful face of man.

Without a sound, without a stir,
    In streets and wolds, on rock and mound,
O, omnipresent Comforter,
    By Thee, this night, the lost are found !

Bend o'er them, white-robed Acolyte,
    Put forth thine hand from cloud and mist,
nd minister the last sad Rite,
    Where altar there is none, nor priest.

Touch thou the gates of soul and sense ;
    Touch darkening eyes and dying ears ;
Touch stiffening hands and feet, and thence
    Remove the trace of sin and tears.

And ere thou seal those filmèd eyes
    Into God's urn thy fingers dip,
And lay 'mid eucharistic sighs,
    The sacred wafer on the lip.

This night the Absolver issues forth,
    This night the Eternal Victim bleeds,
O winds and woods ! O heavens and earth !
    Be still this night.   The Rite proceeds !

AUBREY DE VERE, Poems, p. 62, 1855.

[2] This plank is now a cross in the little chapel of St. Sepulchre at St. Alban's.

progress was necessarily slow until at Kinloch they found a carriage in which they could proceed to Ballachulish. Darkness had fallen before they reached the threshold over which he had passed in the morning sunshine only two days before.

It was in the Bishop's private chapel that during his visits to Ballachulish he had daily made his communions. 'He was ever the first to kneel at our altar,' writes the Bishop, 'and the last to leave it.' And it was before that altar now that they laid him ; the Bishop himself assisting at the last sad offices until all was accomplished, and he lay in Eucharistic vestments with his crucifix upon his breast, and the well-worn Book of Prayers and Offices which had been found upon him, at his side.

Telegrams had been sent to Wantage and to St. Alban's, but it was not possible for any one to leave for Scotland before Sunday night, and Mr. Russell, who started at once, could not reach Ballachulish until Monday evening. As the boat which brought him from Oban touched the shore, the Bishop stood ready to receive him, and when they reached the house, took him into the chapel. 'Though I had watched his face for twenty years,' Mr. Russell said afterwards, when giving an account of his mission, 'I had never seen it as I saw it then. There was no pallor nor any trace of pain, but only such majesty as I had never known before.'

At seven the next morning (Tuesday) the Bishop celebrated, and in the darkness in boats from here and there across the loch there came the clergy of the neighbourhood to receive Communion from his hands, and then the service being over, while it was still dark they carried the coffin over the field to the waterside, where two boats were waiting.

A purple pall with a crimson cross covered the coffin, and in the stern of the boat the Bishop took his place beside it. The snow was falling thick and fast, and all the hills were hidden by it. There was no sound of life about except from one great white sea-bird which rose up and flapped its wings, and led the way before the boats—even the very oars seemed muffled as the boats moved noiselessly down the loch. By the time they reached the pier-head the coffin which they had veiled in purple was veiled in white. It was like an absolution from the Hand of God. Then suddenly as the ship took them on board there came a change in the sky. The snow stopped falling, the clouds and mists rolled away, the sun shone out, and all at once the mountains which yesterday had only been patched here and there with snow, now stood revealed, clothed in virgin white from head to foot.

And so most fitly amidst beautiful sights and sounds that sorrowful journey began, and with sad hearts and loving reverence they bore him onwards towards his last earthly resting-place.

London could not be reached before Thursday morning, but it was known in the parish when the train was due, and as the hearse passed up Gray's Inn Road crowds lined the streets standing bareheaded, silent, and awestruck ; watching until the body in its plain coffin of Scotch pine, the work of the village carpenter, was met by the surpliced clergy at the entrance to Bell Court, and carried into the beautiful little mortuary chapel. The windows surrounding the court were filled with spectators, and on the pavement below the poor people stood shoulder to shoulder or knelt as the coffin passed. It was no wonder. For twenty years he had gone in and out amongst them. Often misunderstood and patient under much provocation, upon how many now well-remembered occasions had that compassion for the weak and sinful shone forth which had been the solitary passion of his life. To how many of those now gathered round his coffin, from the group of his own near relations to the poor people standing in their doorways, had he not been at once a father and a friend! And as soon as the first Eucharist was over, all day long and through the night until the funeral on Friday, the footsteps of those who loved him passed softly in and out of the little chapel, as they came in silence to take their watch beside their dead.

At solemn vespers for the dead on Thursday, the church was filled to overflowing, and the coffin was brought from the chapel into the church, where it lay in the chancel surrounded with tapers and almost hidden by flowers, whilst after the service was over Mr. Russell told from the pulpit the story of his journey (from which we have already given extracts), and related the circumstances of the death to the sorrowing congregation.

On Friday morning there were successive celebrations of the Holy Eucharist from a very early hour, at which numbers communicated, and at eleven the Requiem began. Admittance had been by ticket as a necessary precaution against a crush; nevertheless, the church was crowded in every part, and hundreds of persons were unable to obtain admission. As the service ended the procession formed in perfect order, the vast assembled crowd reverently and silently co-operating with the police so as to avoid any confusion.

The large silver Crucifix was followed by the members of the choir, and after them by about fifty clergy in surplices, then the bier with lights on either side, the pall-bearers being all clergy connected with St. Alban's. His own near relatives and friends followed in carriages, and then came the Sisters, members of the Confraternity, Parochial Guilds, and hundreds of clergy and laity walking four abreast. There were representatives of every age and class. The Holborn flower-girls; Lord Halifax as President of the English Church Union; the members and officials of the Church of England Working Men's Society, the men and women he had guided, his own spiritual children, clergy from remote country parishes, the children he had taught in his schools —in literal truth it might be said that ' his works did follow him.'

The long procession moved slowly on amongst the crowds of people who lined the way, down High Holborn and Chancery Lane, and along the Strand to Waterloo Station; and the hymns, sung at intervals as they passed along, rang out clearly above the mingled sounds and the roar of the City. For once the incessant traffic in the great thoroughfares was arrested. London was startled into wonder. Death had hushed even those who had once condemned him into silence, and the wave of feeling swept from the train of mourners over curious and indifferent spectators, as with tears and prayers, and yet in a sort of triumph, they carried him to his grave.

Woking was reached by the special train, which carried some hundreds of people, in the early brightness of a fine winter's afternoon. Even the bare heath seemed to hold a promise of spring, flecked as it was by light clouds and sunshine. For about half a mile the coffin was carried on a hand-bier to the burial-ground of the St. Alban's people. In the centre there stands a granite shaft supporting a crucifix, and it was at its foot that the grave had been prepared. The Rev. A. H. Stanton read the service, and 'Lead, kindly Light,' with its singularly appropriate reference to the circumstances of his death, was sung at its conclusion. Mr. Suckling, the Vicar of St. Alban's, then read a telegram from the Bishop of Argyll, dated from Ballachulish :

How I wish I could be present with you to-day, but though separated by space we are united in the same sorrow, and the same prayers for our dear departed friend, and in the same hope through Jesus Christ our Lord. May His peace be with you all.

They were the last words spoken, and as the mourners drew closer round, the grave was filled in, and the flowers, sent in almost overwhelming quantities, deposited upon it.

And so they left him—where he would most have wished his body to be laid, amongst his own people—and reluctantly turned their faces homewards.

To some it may well have seemed that a quiet grave on the Scotch hillside would have been his most fitting resting-place, in that deep seclusion where, far from the turmoil of a city, he had so often communed with his God. But his home was at St. Alban's ; no earthly tie, except that of near relationship, could be stronger than that which bound him to his people. Almost the whole of his ministerial life had been spent amongst them ; his lot had not been cast in the shady by-ways, but in the glaring thoroughfares of the world.   It was there that the battle had been fought, and now that the victory was won, it was in the neighbourhood of the battle-field that he was most fitly laid to rest.

A cross of Scotch granite marks his grave, with the Chalice and Host engraved upon it, and the simple inscription :

JESU MERCY.

I. H. S.

IN PACE.

ALEXANDER HERIOT MACKONOCHIE,

PRIEST.

15 *December* 1887.

And a cross will be erected upon the spot where he died ; but his fairest memorial is in the hearts of those who loved him, in the lives of those to whom he ministered —those hearts in which the flame of love to God and man burns brighter, those lives which are stronger and purer since Alexander Heriot Mackonochie has lived and died.

THE GRAVE AT WOKING.

APPENDICES

APPENDIX A

The Mackonochie Memorial.

A CROWDED meeting was held on the afternoon of Monday, February 13, 1888, in the Freemasons' Tavern, to consider the question of a Memorial to the Rev. A. H. Mackonochie. The chair was taken by Earl Beauchamp. Sir Walter Phillimore moved—'That it is fitting that a Memorial should be raised to the late Rev. A. H. Mackonochie, and that public subscriptions be solicited for the same.' The resolution was seconded by the Rev. Prebendary Eyton.

The second resolution, 'That the actual form of the Memorial be a chapel built as part of the fabric of the Church of St. Alban the Martyr, Holborn,' was moved by Canon Carter and seconded by Rev. A. H. Stanton.

The third resolution, proposed by the Rev. Berdmore Compton and seconded by Mr. G. W. E. Russell, gave authority to an Executive Committee.

These resolutions were carried unanimously. The amount collected up to the present time is about 6,000*l.*, thanks in large part to the zeal of the Honorary Secretary, the Rev. G. R. Hogg.

Of this sum, rather more than 2,000*l.* has been spent in securing and pulling down a line of miserable tenements in close proximity to the church, and which have been for years a physical and moral plague-spot in the parish. Mr. Mackonochie had left no means untried for mending the unhappy condition of the buildings and their inhabitants, but in vain. That the houses now no longer exist is the fulfilment of a wish very dear to him. Upon part of this site the Memorial Chapel will be built. The plans are complete, and will be carried out immediately upon receiving the necessary permissions from the authorities.

The scheme includes a tomb with a recumbent figure.

APPENDIX B

History of the Ecclesiastical Courts.

IT is needful, for the clear understanding of the issues involved, to sketch the history of the Courts wherein the suits were tried, and of the law which fell within their province to administer.

The Norman Conquest may be conveniently taken as the starting-point, because the system of ecclesiastical law and procedure which it brought in its train differed in several important particulars from that prevalent here in Anglo-Saxon times, and continued in force as a whole down to the Reformation, and indeed continues, with certain further modifications, to prevail still.

The two principal changes introduced under the Norman sovereigns were (1) the addition of the main body of the local Roman canon law to the ecclesiastical code of England, which had previously been made up of Scripture, the canons of General Councils and some few ancient local councils, and the Church laws of native origin, either enacted by the clergy in their synods, or as temporal laws by the Witenagemot, wherein both clergy and laity sat jointly ; and (2) the substitution of the Roman civil law in matter of procedure for the mixed jurisdiction of the Anglo-Saxon shires and hundreds, wherein no clear line of demarcation was drawn between civil and ecclesiastical causes, save that the Bishop presided in the former case, and the Ealdorman in the latter ; and that, even with this apparent right of lay cognisance of spiritual questions, the fact is that the Church was then much more powerful than the State, and it is more accurate to say that the bishops and abbots had power over the laity in temporal matters than that the lay magistracy had power over the Church in spiritual causes.

The first important change brought about by the introduction of these new principles into the ecclesiastical laws of England was the withdrawal of all ecclesiastical causes from the cognisance of the secular Courts, in virtue of an edict promulgated by William the Conqueror. This involved a reconstruction and development of the Church Courts, and from this time the Court of the Archdeacon dates as a tribunal of first instance in spiritual causes, from which an appeal lay to the diocesan Court of the Bishop, presided over by his Official ; and appeal lay from this Court to the Provincial Courts of the two provinces, of which there were four in Canterbury and two in York, while there was a further appeal in practice to the Pope, though this was resisted and restrained at various times by the English sovereigns, and indeed by the Archbishops of Canterbury also, who, as being *ex-officio* Papal Legates, contended that no appeal beyond themselves, sitting in their legatine character, was needful or even legal. Whenever temporal interests were involved in any ecclesiastical causes, the Crown claimed and exercised a right of interference, as in the matter of advowsons ; and further, the right of staying all proceedings in the ecclesiastical Courts by means of a writ of prohibition, whenever it seemed that the Church Courts were either encroaching upon the secular jurisdiction, or prejudicing the rights of any subject in a way entitling him to the aid of the Crown for his protection. But there are no examples found of any interference by the secular authority in matters of faith, morals, or ritual during this entire period.

The legislation of Henry VIII. constitutes almost a revolution in the system of Church law which had thus prevailed from the

Conquest.   The more important statutes were the Act of Citations, 23 Henry VIII., c. 9, restricting the Archbishop of Canterbury's power of hearing causes of first instance ; the Statute of Restraint of Appeals, 24 Henry VIII., c. 12, which prohibited recourse to the Pope as final arbiter ; the Act for the Submission of the Clergy and Restraint of Appeals, 25 Henry VIII., c. 19 ; the Act for the Non-payment of First-fruits to the Bishop of Rome, 25 Henry VIII., c. 20 ; the Act concerning Peter-pence and Dispensations, 25 Henry VIII., c. 21 ; and the Act of Supremacy, 26 Henry VIII., c. 1.

The net result of these enactments was not only to recover for the Crown various incidents of its prerogative and powers which had passed into the hands of the Pope, but the erection of the Crown itself into the position of Supreme Ordinary and fountain of all ecclesiastical authority within the realm, right of inquisition into cases of heresy, thus bringing doctrinal matter for the first time within the purview of the civil authority.   Further, the clergy could neither assemble in their Convocations, nor enact any new canons or constitutions therein, without the King's writ and licence ; and the King was also empowered to nominate a commission of thirty-two persons, half clerical and half lay, to revise the then existing code of Canons, and to abrogate all therein which the majority of the commissioners should think fit to be abolished. Besides these defined powers, there was a large additional area less determinately limited, whereby the Crown could declare doctrines, to be laid down by a body of ecclesiastical advisers, and could also confer extraordinary powers upon Archbishops and Bishops, enabling them to exercise jurisdictional authority over and above that inherent in their spiritual office.   And lastly, an appeal was to lie to the King in Chancery in the case of lack of justice in any Courts of the Archbishops, and be exercised through a Commission under the Great Seal, whose members should be nominated by the King.   The virtually Papal authority thus conferred upon the Crown did not prove durable, the new laws touching heresy were soon abrogated, the absolute headship claimed for the Sovereign did not enter permanently into the Reformation settlement, and the proposed revision of the Canon Law was never completed. But the Royal Supremacy, as the term is now understood, dates from this legislation of Henry VIII., and rests now upon the footing on which it was placed by the legislation of Elizabeth, after it had been still further extended under Edward VI., and then again limited by the statutes of Philip and Mary, repealing many of the recent ecclesiastical statutes, and restoring the Papal authority, though not to its original extent. The chief Elizabethan statutes are the Act 'restoring to the Crown the ancient jurisdiction over the State ecclesiastical and spiritual, and abolishing all foreign power repugnant to the same ; ' and the Act of Uniformity, these being the two earliest enactments of the new reign. These statutes abolished the Papal authority anew, but also considerably narrowed the bounds of the Royal Supremacy, specifically abandoning the claim to Supreme Headship, and modifying the visitatorial and corrective authority vested in the Crown by the Act of Supremacy, 26 Henry VIII., c. 1.

The net result of these changes was to add the ecclesiastical statutes enacted in Parliament to the body of unrevoked canon law as part of the system to be administered by the ecclesiastical tribunals, to require the consent of Parliament as well as of the Crown to legislation in Convocation, to enable the Crown to issue Proclamations and Injunctions or Advertisements having the force of law in ecclesiastical matters, and the erection of two new Courts of Appeal from the provincial, consistory, archidiaconal, and peculiar Courts, which had survived throughout all the changes of the three preceding reigns. These Courts were (1) the Court of Delegates, already constituted by the Act of Submission under Henry VIII. but set aside by Philip and Mary, which continued to be the Final Court in ecclesiastical causes until 1832 ; and (2) the Court of High Commission, which originated under Elizabeth herself, and, after earning the worst possible reputation, was abolished by an Act of the Long Parliament, 16 Charles I., c. 11.

The Court of Delegates, when sitting to try testamentary and matrimonial causes, appears to have been constituted of common law judges and civilians of Doctors' Commons only, but when questions of a more strictly ecclesiastical character came before it, Bishops were added to the list.

No direct change was made in the constitution of the Court till within living memory, but in the meantime an event had occurred which seriously conditioned the validity of the change when it did take place. That event was the suppression of Convocation from 1718 till 1852, with the exception of two brief meetings for the transaction of business in 1728 and 1741, a hiatus for which the Metropolitans and Bishops who sat during this period of 134 years are even more responsible than the civil advisers of the Crown, seeing that the writs for the assemblage of Convocation were issued regularly along with those for summoning each new Parliament, and might have been equally acted on. But the constitutional result of this abeyance was precisely that which would happen in the temporal sphere by a like failure of Parliament to meet ; in which case no new statutes could be legally enacted, and no old ones repealed. This position will be made clear by citation of the preamble of Henry VIII.'s Statute of Appeals : 'This realm of England is an empire . . . the body spiritual whereof having power, when any cause of the law divine happened to come in question, or of spiritual learning, then it was declared, interpreted, and shewed by that part of the said body politick, called the spirituality, now being usually called the English Church, which always hath been reputed, and also found of that sort, that both for knowledge, integrity, and sufficiency of number it hath always been thought, and is also at this hour, *sufficient and meet of itself, without the intermeddling of any exterior person or persons*, to declare and determine all such doubts, and to administer all such offices and duties, as to their rooms spiritual doth appertain . . . . And the law temporal, for trial of property of lands and goods, and for the conservation of the people of this land in unity and peace, without rapine or spoil, was and yet is administered, adjudged, and executed by sundry judges and ministers of the other part of the said body politick, called the temporalty ; and both their authorities and jurisdictions do *conjoin together* in the due administration of justice, *the one to help the other.*'

That is to say, while both the spirituality and the temporality form part of the same body politic under the same Crown, from which both of them derive their coercive jurisdiction, each is restricted to its own sphere, and neither is empowered to intrude into, or encroach upon, the domain of the other ; but when any matter affecting them both arises, they are to entertain it conjointly. Now what this means is that no statutes of the civil Parliament affecting the spirituality have any constitutional validity without the concurrence and assent of the ecclesiastical Parliament or Convocation ; nay, it may even be doubted whether any such statutes can be lawfully initiated in the secular Parliament, even if afterwards accepted by the Church. Enactments of the kind are in violation of the first paragraph of Magna Charta :

'In the first place, that we have conceded to God, and have confirmed by this our present Charter, for ourselves and our heirs for ever, that the Church of England is to be free, and to have its rights (*jura*) unimpaired, and its liberties unmolested.'

And there can be no reasonable doubt that the word *jura* here used includes and covers all such matters as the constitution, erection, and commission of ecclesiastical courts and officers. Magna Charta, moreover, does not rest merely upon its original concession by the Crown, it was enacted as a statute in 9 Henry III., and is one of the fundamental supports of the English Constitution, so that any Act conflicting with it is constitutionally null and void. Apart from this objection, the legal status of an Act of Parliament affecting the Church, but not concurred in by the spirituality in its own assemblies, is precisely that of a Bill which has passed one of the two Houses of Parliament, but has not been so much as introduced into the other—it is no lawful statute of the realm, but is wholly illicit and null. This, then, is the position of the four following statutes which have within living memory altered the ecclesiastical jurisdiction :

I. The Act 2 & 3 William IV. c. 92, transferring the powers of the High Court of Delegates to the King in Council ;

II. 3 & 4 William IV. c. 41, constituting the Judicial Committee of Privy Council as the tribunal for exercising the Crown's appellate jurisdiction over causes arising within the realm, and its original jurisdiction over causes arising outside the realm, but within the empire ;

III. The Church Discipline Act, 3 & 4 Victoria, c. 86 ; and

IV. The Public Worship Regulation Act, 37 & 38 Victoria, c. 85, the last of which was not merely enacted without the assent of Convocation, but in the teeth of its repudiation and protest, and thus has never been even presumably a valid statute of the realm.

It may be added here that the grounds urged in 1832 for the transfer of the powers of the Court of Delegates to the Privy Council were the delay and costliness of the procedure ; but no charge was brought against the Court on the grounds of competent knowledge or of substantial administration of justice. In fact, as respects the intellectual competency of the Delegates, it has to be borne in mind that the majority of the judges always consisted of civilians and doctors who had specially studied canon and civil law, while the advocates who pleaded before them were also specialists, familiar with the particular branch of jurisprudence within the cognisance of the Court.

The three main objections to the so-called Ecclesiastical Courts which have been substituted for the Delegates, apart from the legal objection to their validity as not set up by lawful statutes, are these : that the Crown in exercising ecclesiastical jurisdiction by and in them, transgresses the constitutional limits of the Royal Supremacy, which must act in all cases through the proper channel, through spiritual Courts and persons for spiritual causes, through temporal Courts and persons for civil causes ; and can no more provide for the hearing of a spiritual suit in a lay Court than for the trial of a civil action by Convocation; that the setting up of the new Courts by parliamentary action is precisely that 'intermeddling of exterior persons' repudiated by the preamble of the Statute for Restraint of Appeals, seeing that since the Union with Scotland in 1707 and the Roman Catholic Emancipation Act of 1829, whereby Presbyterians and Roman Catholics sit and vote in Parliament, and the further legislation which permits non-Christians to sit there also, Parliament is no longer even colourably the laity of the English Church by representation, but has become 'exterior' in the fullest legal and moral sense of the word; and finally, that there is no provision whatever to secure competent acquaintance with the subject-matter of ecclesiastical suits on the part of so much as a single member of the new tribunals. It is often heard that lawyers must needs be, from their technical training, much better able to adjudicate upon legal questions than ecclesiastics can possibly be, and that there is thus a greater security for justice. But this plea obscures the real issues. For law is so difficult, intricate, and minutely differentiated, that highest eminence in one branch of it does not in the least imply so much as a smattering of knowledge of other departments even in the same category, and the opinion of a great criminal lawyer would not be accounted of the slightest value in the class of suits which come before the Chancery Division, or that of a common lawyer in a complex question of international law. But the law ecclesiastical is of an even more complex and technical character than any branch of the temporal law, it ranges over a far wider area, and not only are the temporal lawyers, as a class, profoundly ignorant of its principles, but they have had, from their first appearance as a separate order in the nation, an acute jealousy and dislike of it, inducing them rather to oppose and defeat it where possible, than to comply with the counsel of the Statute of Appeals, and 'conjoin together in the due administration of justice, the one to help the other.'

And such has been the practical result. Not only by applying the terminology of secular law to matter which is not susceptible of being so treated, but by unfamiliarity with all that large mass of ecclesiastical learning lying outside the bare text of the formularies of the Church of England, but essential for the determination of questions of doctrine and indeed of discipline also, the new Courts have on several occasions displayed complete ignorance of matters of fact directly bearing upon the causes before them, and have, in a majority of the suits they have decided, misrepresented the law, in some instances even to the extent of total inversion of the merits.

To establish the truth of these charges, it will be necessary to give some illustrations from decisions which it is difficult to reconcile with legal fairness and freedom from prejudice ; and which in fact have never been accepted by competent authorities as being reasonable expositions of the law—a proof of which is found in the contradictory pronouncements of some of the decisions and in the evident unfamiliarity of the Judicial Committee with much which it was its business to know. For the present, the specimens offered are taken from decisions of an earlier date than the litigation in respect of the services at St. Alban's, Holborn. And they will be fitly preceded by a few words upon the theoretical character of the Judicial Committee, and of its own view of its functions. Properly speaking, then, the Judicial Committee is not a Court of Law : it is simply a body of private advisers of the Crown to assist it in the exercise of the royal prerogative. And consequently, the constitution of the body has from the very first shown that it has not inherited the powers of the Court of Delegates, and can neither pronounce a final sentence in any cause, nor act as a Commission of Review. What it is supposed to do, is to tender advice to the Crown as to the best manner of dealing with cases coming up for decision, and to that end the opinion of the majority alone is, as the rule, reported to the Crown as the joint finding of the whole Committee, the dissentient views of the minority being suppressed. Nor does this report to the Crown take the form, or possess the authority, of a legal judgment ; it is of no force till it has been given weight and currency by an order of the Crown in Council. And it can be seen at a glance that such an anomalous position and character must tend seriously to impair the sense of responsibility on the part of members of the Judicial Committee. For the view almost forced upon them by the conditions of their office is that they are much less a Court to do justice upon the merits of questions brought before them, than a Board of advisers of the Crown as to what is expedient to be done; and that, as the Crown is not technically bound to accept their recommendations, but may decline to follow them up with the Order in Council necessary to validate them, the whole moral responsibility may be shifted from their shoulders to those of the Ministers who cause any such Order to be promulgated. But in point of fact, the Judicial Committee has customarily acted as though a real Court of Law, and has moreover practically acted as not merely the Final Court of Appeal for the Church, but its final legislative body also, because by putting certain constructions upon the formularies of the Church, it makes those constructions part of the law; and whereas bad judge-made law can be abrogated in secular matters by means of Parliament, the abeyance of the Church legislature prevents any remedy from being applied in the only adequate way to spiritual questions; and thus the only available course for aggrieved Churchmen to take is, to ignore the recommendations of a body so thoroughly unreliable as the Judicial Committee has proved itself to be.

As to the account which the Judicial Committee has given of its own character and functions, a few paragraphs culled from the Gorham Judgment will suffice in evidence.

'It is not for the Court to decide whether opinions are theologically sound or unsound, but whether such opinions are contrary or repugnant to the doctrines which the Church of England, by its Articles, Formularies, and Rubrics, requires to be held by its ministers.'

'The Court will apply to the construction of the Articles and Liturgy the same rules which have been long established, and are by law applicable to the construction of all written instruments, assisted only by the consideration of such rational or historical facts as may be necessary for the understanding of the subject-matter to which the instruments relate, and the meaning of the words employed.'

'The Court has no jurisdiction or authority to settle matters of faith, or to determine what ought in any particular to be the doctrine of the Church of England ; its duty extends only to the consideration of that which is by law established to be the doctrine of the Church of England, upon the true and legal construction of the Articles and Formularies.'

Now, if this programme had been observed in practice, Churchmen would have been ready to overlook the constitutional and theological objections to the validity of the Court, content to get substantial justice, even if not through the most appropriate channel ; but the application of modern undogmatic religious teaching and lax ecclesiastical custom to the interpretation of the doctrinal and ceremonial law of the Church of England, which has so greatly marked the rulings of the Judicial Committee, has made any such acquiescence impracticable, if the doctrines and laws of the Church are not to be surreptitiously juggled away under the pretext of interpreting them.

The Gorham case is a palmary instance of such misinterpretation of the law, as will appear from a brief statement of the facts. Mr. Gorham then held a view concerning baptism which is not only contradictory to the plain meaning of the English Baptismal office, but which, if not absolutely peculiar to himself alone, at any rate had never been adopted by any Christian communion, nor accepted by any appreciable number of theologians. It was as follows: He held that, 'As infants are by nature unworthy recipients, being born in sin, and the children of wrath, they cannot receive any benefit from baptism, except there shall have been a *prevenient act of grace* to make them worthy.' The result of this is that, while it is possible that some children may be beneficially affected by baptism, yet this can never be asserted of any one child in particular, in the absence of knowledge upon our part whether that child has been

secretly made the recipient of an act of divine grace to give it
eligibility for being baptized at all. Now, Mr. Gorham acknowledged that this tenet nearly stopped his ordination by Bishop
Dampier of Ely so far back as 1811, a time when very rigid inquisition into the orthodoxy of candidates was not practised. And
there can be no question at all of its precise contradiction to the
language of the Prayer Book, which is express in declaring that
each individual child brought to baptism is then and thereby
regenerated. Two brief quotations will suffice in proof : ' Seeing
now, dearly beloved brethren, that this child is by Baptism regenerate, and grafted into the body of Christ's Church, let us give
thanks unto Almighty God for these benefits ' ; ' We yield Thee most
hearty thanks, most merciful Father, that it hath pleased Thee to
regenerate this infant with Thy Holy Spirit, to receive him for
Thine own child by adoption, and to incorporate him into Thy
Holy Church.'

Nevertheless, the Judicial Committee decreed that ' the doctrine held by Mr. Gorham is not contrary or repugnant to the
declared doctrine of the Church of England as by law established.' And the Judges were not content with this : they
alleged a particular view of baptism as being Mr. Gorham's,
setting it out in a paragraph too long to quote here, but which
differs essentially from that which Mr. Gorham actually did hold
and had publicly asserted, not even containing the term ' prevenient grace,' which is the keynote of his theory. And indeed,
Mr. Gorham himself, after taking possession of the benefice of
Bramford Speke, which had been the matter directly in litigation,
with a cynicism rivalling that of his judges, publicly repudiated
the doctrine they had invented for him and put into his mouth,
declaring that he did not hold, and had never held it, though it
was only on the faith of his doing so that he had secured institution to his living.

In the case of Liddell *v.* Westerton, Liddell *v.* Beal, usually
known as the Knightsbridge Judgment (1857), the first of the
Ritual suits, the Court, when speaking of the Second Prayer Book

of Edward VI., alleged that 'the prayer for consecration of the elements was omitted, though in the present Prayer Book it is restored:' the fact being that the prayer stands in the Book of 1552 exactly as it does in the present one, with the exception that there is no 'the' before the words 'remission of sins.' And upon this amazing blunder an important part of the judgment turned. When the blunder was detected, as happened speedily, a correction was introduced into the authorised report of the judgment, in these words: 'Material alterations were introduced into the Prayer of Consecration;' but the error in the judgment due to the original mistake was not amended; and the erroneous statement that a great change had taken place in the Eucharistic doctrine of the English Church between 1549 and 1552 was maintained, though directly in the teeth of the Act of Parliament ratifying the Second Book, which says expressly of the First Book that it contained nothing but what was 'agreeable to the Word of God and the primitive Church;' and further 'that such doubts as had been raised in the use and exercise thereof proceeded rather from the curiosity of the minister and mistakers than from any other worthy cause.' But although these faults marked the finding in Liddell *v.* Westerton, and its rulings were erroneous in some particulars (notably in prohibiting the stone altar), yet it is honourably distinguished from its precursor and from the cognate judgments which followed it, by being a genuine statement of the law, as the Court supposed it to be. And two maxims of interpretation which the Court laid down would have effectually put a stop to all the subsequent litigation, had they been consistently maintained and acted on.

These maxims were: 1. 'The Rubric to the Prayer Book of Jan. 1, 1604, adopts the language of the Rubric of Elizabeth. The Rubric to the present Prayer Book adopts the language of the statute of Elizabeth, but they all obviously mean the same thing, *that the same dresses and the same utensils or articles which were used under the First Prayer Book of Edward VI. may still be used.'*

2. 'Their Lordships entirely agree . . . that in the performance of the services, rites, and ceremonies ordered by the Prayer Book, the directions contained in it must be strictly observed ; that no omission and no addition can be permitted ; *but they are not prepared to hold that the use of all articles not expressly mentioned in the rubric, although quite consistent with, and even subsidiary to, the service is forbidden.'*

The particular point ruled in the judgment by this second maxim was the legality of a credence-table, as a convenient place for the bread and wine prior to their being placed upon the communion-table at a specific time in the service ; and the judges cite several kindred examples, such as organs, pews, pulpit-cloths, &c.

It is from the delivery of this judgment that the Ritual movement really dates. On the faith of the two maxims just cited, that whatever was lawful under the First Book of Edward VI. remains so now, and that any articles reasonably subsidiary to the service may be used, though not expressly prescribed by any rubric, a very general improvement in the conduct and accessories of public worship in the Church of England began : and the fact that it did not begin till after the delivery of this judgment by an exceptionally strong Court,[1] amply refutes the charge of 'lawlessness' frequently urged against the Ritualistic school.

The gross miscarriage of justice which had marked the Gorham Judgment was followed by a similar distortion of the law in the joint suit known as the 'Essays and Reviews' case (1863), and more exactly as 'Williams *v.* Bishop of Salisbury and Wilson *v.* Fendall.' It is true that the condemnation of the two appellants by the Arches Court had not been so complete as that of Mr. Gorham, but nevertheless they were condemned upon all the main articles alleged against them, and acquitted upon a few minor points only. But the Judicial Committee reversed the Arches Judgment, despite the plainest evidence of the novelty

---

[1] Lords Cranworth and Wensleydale, Mr. Pemberton Leigh (afterwards Lord Kingsdown), Sir John Patteson, and Sir W. H. Maule.

and heterodoxy of the views formulated and published by the two clergymen concerned.   Such was the record of the Court when the troubles in connection with St. Alban's, Holborn, began.

R. F. LITTLEDALE.

APPENDIX C

A Letter addressed to the ' Record ' newspaper. Corrected and amended. By A. H. MACKONOCHIE, Perpetual Curate of St. Alban the Martyr, Holborn, 1870.

MARTIN *v.* MACKONOCHIE.

SIR,—Will you allow me space for a few remarks?

In your very excellent article on this case in Friday's issue, there are one or two things on which I hope you will allow me to comment, in order to correct wrong impressions which might otherwise be formed about myself personally.

First, I find the following, near the beginning of the article :— ' The judgment was delivered on Friday, but up to Sunday morning it had not been legally served, and in accordance with the casuistry exhibited by the party throughout, the Incumbent of St. Alban's still considered himself at liberty to preach.'   This is quite true in fact, but, without a word of explanation, may mislead.   The truth is, that the only report of the judgment which I had seen was that in your columns of the previous Friday.   I believe it is the best which has appeared.   At any rate it contains these words,—' They order that he be suspended for the space of three calendar months from the *date of the Notice of Suspension*.' I must call special attention to these last words.   The ' date of the Notice of Suspension ' must mean, I presume, the ' service ' of that notice, as, until its service, I could know nothing of its date.   Therefore, I waited to obey it, till it was served. When I knew less of Law Courts, I might have done otherwise, but experience has taught me some few things about Law words and forms. If you say to your servant, ' Mind you lock the door as soon as you hear me go out,' you do not complain that he neglects his duty if he waits till he does hear you go out, before he locks the door. If this is 'casuistry,' I venture to think it is very good casuistry.

The second point is somewhat different. You say, ' If we regard the acts as mere acts, complete in themselves, having no ulterior meaning, having neither beginning nor ending in anything but themselves, then we say that the Incumbent of St. Alban's and his friends are perfectly justified in their complaint. They had no reason to expect a decision so clear and trenchant, and they have a right respectfully to complain.' Now, Sir, this hypothesis exactly states the true view of the matter for the purposes of the present decision. The sentence pronounced against me purports to be a punishment for [1] having disobeyed a previous decision. But then, disobedience is ' doing what I am told not to do.' It is, however, a principle of English justice that the accused in any case can only be condemned within the letter of the articles under which he is charged. If then I have disobeyed, I must have disobeyed the articles charged. The Order in Council bids me to abstain from doing certain things ' as pleaded in the articles.' If then, for the purpose of the decision, these acts have any ' ulterior meaning,' any ' beginning or ending in anything but themselves,' such meaning—such beginning or ending—must be found alleged in the articles pleaded in the case. I do not mean that the acts have no ' ulterior meaning,' but that no such meaning is alleged in the articles to which the attention of the Court was bound to be confined by the principles which rule all administration of justice in England. In support of this proposition, I will cite at length (if you will allow me) a clause in Dr. Lushington's judgment, as Dean of the Arches, ' on Admission of Articles,' Joint Appendix to the above case, pp. 14, s. 36, to pp. 15, s. 10. ' I am decidedly of opinion that it is not necessary for any purposes

---

[1] ' Contempt of Court in ' is omitted here.

of justice that intention should be pleaded in this case. For the purpose of considering the admissibility of these articles, I shall presume, without giving any opinion of my own, that, intention apart, the practices which are set forth in them come within the category of ecclesiastical offences. The proposition is, that though the matters in themselves may be perfectly indifferent and absolutely innocent, yet if they are used by clergymen in their church, and are not found within the limits of the Book of Common Prayer, and the Canons, and that which constitutes the law of the Church of England Ecclesiastical, they are in themselves offences. Now I do not say one word as to the truth of that proposition. That is the great question which is to be argued hereafter. It is one of the utmost importance, and many will think it one of the greatest possible difficulty. But for the purpose of considering the admissibility of these articles I presume it to be law. I think it wholly unnecessary to plead *quo intuitu*, and I may say, indeed, that I should be forcing the promoter to do that which might seem an injustice to Mr. Mackonochie if I hold otherwise. I know not with what intention Mr. Mackonochie has done these things which are specified in the articles. He may be not only innocent, but he may be most praiseworthy. He may have followed the dictates of his own conscience, to adopt and to persevere in carrying out these views as a necessary part of religion, and I have no right, I think, to compel the promoter to charge that in causing the service to be performed in this manner he therein was actuated by any improper motive ; I will not do so. I do not think it necessary for the purposes of justice. If, as I say, I presume that the doing these things without the sanction of the Book of Common Prayer, or any statute or canon, is an ecclesiastical offence, that is sufficient, without attempting to impose upon Mr. Mackonochie any improper motive.'

I have quoted this passage at full length, because I do not see any other way of showing how explicitly Dr. Lushington excluded the ' ulterior motive ' from the case against me. Dr. Phillimore and Lord Cairns, acting upon the same principle, more than once interrupted the counsel for the promoter with the observation, 'You cannot plead intention,' or 'You cannot charge adoration,' it is not in the articles. In fact, it has been kept out from first to last, until Lord Chelmsford dragged it into his judgment on the 25th ult. I claim, therefore, the benefit of your conclusion that, inasmuch as, for the purposes of the Court, these acts stand simply on their own merits, I have 'a right to complain of the judgment.'

I will now presume so far as to ask you further to allow me to say something as to the history of my action in this case. I would not do so were it not that you have, in an article otherwise most fair, given expression to the old sneer of dishonesty, or, as you call it, 'casuistry' against us; while yet, judging from the notices which have appeared lately in your columns, you desire yourself to give an accurate and unprejudiced account of facts. If I am right in this estimate of your intention, I think you will not grudge space for my statement.

I begin with the articles of the case. They alleged against me :

1. 'Elevation of the paten and cup above the head during the prayer of consecration.'

2. Kneeling or prostration before the consecrated elements during the prayer of consecration.'

3. 'Lighted candles on the communion table during the celebration of holy communion.'

4. 'Use of incense for censing persons or things.'

5. 'Use of incense, alleged to be unlawful, but not for censing persons and things.'

6. 'Mixing water with the wine used in the administration of the holy communion.'

You will notice that none of these allege any 'intention' or 'ulterior motive.' Also, I beg you to notice that Nos. 1 and 4 applied only to certain days in the year 1866, and not to the day, January 13, in the year 1867. The reason of this was, that on the Feast of the Epiphany 1867 I made certain alterations in the mode of conducting the divine liturgy. One was to discontinue the elevation of the paten and chalice *above* the head, and to substitute a lower elevation *as high as* the head ; another was to give up the practice of 'censing persons and things,' and to substitute for it the use of incense during the service, in a way which seemed likely to be less provocative of offence in those who differed from us, while it was sufficient to keep us in union with the spirit of Catholic worship from the earliest times. An account of these changes was published in an address to my parishioners, with the reasons of them, and the means of reconciling them to Catholic usage. This address was in the hands of the promoter, and annexed by him to the case. With this full knowledge of facts, while he alleged the lesser use of incense on January 13, he did not allege the lesser elevation on the same day. Yet it is for this elevation (if for any) adopted on January 6, 1867, deliberately omitted by the promoter from the charges against me in March of that year, and to which I have kept strictly ever since, that I am now, in fact, condemned by Lord Chelmsford.

In the Arches Court the judgment was given on each of these six articles on March 28, 1868.

At the risk of being tedious, I will, for the sake of distinctness, put down once more each article as pleaded, in parallel columns with the judgment and my action upon it.

Article	Judgment of Arches Court	Action thereon
1. 'Elevation of the paten and cup' *above the head*, during the Prayer of Consecration,' *i.e.*, the use followed in 1866, but discontinued in January 1867, before the suit began.	Do not recur to it.	I have not recurred.
2. 'Kneeling or prostration before the consecrated elements during the Prayer of Consecration.'	Not illegal.	Continued till the Privy Council reversed the judgment : then given up.

Article	Judgment of Arches Court	Action thereon
3. 'Lighted candles on the communion table during the celebration of Holy Communion.'	Legal.	Continued till the Privy Council reversed the judgment : then given up.
4. 'Use of incense for censing persons and things,' *i.e.*, the use which was given up before the case began.	Do not recur to it.	I have not recurred to it.
5. 'Use of incense, alleged to be unlawful, but not for censing persons and things.'	Some use of incense lawful, but not this. Abstain for the future.	I have abstained from it.
6. 'Mixing water with the wine used in the administration of the Holy Communion.'	Abstain for the future.	I have abstained according to the judgment.[1]

Let me ask you to consider my position towards these articles. You will think me wrong ; but, in looking at the question of honesty, you must take my points of view into consideration. Please also to remember that I do not condemn, in what I am going to say, those whose deep convictions contradict mine. If they are wrong I leave them to their Master, with whom I trust they will find mercy, even as I hope that, if I am wrong (which, as I trust not my reason but His Word, it is almost blasphemy in me to suggest), I may find mercy with the same All-Loving Master. My position is this—

1. [2] I believe that the Lord Jesus Christ is present, really

---

[1] This passage is altered in form, but not in substance, from that in the *Record*.

[2] This passage has been re-cast. In the original letter in the *Record* it stood thus, 'I believe the doctrine of the Real, Objective, Spiritual and Heavenly Presence of Our Lord, in the Holy Sacrament, as being as true as God is True.' This seemed to me to be sufficient : but was objected to by the *Record* in its leading article, as stating no more than all 'Orthodox Protestant Churches hold ;' whereas I ought (it was said) in order to state my own teaching, to have used the words, 'Our Lord's Natural Body and Blood.' Now, when I thought of Our Lord as Present in the Holy Eucharist, I could

and objectively, in the highest and truest sense after an heavenly and spiritual manner, in the Blessed Sacrament, in the truth of His Deity, and in the perfection of His Manhood, conceived by the Holy Ghost and born of Mary. I believe this to be as true as God is True:

2. I believe it to be taught by the Church of England, as by all the rest of the Catholic Church from the beginning. I do not see how I could have accepted the Catechism, the service for Holy Communion, and more than all, the Sacramental Articles, without believing it.

3. I believe that it is the essence, the very life of the Church of England, that she is bound up in the Life of Her Lord, as being simply the same Church which He founded by the hand of some of His servants in this land, in the earliest ages of Christianity, centuries before the coming of St. Augustine, which He revived by His Spirit working in that holy man and his companions, and which has come down in unbroken line of spiritual descent to this time ; and that therefore all in doctrine, discipline, practice, and ceremonial which ever has been Hers, and has not been set aside by express words, or the strictest necessity of inference, is Her law still. How was I to act with these convictions under this judgment ? Could I leave the Church of England ? It was no

only think of Him as Present in His Body and Blood, because those are His own words, in which He defines that Presence. The word ‘ natural ’ I decline to use, because it has more than one sense. If natural be used as opposed to supernatural, or glorified, its use would be heretical, I believe, ever since the first Easter Day. It would be difficult, not to say impossible, to quote any theologian of eminence in any part of the Catholic Church who has, in any age, taught such a doctrine. If the words be used to signify Our Blessed Lord's Manhood, Born of Mary, Inseparable from His Godhead, and now Existing in a Supernatural and Heavenly manner, both on the one Altar in Heaven, and on the countless Altars on earth, then I accept it as necessarily involved in the belief in the ‘ Real, Objective, Spiritual, and Heavenly Presence of Our Lord in the Holy Sacrament.’ I cannot say how thankful I am to know that this is the faith of all orthodox Protestant Churches. This assurance, on so high authority, confirms, more than anything I have heard, the profession of Dr. Pusey (*Eirenicon*, p. 5, ll. 1 and 2), ‘ their belief is in many points truer than their words.’

question with me of giving up temporalities, for I have none to give up. But, then, to me the Church of England is in God's Providence the only channel ordained of Him through which His Grace can reach my soul. Well, but why should I think of leaving? What was the bearing of the judgment? I might know or suspect the *animus* of the promoter; but was there anything in the judgment which gave such expression to this *animus* as to compel me to say that the doctrine of the Church was impugned?

The answer to this last question was easy enough. The basis of the judgment was Catholic, although the conclusions drawn from it did not altogether stand square on so Catholic a footing. It was no discredit to the judge to see that he was acting, or trying to act, as arbitrator rather than judge; but this fact set him quite free from the suspicion of endorsing the *animus* which lay hid under the articles. What, then, about the Court? Was it an Ecclesiastical Court in such a sense that its judgments were of force in the name of the Church? In form, no doubt, it was so. The judge was appointed by the Archbishop, and sat as his representative, delivering judgment in his name as Primate of All England, invested with powers which belonged to him (I believe) originally as legate *a latere* from the Pope. So far all seemed in order; but then by a more recent arrangement this Court has entirely lost its ecclesiastical character by being reduced to the position of a mere function of a civil tribunal—the Judicial Committee of the Privy Council. If, therefore, a civil Court interfered with Church law, this could be no ground for leaving the Church of England, but rather ground for clinging to Her in order to protect Her from such attacks from without. The only question, then, was whether or no it were possible to comply with the demands of the Court without thereby being untrue to the Church's catholicity. As far as my own conscience was concerned, it could not be necessary to recur to what I had already, though under protest, given up: but could I give up more? Two things, lights and kneeling, were declared legal; while the ceremonial mixing of water with the wine was the most important of the things forbidden. This was no doubt, a very great matter to yield, even under protest ; still, upon the whole, it seemed possible to comply, and by pleading before the Court I had almost, if not quite, pledged myself to obey. Therefore, at once, without waiting for any monition, I yielded and obeyed.   Then came the appeal against the small remainder which was left to us.   Should I plead again ?   Should I own any authority in the Privy Council?   It was a difficulty.   I did not believe it to have any.   But still, if the State could be hindered by my pleading by counsel from doing a great wrong to the Church, it seemed as if I ought to plead.   Then came the ' Cairns ' judgment.   Should I yield to this ?   The difficulty in this case was no doubt very much greater.   The Court had not a shadow of ecclesiastical [1] authority.   Still, there came again the complication of having pleaded.   So I gave way.   I was forbidden to ' use lighted candles on the communion table during the celebration of holy communion.'   I disused them.   We had been accustomed to use them during morning service for some time, so that use, not being impugned, was continued.   I was directed not to kneel, so I did not kneel.   The Church knows two acts, quite distinct— kneeling and genuflecting ; being forbidden to kneel I genuflected. As a matter of course I believed my Lord to be there, and must show Him some reverence.   The very principles of my duty to God obliged me to save as much for His Honour as I could, and thus forbad me to obey to a hair's breadth beyond the mere letter of that which seemed to assail His Honour.

Then came the motion of last year, and the judgment thereon, and with it a new definition making genuflexion—indeed, all bending of the knee—to be the same as kneeling.   I found refuge in the Rubric of the Ancient English Liturgy, and substituted an ' inclination ' of the body, without bending of the knee, for genuflexion.   Now I am told that inclining the body over the Altar is prostration ; am fined in the costs, and suspended for not having found it out myself : and am told that I am guilty of ' evasion,' &c., for the same want of foresight, while you own yourself that I

---

[1] See Postscript.

could not have foreseen it. Much has been said about the little-
ness of fighting over such minute details. But who fights over
them? I find myself in the Presence of my Lord, and am conscientiously bound to do Him reverence : nor am I forbidden by
my own branch of the Church Catholic from doing that which all
the rest of the Church has done, in one form or another, from the
beginning. I adopt, therefore, a different act of reverence from
that which has been forbidden—one which is ecclesiastically quite
distinct. Who fights over this distinction, and seeks to force me
from it? Clearly the promoter. Again, I get a definition from
the Court, 'all bending of the knee is kneeling.' Truly it is a most
unforeseen definition : but I obey, and now at least I am safe—my
act of reverence must be without bending the knee. I do not
bend the knee. Who follows me to prove that I may be held to
kneel, nay, more, to prostrate myself, without bending the knee at
all, and with an Altar of considerable height immediately in front
of me? Surely it is not I who raise such an apparently impossible
proposition, but the promoter.

Let me ask you, Sir, who drove Wesley from the Church of
England? The Bishops and the Upper Middle Classes in Church
and State. In fact the 'Chief Priests with the Scribes and
Pharisees.' Who tried to drive the early Evangelicals from the
Church? The same 'Chief Priests with the Scribes and Pharisees.'
Who are now trying to drive from the Church those who are the
fruits of the labour of Wesley, and the old Evangelicals? The
same 'Chief Priests with the Scribes and Pharisees.' An old
and most highly respected priest of the Evangelical section of
the Church, lately gone happily to his rest, used to say, 'If you
want to find an old Evangelical, you must look for him in the
ranks of the extreme High Churchmen.' He was 'Evangelical'
to the day of his death.

Now, as regards this sentence of suspension, let me say again
what I said to the *Times*. You Evangelicals believe, as well as
we do, that there is something, in the sacred ministry, which God
gave, which only God can give, and which, therefore, the Queen

cannot take away, and cannot suspend.   We differ as to what it is.
but the essence of the ministerial life we both believe to be God's
alone.   Do not, then, let me be misunderstood.   I accept this
suspension as purely and simply a legal compulsion.   I must
accept it, or do that which I believe would displease God more ;
but it is only the world's suspension.   In the presence of God,
and in the forum of my own conscience, I am as free as if no
suspension whatever had been issued.   Having elected to obey it,
I will do so in all ways in which I can obey it without disobeying
God, but I do not for a moment accept it as depriving me of privileges, or releasing me from duties which God has enjoined upon
me as a priest, and from which He only can release me.

Long as this letter unhappily is, its limits have compelled me
to treat much very imperfectly, but I hope it may help your
readers to form some notion of the motives of truth by which I
have been guided.

Yours faithfully,
ALEX. HERIOT MACKONOCHIE.

Postscript.

Some people find it difficult to understand how we can say
that we 'acknowledge no authority in the Judicial Committee of
the Privy Council.'   They say, 'You are clergymen of the Establishment ; is not this Court duly appointed by Act of Parliament,
and are you not, therefore, bound to obey it ?'   This is a short
question which requires a long answer : just as some one might
say, 'Why does not the sun fall down upon us ?' a very short
question, but one which can only be answered by enunciating the
whole philosophy of the law of gravitation.   Still, it may be worth
while to try and say something about it.

The expression 'Established Church' contains two ideas
quite distinct from one another : first, the CHURCH ; secondly, the
ESTABLISHMENT.   The Church is the Body of Christ : the Establishment is that Body of Christ, in a certain relation to the State.
Whether that relation is right or wrong is not the present question ;

but 'what is the relation?' It has grown up, in many Christian countries, under different circumstances, and during many centuries. In England we find it assuming a definite form in the 'Magna Charta' of King John. The king, being recognised as supreme ruler over everybody in the land, in all causes, bound himself to decide ecclesiastical questions by the 'Spiritualty,' as it is called—*i.e.* the Church in her Councils and Courts. This relation of the Church to the State is recognised in 'His Majesty's Declaration' prefixed to the 'Articles of Religion' in the Prayer Book, and is the 'Constitution of this Realm of England in Church and State.' Therefore, no Act of Parliament has power to make any Court for the Church ; and any such Court, being made by Act of Parliament, is a violation of the Constitution. Then some one says, 'But you have signed a declaration, acknowledging the Queen's Majesty to be, under God, the only supreme governor of this realm, . . as well *in* all spiritual or ecclesiastical things or causes, as temporal : how do you explain that?' I explain it of myself in the same sense as I should explain it of a dissenter, as the words, both of it and of Article xxxvii., require : viz. that the Queen has authority over my body, my goods, my position in life, in fact all that this world has to give me of good things, even though they be mixed up with the spiritual things which God has given me ; but over those spiritual things themselves, she has no authority.

I deny, therefore, the jurisdiction of the Judicial Committee of the Privy Council. First, because it is a Civil Court imposed upon the Church by the State, contrary to the constitution of the Realm. And, secondly, because it has taken upon it to adjudicate in the things of God, over which it can have no power. I deny its jurisdiction just as much in regard to questions in which I may think its judgments true, as in regard to those in which they are false.

A. H. M.

IN THE BILL OF COSTS

Presented by the Proctors for the Church Association to the Rev. A. H. Mackonochie, exceeding, before taxation, four hundred pounds, and relating only to that part of the case heard on December 4, 1869 (*i.e.*, the case preceding this), the following items occur :—

July 1869.

	£	s.	d.
Attending Mr. Pond, instructing him to attend St. Alban's on Sunday, July 11	0	6	8
Taking his statement and fair copy	0	18	4
Paid him for his attendance	2	2	0

	£	s.	d.
Attending Mr. Pond, instructing him to attend the early Communion on July 12 (*i.e.*, the next day, Monday) and four following days	0	6	8
Taking his statement and fair copy	0	18	4
Paid him for his attendance	5	5	0

(Two guineas for Sunday, one each week-day.)

Three persons were employed.

Similar entries occur all through, exceeding in the whole one hundred pounds.

Though judgment was given in Mr. Mackonochie's favour on two charges out of three, he was ordered to pay the whole costs.

THOMAS LAYMAN,
ELIJAH CORNISH,
Churchwardens, St. Alban's.

APPENDIX D

As an evidence of the widespread regret evoked by Mr. Mackonochie's death, the result no doubt in a great measure of his own wide sympathies, we may quote the following letter from the Roman Catholic Archbishop of Armagh :—

'Armagh, Dec. 23, 1887.

'My dear Mr. Russell,—Permit me to convey to you and your colleagues at St. Alban's the assurance of my sincere sympathy with you in the very severe affliction which the early death of the Rev. Mr. Mackonochie must have been to all.

'I would have written at once on seeing the sad news in the papers, but it is so long since I have had any communication with St. Alban's that I was not sure whether either you or the Rev. Mr. Stanton, the only members of your community besides poor Mr. Mackonochie with whom I was personally acquainted, were still there. I am very glad that the mention of your name in the papers as having delivered an address at St. Alban's yesterday evening affords me an opportunity of paying this debt of gratitude.

'I cannot forget how nobly you and your brethren at St. Alban's, including the lamented deceased, came to my aid when my poor starving people in Donegal stood in such need of sympathy and assistance.

'Would that I could give you some more pleasing token of my remembrance and gratitude than that of condoling with you on the death of your dear friend ; but since it has pleased Divine Providence to visit you and your brethren with such a heavy cross, I am sure a word of sympathy will be grateful to you.

'I am, dear Mr. Russell,

'Yours most faithfully,

'† MICHAEL LOGUE.'

In pulpits all over the country reference was made to Mr. Mackonochie's death both by the clergy of his own communion and by others. Canon Liddon in his sermon at St. Paul's Cathedral spoke of him as one of ' those to whom the service of God is the main object of their lives, . . . a man whose name was very prominently before the public a few years ago, and whose life as a true servant of God and friend of the poor will be more fully recognised now that he has gone from us.'

And Canon MacColl ended a short ' In Memoriam ' notice with these words :—' Thus has closed the once stormy, active life of a man by nature simple, loveable, most affectionate and loyal—a man of great force of character, of iron will and indomitable determination in all that he conceived to be his duty to his Church and his Master. Future ecclesiastical historians will do him justice. He fought hard and long for the spiritual rights and liberties of the Church of England ; his work in London remains and prevails. . . . Amongst his faithful people he led a most self-denying, self-sacrificing life ; he acted and lived what he believed to be the truth, and doubtless he has his reward, where the pure and holy, and the weary are at rest.'

University of Cambridge, Nov. 8, 1888.

The following was the speech delivered by the Public Orator, in presenting the Right Rev. J. R. Alexander Chinnery-Haldane, LL.M., Trinity, Bishop of Argyll and the Isles, for the degree of D.D., *iure dignitatis* :—

' Dignissime domine, domine Procancellarie, et tota Academia :—

' Nuper in hoc ipso loco, magna praesente episcoporum frequentia, Caledoniae laudes non sine desiderio prope intactas praeterivimus. Eo maiore igitur gaudio sedis Caledonicae vetusissimae praesidem, tot episcoporum Lismorensium heredem, Academiae nomine hodie salutamus. Salutamus insularum septentrionalium episcopum, quae fidei Christianae focum antiquum, Ionae insulam, Sancti Columbae tamquam nidulum in asperrimis saxulis adfixum, non modo rupium praeruptarum serie perpetua coronant, sed etiam laborum piorum corona quadam immortali cingunt. Episcopi autem huiusce auspiciis (ne plura commemorem) Caledoniae fauces illae formidolosae, caede crudeli quondam infames, religionis mitissimae mysteria, adsistente venerabunda indigenarum multitudine, patrio in sermone saepenumero celebrata viderunt. Eiusdem e domicilio (ut meministis ipsi) hospes exiverat presbyter ille Anglicanus qui in vita plurima perpessus, hieme proxima nemoris remoti inter nives quietas mortis pacem defessus invenit. Illo vero die fatali, viri fidelis relliquias, ab episcopo fideli per noctem frustra quaesitas, solis ad ortum, domini ipsius in adventum, fida canum custodia fideliter conservavit. Fidei autem tantae dum exempla inter homines recordamur, mentesque a terrestribus ad caelestia paulisper revocamus, verba divinitus dicta procul audire nobis videmur :—"haec dicit primus et novissimus, qui fuit mortuus et vivit. Esto fidelis usque ad mortem et dabo tibi coronam vitae."

' Duco ad vos episcopum fidelissimum, virum in laboribus piis obeundis indefessum, in donis plurimis ecclesiae dandis munificum, IACOBUM ROBERTUM ALEXANDRUM CHINNERY-HALDANE.'

[Translation.]

' Not long ago, speaking in this very place in the presence of a large gathering of Bishops, we left—but with regret—the praises of Scotland without mention. It is therefore with the more pleasure that, in the name of the University, we welcome to-day the Prelate of the most ancient Scottish See, the successor of the long line of Bishops of Lismore. We welcome the Bishop of those northern isles which not only enwreathe Iona—with their unbroken range of precipitous crags—that early centre of the Christian Faith —St. Columba's nest, as we might call it—a nest built on the roughest shingle—but also bind on her brow an unfading wreath of zealous piety. It is by his initiative—I select a single instance —that the sacred mysteries of the religion of peace [love?] are often celebrated—before reverent throngs of the inhabitants and in their mother tongue—in that dread Scottish pass, which is notorious in history for a merciless act of butchery.

' From his house too, you well remember, and as his guest, that noble English priest had gone forth, who last winter found, after a life of heroic endurance, amid the still snowdrifts of a secluded glade—rest for his weariness in death. On that fatal day, indeed, the mortal remains of that faithful hero, for which the faithful

Bishop had all night searched in vain, were loyally guarded by the loyal watchfulness of the dogs until the sun rose and their master himself had come.   But while here below we commemorate constancy such as this, while for a moment our minds are recalled from things on earth to things in heaven, we seem to hear, afar off, the words spoken by divine Lips, "these things saith the First and the Last, which was dead and is alive. Be thou faithful unto death, and I will give thee a crown of life." I present to you a Bishop most faithful to his duty, a man unwearied in good works, an open-handed benefactor of the Church, JAMES ROBERT ALEXANDER CHINNERY-HALDANE.'

APPENDIX E

A GREAT deal was written both in poetry and prose about the place and manner of Mr. Mackonochie's death, but space forbids us to give more than the following poem by Mrs. Hamilton King author of the 'Disciples,' &c. It is taken from her volume entitled 'Ballads of the North.'

FATHER MACKONOCHIE.

ROSE-RED o'er Ballachulish
    The sunset dies away,
And glorious to the last expands
    The short December day ;
The purple islands of the West
    Stretch down the ocean way ;
The great and lonely mountain-land
    Looms inland ghostly-grey.

Suddenly with the evening
    The snow begins to fall,
And wailing voices of the North
    In the wild winds to call ;
And night wears on, and still they wait,
    Nor hear within the hall
Thy homeward steps, O father
    And friend, beloved of all !

Oh, dark upon Loch Leven
   Comes down the winter night ;
The desert spirits that love not man,
   The lonely hills affright ;
The blinding whirlwinds and the snow
   Beat out all sound and sight ;
No moon is there, nor stars to give
   The wanderer any light.

Oh, many on wild winter nights
   Have been out here too late,
And left among the haunted glens
   A hearthstone desolate ;
Poor men and women, none have marked
   Their name or their estate ;
And now the father of the flock
   Has come to share their fate.

Oh, awful is the wilderness,
   And pitiless the snow ;
But down in dim St. Alban's
   The seven lamps burn aglow,
And softly in the Sanctuary
   The priest moves to and fro,
And with one heart the people pray ;
   And this is home below.

And higher, in the House of God,
   Seven lamps before the Throne,
The golden vials of odours sweet,
   The voice of praise alone ;
With the belovèd, the redeemed,
   Whose toil and tears are done,—
And this is in the Father's Home
   That waits for every one.

O Priest, whom men unkindly judged
   Too fixed on rule and rite,
In this thine hour no ritual comes
   To help thee through this night ;

None but the Everlasting Arms
　　Support thee with their might,
None but the unseen Comforter
　　Upholds thy soul in flight.

For thee no priest, nor passing bell,
　　No holy oil or wine,
No prayer to speed the parting soul,
　　No sacred word or sign ;
Long as thou hast by dying beds
　　Ministered things divine,
Nor voice nor hand of earthly friend
　　May minister to thine.

There is none other left but Thou,
　　O Jesus, now give ear !
Far off is every help and hope,
　　O Jesus, now draw near !
The heart is sinking and the flesh,
　　O Jesus, save and hear !
Darkness and death—Oh, show Thy Face,
　　O Jesus, Lord, most dear !

.　　　.　　　.　　　.　　　.　　　.

One kneeleth in his chamber,
　　Near midnight, at his prayer,
He feels a cold breath suddenly,
　　A presence in the air :
The white wraith flits before his eyes,
　　Awe-stricken and aware ;
Yet till the morrow all unknown
　　Whose visiting was there.

No funeral tapers round thee burn,
　　No hand thy bed to dress,
No watchers kneeling round in prayer
　　And tears of tenderness.
The vigil and the fast are kept
　　Beside thee none the less,
By the dumb creatures in their love
　　And living faithfulness.

The deerhound and the terrier
  Lie watching foot and head,
They only left of all on earth
  To guard thy dying bed.
Two nights and days the searchers toil,
  The trackless wastes they tread,
In howling darkness, storm, and snow,
  Until they find the dead.

Thy feet are bruised upon the rocks,
  In struggle stiff and sore,
Thy corpse is frozen in the snow,
  With snow-wreaths mantled o'er ;
Thy face is calm,—the smile of one
  Remembering pain no more ;—
Their hearts were lightened of a load,
  Seeing the look it wore.

Ill-omened Pass ! laid under ban
  By curse from sire to son,—
The elemental powers have raved
  O'er torrent and o'er stone ;
Untamed and hostile hitherto,
  At last their worst is done,
A holier death has hallowed thee,—
  The Cross its place has won.

The funeral barge is on its way
  Across the pearly seas ;
One great white sea-bird flies before,
  With waving wings of peace ;
All shrouded white, the mountain-heights
  Still silently increase ;
Thy violet pall with flakes that fall
  Has grown snow-white as these.

They wait within the city,
  Stricken with grief, to lay
Their dead within St. Alban's,
  For one sad night and day.

Around thy bier the music wails,
  Thy people weep and pray ;
Thy mourners fill the streets on foot,
  Along the funeral way.

   .   .   .   .   .   .

O soul, that hast already passed
  Beyond this earthly bourn,
In London, in the narrow streets
  They miss thee, and they mourn ;
Thy face still haunts the holy house
  Where thou wilt not return ;
The hearts are aching day by day,
  With whom thou didst sojourn.

Is not thy sleep the smoother
  Because of hearts that ache ?
Is not thy rest the deeper,
  That thy own heart did break ?
Because to-day the sick and sad
  Are weeping for thy sake ;
Surely their sighs have gone before,
  Thy bed in heaven to make.

To fast among the hungering,
  To serve among the poor,
To toil among the weary,
  Among the sick endure ;
To intercede for sinners,
  The tempted to secure : —
Thy lifelong path of pilgrimage,
  Most strait, most steep, most sure.

Sleep on in Christ.   ' O Lamb of God ! '
  Resounds the Passion hymn ;
And heaven is opened, and we join
  The song of Seraphim :
One Presence fills, unites, transforms,
  Beneath these arches dim,
And they who wake, and they who sleep,
  Together live in Him.

INDEX